RISE OF THE SOURCE

THE PHANTOM COBRA

Don Universe

Copyright ©2023 Donald R. Williams
Los Angeles, California
All rights reserved
Printed and Bound in the United States of America

Published By
Building Block Enterprises
Los Angeles, California
Email: universedon8@gmail.com
Website: donuniverse.com

Packaging/Consulting
Professional Publishing House
1425 W. Manchester Ave. Ste B
Los Angeles, California 90047
323-750-3592
Email:.professionalpublishinghouse@yahoo.com
www.Professionalpublishinghouse.com

Cover design:
First printing March 2023
Digital Cover Art: Molly M. Kaplan
Cover Design: TWA Solutions
9780984-207-206
10987654321

Acknowledgments

First, I'd like to thank The Source of the universe who has made this book possible with the mysterious gifts of experiences and the gift of creative intelligence.

I'd like to thank my good friend and writer, Roxanne Jones. She was the first person I told about my idea of writing a script. She told me I had something and urgently told me to write it down, and I did. Thank you, Roxy.

To artist and documentarian, Emmett Gates, thank you for your continuous undying support, prayer/meditation partnership, and technical support.

Thank you, Hylton Mayne. Your mock renderings got the cover art vision going.

To Molly Kaplan, thank you for your great digital artwork on the cover. The back and forth on the Phantom Cobra was worth it.

To Dr. Rosie Milligan, my neighbor found an article on you in the newspaper and gave it to me. Thank you for your guidance, networking, honesty, business acumen, teaching, and support.

Thank you, Jeff Wallace, for thinking of me and giving me that article.

To Eric Lewis and Greg Ware, thank you for listening to those pages and for the feedback on the artwork.

Last but not least, thank you to the editor, Jessica Tilles. Thank you for your due diligence and God-given talents. You've dressed me up and made me presentable to the world.

CHAPTER 1

In the desert belt of the distant planet Larus, laser guns were blasting and bombs bursting plums of dirt, sand, and rock into the air in one hundred fifteen degrees or 46.1 Celsius. It was a cooler day, with the temperature having dropped ten degrees from the previous twenty-four hours. The dust cloud was now so big that it generated its own weather with electrical charges sparking about, none of which stopped the alien dogfight of flying saucers swirling around the desert storm as the Larian Federation, aircraft patrol, pursued the planet's galactic pirate, Rhynous. He was the only criminal threat on the planet, with an army of followers who were now firing on the Federation saucers pursuing him. The speeds of these electromagnetic saucer fighters were incredible. Powered by a core engine charged by the light of their two suns, and with plenty of sun, they glowed a hot metallic white fully charged.

Rhynous saw one of his guard ships take a direct hit with a starlight laser blast and spun out of control in a sea of sparks and fire as it hit a canyon wall and skidded half a mile on the desert floor. The highly trained Federation pilots were the best in the galaxy and had taken down their fifth kill today, leaving only Rhynous the point in a six-saucer diamond formation. Now he was on the run as a lone renegade, but he, too, was highly trained, having done a stint in the Larian Space Force before greed and darkness consumed his mind. He switched on his cloaking device, as his perimeter cameras projected the desert floor on the top and bottom of his craft now flying at three thousand five hundred miles per hour and gaining speed. This didn't fool the Federation forces, as their computers were still engaged, though it made visual identification difficult. As they approached the helium gorge, a canyon that makes the Grand Canyon look like a short ditch, Rhynous dove into the gorge with the

1

eight Federation saucers on his tail. Suddenly, heavy laser fire came from the walls of the canyon, hitting the fourth Federation craft and taking out the fifth as the last three saucers in their formation avoided the fiery crash. They now knew it was a trap and, in milliseconds, ascended to thirty thousand feet above the gorge and out of the line of fire.

Rhynous stopped on a dime and zipped into a huge cavern at blink speed, short for a blink of an eye. The Federation forces had now lost their lock on the renegade saucer, now blocked by the helium-3 and mezmerite crystals in the gorge. The Larian forces circled around and called for backup, but Rhynous was nowhere in sight.

They stayed for hours in the desert's night, hovering, floating, sailing by as if on water and camouflaged as clouds, but Rhynous appeared to be long gone. At midnight, flashes of lights were the order for the Federation crafts to return to their Larian air base, disappearing into the night. Cheers echoed from the canyons below as Rhynous's men declared victory over the Federation and in celebration of protecting their majestic leader heralded as the first future ruler of Earth. At exactly 0400 hours—4:00 a.m. on Earth—a dark craft slowly rose from the helium gorge, no flashing lights or perimeter lights, as if it were a balloon floating away. Once the darkened saucer hit fifty thousand feet, its lights flashed, and it blasted to four thousand miles per hour in three-point-nine seconds, reaching five thousand miles per hour, as it punched through the Larian atmosphere, heading back to the stationary wormhole that would soon be lit up by the twin stars of Zeta Reticuli.

Back on Earth, it was a sunny September day in Los Angeles, California. Vic, a forty-four-year-old who started putting money away early for retirement, had just retired. Many people, colleagues, and friends wondered how he did it. When they would ask, he would just say, "Planning is everything." Having retired in June, he had a few months to recuperate from the drain of students and the long school year. In the teaching profession, middle school was the most brutal. Teachers at this level of education were known as gluttons for punishment. A deviant twelve-year-old could smell fear or weakness in a teacher, some of whom had quit at the end of one week. To have survived twenty-two years at inner-city schools was no small feat, but all behind him now.

Vic was now heading to his friend's house in the unincorporated area of Altadena, north of and next to Pasadena. If it were not for the sign, one wouldn't know they had crossed into the unincorporated area. However, he was coming from Los Angeles to make good on a promise to smoke a joint with his friend, Greg. Vic hadn't smoked marijuana since college and had always refused Greg's offers on his numerous visits. Having known each other since high school and being former roommates, the two had been friends for a long time. Greg, also a former educator, retired because his brother, a wealthy entrepreneur, rewarded him with a million-dollar annuity and he, too, was now pursuing a career as a comedian. Not only was Vic heading up to Greg's, making good on a promise, but he also wanted to put his car to the test on the winding Pasadena freeway with all of its twists and turns. He saved for a few years and, with the help of his wife on the down payment, got one of his dream cars: Porsche 911. He loved going up the 110 freeway past Dodger Stadium to enjoy the slalom. The problem in L.A. was traffic. One must know when to leave to miss the morning rush and a late return helped to avoid the evening rush that could delay a trip by thirty minutes in either direction.

As Vic headed up the freeway and got past downtown, things opened up and the adrenaline flowed just past Avenue 26 into the first turn. Being aware that many a person had died on this stretch of dangerous highway, Vic knew he couldn't become too enamored with speed and that he must continually monitor the tension of the G forces on the car and have a sense of its limitations based on feel and experience. A Porsche 911 could easily cut into a turn like a knife through butter, but if the speed was too great, the weight and position of the rear engine could swing the rear end out, throwing the car into a side spin or complete spin out if the driver should turn the stirring wheel in too deep into the turn. All of this added to the excitement and sensation, a balancing act. Knowing the limitations of speed and turning so as not to generate over stir, it was important to be in tune with the car, knowing its characteristics and limitations. The car's sensors would kick in and one of the gages would change automatically from the recent calls paired with his phone to the oscilloscope measuring G forces. It was like a small jet on wheels in constant need of a lion tamer to control the vehicle and the need for speed.

As Vic kept one eye peeled in the rearview mirror, in respect of officers monitoring the roads, a new Honda Accord passed him.

"These damn Hondas always want to race. I'm on you now. I've got you."

He pulled even and noticed it was a young female in her early twenties as they approached the dead man's curve when she pulled a dangerous maneuver by accelerating and cutting in front of him with only two feet to spare.

"Okay, heifer, I see you're crazy and willing to wreck your car, but I'll be damned if I'm going to wreck mine." Vic eased back. "But you can't get away in a damn Honda. Give me a break."

As he approached the Orange Grove exit, he let her go and kicked himself for letting a young reckless girl suck him into a duel on a dangerous stretch of road. Now driving like a model citizen, Vic turned on to Greg's street, down shifting to hear the whine of the engine.

Once out of the car, he knocked on the side service entrance door off the driveway. Greg, who was thin for six feet tall and had distinguished graying temples and a youthful face, opened the door.

"Hey, I see you made it."

"Yeah, I'm here, G. Can I bother you for some water?"

"Yeah, look in the fridge."

"Cool, thanks."

Greg gathered his wallet and keys. "You ready to go to the store

Vic looked confused. "What store?"

"The weed store."

"I thought it was called a dispensary?"

Greg, not impressed with the correction, shrugged. "Whatever. Let's go."

Vic was in anticipation of his first trip to a weed shop. "Okay, let's do it, and what do you think about stopping to get something to eat on the way back?"

"No, I've got food here."

Vic looked disappointed. "Like what?"

Greg thinks for a second. "Hot links, beer, and condoms."

Vic was completely shocked and disgusted. "What? Okay, I'll have the beer and links. You eat your own dam condoms. What the hell? Condoms?" Vic chuckled, going out the door.

Upon seeing the Porsche, Greg remembered his first ride and exclaims, "Hey! No fast driving."

Knowing Greg's fear of speed, Vic put him at ease. "Of course, not, old man. I know you can't handle it."

Greg nodded, with no shame. "That's right."

As they arrived and entered the shop, a very pleasant and attractive woman came to the front counter.

"Hello, gentlemen. What can I do for you today?"

Greg jumped into action. "Hi, I'm Greg. I'm bringing you a new customer today and this is Vic."

Hi, Vic. I'm Linda."

Vic tried not to look at her cleavage and succeeded. "Hi, Linda. Nice to meet you.

As Linda explained to Vic what benefits he'd receive as a new guest, Vic looked at all the different types of marijuana buds with names he'd never heard of. He noticed Greg peering into the glass counter display like a demented kid in a candy store, drooling over his favorite flavor.

Linda was still reciting her script. "Vic, if you buy fifty dollars' worth of product, Greg will receive a free bag of his choice."

Greg smiled like a wild jackal.

"Vic, do you have any questions?"

"No, Linda, I'm a newbie here. I just need a few minutes to see what you've got."

"More like a virgin."

Vic snapped his head around and looked at Greg. "What?"

"Nothing."

Linda smiled, realizing Greg was a nutcase. "Okay, Vic, take your time. I'll be back here. Just let me know when you're ready."

Vic responds with a "Thank you" and heard Greg talking under his breath.

"Oh, baby, I'm ready, too. Got a rock in my pocket ready to turn into a rocket."

Embarrassed, Vic mouthed, "Shut up!"

Greg gave Vic a what-are-you-talking-about look and mouthed, "What?"

Vic continued to look at the green furry-looking buds. Back in the day, there were names like Columbian red, Acapulco gold, Thi stick, and Kona gold. Those names were long gone as Vic tried to figure out these new names and more potent strains of weed. Names like Purple Haze, King Kush, Mellow Lady, Sticky Gorilla, and Exotic Blue.

Vic called Linda over. "Okay, I think I'm ready."

"Okay, what will it be?"

Vic felt he had it figured out. "Let me have a bag of the Mellow Lady, a bag of the King Kush, and some gummies. I'm assuming that the Mellow Lady isn't as strong as the rest of this stuff?"

"That is exactly right. It's for relaxation and tranquility."

Vic was now feeling more confident. "These gummies, what do you recommend as a dose for a first timer?"

"Well, I would start with one and no more than two at max, but stick with one for now."

Vic agreed, already satisfied with her assessment.

Linda looked at the box and added, "Yes, one is the recommended dose on the box."

Feeling satisfied about his choices so far, Vic asked, "Linda, do you have any brownies?"

Linda responded with a perky and surprised tone. "Yes, we do."

Vic was thrilled." Can I see one?"

Linda turned to head for the back room. "Yes, you can, and your timing is perfect. They're freshly baked."

Great!"

"Don't forget about me. " Greg said, now feeling left out.

"I have absolutely not forgotten about you, Greg. " Linda said, disappearing into the back.

Out of left field and again half under his breath, Greg said, "I can't forget about you, Greg, not with that erection. " As if Linda was digging his erection fantasy.

She returned quickly, surprising Greg. "Huh? Were you saying something, Greg?"

"Oh, no, I was just talking to myself."

Vic was now looking at Greg in disbelief and embarrassed. In Linda's hand was a moist, juicy looking brownie.

Vic smiled. "So this is it?"

Linda smiled. "Yes, nice and fresh."

Vic marveled at the fact that it just looked like a regular brownie, delicious and ready to eat with a glass of milk.

"Hey, man, you need to be careful with that brownie. That's some really strong shit. You want to eat that in really small portions."

"Okay." Vic looked at Linda.

"I agree with that, Vic. This is very potent stuff."

Looking at the brownie, Vic was trying to grasp the truth. "It's that strong?"

Greg nodded. "Hey, that's five hundred milligrams. That's a lot."

As Linda nodded, she asked, "Do you still want the brownie, Vic?"

"Yes."

She returned to the back to bag the brownie.

Greg shook Vic's hand, slipping him a twenty-dollar bill. "Get me a bag of that Sticky Gorilla."

Vic nodded.

Linda returned with the brownie. "Okay, Greg, what would you like?"

Keeping it clean this time without an X-rated comedy routine, Greg gives a straight answer. "Oh finally, I'll take a bag of that King Kush."

Linda, without looking up, said, "King Kush, it is. Will that be it, guys?"

Vic, bidding for his friend, said, "No, I'll have a bag of that Sticky Gorilla."

Linda collected the two bags and asked again if that's all. Vic agreed and Linda totaled the purchases.

"Okay, Vic, that's going to be fifty-five dollars even."

Back at the house, Greg shouted, "That's what I'm talking about!" He slapped Vic high five.

Vic wasn't clear about what the excitement was about. "And what are you talking about?"

Greg was now on a self-proclaimed high. "That's how you go in and take advantage of all the discounts and everything that's free."

"Oh, okay, I guess we did clean up on all the deals."

"You doggone right, we did." Greg was still shaking Vic's hand, who was now ready to convert the glee into some food.

"G., where are those links you were talking about?"

Greg was still pumped up over the haul. "Yes! Let's get some links going and I've got chips. What do you want to drink? I've got beer, soda, water?"

"Hey, I'll take a beer, thanks."

"Coming right up."

Greg was an everyday smoker of marijuana and was ready to smoke a joint. However, Vic was not so willing, but Greg prepared the links and chips as Vic watched football in the den, a nice space that stepped down from the living room onto a marble floor with French doors and a large window that looked out on the pool. It was a respectable place when he bought it, though not enough for Greg who spent money to install the marble floor, remodeling the pool, furniture around the pool, stuccoing the back wall and lights, adding two palm trees, a big table in the patio area with a barbecue grill and sound system that could blast from the pool house. Vic liked the entertainment set up except for one thing: Greg seemed to adore his cactuses. There were cactuses in front of the house, on the side of the house and throughout the backyard, around the pool. It wasn't a place you could get drunk and fall into the bushes because that would be on a cactus.

Once the guys finished eating, Greg was ready to fire up a joint. "Are you ready to smoke?"

Vic was now thinking about the drive home. "Hey, man, I'll take a puff, but I've got to make that drive back to the big city."

Greg grew disgruntled. "Come on, man, a puff? I thought you were going to smoke with me."

At that moment, the doorbell rang.

"Now, who is that? I didn't invite anybody but you."

Greg answered the door and returned with his best friend Steve, and made a beeline to the kitchen.

Steve was also an avid smoker, but a very nice guy, a college graduate, and very conservative looking with a professional career.

Vic looked up and saw Steve. "Hey, Steve! How have you been?"

"Good, Vic. Good to see you. " Steve said in his calm, mild mannered way.

Greg returned from the kitchen with a bottle of tequila. "Okay, let's fire it up!"

Vic was now feeling a little more festive with Steve there. "Okay, G., you do the honors."

So Greg happily fired up the joint and as the guys laughed and talked, there was a knock at the side door. Greg sat up straight with an inquisitive smile on his face. "Now who could that be?" As he goes to see, Steve explained the mood.

"Greg, it's Friday night."

So, there it was. The working class was off looking for a spot to relax and wind down for the weekend in a private, safe environment. Those who knew the party guy, Greg, knew he loved to entertain. The doorbell continued to ring until it was a party of thirteen uninvited guests. However, they were no slouches. Everyone brought something. More weed, beer, and another bottle of tequila for Greg. All good people, Greg introduced everyone, and now he was in his element, returning with a glow on his face, the consummate host. The only person better at hosting was his wife, who was still at work. Vic had to admire Greg's attitude; so welcoming without any notice, but that was who Greg was, and he loved the attention. Vic thought about how he had changed now to being more private and definitely not into hosting unannounced guests or going to parties anymore, but here he was.

Greg came into the den with a joint in his mouth and made an announcement. "Well, it looks like a party, so it's party time. Let's all head to the back." With that, everyone filed into the backyard and around the pool.

The day passed quickly. It was now 8:00 p.m., and Vic hit the joint four or five times in the next hour, along with a few beers, and it was all taking effect. He was now finding humor in everything, but one element differed from twenty-two years ago: the faces of the people at the party were changing. At first, Vic believed it was just a hallucination from the marijuana. Then, the thought came to him, and he wondered if this could be a visual manifestation of their true essence, who they really were on the inside. But he dismissed the idea, knowing he was high, but the thought remained.

Greg walked by, talking to some guy from across the pool. As he passed Vic said, "That guy's a werewolf, you know." Greg looked at Vic as if he had just grown a tail and ignored the comment as he continued the conversation from across the pool. Before Greg got away, Vic asked, "Where's Alondra?"

Greg looked back. "If she's not here in the next hour, that means she's still tied up in the basement." They laughed. Vic's first thought was to go look and then remembered Greg didn't have a basement.

As Vic looked toward Greg's friend from across the pool, he noticed a woman in the shadows watching him. She was one of the seven women there and even in the shadows, there was something dark about her presence. Her face had sharp angles to it with high arched eye brows, high cheek bones with a pointed nose and chin. Vic wondered if anyone else was seeing the faces he was seeing. When he looked around the backyard, he noticed everyone else having a great time and realized that it was only him. When he looked to his right, the woman with the angled face was standing next to him. Now startled, he saw her in the light of the romantic lamps and pool lights. She looked like a witch. Not ugly but scary, and in an instant, Vic imagined being with her as a partner in life and saw himself being tormented, manipulated, and mentally and physically tortured—

"Hi, Vic. I'm Ann. Are you okay?"

Vic was shaken. "You need to know I'm married and I don't talk to witches."

Ann, the thirteenth and last person to join the party, retorted by gathering the winds from east and west and puffed up like a poisonous blow fish. "What did you say?"

Vic now focused on the ghostly blur on her face. "Well—"

Now in a rage, Ann pushed him into the pool.

At that point, some people thought he had jumped in and shouted, "Yeah!" Others gasped while the rest just laughed.

Ann stood at the edge of the pool, now being the witch Vic thought her to be. "Who the hell do you think you are?" Kneeling on the edge of the pool, with her fist balled up, she tried to lean in and punch him in the head without falling into the pool.

Vic drifted her way and just as she cocked her arm to swing, Greg catches her, pulling her back. Now under Greg's arm, he explained to her that Vic was under the influence, high out of his mind, for the first time in twenty-two years. She calmed down, but continued to glare at Vic, who was now splashing around in the deep end of the pool, claiming there was a shark. "Get me out! Hey! It's a shark!"

A mutual friend and chiropractor, Marty, came over with the pool cleaning net on a pole and pulled Vic over to the side of the pool. With help from Marty, Vic pulled himself out of the pool.

"Hey, buddy. You okay?"

"I'm good, Marty. Thanks for helping me out, man. You saved my life."

Marty laughed. "I don't know about all that, but glad I could help."

Vic went back to where he was sitting and said nothing to Marty about him looking like a bear. He made it a point to locate Ann, who was now talking to a friend away from Vic in the patio area between the house and the pool.

Greg came over with a concerned smile on his face. "Man, what have you done now? Why did you call her a bitch?"

Vic looked surprised. "No, I never called her a bitch, G.!"

Greg shushed him. "Okay, okay, keep it down."

Greg sent Vic into the house to get a towel. He returned a few minutes later, wrapped in a fluffy green one, almost dry in the warm summer evening. With the action now over, things had calmed down, but a still-agitated Ann seemed to be planning something with her friend. While Vic and Greg surveyed the atmosphere, a shapely figure walked through the house from the kitchen to the den and into the light of the patio. It was Greg's wife, Alondra. Guests were stopping her, Greg walked down to greet her.

"Hey, dear, how was work?" He leveled a peck on her lips.

"Work was okay, but it looks like you guys are having a nice time. When did you decide to have a party?"

Greg chuckled. "I didn't. They just showed up, so I moved it outside. And things got upside down when Ann and Vic had a little blow out."

Alondra was now drawn in as if watching a reality drama. "Really? What happened?"

Greg walked her away from Ann and her friend. "Vic is high out of his mind. I probably let him have too many hits on the joint. He hasn't smoked in over twenty-two years. Ann goes over to ask him how he's doing and he called her a witch, but she heard bitch. And that's when things got wild."

Now, knowing what had happened, Alondra shook her head. "Oh, Vic. Poor baby. Okay, I'm going to go talk to Vic. You make sure Ann's okay."

Shaking his head, Greg was reluctant. "Whatever."

Alondra gave the whole situation another thought and giggled.

"Good luck. " Greg said to Alondra, as she went over to talk to Vic, who was now staring off into space.

Vic noticed Alondra approaching from the corner of his eye and looked in her direction. His eyes widen. "Oh, wow. Hey, Alondra."

By his response, she realized that in his mind, he's still out there somewhere. "Hi, Vic. How are you feeling?"

"I'm good." Vic seemed in awe of her presence. His focus on her felt a little uncomfortable.

"Why are you looked at me like that?"

He realized she was feeling visually molested, and he felt compelled to tell her the truth. "It's that you have this bluish glow around you with something on your back."

Alondra looked over her shoulder to see if she could get a visual. "On my back? Like what?"

"I don't know for sure, but you're the only person here who doesn't look like a vampire, an animal, or a witch."

"Okay, what do I look like, then?"

"You look like an angel."

Pleased not to be a demon, Alondra appeased Vic. "So maybe these are wings on my back?"

"That's what it looks like."

Greg reappears. "You're not dead yet?"

Vic gives Greg a dirty look and a smirk. Greg explained Ann was better, and that he had walked her out as everyone was leaving to make sure she didn't key Vic's car. Vic was grateful and asked if he could spend the night.

"Greg, I think I need to borrow your couch for the night. I don't want to chance driving home."

Alondra nodded. "I think that's a good idea. I'll put out a blanket for you, Vic."

Grateful, Vic thanked her as she walked away. "Greg, you okay with me staying the night?"

Greg swung into verbal action. "Yeah, as long as you don't die on my couch."

"I'm not going to die on your raggedy little shit couch."

They both laughed.

"Hey, you're the one running around here talking about witches and sharks, man. I don't know."

As they walked into the house, Greg explained he paid a lot of money for the couch and that Vic should be proud to die on it.

Greg bade Vic a good night and headed for the bedroom.

Vic disrobed and covered up in the blanket and tried to forget the events of the evening. Now, with his eyes closed, he can still see the faces of the people at the party. A chill came over him when he remembered that Laura, who looked like a vampire, had just divorced her husband and drained him dry, leaving him with a mortgage for a house he no longer lived in and a child support payment. Now, with an increased heart rate, his mind came back to the idea of the faces being a manifestation of their true essence. He fought off the idea again, knowing he was really high and convinced himself it was impossible. He fell into a deep slumber and into a dream, with men walking around in what seemed to be a cave, none of which made any sense.

It felt as though he had just fallen asleep when he heard Greg's voice.

"Sleeping Beauty, are you awake yet?"

Vic's eyes were still closed. "Do I look awake, dick head?"

Greg smiled, responding in a calm voice. "Oh, you're welcome for me letting you spend the night and not allowing you to get smashed up in your car last night."

Suddenly, Vic remembered he hadn't called his wife the night before, and surprised Greg when he threw the blanket off. "Damn it! I forgot to call Tina last night! What time is it?"

Greg looked at his watch. "It's nine-thirteen."

"Of course it is."

Greg looked confused. "What's that supposed to mean?"

Vic got dressed and put on his shoes. "It's just some weird time thing. It's nothing."

Greg chuckled. "Boy, you may not have died last night, but I doubt that you're going to be lucky enough to make it through the day when your wife gets a hold of you."

Vic knew it could be problematic, but felt confident because of his track record. "Well, my saving grace is that I always let her know where I'm going, so she knows I'm here." Vic excused himself to the bathroom, quickly rinsed his mouth and threw water on his face before hurrying back to the den to fold the blanket. "Greg, thanks for putting me up. I appreciate it. I'll talk to you later."

Greg pulled out Vic's bag from behind the couch. "Don't forget about this."

Vic was pleased to see the goods that he almost forgot. "Oh wow, you're a lifesaver, thanks."

Greg reminded him he still may not make it through the day, so he couldn't take credit for being a lifesaver. They chuckled as Greg saw him out.

"Greg, I know this is a strange question, but did you notice anything unusual about people's faces last night?"

Greg was now ready to give Vic a punch line in the face, but thought better of it. "No, not really," he said in a disappointed tone for having passed up the joke.

"Okay." Vic was now convinced it was him on a bad trip, saying the wrong thing to a lady who was probably looking for a man or just trying to be nice. He's overcome with regret and wished it hadn't happened. *If only I could fix it*, he thought, but knew this was one that he should just leave alone.

He fired up the car and heard his late grandmother's voice in his head, telling him like she had on so many occasions, *Time heals all wounds.*

CHAPTER 2

Back in Los Angeles an hour later, Vic's garage door rolled up, and he pulled in next to Tina's light green Camry. He hopped out of his sports car, grateful he didn't have to make up some lie to cover for an act of infidelity. As he walked into the house, Tina was standing in the kitchen.

"Hey, babe, good morning!"

Tina knew Vic was at Greg's, but was still not pleased. "Don't you 'Hey, babe' me. Where have you been?"

"I told you I was at Greg's. I left you a message."

"Yes, I know that. If it was going to be all night, I think I should have gotten a phone call."

"Yes, you are absolutely right, babe, and I apologize for not calling, but we went to the weed shop, bought a bunch of weed, and I was completely blasted. My first smoke in years and I overdid it. There was no way I could have driven home last night, and I just didn't remember to call. But look at this." Vic pulled out the brownie.

Tina's mood changed from dark and cloudy to sunshine and blue skies. "Oh, is that a marijuana brownie?"

Nodding, Vic smiles. "Yes, it is."

With a fresh air of excitement and wonder, Tina looked at the brownie like it was a new science project. "It looks absolutely gorgeous. Like a regular brownie; it really looks good. So, when are we going to try it?"

The smile was now gone from his face. "Okay, look we can't rush into this. Let's do it when we're both off and maybe the day before a holiday. I need you to understand what I'm still trying to learn and that's the fact that this marijuana, nowadays, is so much stronger than it was back in the day. This stuff is nothing to play with, so when the time is right, we'll have a very small portion of it."

Tina's brow rose. "A small portion? How small?"

"Maybe an eighth of it or less. We'll have to figure it out."

Tina was now baffled. "Really? Just that little bit?"

He smiled. "Yes, just that little bit. Like I said, this stuff is strong. That's why I didn't make it home last night."

His last words seemed to confuse her and deflate the mood. "Okay…well, let me know when you want to try it."

"Look, the time has to be right, being that you're a doctor. I don't want you to get high and then go into work the next morning. We need to be careful."

She scratched her head. "I appreciate your planning and concern, but the stuff is legal now."

Her response hit Vic like a bright light in a dark room. Though he knew it was legal, somewhere in his subconscious, he realized he had been operating as if it were still illegal. The nervous fumbling of the money in the shop and half of the concern about Tina getting high then going to work was an old-school knee-jerk response that he couldn't help. The last time he had smoked weed before yesterday, it was illegal and somewhere in the back of his mind, that was what he still believed. However, the realization that he had just come too, ignited by Tina's statement, had just freed him in some kind of deep-seated way and he felt a relaxation come over himself. Deep down in his spirit, he felt lighter and happy, then tickled. *How strange it is*, he thought, that there seemed to be two parts to his inner being. One part of him knew the freedom of smoking weed and the other still operating as though it was still a federal offense. *The subconscious mind is still in protection mode*, he thought, and then gratefully let it go and headed to his man cave.

Vic walked into the room, looking for a place to put his bag of goodies and edibles, quickly deciding to put it on the bookshelf. He took a seat in his office chair, his favorite seat, and breathed a sigh of relief that things had gone so well with Tina concerning him being out all night. He was glad he had bought the brownie; it had saved him from hours, maybe days, of attitude and drama or worse, manipulation. He realized that without the brownie, Tina would have possibly subjected him to interrogation and leverage, favoring her in the constant power struggle that could go on in a marriage.

He shifted his mind to more important matters, like their real estate endeavors and trying to buy more of it. The couple had already bought income property in Los Angeles and Long Beach and would have to save more money for the next two years to purchase another place in town with West Coast sky-rocketing prices. Vic had his eye on Detroit. A city that had been making a comeback since the recession of the previous decade. He spent hours online, researching that city's resurgence and would not have found it of interest if not for the commitment of major corporations like Ford and financial institutions to bring back jobs. It came to his attention through friends and acquaintances that had bought there or knew someone who had bought there for a minimal amount of money and generated an income stream. He thought he and Tina could do the same thing. She had been warming up to the idea because of the minimal amount of money needed to acquire a property through a bidding process. They both agreed that Vic should go there to see firsthand what was going on there and what it looked like. This was a good opportunity to go look, but still late in the game because it had been ten years of contractors and real estate speculators going in and purchasing properties to flip for a profit. He understood that there probably wasn't much left, but needed to see for himself. And like any city, foreclosures were an ongoing thing, so it was worth a shot. However, it wasn't lost on him that Detroit had the reputation of potentially being a dangerous place if caught in the wrong place at the wrong time. That could happen in any big city,but Detroit had the dubious distinction of being the murder capital of the world twenty years earlier, and so it wasn't a place to be roaming around by yourself. So Vic needed a sidekick and a wingman, and only one person came to mind: Steve Macintosh.

Years before Vic and Tina had married, Vic and Steve had traveled the world together in Europe and South America. They had been friends for years. Steve was his first choice and being they had traveled so much in the past, Vic knew there would be no surprises. Steve had started traveling with Vic when they were in their early twenties and Steve had gotten the travel bug and never stopped traveling. He had adopted Rio de Janeiro as his second home, but could be anywhere between Chicago and Australia. Thanks to modern technology, cell phones, and some phone carriers, it was easy to stay in touch with anyone around the world.

Vic picked up the phone to locate Steve on Whats App.

"Hey, Steve-O, how's it going?"

Steve was pleased to hear a familiar voice. "Victor, Victor, Vic. What's going on?"

This was the perfect question for Vic to get right into his reason for calling. "Well, I'm glad you asked. What do you think about going with me to Detroit?"

"Detroit?" What's going on in Detroit?"

Steve was interested in traveling to many places, usually abroad, but Vic could tell that Detroit wasn't Steve's first choice. Vic explained the venture, but Steve was not convinced. "Steve, where are you right now?"

"I'm in Brazil, but I'll be headed back to Chicago in October."

Vic now saw the plan coming together. "That's great because I was thinking October would be a good month to go. That would give us some time to plan and head back before winter sets in up there. I was thinking I could meet you there and I'll pick up the tab on the room. Hey, you might even find a property you're interested in."

Steve asked for a few minutes to think and returned with, "Okay, I've got a better idea. Why don't you meet me in Chicago instead? We can rest up for a day or two, then go to Detroit from there. Once you're finished in Detroit, you come with me down to Louisiana to look at that land I've told you about and see if you might be interested in investing in a project with me. It's just a look-and-see. I haven't been down there in a while, but I have some ideas. What do you think?"

Vic was now enthusiastic. "I think we have a road trip."

"That's what we need, Vic, a road trip like the good old days. So look, I can put together an itinerary just to give us a time frame so on the way back, we can make sure you get to Chicago on time to catch your plane back to L.A."

Vic agreed with the itinerary and Steve told Vic he'd get back in a few days with the schedule. They talked a while longer to catch up and ended with Vic letting Steve know he was looking forward to hearing from him in a few days.

The next day, Vic felt satisfied things were getting done and decided to try a gummy edible. Before doing so, he called Greg for more information. Greg answered the phone while he was choking, so Vic initiated the conversation.

"Hey, G."

Greg lets out a strangulating cough. "Hey, what's up?"

Vic realizes Greg was in the middle of smoking a joint. "You know, one of these days, you're going to choke to death on that shit."

Greg grabbed some air and said, "What a way to die," as if it would be a heroic ending with a military burial.

Amused, Vic shook his head. "Yes, you're as nutty as they come, and a true weed head."

"Yep!"

"Look, man, I'm getting ready to eat one of these gummies. Should I eat one or two?"

"Remember she told you one, so if you do one you need to wait an hour or two for it to kick in. It's not like smoking. It takes longer when you ingest it."

"Yes, she did say that. Okay, that's what I'll do."

"You may just want to take half, but definitely not more than two."

Vic agreed and felt like he had a measurement that would keep him from overdoing it. "Okay, I'll remember that. I'll call you tomorrow and let you know how it went."

"Have you tried that brownie yet?"

"No, not yet. I'm waiting for Tina to be off and then we're going to try it together."

Greg raised a brow in surprise. "Tina's going to try some brownie? That's a surprise."

"Yeah, she caught me by surprise, too."

"Let me know how it goes with the gummies."

Vic nodded. "I will."

Vic's call with Greg energized him to try a gummy, as he opened what looked like a candy box from his childhood. Again, he marveled because it just looked like a gummy candy or vitamin. Vic popped one in his mouth, feeling like he was eating a kid's candy, then sat and waited anxiously with some excitement while watching TV.

An hour goes by with no results, so he started paying some bills and throwing away papers, but at an hour and a half, Vic figured he should take another gummy because it was obvious to him that it wasn't working. So he popped another gummy in his mouth almost two hours later and felt content that he was at the limit of what he should take. And so, he continued sorting papers and through the mail, only to find more bills. He then started paying another bill with the TV on, watching college football. Being a big football fan, Vic would stop whenever there was a big play and then go back to paying the bills. Reading, then tossing more letters, and then at approximately two hours and thirteen minutes, he felt something. It was a feeling that came up from the depths of his gut and flared out to his brain and the rest of his body. *It feels good, and I feel good*, he thought, as he smiled. Vic's eyes became busy with electrical activity around his peripheral vision, creating a tunnel effect, a short tunnel vision. At this point, Vic knew that he was high but goes back to ridding his desk of the endless flow of mail. Letters from Realtors looking to buy him and Tina out, bills, finance companies offering loans, insurance statements, and more junk mail. Now he's even higher, as his mouth dries out and his ability to think and process information gets cloudy. Vic put down the paperwork and went to sit on his leather couch. He was now a little disgruntled that his head was not clear so he could focus on the bills, his trip to Detroit, repairs that needed to be done, and sending his niece, who was away at college, some money. It was all too cloudy now.

The gummies intensified, flooding out the euphoria. It was like someone had flipped a switch that was now pumping his gut full of nausea. Vic's head was now racing as he sat in disbelief at how fast his mood had gone from happiness to illness. If the cannabinoids in his system went down, he could overcome the nausea. He tried to think positive thoughts and watch the football game, but the crowd noise and the sound of the announcer's voice were making him feel worse, so he turned off the TV. He sat wondering if he'd be able to make it to the bathroom if the nausea intensified. Now he knew he had to get to the toilet. Feeling his stomach rumbling like a volcano nearing eruption, Vic rushed to the bathroom, as he kneeled before the toilet in the nick of time as his lunch and fluids exploded from his mouth.

He felt some relief for about fifteen minutes and was grateful he could make it to the porcelain throne in time, sparing himself the awful cleanup. However, the two gummies were too much, and he felt the buildup of nausea again and made his way back to the bathroom. This time to the sink to throw water on his face and neck, but to no avail, he hurled again, knowing he had emptied his stomach and felt that should be it, but it wasn't.

The third and the most painful time, his gut wrenched so hard he almost blacked out, but what he saw dazed and shocked him. It was a green bile he had never seen before. Vic wondered if he had ruptured his pancreas, but the pain subsided though the nausea did not. He had been sick now for an hour, but this cycle would continue for another three hours with dry heaves.

By that evening, when it was all said and done, Vic was extremely weak, dehydrated, and exhausted. He went to bed after drinking a glass of water around six o'clock in the evening. Tina got home at seven, surprised to find Vic in bed so early. He explained to her of his ordeal, and she went to the store to buy 7 Up and Pepto-Bismol to help settle his stomach. Vic passed on the Pepto, but drank 7 Up and felt better. He fell asleep.

The next morning, Vic woke up with a clear head. He got out of bed and as he turned, the pain hit him and he fell back onto the bed. It was as if three gangsters had held him up and beat him in the ribcage for an hour. He couldn't move. *This is it,* Vic decided. He was done with this shit. No more edibles or marijuana. He felt he was trying to get back into a game that had passed him by. He could never smoke that much weed back in the day anyway, and now it's even stronger. Yesterday, he could not focus or think clearly and it was a helpless feeling knowing he had things to do and couldn't function. It was frustrating. So, that was it. He had fulfilled his promise to smoke with Greg and decided he didn't need it. Now, the thought of it made him ill. Vic lay there until he could figure out how to avoid the pain and to avoid twisting his torso getting out of bed. He swung his legs over the edge of the bed and sat up. He smiled, glad to be in his right mind. Then, he stood up without a problem and headed downstairs.

Vic reached the bottom of the stairs, holding the rail, and saw Tina standing in the kitchen. It was now Saturday morning.

"How are you feeling?"

Vic happily replied, "Better, much better. But that's it. I'm done with these weed products."

"Are you serious?" she asked, without disdain or malice and with lots of concern. "You just started. Do you want some breakfast?"

Vic was now sitting at the table. "Yes, but I think I'm just going to have some oatmeal."

She went to the cabinet for the oatmeal.

"I was going to fix it," he said.

"I've got it, relax." She pulled out an apple and cinnamon packet. "Have you told Greg yet?"

"No, but I'll call him sometime today."

"Okay." She pulled the oatmeal out of the microwave, piping hot, and set it on the table in front of Vic.

"Thank you, Tina. I appreciate it."

She acknowledged his gratitude and went upstairs to get ready for her hair appointment. He sat eating his porridge and listening to his stomach moan and groan with delight. *Surely, its glad that it isn't a gummy,* he thought, and smiled, pleased his thought processing wasn't altered. *How do people like Greg smoke that stuff and continue to function?* One thing he was sure of, he wasn't one of them, and that was okay. He wasn't going to lose any money because he wasn't like them and that at some point over the years, his mind had shifted into high gear and was always processing information and nuances in his life.

That weekend, Vic realized how important it was for him to keep that mental motor running and that he was retired but not finished. There was still plenty to do. Like continuing to increase his bottom line but also to figure out strange little nuances he'd been experiencing lately. Like the faces of the people partying at Greg's house and the constant strange reoccurring dreams and number 13. Vic now pushed those thoughts to the side, as there was plenty of time to figure those things out. He finished his oatmeal as Tina was walking out the door. They say their goodbyes and Vic retreated to his man cave to call Greg. After yesterday, he felt no remorse in letting Greg know how he felt as he dialed his number.

"Hey, how were the gummies?" Greg asked, just before taking another hit on the joint and then the cough as usual.

Vic now wondered, *when does he not get high?* "It was terrible. I took one and waited almost two hours with no result so I took another one and that proved to be too much. I was sick as hell and I'm done."

With surprise, Greg asked, "You're done as in no more getting high?"

"That's it, no more for me."

"You mean you were throwing up sick?"

"Explosive throwing up sick, for hours. Yes, it's all yours, G. I'm done. I get sick just thinking about edibles and weed now."

Greg nodded with compassion. "I can understand that. Well, I guess that means more for me."

Vic got a kick and relief out of Greg's response and chuckled. "Hey, it's all yours, pal, have at it."

Greg took another hit. "So what are you going to do with the brownie? Are you going to let your wife have it?"

"Oh, hell no! If she gets high, it won't be with me."

"Then let me have it."

"You got it, G. I'll bring it to you the next time I come up."

Greg expressed his appreciation and Vic cut the conversation short, explaining he had only called to let Greg know how it went. They exchanged goodbyes but just before Vic hung up, Greg asked, "Hey, where are you keeping it?"

"What, the brownie?"

"Yes."

"I've got it on the bookshelf."

"Hey, can you put it in the freezer until you bring it up? That will keep it fresh."

"Sure, no problem. I'll do it right now."

Greg was appreciative, and they ended their conversation. Vic, true to his word, walked to the bookshelf and took the brownie, still in the white bag, to the kitchen, and into the fridge.

Vic opened the bag and again, he marveled at how good it looked but was now somewhat aware of how potent it must be. Vic opened the freezer and bent down, putting it on a lower shelf and in the back where it wouldn't be easy to find behind the meat and under the vegetables. He would also forget to take it to Greg's on his next trip to Altadena, but Vic assured Greg it was in the freezer and that it would be all his on the next trip up.

The following week, Vic got a call from Steve with a schedule for the trip to Detroit. It was complete with motel choices and alternate time frames in the event there was a delay. For a guy who had not finished college, Steve was organized, well-read, and up on all the latest politics. Steve's military training had sharpened him like a pencil. Although Vic didn't agree with all of Steve's conspiracy theories, he enjoyed the banter of Oxford-style debates and arguments on various topics, including sports. The guys would take the two-and-a-half-hour ride to San Diego's gas lamp district as a guy's night out on the town, talking about everything under the sun and the latest news on the way there and back. Vic remembered back in their twenties the time he and Steve were in Spain and had run out of money in the dead of winter. They had come up with a plan to get on a train leaving Valencia, Spain, at about ten o'clock at night so they could sleep in a warm train car. The plan was to set the alarm and catch a train going back to Valencia from one of the small towns south of Barcelona. Having a train pass would get them a free night of sleep in a train car and take them back to where they started so they could catch their scheduled train to Leon, France, for their flight home. Make no mistake, this was a very clever idea thought up by Vic, who at the time thought of it as a stroke of genius. However, when they got off the train in the small town, whose name no one could remember, the train station rail man explained to them in Spanish that there was no returning train to Valencia from that town. The problem was, if they didn't get back to Valencia to catch the train to France, they would be stranded in Europe. The amazing thing about Vic was that he hadn't had a Spanish class in twelve years, not since night school. To his amazement, some words came back to him like bus, six, and church in Spanish. With Steve chipping in on the translations, they could figure out a bus was leaving the big church at six o'clock that morning going back to Valencia. Vic had just enough money in his pocket to get them on the bus to a town with a Western Union. The bus driver said it would be a thirty-minute stop and pointed them in the right direction. Vic and Steve began speed-walking up the cobblestone street of another old village town.

Passing chickens and goats being herded to market, the two felt as though they had suddenly been transported to the 1700s. They looked up the street and noticed it forked in two different directions. Vic said left and Steve said right. There wasn't a lot of time to ponder or debate, so the idea of splitting up was about to be initiated when Steve said that the bus driver said *derecha*. Vic didn't remember that from the old Spanish class, but Steve said he thought it meant right. Steve was now channeling his old Spanish class. So the two went right and within five minutes came to the *cambio* with the Western Union sign. The money had been sent and was waiting. The guys came charging out of the *cambio* because the bus driver made it clear he was leaving at 7:00 a.m. and would not wait. So, the guys were now on a brisk trot, dodging chickens, donkeys, and goats on the way back. Vic and Steve were three minutes late, with their hearts in their throats as they turned the last corner of that ancient town in Spain, worried and seeing day dreams of an empty space where the bus had been. They now jumped for joy as their eyes fixed on the gleaming white modern tour bus, looking futuristic and out of place in the old town. As Vic recalled the adventure in his mind, he realized why Steve was his first choice.

CHAPTER 3

Vic had worked hard getting Tina on board to buy income property in Detroit. They both agreed that Vic would purchase nothing without talking to Tina about it first and that they both had to agree to go through with any deal or opportunity. Vic had filled her in on the financial crash of that city and how the population had fallen from three million to eight hundred thousand because of the loss of jobs and people on drugs, but Detroit was making a comeback. The major car manufacturers had committed to bringing jobs back, and financial institutions were also committed to helping in the resurrection of the city. That made it a prime location to invest in income property because, as the jobs came back, the people would follow and the price was right for anyone who could see it.

The next morning as Vic got ready to get up, he wanted to look at the clock but didn't because of the strange happening with a certain number, so he waited to look at the clock. Once he felt it was okay, he looked at the digital clock under the TV, and again it was 8:13 a.m. It didn't matter what the hour number was 8, 9, or 3, but the minute number was 13 most of the time. He wondered how that could be. If he woke up in the middle of the night, it was 2:13 a.m.— this had been a recurring theme for over two years. It was as though something or someone was trying to give him a sign or inform him of something unknown to him. Vic hadn't mentioned it to anyone yet but knew something was going on and yet he couldn't put his finger on what it was. If he decided to check the time in the evening, it was 6:13. So now he had stopped trying to avoid it. It was an occurrence that he had accepted, He knew it meant something, but he just couldn't figure out what. Be that as it may, he still sometimes found it annoying, but went about his daily business and, on occasion, wrote it off as a coincidence.

So on this day, he shook off this oddity with an air of excitement because it was his golf day. After a prayer, Vic bounced out of bed and to the middle of the floor to stretch. If he could touch his toes, then stand up straight without too much pain, he'd be ready to go. He loved the open space of the golf courses with their ecosystems of lakes, streams, fish, birds, coyotes, foxes, and, his favorite, rabbits. Most of all, what kept him coming back was hitting a great shot or making a putt for par or birdie. As he rushed out of the house to make his tee time with the guys, he looked at the clock. It was 9:13 a.m. But this morning, he ignored the occurrence and headed for the Westchester Golf Course just north of LAX, short for Los Angeles International Airport.

After his round of golf, Vic headed back to the house to go online to find more properties on the Detroit Land Bank website. He would spend the next two to three hours jotting down addresses and looking at pictures of properties. Most of them still had furniture and trash inside, as though people had just grabbed only the items they valued and left the rest. And why would they care? They were having to move from their longtime home sweet homes that they'd been paying on for years and now all their investment was lost along with family history and memories. Before the Land Bank was set up, Vic had heard that the auction process was held in person at a given site. People were there to bid on a given house with limited knowledge of the property, only to find that the previous owner who had lost it through foreclosure was also there trying to buy it back. This made for some tense encounters with people pleading with opposing bidders not to bid so they could buy their homes back. So, the bidding process went online to quell the drama. Now, ten years after the crash, those scenes were long gone and Vic was hoping to find a two or four-unit property that was in good shape or at least not beyond repair. Vic was surprised when the garage door opened and he heard his wife's car pulling into the garage. He looked at the clock. This time with no occurrence, and it was 5:45 p.m. Then he heard Tina walk in the garage door, letting out a long sigh of relief. Vic walked out from behind his desk in the man cave to greet his wife, kissing her on the cheek and hugging her.

"Hey, babe, how did it go today?"

Tina's face soured at the thought of the day's interactions at work with her patients. "Oh, these people! They just won't do what you ask them to do and then they want to know why their condition is getting worse."

Vic knew this was going to lead to a long outpouring of complaining and frustration, but knew she needed a sounding board and a voice of reason. So this time, he didn't run back into his cave, especially since he was now retired and didn't have to shoulder his work problems with hers. "So what happened?"

Now that Tina knew she had a listening ear, she quickly started pouring it out. "These patients know they need to lose weight and restrict their diet to get their blood pressure down, and I tell them what they need to do. I tell them that their lives are in danger if they don't change their eating habits, exercise, and follow doctor's orders. And still, they don't do it. They come back heavier, blood pressure through the roof, with one foot in the grave just days away from a heart attack or stroke. Then I'd ask, 'Did you take the medication?' No. 'Did you follow the diet restrictions list?' No.' And then they'd ask, 'What can I do?' I've had two patients die this month, and they didn't have to. They could still be alive."

Vic understood how she was feeling. "Listen, Tina, I know it's frustrating and I know you feel responsible for these people as their doctor, but you can't care more than they do. You're a good doctor and you give them what they need to be successful, but if they don't follow through for themselves, it's not your fault. You've done your job by giving them good care, medical advice, and instructions. The only thing left is their part. They have to follow through and do what they need to do to live. And you have no control over what they need to do. That responsibility lies solely on them. What you need to do is protect you."

Confusion washed over her face. "What do you mean?"

"Look, I know you document everything, but you have got to find a way to build some kind of mental toughness, a barrier, or mental callous. A disconnect between you and that patients' poor results when they fail to follow plans that are designed to save their lives. If you crash and burn every time this happens, your health will be at risk and you'll be living out of a shrink's office."

Tina was now in deep thought. "Yes, I see your point, and you're right."

Vic knew he had to stop talking because this was her time to empty her baggage, but felt he needed to add one more thing. "Hey, I know it's easy for me to sit here and say this is what you need to do, but I know it's difficult to accomplish. These are people you know and felt responsible for medically and it's gonna take some time to build that barrier but you have to get to the point where you could say, 'Well, he or she knew what they needed to do and for whatever reason refused to do it.' And then you say to yourself, 'Oh well, I did my part. I did the best I could do.' And then you work to push their demise to the back of your mind and move on to protect you."

Reluctantly, Tina agreed. "It shouldn't have to come to that, but I know I have to do something to save myself emotionally and commit to working on it."

Vic continued to listen for another half an hour until she had emptied her soul and felt better. Tina thanked her husband for his support and hugged him before he retreated to the cave to watch what was left of a football game and to get ready for his upcoming trip.

Vic and Steve were in daily contact, making sure everything was in place. The three weeks had passed quickly and Vic was leaving that afternoon at 3:00 p.m. His bag was packed and it was Tina's early day getting off from work so she was taking him to the airport. He spent his last free hour looking at Google maps of Detroit online. He was locating the properties he had found at the Land Bank and

32

began numbering them in order so they wouldn't be zigzagging across town, wasting time and gas. Once they saw all the places in a given area, they would leave that part of town for good.

Vic looked at the clock on his phone, and his hour was gone. It was one o'clock. Then he heard Tina pull into the garage. He realized that he'd have plenty of time to finish the order when he got to Steve's house in Chicago.

Tina walked in. "Ready to go?"

Vic nodded and took one last look at his desk to make sure he was not leaving anything. He had his larger blue cool water sports bag already downstairs, and that was it. Vic prided himself on packing light and put his notepad on top and zipped up his bag. "I'm ready," he said, throwing his bag in her car and they headed for the airport. Vic was wearing black slip-on casuals for going through security, golf slacks, a long sleeve shirt, and his favorite hoody to keep warm at thirty-five thousand feet.

Tina was still in her scrubs and started double-checking the plan. "So, Vic, you're not going to put in a bid until we've talked first, right?"

Her line of questioning instantly annoyed Vic. "Didn't we go over this for the third time last night?"

Tina had forgotten they had thoroughly discussed it. "Yes, I know, but I just wanted to make sure."

Vic felt an unwarranted lack of trust and fear that had never been present in their previous deals, but this one was out of state and she wouldn't be there.

Tina was now upbeat. "So, when are you coming back?"

Vic knew he had already told her, but to keep the peace, he just answered the question. "I'll be back on the twenty-first. I'm sure you'll enjoy your time without me."

Tina smiled. "That's ten days, so I guess I will."

They both chuckled and watched the departure sign go by as they entered the airport. The Southwest terminal was the first one

33

they came to at LAX and Tina pulled up and stopped. Vic gave her a peck on the lips.

"Call me when you get to Chicago," Tina said.

"Will do." He closed the car door and headed to the security line, having already checked in and downloaded a boarding pass online.

Once on the plane, Vic found his window seat and put his bag under the seat in front of him. He loved looking out the window and identifying different landmarks. Usually, the planes took off heading west out over the Pacific Ocean and circled around, passing over near Santa Monica. Then the Wilshire district, Hollywood, and downtown Los Angeles, if the plane was headed east, which this plane was.

A young man puts his bag in the overhead bin and sat down in the aisle seat. Vic looked over to make eye contact, but the fellow never looked up. He then pulled out his laptop and focused on that. He appeared to be a quiet person who stayed to himself. Vic looked back out the window, watching the ground crew move around the plane as they loaded the rest of the baggage and inspected the plane.

Vic took a deep breath and felt a deeper sense of relaxation as people continued to board the plane when suddenly there was a commotion four rows back to his left on the other side of the plane. Vic looked back when he heard a guy say, "Sir, you're in my seat." A nerdy, husky-looking guy with glasses. The conversation goes back and forth until the flight attendant appeared and asked what the problem was. She asked the man, who was seated, for his ticket.

"Sir, you're in the wrong seat," she said.

"My wife and I received seats in different aisles and I was just trying to sit with my wife."

The flight attendant, now annoyed, explained to this poor idiot that just because he didn't book his reservation in time to get two seats together didn't mean that he could take someone else's seat. She then asked him to move and go to his assigned seat. Problem solved.

Then the guy who was asking for his seat said," That's okay, I'll just take another seat."

So, the flight attendant looked around and saw the middle seat next to Vic and said, "There's a seat next to this gentleman here."

Vic, with his bag under the seat in front of him, had his left foot on the leg of that seat when, from the aisle, nerd boy, out of frustration, threw his heavy backpack into his space and missed, hitting Vic's foot.

With his foot smarting, Vic immediately retorted, "Hey, you hit my foot!"

"Your foot should have been on your side."

Now angry and surprised at the rude remark, especially since his foot technically was on the border of the spaces, Vic was now burning a hole in the nerd's face with his stare. He held his tongue in restraint and said nothing while sizzling under the collar. Vic looked away, trying to put the incident behind him, but thought, *What an asshole.*

A few minutes went by when, out of the blue, the nerd leaned over and said, "Now I know you think you're the most important person on this plane, but you're not."

Vic had enough. "Listen, you turd, if you say one more thing to me, I'm going to break your face. You must be some kind of fucking idiot."

The nerd, for the first time, looked Vic in the eye and saw a raging forest fire moving fast and burning uphill toward him. He looked down and shrunk into his seat. Vic realized he had raised his voice and looked at the guy sitting in the aisle seat. He was too close to have missed what was said, but never took his eyes off his device, nor did he turn his head for a glance. People in front and behind got quiet, but no one said a word. All of this and the plane hadn't even left the runway. As the plane taxied from the gate, Vic realized he needed to calm down. A physical altercation would get them both thrown off the plane with all the planning, road trip, investment opportunity, and ticket money gone down the drain. Vic looked at his watch. It was 3:13 p.m. *This is a hell of a start*, he thought and marveled at how one knucklehead deciding to change his seat altered the energy and dynamics on the airplane. At that moment, the jet turbines revved up, and he realized they were on the runway, facing west, and suddenly, a thrust forward, pulling him back in his seat. The acceleration from zero to one hundred eighty miles per hour on the ground was a sensation he'd always loved. He then looked to the right and saw his golf course go by, then the bumping of the wheels stop as they soared out over the Pacific Ocean, then back to the right and off to Chicago.

As Vic got off the plane in Chicago and started up the ramp, he noticed the jackass who sat next to him looking back and walking faster. So Vic stopped in the restroom to put some distance between himself and this guy so as not to appear to be following him and to hopefully never see him again in life. When Vic came out of the restroom, he stopped for a minute to call Steve and continued to the front of the airport.

"Hey, Steve-o! I'm here."

Steve was in the car close by. "Cool, I'm about ten minutes away. I'm in a gold Nissan."

Vic had his earpiece now connected. "Okay, I'll call you back when I get there with an exact location."

Steve agreed and Vic continued to the front when he saw an original Blackhawks jersey next to a new one and stopped for a minute to admire them both but loved the colors on the new one—black, red, green, and yellow, mostly in the feathers. Then, he quickly started moving again to get out front. He was glad it was closer than he had thought. When he got there, he moved to the outer island and Steve was three minutes away. He spotted Steve and waved. Steve pulled over. Vic threw his bag in and the two exchanged pleasantries.

"Vic-O! Good to see you, man. You look well. Taking good care of yourself I see."

The two shook hands and bumped shoulders.

"Hey, I'm trying to, but what about you still looking twenty-five? How is that possible?"

Steve knew it to be true, which was why he also dressed the part to attract younger women. "Hey, still drinking my smoothies with antioxidants?"

"Yeah, I still have that berry recipe you gave me and I still make it from time to time, but after seeing you, I think I'll get back on it." They both laughed.

"Hey man, you hungry?"

Vic gave a resounding, "Yes!"

"Great, let's go grab some Chicago-style pizza."

Vic had been coming to Chicago for years and Steve remembered he had never had a Chicago deep-dish pizza.

"Man, that's a great idea, Stevie. Where are you planning to go?"

Steve, with his eyes glued to the road and traffic, gave a light nod. "The place I like to go, and one of the places I think is the best, is Lou Malnati's. There's one here near Midway airport."

Vic's interest was now peaked. "Yeah, that sounds great."

When the two walked into Lou Malnati's, Vic immediately acknowledged that it was a real restaurant with a Cheesecake Factory feel. He noticed there were people there from every racial background. As world travelers, they both liked that kind of environment.

A hostess came over to seat them right away, leaving menus. Steve recommended the deep-dish. After looking at the menu for a minute or two, the waiter came up and introduced himself, and took the order.

"So what's going on in Detroit," Steve asked.

Vic filled him in on the crash of the economy, how people walked away from and lost homes, and how car manufacturers and financial institutions were committed to bringing back jobs and financing. Steve now understood the vision and opportunity of finding a good property for a fraction of the cost and building equity over time while adding to the monthly cash flow. Steve then asked about managing it from California, so Vic explained the key to success would be to find a good property manager there in Detroit. Vic could see the light turn on in Steve's eyes as he now understood the big picture.

Just as Vic was ready to ask about Steve's property in Louisiana, the waiter returned with the deep-dish pizza and drinks. Steve had ordered pepperoni and Vic the same with black olives. It was so thick

Vic wasn't sure how to proceed. Steve informed him that a knife and a fork might be the best way to go. Even though the waiter had cut it into quarters, Vic took Steve's advice and used the knife and fork. The cheese was so heavy and thick; it was like pulling on a rope, but that first bite was delicious and different.

Steve wasn't sure of the outcome, so with a curious smile and fixed eyes, he asked, "Well, what do you think?"

Vic didn't answer. Not because he didn't like it, he just didn't have the words to describe it. "Man, I like it, but it's different."

Pleased that he liked it, Steve agreed that it was nothing like pizza in Los Angeles.

Vic continued to quantify the new flavors and textures. "This cheese is so thick and flavorful. It's not really a pizza, it's a pie. I get it now. That's why people on this side of the country call it a pizza pie. Now it all makes sense."

Steve smiled. "You got it."

Vic now swigging down a Coke that mixed so perfectly with the crazy good cheese, pepperoni, black olives, and the tasty crust that was more like baked perfection. "Hey! This is like a complete meal. You don't need anything else after this."

Steve's only response was, "Nope."

The guys savored the meal for another thirty minutes and then resumed their conversation in the car.

"So, Steve, what's going on in Slidell?"

Steve perked up with enthusiasm to share his leg of the trip. "Well, my grandmother left my brother and me fifteen acres, as you know, but I've got a couple of ideas. One is to put some mobile or modular homes in to generate some extra income and the second thought is to look into allowing a company to lease the property to install a solar farm."

Vic had heard Steve's ideas before but wanted to make sure his plan hadn't changed.

Steve then added, "But I'm leaning toward the mobile or modular idea."

Vic agreed that the traditional income property route would be faster. The two talked about the timeline and then left the parking lot, headed to Steve's family home to greet Nadine, Steve's mom. Vic looked forward to seeing her because of her spiritual and numerological knowledge and understanding. He felt she was the only one he knew who would have some understanding of this number phenomenon of reoccurring 13s.

On the way to the house, Vic said nothing to Steve about the strange number occurrences and they continued discussing Detroit and Slidell until they pulled up to a quaint home in a Chicago suburb. Vic liked the look of the brick single-family home with a neat lawn and short black wrought-iron fence with a round globe-like yard light on a pole—every house on the street had one.

Steve asked, "Need help with the bag?"

Vic shook his head. "Nope. Don't have any tip money."

They both laughed.

As they went through the gate and up to the front entrance, Vic noticed a new storm door and front door. Steve opened the front door and called out Nadine's name, but she was not there. So he led Vic through the living room, dining room, then the kitchen, to an entrance at the back of the house, and up a flight of stairs. Once there He realized it was an attic that had been remodeled into an upstairs bedroom, bathroom, and closet. As Vic walked in at the top of the stairs, he saw a window at the other end of the room straight ahead that looked down on the front of the house with Steve's single bed on one side and a couch on the other side of the window.

Steve nodded toward the couch. "You can put your bag down."

Vic dropped his bag by the couch and walked over to the window and looked out. "This is a nice view from up here. I can see everything up and down the street."

Steve was now at his dresser near the closet. "Yes, it is. This was my childhood home after my mom and dad divorced. And this was our bedroom, Mike and me." Mike was Steve's brother who now lived in L.A.

"Okay, this is a really cool spot up here, man, I like it. As a matter of fact, I have a name for it. The bird's nest."

Steve smiled. "Hey, that is a good name for it."

After Steve's history of the room, it all made sense. The single bed and room at the top of the house for the boys. Steve then pulled out a cot-like mattress from the wall side of the bed.

"Okay, Vic, I'm going to give you a choice of the bed or the cot."

Vic, a man who liked to camp out, had no interest in putting Steve out of his comfort zone by sleeping in his bed. "The cot is all I need; that's fine."

Steve then clasped his hands. "Oh thank you, bro. This is the first time I get to sleep in the bed when someone else is here."

Vic was glad to help, and Steve was grateful. "Hey, no problem. I'm glad to be saving the hotel money, but who else is up here with you?"

"Oh, I'm talking about Mike when he comes. He always has to have the bed."

"Why is that?"

"He said his back is messed up, I don't know."

Vic was surprised, considering Mike was about five-eleven, muscular, and worked out all the time. "Really? Mike has a bad back? Okay."

"Hey, he could be getting the best of me on that one."

Vic looked at Steve and they both laughed.

"Hey, if the man said he has a bad back, I guess you have to take him at his word."

Steve agreed, and they laughed again. At that moment, they both heard a voice from downstairs.

"Steven! Are you upstairs?"

"Yeah, we made it back."

"Okay."

Steve was glad he was upstairs to get a break from Nadine's long honey-do list and long conversations, but Vic said he wanted to go downstairs and say hello.

"All right," Steve warned, "by doing that, you may be stuck down there for hours in an incessant hell of suffering."

Vic laughed and said, "Stop," as he started down the steps.

"Okay, you like punishment, go for it."

Vic stalled on the steps, realizing how steep they were, and almost stumbled. "Oh shit, I didn't realize they were so steep."

"You're going to wish you had fallen in about an hour."

When they got to the living room, Nadine was sitting in front of the TV in her favorite chair and saw Vic.

"Hey, Vic, you made it. Good to see you and welcome to our home. It's not much, but it's what we have."

This was the first time Vic had been to the Chicago house. He met the McKibbens over twenty years ago through an entertainment lawyer in L.A. Actually, he met Nadine first, who was an established screenplay writer who dabbled in songs but was very connected and running in established Hollywood circles at the time. Nadine decided that Steve working with Vic would be a better fit being in the same age group. So no, this was not the Hollywood Hills, Beverly Hills, or San Marino home that many Angelinos aspired to, and maybe that was what she thought Vic would be measuring their house by. Or maybe she was just being humble. But what Nadine didn't know was that Vic was raised in a similar type of middle-class home with the same cozy, comfortable feel.

"Nadine, stop. This is a nice house. You guys really take good care of it and the neighborhood is well-maintained. I like it."

Nadine looked at Vic as if he was just blowing smoke up her butt, then saw he was sincere. "Well, thank you, sugar. Maybe I've just been looking at it too long and can't see what you see."

"Yes, that can happen, but trust me, there are people out there who would give up their first born for a house like this."

Vic earned his real estate license at nineteen and although he was never successful as an agent, he had extensive knowledge about real estate and knew a good home and location when he saw one.

"Thank you, Vic. Glad you like it." Nadine started in on Steve. "Come here, Stevie. Let me look at your eyes."

Steve walked over. "Okay, here we go, what?" As Nadine looks in his eyes. " Stick out your tongue!"

Steve was now embarrassed. "What!" He stuck out his tongue.

"He's getting fat, Vic. I have to check him out," Nadine said.

Vic was cracking up. "Oh boy, you guys are funny."

Steve felt a little better knowing his buddy was not being judgmental. "Now you know what I'm dealing with every day."

"I have to keep him on his toes, Vic, but I'm lucky to have two big old boys to watch out for me."

Vic knew she was over seventy and agreed. "That's right, Nadine."

Steve fired back. "Yeah, but you need to remember I'm forty years old."

Nadine was not missing a beat. "Yes, but no matter how old you get, you still need your mommy."

Steve was now incensed and in disbelief that she said that in front of Vic. "What? Okay, that's it. I'm out of here. Hey man, I'll be upstairs."

Vic was still laughing. "Steve, I used to hear that one all the time, too. We can't get away from that one."

"You're right Vic, but she's in rare form tonight. You guys go ahead and talk, I'll see you when you come back up." Steve disappeared into the kitchen and back toward the stairs.

Nadine held out her hand in Steve's direction, saying. "Pressed down, shaken up, and rolled over, you are blessed."

Vic was impressed and surprised at her prayer for her son because he had always heard that verbiage in church and had never known Nadine to be a church going woman, but he had felt a shift of energy in the room when she said it. Before he could respond, Nadine rolled right into him.

"How's your wife?"

She caught Vic off-guard with a complete change of conversation. "She's good Nadine, working hard, watching out for her mom, and trying to keep up with her TV shows."

Nadine smiled."That's great. She's taking care of business. Such a nice lady."

Vic nodded in acknowledgment. "Thanks for asking Nadine. I'll let her know you said hello and asked about her."

"Please do."

"Nadine, I have a situation going on that I need to talk to you about."

Nadine peered at Vic over the top of her glasses. "What's going on?"

"Well, it has to do with numerology and I know that's your thing."

She nodded.

"I have this number that keeps coming up, you know, appearing. So much so that it is clearly not a coincidence."

Nadine was now clearly interested. She leaned in. "Showing up how?"

Vic got his thoughts together. "Well, it started in the mornings. I would wake up before the alarm and it didn't matter if it was three, four, or five in the morning, the minute number would always be 13. I thought it was odd but tried to ignore it. Then, it started during the day. I would get an urge to see what time it was and no matter what the hour, the minutes would always be 13. It's like someone or something is trying to tell me something, but I don't have a clue as to what or why. It got to the point that I would wake up and want to look at the clock but wouldn't because I knew what it would be. So I would bury my face back in the pillow and wait, then look, and when I did, the minutes would be 13. I began to feel I couldn't escape it. I'd go to see how much money I have in my wallet—13 dollars. Then I counted my toes the other day, Yep, 13."

Amazed, Nadine peered over her glasses. "Really! Let me see! For real?"

Vic, with a straight face said, "Yes for real. Except for the toes, just kidding about the toes."

They both broke out laughing, lightening the mood that had become mysterious in the darkness of the living room with only the light from the TV on mute.

"Okay, you got me on that Vic. That was a good one but very interesting."

"What the hell is this about? What do you think?"

Nadine was now perplexed. "This is unusual and I understand why you feel there's more to it and there has to be or it wouldn't be happening with such high frequency. Hmm, the universe is trying to communicate, the infinite wisdom. Let me look at some things. What day of the month were you born?"

"The first."

"One times any number is that number, meaning. You could be many things. It's also a strong number and you're a strong individual, usually doing things on your own. Hmm, what I'm feeling deep in my spirit is twelve plus one."

Confusion showed on Vic's face. "Twelve plus one?"

"Yes. Don't ask me why that's just what came to me."She repeated twelve plus one over and over in her head."That's it! The twelve disciples."

Vic was now bewildered and with questioning disbelief. "The twelve disciples? What do they have to do with me?"

She looked him in the eyes and said with confidence, "You're the one. One plus twelve is thirteen. You're going to deliver a message or do something. I don't know what it is, but it's positive and He's going to use you for that purpose. Don't ask me what it is, but that means you'll be around for a while because the universe has chosen you for something. That's all I can tell you. That's what I'm getting."

"And all this just came to you?"

Nadine gave him a don't-blame-me attitude. "That's how it is, Vic. I'm just a messenger myself. And I don't get to read the answers to the messages I deliver. It could be large or small, or I could just be a crazy old lady."

They both laughed. Vic now felt some gratitude. "Yeah, I know your boys think you're out there somewhere, but I don't. Thank you."

Nadine accepted his appreciation. "You're welcome."

Vic hugged her. "Well, I'm headed upstairs to get some rest. It's been a long flight and a long day."

Once back upstairs, Steve was laying on his bed and asked facetiously, "Hey, how did you get away? I thought for sure you'd be down there for at least another five hours."

They chuckled and started talking about the drive to Detroit.

The next day they rented a car for the trip and helped Nadine out at Home Depot, buying items for an empty rental she and Steve had been trying to put back together, working with a contractor. That evening, Steve packed his bag, and the following morning on a Thursday they took off for Detroit. Vic said nothing about his conversation with Nadine or the dreams—those crazy recurring dreams that were broken and seemed to make no sense. Dreams that were usually about men from another time period long ago, walking around and talking among themselves. In a cave or cavern, or some strange place outside of this thing we know as Earth, space, and time.

CHAPTER 4

At the same time, in a state, a few hours from Washington, DC, an alien scientist by the name of Spidis was tweaking his cyber-net mind control program for his boss, Rhynous, at an undisclosed location outside of the US Capitol. An ancient alien, Rhynous has been on Earth since the early days of the Roman Empire. He has traveled between Earth and his adopted home, a planet called Larus, in the outer reaches of the Zeta Reticuli system, still undetected by astronomers and space agencies on Earth.

His head scientist, Spidis, had been experimenting with nanites traveling on laser light to enter a host body and to help alter and control a person's actions and thought processes. The idea of nanotechnology is not an alien invention. It was conceived here on Earth. However, in the hands of aliens with more advanced technology, this maverick alien scientist had the means and know-how to make nanobots a reality, and he did. Spidis created twenty nanites on an earthling laptop after reformatting his alien programs to work on earthling computer operating systems. Then he designed the nanites or nanobots for his boss's desired purpose—mind control. He created each nanobot in the likeness and a cross between an ant and a spider on a micro-level and outfitted it with eight legs, four on each side. The front legs had clamping devices for attaching to brain neurons to short-circuit thoughts from the brain of a host, and to conduct programmed thoughts from the nanobot's nano-processor brain that Spidis or Rhynous would control. The clamps could also be used as wrenches to build or tear things apart. The first of two middle legs are in the form of cutting devices as surgical lasers with a temperature range that could be weaponized and the second middle leg, on each side, had an electrically charged end that could cauterize, mend, or stimulate living organic, or inorganic materials, like the laser but more importantly conduct electrical current from one nanobot to the next. The back legs were like the front, fitted with clamping devices at the end of each leg to grab hold for stability or to clamp onto another nanobot to create a chain of nano wires and circuitry. The nanobot's eyes were cameras for the person or alien at the controls of a cell phone or laptop to see the work being done.

It certainly appeared that Spidis had more ideas in his designs than mind control for these nanites because their capabilities were numerous and potentially dangerous. If the nanites were ever to become self-aware, they, too, could take control of Earth and be lords over mankind. For this reason, Spidis installed a command-only override on their nano processor brains, should one or more become self-aware. Also, this override would be instrumental in controlling nanite replication. Spidis created the first twenty nanobots with his redesign of a 3D printer into a nano printer, an alien design. Each nanite brain processor is a program on how to replicate themselves but it, too, had an override, allowing the programmer to tell the nanites when to replicate, how many to replicate, and when to stop replicating. Very pleased with his progress on this project for his boss, the wealthy galactic pirate Rhynous, Spidis had motives of his own. He was a lustful lover of women and had plans of controlling those chosen by him for his pleasures and scientific experiments. Making him the lesser of two evils as Rhynous's plan was to destroy Earth as we knew it and become Earth's only ruler. But at this time, it's just an unthinkable diabolical plan in the making, unknown to the rest of the world. Rhynous's first target, the president of the United States, and with the help of Dr. Spidis and his young witch, Kali, their plan was quietly coming together.

Rhynous was preparing to leave Earth and return to his home planet of Larus to continue to amass a formidable army and ready his fleet of four alien UFO mother ships.

Meanwhile, Kali and Spidis were carrying out a secret recruitment plan here on Earth and were making good progress. Kali had been visiting the White House on reconnaissance to help execute their plan, and Spidis was testing the cyber-net laser grid nanite web trap. Rhynous, now an inter-dimensional traveler, had mastered the alien science of wormholes and compressing space on Larus and traveled back and forth at will, turning what would be light years into days. On the other side of the Moon was a stationary wormhole Rhynous discovered two hundred fifty years ago. From the Moon, it takes one day to reach the wormhole and once there, it took two days to travel thirty-nine light years to get to Larus.

Unlike scientific speculation concerning visible light at the end of a wormhole, there was not always an ample amount of light from Earth's sun to illuminate the entrance of the wormhole on the Earth's side entrance. Rhynous had to time his departures because the Earth was not stationary as it rotated and circled the sun. When Earth was closest to the wormhole, it was also blocking most of the sunlight from the sun, making the wormhole almost invisible. Rhynous and his scientific personnel had created a detection system to identify the entrance with a technology similar to infrared light that lit up the Earth's side entrance to the wormhole via a computer screen. Rhynous's travel route worked like this, with his alien technology he could open a star gate, with the push of a button, that took him to his small remote base on the dark side of the Moon where he kept his alien saucer. From there, he flew at a quarter of light speed—167.6 million miles per hour plus—to get to the wormhole that bent south of planet Earth to Zeta Reticuli. On his return trip to Earth, the entrance to the wormhole was well lit with Zeta Reticuli's twin stars providing plenty of light. Then once he was on the Moon, it got strange and interesting. Because of the Earth's and Moon's rotations, when Rhynous initiated the star gate, Kali generated a beacon of dark energy through incantations, guiding him back to her compound in a strange mountain town with a weird mysterious energy of its own and a history of alien sightings in the hills and mountains in that region, a few hours away from the White House. Rhynous's true alien looks were masked with a genius of a device that changed his looks by wearing an alien electronic necklace. So, he appeared to be a handsome thirty-five to forty-year-old John Doe. Yet under the surface of what appeared to be a man of average height and a fit build was the raging fire of a genius psychopath whose appetite for power and more wealth was monstrously beyond reason. His dark energy attracted darkness like Kali and Spidis. Kali was smitten by him, but knew she was just a tool in his arsenal and even with that knowledge, she was still like a magnet to his wealth, power, and the ability for destruction. In simple terms, he was a bad boy, and she was a witch in search of one, and Rhynous far exceeded that.

"So when are you leaving?" Kali asked.

"In the morning," Rhynous said coldly.

Even though his reply was void of love and compassion, she was turned on by the ice that chilled his response. The negativity of it somehow charged her, making her want to dig in and win him over, a sign that she was highly dysfunctional and looked for love in all the wrong places. She couldn't realize that her efforts would ultimately lead her to an empty place, just as it had for her mother, who had left California, leaving Kali's father behind who Kali had never known. So she operated in the only way she knew how and contained deep anger and rage at not having known her father. It all seemed perfectly normal to Kali as she was a victim of her mother's drunken rage aimed at the father Kali never knew.

Kali had been a constant reminder of her father to her mother because she resembled her dad in a female body. Kali was a victim who suffered mental and physical abuse at the hands of her mother. She was a pretty girl with a kind smile, and soft green eyes but a hardened soul and a dark endless pit in her spirit that would make one question whether she could be redeemed. For now, she was a wolf in sheep's clothing, going undetected and unsuspected.

"Kali, I need you and Spidis to work out the logistics of the recruitment centers across the country and get this cyber-net web up and running. That's the key that will open the door for my space fleet to arrive without being attacked until we're strategically in position around the Earth and ready for battle," Rhynous said.

"Okay, well, I've been setting them up as homeless shelters, but I'm short on recruiters to run them. As soon as the cyber-net spider web trap is ready, it will kick recruiting into high gear, which all falls on Spidis. He said he's close. I don't think we should try and rush him. He knows the clock is ticking. He hardly sleeps as it is."

"Look! I don't care how you handle it, but when I get back I need that spider web ready to go," Rhynous said with a squirt of venom.

"I will do my best Majestic Leader."

"Don't patronize me."

"Well, that's what your troops call you."

"Stop it." In a rage, he kissed her. "Okay, he has some time. I'm probably going to have to make another trip to Larus after this one, but you need to keep reminding him what's at stake here."

"I think we'll have a better result if you allow me to handle it like that."

"Fine, just handle it," Rhynous barked.

Kali knew she had bought her friend and confidant, Dr. Spidis, some time.

The next morning, Kali fixed Rhynous a light breakfast then packed some water and protein bars in a simple plastic grocery bag as if he were going to work across town. Rhynous nodded without a "thank you" and then pressed the button on a handheld remote, generating a mini star gate. The crackle and hum of electricity in the room was strong enough to burn down the whole house but somehow contained in the space between the floor and ceiling as it hovered in mid-air. Then, from a circular opening, in the space, in the middle, a silvery liquid appeared, held in place by its own energy field. As soon as it appeared, Rhynous walked into the star gate as it opened up and disappeared.

When he stepped through, he put his foot down on the Lunar star gate platform that was built decades earlier by his scientific team with one coordinate to the Moon and one coordinate coming back to Earth. Rhynous took a deep breath of the Moon's fresh unspoiled air. The thin atmosphere on the Moon naturally contained some oxygen, but what made this possible was an unknown race of aliens generating oxygen, miles of it. Rhynous had a small remote compound on the dark side of the Moon and he was not alone.

There were other planets represented there. The gray aliens had a large base visible in the distance, along with the Larian space force thirty kilometers east and too far away to notice Rhynous's little outpost. However, there was an even larger operation at work on the dark side of the Moon but Rhynous had no idea who they were and was not trying to find out what planet they were from. He knew they must be a part of the Federation of Planets because they were operating under planetary federation rules that state: when encountering other beings on foreign moons or planets, come in peace and respect territorial boundaries. That was the law on the Moon and why no Apollo missions were confronted by those on the dark side of the Moon. These aliens were parked in their saucers on a not-too-distant ridge, marveling at the primitive and different types of technology being used by earthlings from the United States.

Earth's propulsion was based on depleting fuel explosions as opposed to gravity-defying electromagnetic energy refueled by an endless supply of starlight energy that existed throughout the universe. The consensus on Larus was that earthlings were evolving and might someday join the Federation of Planets when they learned to come to agreements without war and stopped the use of nuclear bombs that could poison the Earth, along with people and aliens that live there. The Earth is also a research laboratory for federation planets and a resting outpost for those beings traveling to galaxies beyond Earth. Rhynous was a pirate and loved the idea of war and conquest. He had no use for federation guidelines. His goal was to rape and pillage the blue planet and then rule it and extract all of Earth's riches.

What he did have use for were the giant oxygen machines the unknown aliens had erected that supplied a one-hundred-twenty-mile radius of oxygen on the dark side of the Moon to supply their workers with air, freeing them from cumbersome space suits. They had the largest operation on the Moon, mining Helium-3 ore for their home planet a safer cleaner nonradioactive isotope in the rocks that didn't produce dangerous waste products. Their buildings and structures were very organic looking, blending in with the Moon's rocky desert and cratered terrain. They had structures to house their earthmovers, spaceships, and their humanoids. There was a huge underground mining operation on their territory with vents above ground to release dark smoke from their underground machinery. They had what appeared to be a giant organic-looking satellite dish for communications back to their origin planet and to monitor incoming, outgoing, and passing spacecraft. Also, these technologically advanced beings had some type of reactor in a creator that supplied them with an electrical power source. These beings were smart, mining on the side of the Moon that the Earth never saw, depleting Earth's Moon of valuable ore. It was rumored that the United States had knowledge of their presence on the Moon, top secret of course, but intelligently ignored the alien presence because of Earth's inability to compete with such advanced technology. Rhynous had a plan of his own to deplete the Earth itself as he watched the mining operation from a distance in amusement. He then realized that he needed to keep moving and stepped down off the platform and headed for his saucer which was hidden in a makeshift hangar.

Once inside the craft, he immediately checked his power levels and they were good enough to get him out of the shadows of the dark side of the Moon and into the light of the sun that would charge his reactor core and power grid. As he hovered out of the hangar, he shut the door remotely and stayed near ground level, flying in the opposite direction from the other outposts and far enough away to not be identified. Then out over a distant mountain range and up at a high rate of speed escaping the Moons atmosphere and into the light of the sun that caused his craft to glow. The ship's clear solar coating immediately began to surge electricity into the core engine and batteries powering the spaceship's grid, causing it to now generate a more vibrant hum. Rhynous initiated the onboard computer system with the coordinates for the wormhole and then set it to fly remotely by computer. He then got up from his pilot seat and stretched out on the padded bench seat that surrounded the core housing. Rhynous smirked with a sense of relaxation and began digging in the bag of goodies Kali had prepared for him.

The next day back on Earth, Spidis continued to work on the cyber-net. After having made some adjustments to the laser grid with his eyes fixed under a microscope, he saw that the laser grid had a steady temperature of seventy degrees. At seventy, the nannies are no longer falling from the beams of light or being incinerated by the heat. Inside, Spidis was ready to explode with joy and excitement when his mind digressed to thoughts of the beautiful women he would have at his disposal and to do with them as he pleased. As he became aroused by his own lustful and diabolical thoughts, a bucket of cold water walked through the door. It was Kali.

"Hey, Spidis, how's it coming?"

Spidis looked up from his microscope wild-eyed, energetic, and intense. "Take a look."

Kali wondered if this was it, sensing the excitement as if a baby was on the way. "They're not falling. They're not falling!"

Spidis laughed as if he had just struck gold. "That's right! I need to run some more tests but I think we've got it."

As they jumped with joy back on Earth, Rhynous was nearing the wormhole when a computer sensor alerted him of his approach. He instructed the computer to give him a visual on the monitor by voice command, and it acknowledged with the standard sultry soothing non computerized-sounding voice, as the wormhole appeared. Rhynous sat down in the pilot's seat, readying himself to switch on the guidance sensors on the perimeter of the saucer's edge. He could now see the wormhole on the screen in red, still small but getting larger as he approached. When Rhynous reached the giant entrance, he did what he always did, took measurements of the inside circumference of the wormhole. The saucer's computer was busy with measurements, centering the ship in the hole, increasing the speed at Rhynous's command, and cross-referencing the size of the mother ships to the circumference of the wormhole at every point. No one knows what would happen if a space vessel scraped the side of a wormhole. It could stretch, tear, expand the compressed distance, collapse the hole, or damage the ship, and Rhynous doesn't want to be the first to find out.

CHAPTER 5

In Chicago, Vic and Steve started out on their journey early the next morning at seven, each with a single travel bag and a case of water for the road. Steve and Vic were excited to get the road trip underway for different reasons. Vic was more interested in getting to Detroit and Steve was curious about Vic's leg of the trip, but more interested in getting to Louisiana to get his project going and to see the lay of the land that he hadn't seen in years. They both felt great about having a wingman for each leg and before they knew it, they were at the state line, heading into Indiana.

The bulk of their conversation surrounded the outskirts of Rio De Janeiro, Brazil where Steve had an apartment with his girlfriend and a hot dog stand in Nilopolis. However, Steve's hot dog stand had caught fire and burned up during rush hour, his busiest time of the day. And though it wasn't funny at the time of the fire, Vic found it hilarious just imagining the scene. He had asked Steve why he had traveled all the way to South America to open a damn hot dog stand. And that's when he found out Steve was looking at establishing dual citizenship, but starting a small business with a food item that was not popular there—the hot dog—was a gamble. It was all so outlandish and far away, but Vic was never one to step on someone else's vision. Steve's plan had been to grow it into an actual building location, then possibly a franchise. The fire seemed to have also burned up Steve's dream as he was now working on starting an English school and getting Vic to come and help advise him on planning the curriculum. Vic had tried to get Steve to look into tourism, which was a huge business there, but the idea fell on deaf ears. By the time this conversation ended about an hour into the trip, they had passed through Gary, Indiana, and were crossing the state line into Michigan. Vic had found it interesting that when they crossed into Indiana, there was no real change in scenery, but as they drove further into Michigan, the open grasslands shrank into the evergreen of pine trees through Kalamazoo and Ann Arbor up Interstate 94 to Detroit.

About sixty miles out, Vic started calling motels they had mapped out to check for rooms. The first one was downtown Detroit with only street parking and the next one was further away than expected. When Steve started asking about what street to exit on, they decided to work on a room later and Vic went to his notebook for the address of the first property he had mapped out. A street named Stoepel off Interstate 96, which crossed Interstate 94 up ahead. As they merge onto Interstate 96 to the Livernois Avenue exit, Steve asked. "Do we need a gun over here? I don't know this neighborhood. I'm just saying."

Surprised at the question, but understanding the concern, Vic said, "Well, let me see. I wasn't able to get my .9-millimeter on the airplane so no, we don't have a gun. Did you bring one from Chicago?"

"No."

Vic chimed in quickly, tickled and agitated all at the same time. "It's a hell of a time to be asking that question. After days of planning, it came as we're getting off the freeway minutes from the first stop?"

Steve was now on the defensive. "Hey, just checking."

Vic was sensing the chill of cold feet in Steve's size 11. "Here's what I brought, a brain full of diplomacy. If there's a problem, we'll explain it away and it's only 10 a.m., the night people are still sleeping."

"You know, that's a good point. It's early." Even though Vic had explained the plan, Steve's question conjured up thoughts of young thugs hanging out, old timers in the park drinking and gangsters looking for trouble.

Once off the freeway and on Livernois, it was all quiet. And then a left down a street that consisted of mostly demolished homes, leaving green grass, empty lots, and trees for blocks. Then a right on to Stoepel where suddenly there was a block full of older homes. It was quiet and no one was on the street. It was like a ghost town.

Vic said to Steve, "Do you see this?"

Steve was now waffling in a joking manner. "Yes, this is what we were expecting, right?"

Vic was not amused. "Based on your last question, no it's not."

They drove up the street until they came to the address in the notebook. Vic was pleased to see that the duplex looked as it did on the Land Bank website: a modern brick façade with tinted picture windows on both units. What he hadn't seen were the houses next door and across the street that needed work, but were still occupied and standing. It was against the law to enter a property or to jump the fence of a gated property, so since there was no fence, Vic walked down the driveway to look at the back of the structure. It needed some work, but nothing major. Vic made a note of it and headed back to the car.

Steve, who was still at the wheel, asked, "What do you think?"

Vic said in a mediocre tone, "Well, it looks good from the outside, but I'll need to get back on the website to see inside and the neighborhood could be better, but it's still a possibility. Let's head onto the next house."

Before Vic got back in the car, they noticed a boy coming up the street about nine to ten years old. He was their first encounter with another human being in Detroit. He was African American with a smooth, happy face still wearing a pajama top.

Steve got out of the car and smiled. "Hello. How are you doing, young man?"

The boy, in an innocent tone, said, "Hi" and looked at Vic, who exchanged the same pleasantry.

He was just a normal kid who could have been from any town in America, Black, white, or brown. It didn't matter, he was just a kid. Somehow this benign encounter quieted their anticipation of conflict or excessive danger and caused all mental visions of negativity to disappear. They were well traveled enough to leave their antennas up, but much more relaxed and now focused on the task at hand.

They got in the car and Vic found the next street as Steve pulled away. Vic punched the address into the GPS. Vic's planning was paying off. In the next hour they had looked at six more places all in close proximity to one another but none of them being worthy of a bid. Some had dilapidated roofs and tilted porches. Others were not duplexes. The most surprising thing was that many of the neighborhoods had been completely torn down, with only a few homes left standing. And the emptiness of that part of the city had caught them both by surprise. Then Vic remembered the population statistics going from three million to eight hundred thousand. Even so, nothing could have prepared them for blocks of empty streets with nothing but trees and grass. The empty streets seemed surreal, but it was getting to be noon and Vic suggested they grab something to eat. Steve also felt the bite of an empty stomach and pointed out a Mickey D's down the street, so they pulled in.

As they got out of the car, Vic noticed more activity on the streets but he still felt a void in the air, knowing what the population had been. After receiving their order, they found a seat by the window and dug in.

"So, Stevie, what did you think of the Stoepel units?"

Steve took a swig of his drink to clear his throat. "Well, it looked good, but I agree you need to see the inside and like you said, the houses around it weren't great."

Knowing Steve saw what he did, Vic was glad to bounce that off him to confirm his finding. "Yeah, it has some potential but not at the top of the list."

After they finished their lunch, they set out to venture to his next group of properties on the list when Steve poses a question, "So what do you think?"

"I think it's late in the game."

Steve was now confused. "Explain."

"These neighborhoods are ghost towns now and the best of what was here has been sold, and the rest torn down, leaving what we see. So we're combing an empty beach with a metal detector, hoping to find a diamond ring," Vic said.

"So, what exactly are you looking for?"

"I'm looking for two or four units in fair condition in a good to great neighborhood."

Steve pondered for a minute. "That's going to be hard to find."

Vic smiled. "It's out there and we'll find it, but it's a needle in a hay stack. We may not get the bid, but we'll find it. You ready to get back on it?"

Steve now had some pep. "Yes, let's do it."

They headed to a street near Rosa Parks Boulevard, but the place was in ruins so they kept driving and found themselves on McNichols Road looking at a sea of empty blocks leveled down to grass and trees like the area they had just left. Somehow, this stretch of land felt more serene and as they were driving, Vic spotted a patch of homes and on a hunch tells Steve to make a right on that street.

There were four big homes on the left side of the street with a bulldozer in the front yard of the last house. On the right were two homes on the corner they had just passed. Then a fenced area that looked green, but possibly some kind of city yard across the street. Beyond that were empty lots for what seemed like two or three miles around, with an occasional two or three houses here or there. They drove around for a few blocks and didn't see a soul, not even a stray dog. So Vic asked Steve to go back over to where the bulldozer was, believing someone was there but on a break. As they turned the corner, they saw a white truck pulling up to the fenced area across the street from the dozer. A man got out of the truck to go unlock the gate. Vic told Steve to pull over so he could talk to this older gentleman who he presumed to be a city worker.

Vic jumped out of the car and down the driveway. "Hello!" He caught the man's attention, who then stopped and turned to see Vic, unsure of his intentions. "Hi, I'm here from Los Angeles, looking at Land Bank properties and I was wondering if you could help me out."

The man, now a little more at ease, took off his hat and scratched his head. "Well, I don't know how much help I can be, but I'll tell you what I know."

Vic smiled, pleased with the response. "Oh thank you. I appreciate whatever you can tell me. What's your name?" Vic extended his hand.

"James, the name is James." As they shook hands.

"James, do you know where there are any properties still available?"

"No, not right off hand. As you can see there's not much left around here."

"Are you on that bulldozer?"

"Oh no, that guy's on a break somewhere…I don't know."

"So you don't work for the city?"

"No not at all. That's my house next to where the dozer is and this is a community garden. We have to keep it locked up to keep people out."

"I'm way off base. I thought for sure you were a city guy."

"No, but I see why you would think that with the truck and all." Vic was ready to offer an apology and bade him adieu when James said, "But look, I've been thinking about what you're looking for. I can't say for sure, but I think if you go to the corner here and make a left, then go to the end of that street and make a right. When you make that right, stay on that street for oh, two or three miles, and you'll come to a pretty nice area. I can't say for sure that you'll find anything, but I think that's a good place to look."

Vic quickly wrote down the directions without a street name and thanked James for his help, but he couldn't leave without asking a burning question. "James, I know that a lot of the car plants closed and people left, but why are they tearing down all of these houses? Some of them don't look like they need to be destroyed."

James took off his hat again. "That's a good question, young man, for which there is no one good answer. Yes, jobs went away, but there were also drugs. This whole area, as far as you can see, used to be nice twenty-five or thirty years ago. As good as the area I just gave you directions to. All good families, kids playing in the streets during the summers, homes well maintained and in the evenings every house had a yard light. In the evenings the lights would come on and there would be people walking down the streets and kids continuing to play with neighbors sitting on the porch. It was just a great community to be a part of.

"Then, jobs started to go and worst of all the drugs. Then you had some of the parents pass away with the kids inheriting the properties and they let them go to hell. Then, the crack and meth just wiped them out. So you had a bunch of these drug heads still in these homes with no money to pay the utilities. In the winter, the dope heads built fires in trash cans or barbecue pits trying to stay warm and then accidentally would burn up the whole house. Then they would go from empty house to empty house and many of those would end up on fire.

"You see the house where the dozer is?"

Vic nodded.

"One of these zombie drug heads got in there and started a fire. If you look at the side of the house, you can see where the flames were coming out. As soon as that happens, the city condemns the place and tears it down. Some of them are in such bad shape they condemn and tear them down before anyone can get in there. You still see some of these zombies walking around, but not like they were four or five years ago. Well, that's what happened."

Vic was now in shock. "That's quite a story."

James answered with quiet anger. "It's a damn tragedy, if you ask me, and what you see here is the result."

Vic was speechless, not really knowing what to say. "I have to agree that's a real tragedy."

James sensed Vic's need to get going and the awkwardness of the moment. "Yep well, that's how we got to this. It was nice meeting you. Good luck to you guys. I hope you find what you're looking for."

The two shook hands and Vic thanked him for his time then hurried back to the car where Steve had been watching the whole exchange.

"That was quite a conversation, Vic. What did he say?"

Vic took a deep breath. "He said a whole lot, but before I get into that, go to the corner and make a left." Vic explained that James had directed them to a promising area. Once they made the right on to the street that would take them there, Vic told Steve about the drug epidemic and how James had referred to the drug addicts as zombies. And also explained to Steve why so many houses had been torn down. Ironically, no sooner than that conversation had ended, they saw a strange stiff figure walking down the middle of the street, wearing baggy pants and a big winter coat zipped all the way up with the hood pulled over the head and it was sixty-five degrees.

"What's this?" Steve asked, as he veered slightly to the right.

As they got closer he slowed down and they realized the clothes were dirty. As they peered into the darkness of the hood, all they saw were two big eyes fixed straight ahead. As they drove by, the person never looked at or acknowledged their passing car.

"What was that?" Steve asked, with surprise. "A zombie?"

"Yes, it was."

"That's so weird. We were just talking about zombies and then what do we see? A zombie, and James wasn't exaggerating. What a trip," Steve said with excitement.

Vic just shook his head, thinking about the devastation a drug epidemic could impose on a neighborhood or a city.

As they drove for another half a mile, they came to a house sitting all by itself, seemingly in the middle of nowhere. The family was out unloading the car as it appeared someone had been to the store. Steve waved and they waved back. Well out into the distance, they could see a canopy of trees with green grass for a mile in either direction and straight ahead where houses used to be. Vic envisioned Detroit before it was settled in 1701. He was thinking back to the 1600s when it was a wide open Native American land before the French, and realized it must have looked like this, green and wide open as far as the eye could see.

It was peaceful and quiet except for the hum from the engine when Steve finally broke the silence. "Do you think it's up here?"

Vic answered confidently, "Yes, we just need to keep going. We'll come to it when we get to that huge canopy of trees."

"You sure about that, Vic?"

"Yep, I trust what James said and I believe that's where we'll find it."

"Okay," Steve said and continued driving.

As they got closer, Vic senses they're driving into an oasis and begins seeing big well-kept homes through the trees. "This is it, Stevie! This is what we've been looking for."

"Yeah, I have to agree, Vic. It looks like a really good area."

Many of the trees were displaying fall colors in yellow, gold, red, and orange. The snow that would come soon would soon replace the fallen leaves on the ground around the trees and replace their breathtaking colors and mood. Unlike Southern California, the seasons were more defined in the east and Midwest. Like a clay sculptor covering up his figurine with a damp white cloth, so would it be with the coming winter snow. Though for now, it was gorgeous, a sight for sore eyes. It was clear to Vic that this was an upper middle class neighborhood or better and that there would be no duplexes on that immediate stretch of blocks. Still, they combed the blocks, continuing southeast until the appearance of the homes in size and manicure had eased down to middle class. It was like fishing—keep looking for a good spot to cast the line and then *bam!*

"Steve, stop! There's one."

Steve stopped, but kept peering down the street. "That looks like another one down the street."

Vic jotted down the address on Tyler and when they got down the street, Steve was right. It was another fenced duplex with a Land Bank sign. After finding four locations worth bidding on in that area, the well had run dry and they had caught the big fish. Vic had a feeling of satisfaction, knowing he had found what he was looking for and thanked James again, from afar, for guiding them to that area.

Once he finished taking addresses and notes on each property, Steve asked, "So how you feel? You good?"

Vic knew Steve had something on his mind. "Yes, I think that's it here."

"Good, 'cause we need to find a motel."

The sound of those words from Steve's mouth snatched Vic from his euphoria. "Oh man, I completely forgot. That's my fault."

"No, we're good. I just don't want it to get too late."

Vic was grateful Steve was on top of it. "Okay, good looking out. Let's do it."

They had decided to stay a little ways out of the city and settled on a motel in Warren, just outside of Detroit proper. It was nothing fancy. With no women on the trip, the guys had decided to conserve as much as possible and to stay in the suburbs to avoid any trouble. The rule was, if there were two or more reviews online complaining about roaches, that motel was scratched off the list. It was now approaching 4:00 p.m. under a clear October sky and they wanted to get a room before every place filled up, so they headed south down Interstate 75 to Warren, Michigan.

On the way there, Steve was now impressed with the day's work. "Vic, I'm glad I had a chance to see you work it. You said the property was there, and we found it, four of them."

"Yes, glad you enjoyed it, but the hard part is yet to come. I still have to get the bid and it's a possibility they're already gone."

Steve came to 13 Mile Road and Vic thought, *Here we go. It's starting with the number.* When they pulled into the driveway, there were people standing around, talking a bit more than you would normally see at a motel. Steve noticed the way some of them looked.

"Hey, you see this? Looks like some meth heads over there."

"Well, they don't look like they're looking for trouble and look, there's a nice family over there." Steve wasn't so sure, but agreed to check it out, so they headed to the window.

"Hello, how can I help you?" said the clerk.

"Hi, we need a room for two nights."

The clerk asked Vic if it was just the two of them and then started the paper work. Vic pulled out his credit card.

"Okay, we're full on the front with our regulars so I'm going to put you guys on the back side where it's quieter, so you guys will be in number 13."

Vic's heart raced, and he thought, *Of course its room number 13.What other number would it be?* He just looked at the man and eventually said, "Okay."

Steve picked up on the strange vibe from Vic as they walked down the outside hallway. "Hey, everything okay?"

"I guess." Vic handed Steve a room key.

They walked to the end of the hall that let out on a back side parking lot and turned left down the walkway. The first room they came to was room 13. Vic opened the door and noticed a stain on the floor and dust. Vic shook his head and said, "No." He asked Steve for his key and headed back to the window, telling the clerk the floor hadn't been cleaned and requested another room. The clerk apologized and gave Vic keys to room 14. When they walked in, the floor was clean and, more importantly to Vic, it wasn't number 13.

Steve was now believing his friend was a germaphobe or a psychic, but was pleased with the result. "Vic, you were on top of that one. Did you know it wasn't right at the window before we got here? What just happened?"

The reality was that Vic became agitated when the number came up again and when it appeared not to be up to snuff, he fervently marched back to the window and had it changed. Look, I just didn't feel right about it from the start. I can't really explain it."

Steve was satisfied with the answer and the room. "That's the old Vic I know. This is much better."

Still not choosing to tell Steve the whole story, Vic changed the topic to food and the two of them agreed to get something to eat.

On the way out of the room, they discussed and appreciated the wide open view of the parking lot from the room, allowing them to keep an eye on the car. When they returned filled to the gills, they watched TV to catch up on the news.

Vic remembered he never called his wife when he got to Chicago and grabbed his phone. "Hi, Tina. Sorry I didn't call you when I got to Chicago. Things started moving fast and have just slowed down enough for me to remember."

"Well, I didn't hear anything about an airplane crash en route to Chicago so I figured you were okay."

They both laughed and Vic shared the information about the duplexes, letting her know he hadn't looked them up on the Land Bank website yet. Tina was more tired than interested and told him he had woken her up. In his rush to call her, Vic had forgotten about her 9:00p.m.bedtime regime and said he would call back when he knew more. Tina thanked him for calling even though it was after the fact, but she still expressed her appreciation for the effort as the call ended. He and Steve watched a little more of the boob tube and then turned in after a busy day.

The next morning, as they headed to the car, Steve asked, "Hey, you don't mind driving today, do you?"

Vic had a gleam in his eye. "No, not at all."

Steve handed over the keys, sensing his buddy's high energy. "Okay, but no speed racer stuff," Steven said, knowing Vic's need for speed.

They pulled out of the motel lot and Vic made a right, then another right, and down to the next main street without the aid of a GPS, just using his sense of direction. He knew he was headed in the right direction to get on Highway75, but asked Steve to turn on his GPS to get the name of the street. Steve looked it up and said, "We're on 13 Mile Road."

Without looking at Steve, Vic sunk into his seat and said under his breath, "Thirteen, huh? What are the chances of that?"

Steve heard him. "Well, the chances are pretty good since we're on it," he said, and then broke out into a huge laugh and couldn't stop.

Vic looked over with a wry smile and felt a little tickled himself. "Ha, ha, Stevie, very clever. Glad you could find some humor in it, but you are right, we're on it."

"What's the deal? You don't like this road for some reason?"

"No, it's not the road, it's the number."

"Oh, you don't like lucky number 13?" Steve's question was loaded with sarcasm and intrigue.

Vic let Steve in on the strange re-occurrences. "I don't know if I like it or not. It's just that it keeps coming up and I feel it's coming up for a reason."

"And what reason is that, my friend?"

"My good buddy, right now I don't know. I just don't know."

Steve pondered Vic's words and decided not to press for an inquisition, but inquired about the current situation. "So what's the plan, my man?"

"Well, I just want to look at a couple of newly renovated homes just to see what they look like."

So they got off Interstate 75 at Grand and back tracked south, then headed to Shultz Street and saw that the remodel was the same as anywhere else. There were new windows, floors, roof and paint from what he could see from the outside or peeking through the window and a new front door. Once back in the car, Steve noticed Vic in deep thought. "Where to?"

"Stevie, I'm done here. I think I'm going to try to find Mo."

"Who is Mo?"

"He's a guy I've known since high school back in Pasadena. I saw him recently at one of Greg's parties and he's living here in Detroit. He got here just after things started falling apart and people were still walking away from their homes or being foreclosed on in mass numbers. So he's been here for a number of years now, maybe seven or eight, and has bought up some properties. I'd like to go and talk to him about what's happening now."

Steve nodded. "Hey, that sounds like a good idea."

Vic got out his phone and called Greg as Steve pulled into a gas station for fuel.

Greg answered the phone. " Hello." He immediately started coughing.

"Uh, what's up?" Vic was disgusted as usual. "You're going to choke to death one of these days, smoking that shit."

"Yeah well, it ain't gonna happen today. Where are you at?"

" I'm in Detroit."

"Detroit! What are you doing in Detroit?"

"What do you mean? I already told you I was coming to Detroit. If you didn't smoke so much weed, you would have remembered that."

"Okay, score one for you. I think I do remember you saying something about that."

"Well look, I'm trying to catch up with Mo. Could I get his number?"

"Sure, give me a second here." Greg took another drag on his joint and then gave Vic Mo's number."

"Thanks, G. I appreciate it."

"No problem. He'll be able to give you the ins and outs of what's going on up there."

"Yes, I'm hoping he'll be able to give me the big picture. Okay, I'll check with you later."

"Okay, you got your gun?"

"No, Greg. No guns."

"Okay, keep your eyes open."

Vic smiled. "Will do. Talk to you later." Vic understood the concern being that the city had a bad reputation and had led the country in murders years back. But from what he could see from the area he had been led to by Land Bank property listings, it was a few steps away from being a ghost town.

Being close enough in the car to hear both ends of the conversation with Greg, Steve asked, "Does he smoke a lot?"

"Every day! I don't know how he does it 'cause I can't function smoking that shit." Vic decided to call Mo and when he answered the phone, Mo was not sure who was calling. "It's Vic from Greg's party, from high school. You said come to Detroit, so here I am."

Mo caught the voice. "Vic! Hey, man, you're here in town?"

"Yep."

"You said you were coming. I see you weren't playing around. Where are you?"

"Well, I'm near a street named Schulze."

"Hmm, Schulze... let me look it up." Mo saw that it was two miles south of him and told Vic what street to come up to find his house.

"Okay, Mo, we'll be there within the hour and I've got my buddy from Chicago with me."

"No problem, I'm right here on Grand just before you get to the 96. I'll be looking for you."

"Okay, see you in a bit."

"So where is he at?" Steve asked.

"He's only a few miles north of us on Grand."

"Oh wow, he's not that far away."

"Not at all. That works out great 'cause we don't have to spend a lot of time trying to find him."

They made a right on Linwood and headed north.

"Stevie."

"What's up?"

"I think I'm done."

Steve was surprised and then checked to make sure. "You mean here in Detroit?"

"Yep, I've seen what I need to see. If we see something else today, I could just write it down and go online if we decide to bid on it. I don't really need to be here to do that."

Steve felt a bit more relaxed. "Okay, well that helps 'cause it gives me more time down there to do what I need to do."

"Sure it does and I think we should leave tomorrow."

When they got to Grand, Vic made a right like Mo said and saw the high school across the street. They pulled up to a big two-story house and next to it, a house just like it, then a third house the same. As they walked up and knocked on the door, Mo looked out the window and opened the door. The two greet and Vic introduced Mo to Steve. Once inside Mo's, his remodeling efforts were obvious and well done. The old wood floors had been refinished, the kitchen and bath remodeled, with new carpet, but his living room was set up like an office. It had a couch, but there was a desk, a portable display board and a computer. On the display board, he had architectural designs and interior designs of the house. When asked about the designs, Mo started rattling off all the projects he had going on in the house and announced that he was taking the guys on a tour.

First, they headed upstairs, with the guys noticing the refinished stairs and banister. At the top of the stairs was an open landing with three bedroom doors with a hallway leading to the upstairs bathroom and another bedroom, all remodeled. The guys were very impressed, occasionally looking at each other from time to time with raised eyebrows. Then, Mo took them down to the basement but first asked for some help carrying an electric piano keyboard, which caught Vic off guard being that Mo didn't have a musical bone in his body. However, when they reached the basement, it was set up for entertaining. There was a bar, refrigerator, a nice-sized open floor area and murals of famous Motown artists. After helping Mo set up the keyboard, he explained he was down the street from the Motown Museum and gave Motown themed parties for visitors from around the world. And was actually allowing a few of the old artists and musicians to practice and have jam sessions there in his basement for those who were still in town. Mo was a whirlwind of activity and the guys were just trying to keep up mentally. Vic saw a rack or wall of pipes and canisters mounted on a wood-framed particle board.

The pipes were all new copper freshwater lines. Mo explained that he had designed the layout himself and that the clear canisters were filters that looked like something out of a science project. On closer inspection, you could actually see the filter inside the canister, again impressive. The guys were now looking at all the new silver ductwork running along the roof of the basement, going up to all the rooms, new electrical lines and a brand-spanking-new furnace. Just when the guys thought the tour was over, Mo took them to the house next door, the one that looked like the first one. Mo then explained that he bought all three of the houses at auction for pennies on a dollar. On the second house he had not started in the basement but the first floor and second floors were as well done as the first house. Mo explained he had a roof problem in the second house and took them to the attic.

As they cleared the staircase, the first thing they noticed were four or five large cooking pots full of water. Mo began emptying them into the backyard from an attic window. He then pointed to a blue tarp bowed down into the attic ceiling space from a hole in the roof the size of a microwave oven, which Vic and Steve had already noticed. Mo pulled back the tarp and exposed a clear blue sky on the other side. When Mo turned to empty another pot, the guys looked at each other and shrugged.

Vic smiled and scratched his head. "Mo, you've done all that work on both of those floors below and you have a hole in the roof the size of a baby elephant. What's your thinking on this?"

"I know I think I got ahead of myself on this one. I started the work at the same time I was negotiating with a roofer and he never showed up. Then we had a falling out, but the guys downstairs had started, but I'm managing with the buckets and the tarp."

"I know how that could happen. You going to be alright this winter?" Vic asked.

"Oh yes, I'll patch this hole and find someone this winter or spring to do the whole roof. Let's get out of here and head back down."

They headed back down the stairs and Mo explained he hadn't started on the third house yet, so that concluded the tour. When they returned to the living room of the main house, Vic noticed an actual office with a stack of laptops and a printer. When asked, Mo informed the guys that he was a part of a program with the school across the street to teach students how to do computer coding. Mo had majored in computer science in college and had worked for years as a computer programmer. He had also taken some accounting classes and did taxes on the side. All of that was from his earlier life, but Vic and Steve were feeling overwhelmed with all Mo had going on. Their time was growing short and Vic asked Mo about the current real estate market there in Detroit for which Mo told him that most of the really good deals were gone. He said that there were still some things out there, but not like before. Vic asked about the Land Bank and Mo shared that there was also a Wayne County Auction that was held once a year and they had just missed it by a few weeks. Vic looked at his watch and informed Mo that it was time for him and Steve to move on down the road. He told Mo that they were leaving the next day, heading for the New Orleans area of Slidell to look at a property that Steve had inherited from his grandmother. Mo was glad Vic had actually made the trip to Detroit, citing that a lot of people say they're coming and never show up. He was glad to see someone from back home and shared that, if it got too cold the coming winter, he would be on a plane back to Los Angeles for a month or two. The guys laughed and headed for the door when Mo asked, "Hey, have you guys been to the Motown Museum?"

The guys shook their heads, no.

"You have to check it out! It's right down the street, no more than a mile or two."

The guys looked at each other and decided to check it out, since they had never been. Also, knowing they may never be in Detroit again. They gave Mo a shake and a shoulder hug and headed for the car. Vic started the car and made a U-turn headed toward downtown.

Within a few minutes, Steve said. "There it is! You just passed it."

"I sure did. Let me turn around up here." Vic made a left-hand turn, then a right, and spotted a dingy brick duplex in a good neighborhood. They drove around the area for a few minutes and headed back to the museum. Within a half hour, they were on a tour and enjoyed every minute of it. Like Mo said, there were people there from all over Europe, the Middle East, Asia, Africa, Canada and it was packed. It lasted about an hour and the guys felt edified, knowing a little history of the music behind the scenes. They took some pictures and headed back to the car, then to a restaurant to grab a bite to eat.

After their meal, they sat and discussed the day and the two great tours. They laughed about the hole in the roof of Mo's second house and mused over whether he could get it fixed by winter. They were glad to have had those activities as a break from the purpose of the trip. It had felt like a vacation for a few hours, but now it was time to get back to work. They sat a while longer to discuss their route south through Michigan, Indiana, Ohio, Kentucky, Tennessee, Alabama, Mississippi, and into Louisiana. After having worked that out and checking the time, which was heading into late afternoon, they realized the day had gotten away and headed back to the motel. Vic was eager to get back to Steve's laptop to lookup the foreclosure finds of the last two days and was extremely excited to see what the status was on the accidental find near the museum. It was perfect and was now number one on his list.

On the way back, Vic informed Steve that he was going to take 12 Mile Road instead of 13 Mile.

Steve, now reclining in his seat, tells Vic. "You're driving."

Vic smiled and took the exit. When they walked in the door of the room, Vic headed for the computer and brought up the Land Bank site. He typed in the street name and, to his disappointment, nothing came up. He then typed in one of the Tyler addresses and it had sold along with the others on that street. He had a sinking feeling about the dingy brick duplex near the museum, but knew there was always a slim possibility of it being available, so he planned to follow up on the road the next day. It was getting late into the evening and after an hour or so of TV, the guys decided to go back out for a nightcap meal around nine-thirty. They found a burger joint, got their fill and talked some more about the long ride south, mapping motels and estimating where they would need to stop. When they got back, both were feeling the drain of a good but long day. They both brushed their teeth then crashed on to their beds.

About two-thirty in the morning, Vic got up to go to the bathroom. The three hours of sleep had refreshed his energy and, for whatever reason, in the quiet peacefulness of the early morning decided to look out the window. He was shocked to see two suspicious looking guys standing by the car, one with a long metal blade-like device. "Steve! Steve!"

He stirred awake. "Hey, what's up?"

"Get up! Somebody's trying to break into the car."

Steve bolted to his feet. "What?"

"Yeah, two guys, one with one of those door-opening tools."

Steve looked out the window and saw the two men.

Vic called the front desk. "Hello, sir. I'm in room 14 and someone is in the back parking lot trying to break into our car. Could you please call the police? Thank you!"

Steve was now wide awake with anxious fear and excitement, and blurted out, "Hey, hey, there he goes with that metal piece, trying to open the door!"

Vic, now angered and not thinking but reacting with a rush of adrenalin to his brain, opened the door, stepped outside, and shouted, "Hey, get away from the car!" He got a response he was not expecting.

"Who's going to make me?" the thief without the tool asked.

"The police, fool! They're on their way."

One guy said, "Let's go," but Vic's response had angered the big mouth talker and he pulled out a gun.

Upon seeing the pistol pointing his way, Vic broke toward room 13 to the hallway a few feet a head and as he ducked past room 13, he heard shots, two bullets hitting the window as the glass shattered to the ground as he passed then turned the corner. Now up to his old track speed, he zipped into the front parking lot from the other end of the hallway and ducked behind a minivan. He peered from behind that car with one eye open while catching his breath for what seemed like an eternity. A few minutes after that, a fast walking figure turned the corner into the hallway and into the front lot.

"Vic! You there?" It was Steve with a smile on his face.

Vic stood up, his movement getting Steve's attention. "They gone?"

Steve was still smiling. "Oh yeah they bolted when that glass shattered. I ducked when I heard the shots then the glass. When I peeked out they were running out of the lot and into a car on the street and gone. Of course, shortly after that the cops rolled in. You okay?"

"Yeah, I'm good."

The two walked over to the backside lot and made a report to the Warren Police Department. They get back in the room at about 3:45 a.m. and eventually get a few more hours of sleep before checking out. Before the guys hit the freeway, they stopped at their usual breakfast spot, Tim Horton's, for coffee and a muffin and then on the road headed to Louisiana.

CHAPTER 6

As the guys headed south on Interstate 75, down in New Orleans, a palm reader and psychic, Monica Deloche, was opening her shop door down in the French Quarter. Not many people knew her first name because people always referred to her as Madame Deloche. This was out of respect for her abilities dealing with psychic phenomena and energies that existed but went unexplained and, in many cases, unbelievable. Very few people knew she was a science major at LSU and worked for a while at the LSU Medical Center as a research lab technician. Her goal was to merge science, psychic phenomena, and abilities through extensive research, hoping to use science to explain the unexplained and to unveil applicable science to paranormal activities. However, her efforts fell on deaf ears and she was called a quack and a nutcase. She soon realized her forward-thinking into the unknown would not be accepted or understood in most medical and scientific institutions across the country, especially not in the conservative southern hemisphere.

Her ideas were born out of her trying to understand her abilities, which she seldom discussed with other people to avoid misunderstandings and ridicule, but make no mistake, she was the real deal, and where she found her clientele was in the French Quarter, among the shop owners and believers of the unexplained. With palm reading and tarot cards, the reader was only interpreting the meaning of the cards. Anyone who learned the meaning of each card or combination of cards could give a reading of the drawn cards. The drawn cards were by chance, but even with that variable, there was a chance the reading applied to the person or subject of the reading. This would still hold true of a forecast for the future, from the chance drawing, that matched the events that had yet to happen. So depending on the person, their beliefs, and the draw, it could be true or dismissed as hogwash. With palm reading, trade knowledge and understanding of the meaning of lines in one's palm, which, too, were governed by the variable of chance. However, in palm reading, the added variable of the reader, in this case, Deloche, was touching the hand of the subject, looking into their eyes, and talking to them. Depending on the ability of the reader to read people, could increase greatly the accuracy of the reading. What has made Deloche so popular as a reader was the fact that her extra sensory abilities reached beyond the physical plain—she could feel you. She could feel your energy and parts of your personality by touching your hand. She got a larger composite of a person by looking into their eyes, as the eyes are the window to the soul. By just being in your presence, she could feel an entity's heartache, pain, happiness, sorrow, grief, excitement, and peace. When she was at the university and working at the lab, she met Sharon and they became close friends. Sharon, being open to and understanding the paranormal, realized Madame Deloche had special abilities. Sharon, having heard Madame's complaints about attitudes at the job, convinced Deloche to open her own shop and Sharon invested in it with her.

Deloche never looked back as word of her abilities and reputation spread like wildfire and her business has been as steady as a doctor's office. Deloche then hired Sharon, her best friend, partner, and confidant, as her assistant. The attractive Madame Deloche, with her raven black hair and stunning hazel blue eyes, was quite popular with men, young and old, as they piled in for a reading and the possibility of a date. Little did they know, they were being scanned like an X-ray machine inside and out. After their readings, she knew more about them than they would ever want her to know and, in many cases, more than they knew about themselves. The Madame was smart enough to never discuss all that she knew and understood about her clients. The few times she had divulged more than the standard general information, people had become fearful. She learned to temper her insight by asking questions to answers she already knew:"Are you feeling sad today?" and "Why are you so happy today?" When they would say, "How did you know I was happy? I'm not smiling," she would tell them the truth. "I know you didn't tell me, but it's the energy radiating from you." Without getting into the fact that the happiness was based on the client's ex-husband having just picked up the kids for a week. And that the woman was headed home to be with her new boyfriend. Deloche had learned to know that much was unsettling to a person, too much information.

Though Deloche was a devout Catholic, and never dabbled in the occult or searched for demonic entities, she believed in their existence and knew how to stay away or ward them off. With that being said, her abilities go much deeper than the novelty of cards and a person's palm. The unexplained energies or entities that she had summoned and manifested were hair-raising and sometimes not. If the person had gone into the light and moved on to the next plain, Deloche, many times, could still hear them or feel them and translate those feelings into words. And other times there would only be a residue, meaning they had moved on, but she could tell what their state of mind was and pass it on to the family member, and sometimes not. And on this night in mid-October, Sharon had arranged a séance to call on a recently deceased husband.

At the same time, Vic and Steve were barreling down Interstate 75, entering the suburbs of Dayton, Ohio, and making good time with Steve at the wheel again. Vic called the Detroit Land Bank to see if the dingy brick duplex was available. They answered it was not on their books and gave Vic the number to the Wayne County Clerk's Office to see if the property was a part of their inventory. Upon giving them the address, he learned it had just been sold at the past auction, the one Mo had told them about, and that they had missed by two weeks. Vic's disappointment was palpable, then shook it off quickly as he heard the words of an old-time relative in his head. "No use in crying over spilled milk." With those common sense kernels of wisdom, he learned not to ponder over things that were already gone.

He grabbed his notebook and looked through all the properties, and the only possibility left was the very first one they saw on Stoepel. Vic took a minute to breathe and take in the sights of the city of Dayton. From where he stood, it was a pretty nice town. He then decided not to call Tina before looking at all the information on that property.

Steve asked, "Is it gone?"

"That property by the Motown museum?"

"Yes, it went at that auction Mo was telling us about, the Wayne County Auction."

Steve sensed his pal's disappointment. "Oh wow, bummer."

"Stevie, it is what it is. It's gone so moving on."

"I hear you, Vic. That's the right attitude."

"You know what they say, Steve. If it's meant for you, you'll have it. So, it wasn't meant to be."

Steve said in a positive tone, "That's right."

The guys had traveled well past Dayton by now down into a piece of western Kentucky and just outside of Tennessee when he realized his cousin, Clyde, lived not too far outside of Dayton and was mad at himself for not remembering that. It was important because the two had never actually met in person but connected when Vic joined Ancestry.com and Clyde reached out to him and they immediately hit it off. They both had been school teachers and were now doing other things, but Clyde had done some incredible work on their family tree, dating back to 1774 on Vic's mother's side, dating back five generations. So he called him instead and Clyde informed him that a tornado had hit his house, tearing off half of the roof and one side of the house, leaving Clyde still in the bed on the second floor. One of his neighbors down on the street saw him sitting up in the bed with the side of the house gone, disoriented and dazed. The neighbor told him to stay there, then ran up to help Clyde down. Fortunately, Clyde's wife had already gone downstairs and was in the kitchen, but Vic joked with him, telling Clyde he must be living right because under normal circumstances he should have been sucked out of that second-floor bedroom. Clyde agreed and said his relationship with the Source was second to none and Vic knew it had to be true because he was still around to tell about it. By the time he got off the phone with Clyde, he and Steve were in Tennessee outside of Nashville, as the sun was setting behind them. They continued for about three more hours and stopped at a motel in southern Tennessee, almost to the Alabama border. They would be in Slidell by tomorrow afternoon.

At about the same time, back in the French Quarter, Sharon and Madame Deloche were already setting up for their session with Mrs. Gagnon, whose husband passed away in a tragic car accident. She never had the chance to say goodbye and, having been in a rush to get the kids off to school that morning, forgot to tell her husband that she loved him, as she had on so many occasions. She needed closure and to know that he was okay. Mrs. Gagnon was allowed to bring a friend or family member for support but understood that it should be someone who could handle the content of a paranormal activity. In plain speak, not freak out in the presence of a ghost. She had chosen her friend Molly, who was a quiet woman but with a strong-spirited presence. As they came through the door, Sharon greeted them and escorted them into a back room. Sharon locked the front door and put out the closed sign so as not to be disturbed. In the back room sat a round table with four chairs. On it was a candle and incense, no crystal ball. The candle was for light and the incense was to identify any disturbance in the air of the room. With the door closed and the window shut, under normal circumstances, there should be no disturbance in the air.

The ladies chatted for a few minutes when Deloche kindly said, "Let's get started."

Mrs. Gagnon had been asked to bring her questions or statements so she pulled out a small notepad. Madame instructed everyone to clear their minds of every thought and only focus on the deceased, Mr. Jerry Gagnon, or J.G. as he was affectionately known by loved ones and close friends. Madame said a short prayer and began focusing on Jerry.

"Our only thoughts right now are on the pure energy, soul, and spirit of Jerry Gagnon. Jerry, we are reaching out to you in thought and in spirit." Everyone focused on him as they held hands.

Unbeknownst to the other people in the room, something opened up in Madame Deloche's brain, releasing unseen and undetected energy generated from the electrical current in her heart and her brain. Sending out a beacon of energy, a microwave signal if you will, the only thing anyone noticed was the heat suddenly coming from The Madam's hands which Mrs. Gagnon did not feel sitting directly across the table. They sat focusing on the existing energy of Jerry Gagnon for over half an hour. The only thing that had happened was that Madame had shone in the dim light of the candle as she had perspired as her body naturally sought to cool her down. Then Madame said. "Jerry, your wife is here. She needs to talk to you if you're still on this plane."

There was no activity. Then Mrs. Gagnon said, "Please, J.G.," in a pleading tone.

At an hour and five minutes, there was a clear disturbance in the smoke trail of the incense and a flicker of the candlelight. Madame said, "Thank you, Jerry. Mrs. Gagnon, you may ask your questions now."

Mrs. Gagnon was now excited but calm. "Jerry, first let me say I love you so much and I have been so upset that I didn't get a chance that morning to tell you that."

Madame said, "He knows you love him and said, as much as he loves you, he wishes you had been there with him when he left the physical world but was glad you weren't, it was a horrific sight."

Mrs. Gagnon looked at her notepad. "Jerry, are you in pain? How do you feel?"

Madame looked straight ahead, looking like she was in a trance but in actuality, she was focused on translating a combination of words and feelings, being transmitted from the entity. "He has no pain and feels great. He wants you to know that he has resisted going into the light, hoping to contact you to let you know he was okay. He said he was in the house last weekend and wanted to let you know he was there but didn't want to frighten you. He felt he could get into your dream state but you never fell into a deep realm of sleep being awakened by the kids. And that he has been so blessed to be married to you."

Through her tears, Mrs. Gagnon said, "Thank you." She then asked one final question. "Jerry, is there anything you want me to know or tell anyone?"

With her eyes still fixed but focused inwardly as if getting a message on a telephone, Deloche said to Mrs. Gagnon, "Write this down. In his desk, in the bottom drawer filed in the back is an envelope that says rainy day. And behind that an insurance policy from Mutual Life. And call his job to get his retirement benefit. Tell the kids Daddy will always love them."

A light swoosh of air caressed Mrs. Gagnon. The smoke now disturbed began to settle and slow in the depleted air of the room. The room that had been full of electricity or energy was now still and felt empty even with four people in it. They all sat quietly, with Madame and Sharon knowing he was gone, Mrs. Gagnon knowing the same but with an aching heart, and Molly wondering what the hell just happened and in disbelief.

As Mrs. Gagnon dried her tears, Madame Deloche looked at Sharon and nodded to open the door. Once open, the cool fresh air seemed to mark a new beginning for Mrs. Gagnon but most of all, her questions had been answered and a feeling of peace had come over her. Then doubt, and the thought of a cruel parlor trick as she looked for an air machine or a pedal to activate a burst of air. As she looked there was nothing, only a candle and a cone of incense on a plain round wooden table.

Molly looked at Mrs. Gagnon to see if she had dropped something. Madame looked at Sharon and Sharon understood the look, that subtly said, here we go again. The problem was that in the history of séances, ninety-five percent of them were led by frauds and charlatans who had been exposed giving the practice a bad reputation.

Sharon and Madame knew how to handle this reaction and they understood the history. It was just a part of the job.

Mrs. Gagnon was now suspicious. "How do I know this wasn't a parlor trick just for money?"

Madame Deloche was calm. "Well, there are no strings or wires and no knocking of tables."

"Yes, but how do I know that air isn't from the air conditioner?"

"No one has been out of the room, Mrs. Gagnon, but the thermostat is outside the door to your left and I think you'll find that it's off."

Molly went to look and returned with widened eyes and looked at her friend intensely. "It's off."

In thought, as Mrs. Gagnon was about to speak, Deloche cuts her off. "Lady Gagnon, I don't think you're thinking this through so let me help you. If you're having pause about paying me, don't."

"Don't what?"

"Don't pay me. Go home and look in the drawer as he instructed you to. If you find what he said was there, then please return and settle our agreement."

Molly looked at Madame with surprise and then back at her friend who was on the border of embarrassing her.

Mrs. Gagnon now looked as though a light had just come on. "Well, that's a great idea. I didn't think about that. I think that's what I'll do."

"And for the record, we both know I haven't been to your house, ever."

"Yes, I would agree."

"So when you find the truth, when could I expect to see you?"

"Tomorrow, Madame, tomorrow."

"That sounds fine, Mrs. Gagnon. I will look for you tomorrow."

Sharon told the two ladies to have a good evening and escorted them into the front room of the shop and out the front door. When she returned, Deloche was sitting with her head on the table, exhausted which was the norm after a session. Sharon asked Madame if she would like some tea before they leave but she declined, citing the greater need for sleep. They both packed their belongings and headed home in the October midnight sky.

As they walked to the car with no words being passed, Sharon said, "A penny for your thoughts."

Madame was in deep thought which generated the offer. "I could feel how they felt about one another, so powerful. And I could feel their pain and loss. Experiencing both of those emotions in the same hour takes it out of you. I was thinking how wonderful it would be to have that kind of connection with someone and then second thoughts knowing the pain of that kind of loss, it's confusing."

Sharon smiled. "That's a heavy burden." She put her arm around Madame. "But you still have me, dear mum," she said in her imitation of a British accent. They both laughed and continued to the car and started talking about the aura, their new interest as they shake the heaviness of the séance.

The next morning in southern Tennessee outside of a little town named Pulaski and just off Interstate 65, Vic and Steve had packed their bags and stepped out into the morning sun. It was a beautiful day, so calm and quiet. The sky was a pristine clear blue, almost royal. *You don't see that kind of sky in Los Angeles until after a rain*, Vic thought. Across the parking lot on the other side of the fence, were two fantastic-looking horses—a shiny golden palomino and a mostly white appaloosa, both pillars of health and strength that added to the scenery. It was a feel-good morning in the great Tennessee countryside as they checked out of the motel and continued south into Alabama. There was some great-looking countryside to see and as Vic continued to soak it all in, he asked Steve, "So this is Alabama?"

"Yep! This is it."

"Man, I think I like it. I love this countryside. It just feels good, looks pretty and the roads are really clean."

"That's true. Vic, let me ask you a question. What made you step outside that door in Detroit and tell those guys to move away from the car?"

"Look, if they had gotten into the car, they would have taken it and our trip would have been ruined. I wasn't going to let that happen without a confrontation and I wasn't trying to be a hero. Normally people leave when they know they're being watched."

Steven admired the courage. "Well, I'm glad you did."

"Hey, if I had known he had a gun I would have worded things a little differently." Steve broke out with laughter and Vic chuckled. "So what would you have said?"

"Something like, 'Gentlemen, you should know the police are on the way. Please don't shoot.'"

Steve caught a breath. "Ha! Okay, 'cause you stepped out there with that Vic big boss vibe. 'Hey! Move away from the car!' Hell, I thought you had a gun." They laughed.

"Ha! What was I thinking? It wasn't about a gun, I can tell you that. Hey, do me a favor, Steve."

"What's that?"

"Please don't tell my wife about this."

"Hey, no problem. I understand."

"Thanks. I appreciate that. Speaking of her, I need to give her a call. I've got all the information on this property."

"Which one?"

"Well, you know my first choice was Lothrop, but the only thing left was Stoepel. Let's see what she says." Vic called his wife, giving her all the details from the website. He then told Tina the Land Bank gave an estimate of what they felt it would cost to restore the building. "Tina, they think it will cost a hundred thousand dollars, but—"

"A hundred grand! We don't have a hundred thousand dollars to get it back in shape!"

"Tina!"

"No I'm not going to do it. You want to do it? Do it yourself. Are you crazy?" Tina continued to scream and holler like a maniac as if she had been raised in a bad part of town; it was pure ignorance.

It caught Vic by surprise and frustrated him for not being able to get a word in edgewise and he became angry and said, "You're not going to ruin my trip with this crap," and hung up. "Man, screw her! See? This is the shit I can't stand, dumb crap like this."

From the driver's seat, Steve heard the conversation. "Man, she was really trippin'. What were you trying to tell her?"

"That I figured out how we could do it for much less but all that screaming was unnecessary, unprofessional, and disrespectful. All she had to do was say, 'No, I don't want to do it, that's too much money,' and then listen to the rest of what I had to say. And if forty or fifty was too much, no problem, 'cause what I really wanted was gone, no big deal. That really pisses me off."

Steve watched Vic's real estate venture crash and burn. "So you came all this way, spent money and time, then snap, in two minutes, deal gone bad."

Vic was now disgusted. "Yeah, that's how the damn cookie can crumble." Vic said nothing as if he had lockjaw and half an hour later said, "Hey, I'm not going to let her ruin my trip," and they continued on their way.

After a while, Steve sensed the Tina incident had cooled off a little. "Vic I have another question for you."

"Okay, shoot."

"Back in Detroit, you said you were going to take 12 Mile Road instead of 13 Mile."

"Yes, I did."

"So, how did that workout for you?"

"Well, I guess it depends on how you look at it."

"Okay, explain."

"Okay, well, you could say I didn't get shot, the car didn't get stolen, and we had some excitement."

"Okay."

"Or I could say I got shot at, someone tried to steal the rental car and we lost some sleep. It's the glass half full or half empty. What I think you're trying to get at though was the street thing, right?"

"Right! Do you think it would have made a difference?"

"Good question, and we'll never know."

"Yes, but I think you have a little superstition, Vic, and I'm trying to get you to see that it wouldn't have made a difference which way we came."

"I can appreciate that, Steve, but it's not that I'm superstitious. It's that things keep happening to me that I don't understand."

"Like what?"

"When I was a baby in the crib, two or three, there was this scary clown, imp-like character that would show up in the closet. It looked like a hologram with a bluish tint. I don't know if he was sent from the other side to cheer me up and make me laugh or to scare the hell out of me."

Steve was now captured by the story. "Well, did he make you laugh or scare the hell out of you?"

"Both."

"Oh, shit!" Steve was now scared.

"Then, when I got my first car, a British Triumph TR6, many times when I would drive down the street or on the freeway, the streetlights would flicker or dim just before I would go under them. Other times, streetlights would just go out completely."

Steve was now spooked. "What was that about?"

"Hell if I know, but that brings me to this number 13 appearing all the time. I'm just trying to avoid it, but I can't."

"What do you mean you can't?"

"I've tried, but it still keeps coming up. I don't know what it means or why but it's real. I don't know if it's good or bad, but I'm hoping someday it gets revealed and most of all that it makes sense."

"Makes sense how?"

"Right now it's just weird like someone's trying to tell me something. I can't put it together; I just can't figure it out."

Steve couldn't hear anymore. "Okay, that's enough for today. You're creeping me out down here near the voodoo bayou."

"Hey! You asked, I'm just telling you but I understand, it's scary stuff, not for the faint of heart."

The two drive without a word now on Highway 20, cutting across Mississippi just passing Meridian and about to transition onto Highway 55 going south down to Slidell just outside of New Orleans.

Feeling it was time to break the silence, Vic asked, "Okay, so what's your plan for the day, Steve?"

"Well, since we got down here a day early, I thought we would just get settled in, rest up and get a fresh start tomorrow morning."

"Sounds good to me. It's your show from here on out. I'm your wingman. Just let me know when you're ready to get some grub."

"Okay, let's check in first."

The guys go into the Red Roof office and get a room then head over to Carl's for a burger. Steve decided to head over to Slidell City Hall the next morning and then go to the property. Vic had no objection being that he was just going to see what the possibilities were if any, and to support Steve.

Slidell was quite busy around the highway with motels and restaurants but heading into Slidell proper it seemed to be a quiet little town that was growing. Steve's land was further out in a more rural area and he needed to go downtown to talk to someone in the surveyor's office and to get some land maps. In the meantime, they had an afternoon to rest and make phone calls.

One person Vic was not going to call was Tina. He couldn't believe she had flipped out on him like that. She had called back, but he had refused to take the call. He knew there would be repercussions but he would deal with that when he got back. For now, it was nice weather in the south, a slower pace, and peaceful. Vic had no responsibility for a few days, unlike back home. Being completely relaxed he didn't want to ruin it by calling Tina and arguing over something that wasn't going to happen, anyway.

After eating, Steve laid out his plan for the next day and they headed back to the motel. Steve spent time on social media and texting friends down in Brazil. Vic worked on his Spanish with his mobile application. They talked about politics and Steve's conspiracy theories in a respectful debate as they always did but also, sports was a big topic, mainly football. It was dark now, and they turned on the TV to watch a game then back out for dinner and to bed, making sure they would be rested for the coming day.

CHAPTER 7

The next morning around eight, Vic and Steve headed up Main Street and hung a left, heading to city hall. Once there, Steve went in and returned, after having found out it was the building behind them, so Steve went around the corner to pull into the parking lot. As they entered the first floor, they saw the sign: Surveyor and Engineer's Office 5th floor. They headed up to that floor only to find the office closed. They had just passed an office that was open, so they went back to the Titles and Deeds office. When they walked in, the two ladies sat at desks facing each other, with maps on the wall and a copy machine.

"Hi, I'm trying to get a copy of the deed for a property in Slidell perish, the same as a county in other places."

The lady looked up at Steve. "Well, you're in the right place. Are you the original owner or an heir?"

Steve was now digging in his pocket, and smiled as he handed her a one-page copy of the original deed. "No, I'm not old enough to be the original owner."

She looked at the deed from the 1920s and laughed. "Oh no! I guess you wouldn't be, but I'm glad you have this. Now I don't have to spend an hour searching on the computer. I can just punch in the number."

Vic looked at Steve like he had just got an A on a test and gave him a thumbs up. Having that copy saved them an hour on what they expected to be a long day. Steve also asked her for a surveyor's map and she said no problem. Steve looked at Vic with wide eyes and a smile, nodding as if he were saying, *Yes, that's another twenty points for me.*

"What's the address?" she asked.

Steve rattled it off.

"Okay, that's going to be twenty dollars," she said.

"No problem." Steve rushed for his wallet.

She got up for the first time to go to the copier. Vic looked at the other lady who had not said a word, sitting at her desk, scrutinizing some papers. He wondered what she did. Was she a clerk? He didn't know and would not ask but knew it was good work if you could get it. Vic had moved to the back of the office to look out the window that overlooked the parking lot, watching people come and go. He was now curious about what Steve's family property looked like, and figured he would know shortly.

A few minutes later, the clerk handed Steve the maps and a full copy of the deed. The guys said *thank you* and left, amazed at how smooth it had gone, knowing if it had been a big city there would have been long lines and forms for at least two hours. It was nice to be in and out in thirty minutes. They were off to a good start and jumped back in the car, heading to the property. It didn't take long for Vic to realize that it was really rural as they quickly reached the out skirts of Slidell proper and out into the sticks.

"Well, that went really smooth."

"Yes, but this next part won't be," Steve said grimly.

"What part is that?"

"Finding it."

"I thought you knew where it was?"

"I kinda do, but I haven't been here since I was twelve, but we'll find it."

Vic found that odd since Steve had always talked about it as though he had been there many times in recent years and hadn't mentioned that he wasn't sure of the exact location.

On the way, Steve explained that his grandmother, who was the original owner, had sold two acres to a lady who had been bugging her for years about the land and that she had finally caved in and sold it to her, leaving them, thirteen to fourteen acres. They came to another main road, and Steve made a right. In a mile or so, Steve told Vic to look to his right and he saw a piece of land, overgrown with trees and bushes.

"I think that's the back side of it, but there's no access."

Further down were some businesses, trucking, parts, and some kind of shop. In another two miles they came to another main road. Steve made a right and Vic realized they were driving in a giant square. As they went down this street, they came to a little country school.

"Okay, that's the school. I remember that." Steve made a right into this rural community.

Vic said, "Hey, you're doing pretty good for a guy who doesn't know where he's going."

"Yeah well don't speak too soon 'cause it's a little tricky once we get in here."

His words were pure truth as they drove around in there for two hours. Some places were trailer homes, some fixed mobile homes on a foundation, and the rest were regular houses. Finally, they saw a mail carrier for the post office and asked her where it was. She tried to explain it but the guys still weren't clear on exactly where, so she told them to follow her and took them to a small street they had missed. She then pointed down a short access road next to a white house that sat on the street. Behind it was a high fence and down the access road a gate. On one side was a little two-acre horse ranch with a corral and a barn with two trailers as living quarters. On the other side was the same dense forested land with pine trees and brush six feet tall and so thick you couldn't walk through it without a machete. This was Steve's property. Steve had called the owner's son who was living on the property but he was at work and he had someone unlock the gate. Vic got out to pull it open and they drove in. Vic was amazed at the size of the property surrounding the small ranch, but the brush was impenetrable. His imagination ran wild with thoughts of snakes, raccoons, and other varmints that bite. Vic was concerned about not knocking on the door to let someone know they were there, even though Steve had called. Vic had already been shot at and knew a shotgun wouldn't miss, but he shook it off and went over to the fence that had a bush thickly pressed against it from the other side and climbed to the top. By the looks of it Steve would need a crew of men and heavy equipment to cut through it.

Out in the distance, Vic could see a lake strangely quiet with no one on it. There was no sand or beach-like area on the shore. There was soil and roots, then a straight drop off into deep water. It was a scary place that got even scarier when two crocodiles surfaced. This place was completely wild and dangerous. Steve was taking pictures when Vic asked if he was ready to go. He wasn't, so Vic, who still wasn't comfortable, told Steve he would be outside the gate. When Steve was ready, he pulled the car out and Vic closed and locked the gate.

"So behind the ranch and everything to the right of it is yours?" Vic asked.

"Yep, me and my brother's."

"Wow, that's quite a chunk, but it looks like you've got your work cut out for you, Stevie."

"I know. I'm planning to sell some of the pine trees to a mill, hoping they'll cut a swath open so I could get some trailers or mobile homes on it."

"Good luck with that. Hey, you've got another problem. It looks to me that your grandmother sold the entrance to the whole property."

"And you're probably right, that's why I need a surveyor out here to help me find a good spot to create an entrance."

"Got it? Hey it's going on one o'clock. Let's eat."

Steve agreed, and they decided on a Pancake House since there was no Waffle House close. Once there, after being seated, they opened up the menu and Vic was pleased to see some different dishes on the menu. "Hey, they have some creole dishes here, nice."

"You thought it was going to be like the California menu, huh?"

"That's what I thought. " Vic never looked up from the menu. Vic ordered an omelet with pancakes and then decides to have some gumbo to see if it's any good. Steve ordered a B.L.T. and also tried the gumbo.

As they waited, Steve broke the silence. "Look, I need to make one more stop today. You okay with that?"

"Hey, it's your show. Do what you need to do, I'm good. Where to?"

Steve looked at his phone. "Down the highway from the motel about ten miles is a mobile home lot right off the freeway. I just want to see what their pricing is like."

"Okay, let's do it, but I have a question for you, Stevie. Your fifteen acres in the sticks there, your grandmother sold off those two acres of the fifteen total, right?"

"Yes, I see where you're going with this, Vic."

"Well Steve, I just think that's quite a coincidence that you now have thirteen acres. I'm just saying it keeps coming up. Out of all the numbers, there it is again."

"You know, I'm starting to see what you're saying, but it's meaningless."

Vic looked Steve straight in the eye. "Sure it is, Stevie."

After their meals, the guys jump in the car and head down the highway. When they walked into the office, they were greeted by a blond-haired lady with glasses who was very cordial, offering coffee and tea. She asked what they were looking for. "Trailers or mobile homes?"

Steve said it was mobile homes. She said that she didn't handle mobile homes but she would go get the guy who does. She returned with a husky brown-haired guy who came in and said, with a smooth southern accent, "Hello guys, what can I help you with?"

"I'm looking for a mobile home and maybe a trailer."

The guy extended his hand. "Hey, I'm Mike, by the way."

The guys shook his hand and shared their names.

"Okay, Steve, what is this going to be for, 'cause most perishes have banned trailers as permanent homes or fixed homes."

Steve and Vic looked at each other and Steve asked, "Why?"

"Because these perish councils can't tax a trailer. Legally they're not considered real property like a fixed home that has a foundation. Now a mobile home is different because it can be fitted with a foundation and is designed to be fixed to the land with plumbing and electrical."

"Okay, well, it's a mobile home for sure."

"Okay, but before we go out and look, we need to check the perish because there's a lot going on right now. Some of the perishes aren't allowing any building at this time for different reasons so we need to check first. We took a home out to a guy's property only to find out from an inspector that there was a moratorium in that perish so we had to pay to bring it back, then give the guy his money back."

"Oh wow!" The guys said in tandem.

Mike took them over to a computer and put in the address and told Steve that his property was not in Slidell Perish but that it was in Saint Tammany Perish. And then, after searching for fifteen minutes said, "It looks like there's a moratorium there."

"What's a moratorium?" Steve asked.

"It's a freeze on building when a perish is surveying, mapping, or making changes to roads or rezoning."

So Steve asked when it would be over and Mike told him it wouldn't be lifted until spring, but that it could also be extended and explained to Steve to just call in the spring, April or May, to see what was going on. He then asked if they wanted to go look at some mobile homes on the lot. As they walked through, they realized how nice they were, just like a new home. Steve knew this was the way to go and apparently the only way to go. As they left the lot, Mike told Steve he would give him a good deal as they had one last handshake. The guys thanked Mike and piled into the car. Steve, now disappointed and both he and Vic knew the trip was a bust.

"Well Steve, looks like we're both going back empty-handed."

"Yeah, that's what it looks like."

Hearing the disappointment in his voice, Vic didn't respond, not wanting to further agitate his friend. Steve knew Vic was basically saying he wasn't interested. A few minutes later Steve had cheered up, saying the trip wasn't a complete waste, being that they both had gotten great information to move forward with. Vic wasn't so sure about that. He knew Tina wasn't going to do anything and that he still had to face her when he got back. For that moment on the trip, it was pleasant. Vic had seen parts of the country he had never seen and outside of the derailed business deals, it was a good trip.

Over in New Orleans, Mrs. Gagnon had not shown up the next morning as she had promised. Sharon said that they needed to get more information from their customers and was railing on Mrs. Gagnon with some choice words. Madame Deloche was calm, saying she would come. Sharon, not so sure, continued her rant when suddenly Mrs. Gagnon burst through the door in a trot with high heels on.

"There she is. I knew you would come," said Madame.

Sharon, now in shock, tried to cover her surprise. "It's good to see you, Mrs. Gagnon. I'm glad to know you have honored your commitment and returned."

"Of course I returned. I do apologize for not showing up yesterday but everything was as you said it would be."

"As your husband said it would be," said Madame.

"Oh yes, that's what I really meant!" She was tremendously excited." You see, when I called the insurance company, they wanted me to bring the document and before I knew it, the day was over. I do apologize." Mrs. Gagnon reached into her purse and pulled out a cashier's check for three thousand dollars.

Deloche took an audible inward breath. "Why Lady Gagnon, this is for twice the amount. Are you sure you want to do this?"

"Why Madame, in my mind, it's not enough for what you've done for me. I can never really repay you because it's priceless."

The two hugged and wept as Madame felt everything Mrs. Gagnon felt and knew she was sincere. Sharon now joined in, making it a group hug. She offered Mrs. Gagnon a cup of coffee but she refused, citing that she still needed to go to her late husband's job to claim his retirement and a second insurance policy he didn't mention at the session. She thanked them one more time and promised to come back at a later date for coffee and conversation, then briskly walked out the door.

Sharon and Madame smiled at each other and hugged. After the bliss of a successful séance, they talked about auras again and the meaning of their colors. Also, the ability to see them and what that said about the person the aura belongs to. That conversation was now charged with energy since Mrs. Gagnon had walked through that door and lifted their spirits. Sharon had bought a pair of aura glasses to experiment with, something she had seen in a science magazine. The question was, do they really work and under what conditions?

CHAPTER 8

Over in Slidell, Vic and Steve were back at the hotel and laying on their beds, planning their return to Chicago. Steve said that they should leave in the next day or so, disillusioned about how things had gone down concerning the property.

"Man, I didn't need this right now. As far as I'm concerned, we can leave tomorrow."

This got Vic's attention. "Hey! I thought we were going over to New Orleans?"

"Oh yeah, we can do that if that's what you want to do."

"Okay, let's go tomorrow and leave the next morning."

"Sounds good, we could do that."

So the guys relaxed for the rest of the afternoon, watching TV and around six in the evening, went to a restaurant to enjoy a steak. At dinner, Vic told Steve he had never been to the Big Easy and suggested they go tonight. Steve agreed, saying that it was Friday night and it would be off the chain. After eating, they paid their check and headed back to the hotel to freshen up.

As they did so, Vic's phone rang. "What does she want?"

"Who's that, Tina?"

"Yes, but I'm not going to answer. She's not going to ruin my night. Hopefully, it will stop." The phone stopped ringing.

"Looks like you got your wish."

Then it rang again and Vic ignored it.

"You're not going to answer it?"

"I don't think so." And again it stopped.

"Oops, you are planning to go back home right?"

"Yes but not tonight. I'll call her tomorrow."

They then jumped in the car and headed across Lake Pontchartrain to New Orleans, the French Quarter. They drove by the Mercedes

Benz Dome and saw the collapsed Hard Rock Cafe. Later, it was discovered that two men had died and were still buried in the rubble. They continued to drive and Steve parked on Bourbon Street, away from the action.

"Looks like we're far from the action," Vic said."

"Yes, it's hard to find a parking spot closer. It's better if we just walk."

"I see." Vic noticed all the cars. "We'll get there pretty quick."

"Yeah, we're in pretty good shape."

They headed up the street. A half mile up the street was Madame Deloche and Sharon standing out in front of the shop.

"Madame, try on these shades."

"Why? It's nighttime."

"They're ultra violet spectral light lenses. They could help you see a person's aura."

"Can you see any auras?"

"No, that's why I want you to look."

"They're probably fake," Madame happily snapped as she put them on.

"Do you see anything?"

"No, not really. It looks like a starburst from the car lights behind." Madame took them off.

Steve and Vic were coming up the street. "Well it looks like we made it."

"Man, this feels like a seedy place," Vic said.

"What do you mean?" Steve asked as they approached Madame's shop.

Madame told Sharon, "Wait, let me try something." She walked back out of the shop and this time she looked up the street with the car lights to her back. "I'm seeing some things, Sharon."

At that very moment, Vic and Steve walked by, going up the street and she could see Vic's aura and gasps. She can't believe what she's seeing. While all the other auras she could visibly detect were faint and multi-colored like a prism or a rainbow, Vic's was a raging blue. Like a blue flame on a gas burner on a stove top. And though it was the color of a blue flame, it didn't move like a flame. It somehow seemed to be solid but yet untouchable in that it was invisible to the naked eye. It was breathtaking and very unusual. Madame knew that this was something special and needed to find out more about this man and who he was. She needed to touch him, sense him, and look into his eyes to reach into his soul with her incredible and astounding extra sensory abilities. Madame becomes very excited.

"Ah, hey, sir, sir!"

Steve and Vic turned around. "Are you talking to us?"

"Yes, this gentleman here. Hi, I'm Madame Deloche."

"Hello, I'm Vic and this is Steve."

"Nice to meet you. Can I interest you in a reading?"

"No, we're headed up the street, sorry."

"Please, I'll give you a great deal, half off."

"Thank you, but no," Vic said.

"Okay, okay, only for you I will do it for free."

The guys looked at each other and Steve said, "Hey, man, go ahead. We've got time. I'm curious."

Vic looked at Madame. "Okay, lady, why me?"

"Why not you? Come, come, gentlemen. Come have a seat. Steve, you sit here and Vic, please come to the table with me." She handed the shades back to Sharon. "Vic, let me see your hands... hmm, I see a long life and a sudden change. Let me look at my cards."

Vic could feel it coming. "Here we go."

Then Madame said, "I'm feeling very strongly about this number." She slapped down a number 13 card. "I can tell by the look on your face, you know this number very well."

"Yes, I don't seem to be able to escape it."

"This is not a bad thing, but with it comes great responsibility."

What responsibility?" Vic asked.

"I don't know, but this is a powerful number."

Vic was now intrigued. "How?"

"In the last supper, Christ with the twelve disciples makes thirteen. They together have become a worldwide religion and historical figures."

"That's it?"

"Zues, the thirteenth Greek god and the most powerful."

Vic was now captured. "Okay."

"Thirteen is a lucky number in Asia and there are thirteen crystal skulls."

"Okay, Madame, you're on to something here, but I don't know and I don't understand."

"As is often the case, but I can tell you there's nothing to fear from the unknown but be weary of mankind."

"That's not a lot, Madame, but I do feel better. Thank you."

"Here's my card. When you find out more, I can tell you more, but I feel it's bigger than you've ever imagined."

"Madame, you're the real deal, contrary to my first impression."

"Why thank you, that's quite a compliment."

Vic handed her forty dollars.

"Oh thank you, that's very generous of you."

For the first time in this encounter, he noticed how pretty she was, but being a married man, he made no advance.

"Madame, I will be in touch."

They said their goodbyes and the guys continued up the street. When they got a block away, Steve said, "Vic, I don't know what this is about, but I am now a believer."

"Oh you see it now?"

"Yeah, you'd have to with all that I've told you."

Steve was now charged with energy. "When she pulled out that card and put it down, that couldn't have been a coincidence."

"Yes, she was extraordinary in more ways than one," Vic said as they both laughed.

"Yeah, I noticed that, too."

The guys kept walking and stopped at the corner of Orleans and Bourbon Street.

"Man, it's packed. Look at all these people," Vic said in amazement.

Steve looked across the street. "Man, look at this club over here. Now that's a party."

"All of these clubs and they're all jumping," Vic said, twisting his head around to soak it all in.

Steve looked at Vic. "You wanna go in?"

Vic didn't respond directly, being that he really didn't like crowds, especially drunken ones. "Man, they're so packed, this is really crazy."

Steve was now feeling the party vibe energy. "They're starting to party in the streets now." The clubs were so crowded that there was no place else to go but to the streets.

"Hey, I'm starting to feel it myself," Vic said, now bopping his head to the music with rock 'n roll and R&B that was clashing in the streets. Depending on where you stood determined what you would hear and the street crowd continued to grow. Vic knew he was getting a microcosm of Mardi Gras.

Being glad they were in the open space of the streets that was now shrinking, Steve observed. "Hey, I guess this is as good a place as any."

"You got that right, Stevie."

Steve heard a commotion. "Uh oh, look up the street, two guys getting ready to square off."

"Oh man, they're going at it. Don't do it guys!" Vic shouted but they couldn't hear him through the crowd noise and loud music.

Steve noticed some men pushing through the crowd. "There's the police right on time on this one."

Vic smelled the decades of liquor that had been spilled in the streets. The faint smell of sex, people who were too drunk, and the clashing music were grinding on him. "Hey you want to head back to the car?"

Steve looked at Vic with surprise, being that this was all Vic's idea. Steve figured he was in for a long night. And though he said nothing to Vic, he had been there many times with his family as a boy when they would come down from Chicago every summer. And then when he was in his twenties with his buddies and their wild times in almost the same spot. It was old hat for Steve, but he didn't want to deprive his friend of the experience. "Ready to go?"

"Yeah, it's a little over the top."

Steve was now relieved. "Thank you, I like a good party but this is five parties in one. Let's get out of here."

"Yeah and this hasn't been a celebratory week for us. This is for the happy party people."

Steve nodded. "I agree. Let's head back down Bourbon Street. Oh man, the women."

Drunk women did not impress Vic. "Yeah but would you want to marry a party animal chick?"

Steve was being honest with himself. "No, I couldn't hang."

"Me neither."

Steve refreshed Vic's memory. "Remember, I was married to a stripper."

Vic had a light bulb moment. "Oh yeah, and she was fine, too."

"Yeah but every day was a party, and if it wasn't, she was board. The sex was great, but that alone won't sustain a marriage."

"True that."

The next morning, Vic was awake in his bed. He looked at his phone to see what time it was and it was 9:00 a.m. He looked over at Steve who was laying on his bed, facing the other way on his side. "Hey, Steve, you awake?"

"Yep, what's up?"

"What time were you planning to head out?"

Steve was not moving a muscle. "Whenever we get up, but I know we have to be out by noon."

Vic was still talking to the back of Steve's head. "That's right... well I've got to call the wife, so I didn't want to wake you if it gets loud."

Steve was still motionless. "You're good, do what you've gotta do."

Vic tapped out the number, and it rang. "Hey, thanks for getting back. We have some problems here."

It wasn't lost on Vic that she didn't say *hi* or *good morning*. Nor did she apologize for all the screaming and the unnecessary drama from the last phone call. And nor did he apologize for hanging up or returning the call in a timely manner. It was cold, and he knew that down under she was still angry and something was awry, but he said nothing concerning that to maintain the empty calm. "What kind of problems?"

"Well for one, there's water streaming from the foundation in the garage."

Vic was now concerned. "How much water?"

"It's not a river but a steady flow. And Aunt D is really sick. She has a bug, probably a virus."

Vic was now more concerned about his favorite and only surviving aunt. "Oh no, a flu with COPD is nothing to play with."

"Exactly, but she's refusing to go to the doctor."

"What?"

Tina, in a cold, empty explanatory tone, said, "That's why I called."

Vic was now more animated. "Okay, we're still in Slidell. I'll try to catch a plane out of New Orleans."

Tina was now grateful. "I think that's a good idea. Every plumber I call said they don't work on slab foundations."

"Okay, let me try to get back as soon as I can."

"What time is it there?" Tina asked.

"It's about 9:20. Why?"

"Because it's 7:20 a.m. here."

Vic cringed. "Oh I'm sorry. I forgot about the time change, I'll text you later."

Tina said coldly, "Do that, bye."

"Well, looks like the parties over," Steven said, with his back still turned to Vic.

"Yeah, but it was good while it lasted. Let me call the airline. You going to be okay, driving back?" Vic said, now on the move, trying to get his things together.

"Of course, I'm good." Steve finally moved a little." "She sounded angry."

"Too bad. I'm the one who should be angry."

"I get that."

"Hey, have you seen my headset? It was here when we left, right on the night stand."

"No, you had it yesterday."

"I know, but I didn't take it with me. I'll bet the little cleaning chick took it."

"I'd let the office know."

"I don't have time. It was old, but it makes me think of what Madame Deloche said last night."

"What's that?"

"She said be wary of mankind."

"Yes, she did."

Vic packed and called an Uber. He gave Steve some money for the room, then a shake and a shoulder, then headed for the front of the motel. The driver showed up shortly thereafter and was back over the vast expanse of Lake Pontchartrain. Within two hours, he was on a plane headed back to L.A. and landed around 2:15 p.m. Vic was standing at arrivals when Tina drove up. Vic threw his bag in the car and slid in.

"Hello."

"Hi. How was the flight?"

"Not bad, pretty quiet compared to the one going."

"What happened on the one going?"

"Nothing worth talking about."

"Then why did you mention it?"

"'Cause you asked about the flight and I told you the truth, but people don't like the truth anymore, including you."

"What kind of crap is that? I don't like the truth."

"You can't accept the fact that it's not worth talking about, therefore you don't like it."

"Well I don't."

"Then I rest my case."

"Whatever."

"I'm going to the neighbors, Zack. I think they had a pluming problem."

They did, when?"

"A few months ago."

That's great, not that I wanted—"

"I know what you meant," Vic said, cutting her off as he often did to him. "Then I'm headed to Aunt D's house."

"Okay."

When they got to the house, Vic went straight to Zack's and found him in the garage. "Zack, how's it going?"

"Hey, buddy, it's going."

"Listen, you had a plumbing problem a few months ago."

"Sure did."

"Was it a broken pipe in the foundation?"

"Yes it was, you, too?"

"Yep!"

"It's going to cost you twenty grand."

"Twenty grand! Damn, it's just not my week!"

Zack smiled. "Hey, I was just kidding. It was only ten grand. Doesn't that feel better?"

"It still hurts, but only half as much. You're gonna give me a stroke."

"Hey, you may do even better 'cause I had two broken pipes."

"I think I've only got one broken. Okay, my heart's beating again."

"Good,' cause I don't do mouth to mouth."

"Ha, ha, ha. You still have their number?"

"For sure, right here." Zack pulled out his wallet.

"Thanks man, it's hard to find a company that works on a slab."

"That's true, Vic."

"Zack I'll bring this card right back."

"No, keep it. I've got plenty."

"Thanks, I appreciate it." Vic headed back to the house two doors away. Vic walked in and saw Tina. "I got the card, babe."

"That's good."

"I'll call them on the way to Aunt D's."

Tina turned to catch him before he walked out. "Oh before I forget, Mom is coming down to stay for a while. She'll be here the last week in January."

"Okay, great, she's a great chef who's welcome here anytime. And then we need to talk about this Detroit thing when I get back."

"Okay, if you must. For me, there's not much to talk about."

"Okay, I'm going to leave before I blow a gasket." Vic walked out the garage door.

Twenty minutes later, Vic pulled up at Aunt D's apartment complex and hurried to the door and knocked.

"Who is it?"

"It's me, Aunt D. Your favorite nephew."

She opened the door. "Hey, boy. You have to excuse me. I feel terrible. I've got to get back in this bed before I fall. I feel so dizzy."

"Oh my God, you're as pale as a ghost!"

"I am? I know I feel like I want to lie here and die. I feel so bad."

Aunt D was eighty-seven years old but looked seventy. She had worked all her life as a nurse and was in great shape, but she smoked cigarettes for forty years. She quit twenty years ago, but not soon enough. She had a pleasant looking face that could grow mean quickly if she got upset. And that had earned her the nickname Sparky. Today she was miserable and testy from the flu and no one could get her to go to the hospital.

"Oh just let me die."

"Yeah, that's what I'm afraid of, but I can't let you do that."

"What do you mean, you can't let me do that?"

"Aunt D, we're going to the hospital."

"No, I am not!"

"Oh yes, we're going if I have to throw you over my shoulder."

"Boy! You better not!"

"Well, I won't have to if you help me, help you."

Aunt D mocked him. "I won't have to nah, nah, nah, nah, shit. I just don't feel like it."

"And that's how people die, they just don't feel like it."

"Well hell, all my friends are gone. Maybe it's just my time."

"No, it's not your time, Sparky. You're going to live well into your nineties."

"I don't want to. Hell for what?"

Vic gave her the puppy dog eye. "To play cards, to be with family. What kind of nephew would I be if I went along with your plan?"

"That's true."

"Yes, they'd say he just let her die, she said she wanted to die." Stop it!"

"Yeah, even sounds ridiculous to you. Come on, let's get ready."

"Okay, just wait for me in the living room."

"Now that's what I'm talking about."

Vic walked into the living room.

"All they're going to do is stick a bunch of needles in me and poke at me."

"Ahh, let's you know you're alive."

"Shut up! Crazy boy."

Vic laughed. He waited there for fifteen minutes. Then he was shocked when Aunt D walked out. Aunt D never went anywhere without being nicely dressed, with makeup, lipstick, and her favorite wig. Today she was standing there in a pink robe, flat shoes, and a pink turban cap looking like an eccentric wealthy actress from the 1940s.

"Okay, I'm ready, let's go."

Vic's mouth was open in disbelief. "Are you going like that?"

"Yes, what's wrong with this?"

"Nothing, you look cute. I've just never seen you leave the house like that before."

"And you've never seen me this sick before."

"Oh my! You are really sick. Let me get you to the hospital."

"If you must, let's go."

When they pulled into the parking lot, Vic let Aunt D out at the entrance, then went to park the car. When he entered the waiting room, he was disappointed to see that it was crowded but spotted a seat next to Aunt D. "Looks like we're going to be her for a while."

"Maybe not," Aunt D said." I called my doctor from the house before we left and he said he would call ahead, so let's see."

"Okay, great."

"Listen, I have something I want to talk to you about."

"Okay. What's up Aunt D?"

"Well I keep having this dream that my brother has been killed."

"Who Ted?"

"No Nate."

"Did anyone ever find out where he disappeared to, Aunt D?"

"No we didn't."

"I think he slipped into Mexico," Vic said.

"Why do you think that?"

"Because he was in San Diego when he escaped from prison. It's the logical choice."

"I don't know but these dreams are so real."

"Really?"

"Oh, yes. When I wake up it's like it really happened."

"That's interesting."

"Why so?"

"Because I used to have dreams at night that I didn't remember. And then it would happen the next day, Nothing major, a fall, a conversation, or playing with friends. I wouldn't remember I dreamed it until it happened the next day."

"Still a little extra sensory stuff going on there," Aunt D said.

"For sure, do you think it runs in the family?"

"Well, your grandfather was always talking about dreams."

"Like what?"

"I don't remember, but he said they had come to pass."

"I have a question for you Aunt D."

"What?"

"Have you ever had a number that just kept coming up?"

"No, that's a new one for me."

"Well—."

Before he could finish, a nurse stuck her head inside the waiting room. "Mrs. Dorothy Venable?"

"Yes! That's me."

"Hi, come on back. Your doctor called and so we're going to run some tests and give you some treatment for your breathing."

"Okay, that sounds great, and this is my nephew."

Vic waved.

"Hi, come on back." The nurse took them back to a small room down the hall.

In the back, things were less crowded. Doctors in their smocks, rushing around and nurses tending to other patients with maintenance men cleaning and repairing things. Once in the room, they took Aunt D and wheeled her around so that she was facing the door and was now next to a machine with tanks on the bottom and clear hoses running up a board and hanging from a clamp. At the end of the hoses were clear masks to cover the mouth and nose. The nurse took one of those and put it over D's head with the strap to hold it to her nose and mouth. She then explains that it's oxygen mixed with steam and medication to help open up her lungs. She was down to half a breath. As the nurse was instructing Aunt D to breathe deeply, a crew of doctors and nurses ran by and Vic heard the words: code blue. There was so much energy and commotion outside, the nurse closed the door. It now felt like being in a closet but quieter now, and cozy with the nurse coaching Aunt D.

"Breath in deep and slow," the nurse said. "Close your eyes and relax, exhale, breathe deep, slow it down. Let's get a rhythm slow and deep.

"Okay, I have to step out for a minute. Just continue what we've established here and I'll be right back."

As soon as she walked out the door, Aunt D started talking. "Oh, I feel so much better. What does that mean, code blue?"

"I don't know, Aunt D, but if I had to guess, I would say it was a life or death situation like someone who stopped breathing or went into cardiac arrest."

"Yes! That's what I was thinking because when I worked at a hospital we had a code, but it was code red."

From there, Aunt D seemed like she was back to her old self. Talk, talk, talk nonstop, without anyone getting a word in edgewise. But Vic was glad to see some semblance of the auntie he knew. A few minutes later, the nurse walked back in and Aunt D was still talking a mile a minute in between breaths.

"Now, Mrs. Dorothy, I need you to stop talking. That's not helping your treatment, the nurse said.

"Oh! I'm sorry. You said deep and slow."

The nurse gave her a cadence to breathe by. Vic stepped out of the room so as not to tempt Aunt D to talk. Things were quiet again out in the hallway as he walked down to the restroom. He noticed the police come in with a man in chains. This man looked like a wild animal, big hair, beard and dark as night. He looked African. As Vic walked past, he heard the man say, "He's a seer, dis man." Vic looked at him and realized he was talking about him. He started yanking and pulling on his chains on his prison wheel chair as if to break them. Vic looked into his eyes and saw anger and fear, then he started hissing like a big cat as if trying to get away. Then his eyes turned colors from brown to green to gray.

"What the hell?" Vic said.

"He's from Haiti; weird stuff all the time," the man's police escort said. "Hey Sha' man, calm down."

Then Sha' man said, "The last one like him tried to kill me. Use it for good or die garcon."

"What!" Vic exclaimed.

The officer told Vic to ignore him if he could, citing that the prisoner was a mental case and was way out there. Vic nodded and said "Thank you" to the officer and headed back to the room.

"Oh there you are," the nurse said to him as he walked into the room. "Looks like we're going to keep her."

Vic looked at his aunt. "Aunt D, you going to be okay?"

"I guess so, I'm dressed for it."

"Yes, you are. Well, I'm going to head home and I'll let the family know."

"I just hate I'm going to be here 'til the weekend."

"No big deal. You'll be alive and we'll be here." Vic thanked the nurse and headed home.

CHAPTER 9

One week later, Tina was on the phone, with the speaker on, as Vic came down the stairs.

"Mom, try not to bring too much stuff. We have a washer and dryer, you know."

"I know, but if we decide to go somewhere, I want to be presentable."

"You'll be fine, it's L.A. Bring some jeans and a jacket, it's winter," Tina said.

"What if I want to go to church?" Lilly said.

"Okay, bring a dress or two, not ten."

"Okay, okay," Lilly said.

"Alright, Mom, gotta go. We'll talk before you get here."

"Okay, talk to you later."

Vic was now in the kitchen. "When is she going to be here again?"

"Next week," Tina said. "Can you pick her up from the airport?"

"Of course."

"Thank you. I may have to work, but if I can get there, I'll pick her up."

"Sure, I want to talk about Detroit."

"What's there to talk about?"

"There's plenty to talk about."

"Like what?"

"Like the fact that you let me fly halfway across the country to look at property that you knew you didn't want us to buy."

"I was interested until you started talking about a hundred grand. We don't even have a hundred grand."

"If you hadn't flipped out and so disrespectfully cut me off before I could explain that it wouldn't have cost that much."

"At this point I don't care how much it costs. I'm not doing it."

"Why not!"

"What about the three properties here? What if something goes wrong here? Where's the money going to come from for that?"

"We both have money coming in. You're afraid of taking a chance on a great opportunity."

"Whatever you want to call it, I'm not doing it."

"Fine, I just don't see why you had to waste my fucking money and time to say you didn't want to do it."

Tina was now feeling cornered. "You done? Get it all out, 'cause I don't want to hear about goddamn Detroit again."

"Kiss my ass, Tina."

"No thank you."

It was the third week of January and Tina had picked up her mother, Lilly, from the airport. Vic and Tina were still barely speaking but knew the routine of how to put a good face on it for Vic's mother-in-law. Tina called Vic on the way back. "Hey, Vic?"

"Yeah, what's up?"

"Mom and I are on the way back from the airport. Can you come out when we get there and help with the bags?"

"Sure."

"Thank you. We'll be there in a minute."

A few minutes later, the garage door opened and Vic walked out into the garage. Lilly got out of the car. "Hey, Lil, how are you?"

"I'm fine, Vic. How are you?" They hugged.

"I'm good, and good to see you. Let me grab that bag for you."

"Yes, thank you."

Vic took the big bag upstairs to the guest room."

"Mom, do you want something to eat?" Tina asked.

"No, not really."

"Do you want to go out somewhere to eat?"

"No, I was planning on cooking for you guys."

"Okay, if that's what you want to do. I thought you might be tired."

"No, not at all." Lilly was five-foot-seven with brown hair and brown eyes with smooth skin. She was a quiet and calm lady, very pleasant to be around. Lilly was knowledgeable and wise at a young seventy-nine years old and in better shape than her daughter and a fantastic cook.

Vic came back down the stairs. "Lil, I left your trunk on the table at the end of the bed."

"Okay, thank you, Vic. Trunk! Was it that heavy?"

"Yes." They both started laughing."

So, Vic, I'm getting ready to cook. Do you have anything in mind?"

"Cook! You just got here. You don't want us to take you out for dinner?"

"Not really, I'd rather just whip something up."

Well, Lil, you have a whole freezer full to choose from. Whatever you decide."

"Okay, let me go in here and see what you've got."

Vic walked back to his man cave. "Thank you, Lil. Nothing like a home-cooked meal."

Tina chimed in from the living room that's open to the dining room and kitchen. "Yes, thanks, Mom. I'm usually too tired to cook and we end up eating out a lot, and that's not good."

"No, it's not, but glad I could help out."

"It's a big help."

"I see you have this ground meat defrosted in the fridge. I'm gonna make a meat loaf with mashed potatoes, gravy, and broccoli. How does that sound?"

"Hey, that sounds good, Mom."

Later, at the start of dinner with the three of them seated at the table ready to dig in, Tina asked. "Vic, can you say grace?"

Vic started in so as not to waste any time. "Yes… Dear Lord, thank you for this food we're about to receive. Let it nourish and restore our souls. Amen."

"Nice and short," Lilly said.

"I've always hated long-winded prayers, especially when people are hungry." They all chuckled and agreed.

"There's always one who thinks they're a preacher," Lilly said.

Vic was now focused on the food. "Mmm, this is really good meat loaf, Lil."

"Sure is, Mom," Tina added as not to appear less appreciative than Vic.

"Well, I'm glad you guys like it."

"We don't like it, Lil. We love it."

"Right," Tina said.

"Oh stop, you guys, it's not that good."

"Oh, yes it is," Vic said.

Tina chimed in again. "We try to eat healthy, salads, and less greasy stuff, but it's still not like this."

"Well, I'll try to keep the meals coming while I'm here."

"That sounds nice," Vic said.

"Vic, don't you cook?" Lilly inquired.

"Yes, if you like burned leather," Tina said, garnering a big laugh from both Vic and Lilly.

"Hey! I have a couple of dishes I can cook, but your daughter will cook what I made and say, 'I like mine better,' so I let her do it, Lil."

"Oh, well that explains it," Lilly said.

"She'd rather bring food home than eat my cooking."

"And he cooks his chicken 'til it's dry, Mom."

"And yours is always brown on the outside and raw on the inside. Lil, I'm glad you're here."

As Vic and Tina go back and forth like kids would do complaining to Mom, not wanting to be outdone by the other as they conceal the bad blood well under the surface.

"You guys are a mess. Well, there's plenty in there for me to cook."

Tina nodded. "Yep."

They finished their meal, then Tina headed to the couch. Lilly washed the dishes, and Vic headed to the man cave.

The following week, Vic was in his man cave and the phone rang.

"Hey, what's up, Greg?"

"Hey, you have me on speaker?"

"Yes."

"Can your wife hear me?"

"No, she's at work and my mother-in-law is upstairs. You're good."

"I wanted to run some jokes by you."

"Okay, shoot."

"I came home pretty high and started making love to my wife. When I finished I realized it was her sister. I asked her, 'Where's my wife?' She said, 'In your bedroom.'"

"Ha! Not bad."

"Here's another one. My wife asked me to remodel the kitchen, so I took down the stripper pole."

"Clever, clever. I see you've been putting in work."

"Yeah, trying to get ready for the next show."

Okay, okay."

"So which one do you like the best?"

"The first one."

"Okay, that maybe an 'A' joke."

"Maybe," Vic said nonchalantly."

"Let me make a note of that." Greg started writing.

"So Greg, when's the next party?"

"Party! They're still talking about you from the last party."

"Really?"

"Yes, really."

"You can come but you're banned from smoking. You scared some people."

"What? How?"

"Demons, witches, vampires, werewolves. And I think that chick still has it in for you."

"Why?"

"She still thinks you called her a bitch."

"No, I wouldn't say that to a stranger."

"Well, I'm just saying.

"Hey! You know I will not be smoking."

"Okay!" Greg said to assure Vic.

"So when is it?"

I don't know, but let the dust settle from the last one. More like a dust storm. Boy, you were in rare form."

"Or beyond form."

"What is that supposed to mean? What if I was seeing the true essence of who they are?"

"Were you?"

"I don't know. It was just a hypothetical question."

"Hey, I don't know either but no more hypotheticals. I've gotta get out of here, I'll catch you later."

"Okay, catch you later."

The following week, Vic was out hitting golf balls. Tina and Lilly were discussing dinner. Lilly was pulling food out of the freezer. It was the first week in February, icy cold at night in California, then warming in the day.

"Mom, what are you cooking tonight?"

"I think I'm going to make some spaghetti tonight."

"I like the sound of that. It should last us a few days."

"FYI, I'm starting to empty out your freezer here. We're going to have to go to the store in a week or so."

"Not a problem, but don't forget that top freezer shelf."

"Okay, yes, I see a few things up here."

"And there's some steak at the very bottom."

Yeah, where?" Lilly asked.

"Probably under the vegetables. When it gets full, I just put stuff where I can."

"I see it. I think I'll do the steak next week."

"That sounds good Mom."

Vic walked in the front door. "Hey, people."

"Hey, Vic, I'm fixing dinner in case you're hungry."

"Sounds great, Lil. I think I've worked up an appetite."

Later that night, Tina and Vic were in their bedroom. "Did you finish the roof on Rexford?" Tina asked Vic, hoping to question why he was out working on golf.

"That was done last week."

"Well, you never said anything."

"Every time I try to talk to you about things, you get an attitude because I'm interrupting one of your drama, gossip, reality shows, so now I don't bother."

"Well, I need to escape for a little while after work."

Yeah, that's clearly more important."

"Hey, you're retired. That's easy for you to say."

"Since you're in the mood to talk, I found out that the place in Detroit sold for three thousand dollars. Three grand."

"Why are you telling me this?"

"Because I want you to know we missed out on a great opportunity. For fifty-three thousand or less we could have had a duplex, paid off and renovated."

"So why don't you use your money?"

"You know my money is all in annuities."

"So, take some out."

"I thought we were a team."

"Well, I changed my mind."

"You're the one who said that's what the money was for. To buy or fix something. And why the hell didn't you tell me you changed your mind?"

"I don't know. I'm telling you now."

"You don't know?"

"And I don't know if I want to stay in this marriage," Tina said.

"What! So it's like that? Okay, well, you let me know when you figure it out." Vic turned his back, retreated to his side of the bed and lay awake a few hours before falling asleep.

One week later, on February 13, Vic came out of his bedroom with clothes to wash and ran into Lilly in the hallway upstairs. Being a newer home, the laundry room was on the second floor, a big convenience, not having to walk down to the first floor or the basement. It's a spacey upstairs landing wider than a hallway, a room in itself with tan carpet and tan walls.

"Good morning."

"Good morning, Lil. How are you feeling?"

"Pretty good. How about you?"

"Good, good, are you getting ready to wash?"

"No, but I do need to get a few things out of the dryer."

"Oh okay, yeah, I'm headed to a funeral next week so I need to make sure I've got a clean white shirt."

"I'm glad you mentioned that. I need to make a payment on my plan. I'm still trying to figure out if I'm going in the ground or a crypt."

"Yes, that's something to think about," Vic said.

"Have you and Tina decided on your arrangements?"

"Well, we're planning on cremation. It's just so much cheaper. I've watched the price of these funerals go up and up. It's a racket."

"I know, but I just can't wrap my mind around cremation."

"And a lot of people can't, Lil, but remember, the body is just a dead shell at that point."

"Yeah, but I don't know."

"Remember, the Vikings used to put their remains on bales of hay, or on a boat full of hay and wood to cremate."

"Yes, but I'm not a Viking," Lil said. They both laughed.

"I know, just food for thought. Hey, there was a guy who said, 'Just put me in a trash can and take me to the dump when I'm gone.'"

"What! Now see, that's too crazy."

"I know, that's way over the top, but what difference would it make? His spirit will be gone," Vic said.

This conversation had gotten the attention of the ancient guardians from another dimension, who had once walked this

Earth and who were waiting for Vic to come into the realization of who he was to become and to understand the signs they had been leaving him. These statements had possibly expedited things as The Guardians were angered from the other side and looked to expedite things.

"But what about family?" Lil asked.

"Absolutely right, I'm with you."

"Okay, well, I'm going down stairs for some coffee."

"Okay, Lil, somehow I don't think I helped much."

Lilly chuckled. "No, not on this one."

"I'm sorry."

"Everyone's different. You want anything for breakfast?"

"No Lil, I'll just fix some cereal when I get down there, thanks."

"Okay."

Vic went back into his bedroom to see if he had missed any dirty clothes. Not finding any, he started to go downstairs for breakfast and more conversation with Lilly, but decided to shave first and got downstairs ten minutes later. He didn't know why; maybe a quiet voice in his head, but this seemingly insignificant short delay would change the course of his life.

At 9:30 a.m., Vic headed down the stairs and saw Lilly sitting at the end of the table. "Lil, I see you've got your coffee."

"Yeah, I found a little something to go with it."

"Lil, what's that?" He moved in for a closer look.

"It's a brownie and really good, too. I didn't think anyone was going to eat it."

Vic's shock was turning into a quiet panic. "Lil, please tell me you didn't get that out of the freezer."

"I did. Why, is it bad?"

"Oh, my God, you've eaten almost all of it."

"I was getting ready to finish it."

"No! Lilly, it's a marijuana brownie. Don't take another bite."

"What! Are you kidding?"

"No I'm not. I know there's only that one bite left, but you've already had too much, way too much."

"Oh no, I should have asked. I found it all the way in the back. I didn't think anyone wanted it."

"I just can't believe you found it, and ate the whole thing."

"Am I going to die?"

"I don't know, I need to call Tina..." Vic pulled his cell phone from his pocked and called his wife. "Tina!"

"Yes, what's going on?"

"Some crazy shit."

"What? What happened?"

"You're not going to believe this. Lilly found the brownie and ate it. All except one bite."

"What! Are you serious? Did she ask you?"

"I'm serious as a heart attack and no, she didn't. I came down stairs and she was almost finished."

"It's my fault, I should have asked," Lilly said.

Tina giggled. "Well, I don't think she can OD. You need to find out, but you're on your own. I can't leave work. Is she high yet?"

"No it hasn't kicked in yet. I'm going online to see if she can OD as we speak and this article says...No one has ever OD'd on marijuana, uh, but I expect that she's going to be really sick so I've gotta get prepared. I'll talk to you later."

"Okay, text me, bye." Tina hung up and Vic looked at Lilly.

"Well, I don't feel anything yet."

"That's good, but I need you to drink some water, Lil. I think that will help."

"Okay, let me grab a bottle from the fridge."

"Okay, and I'm going to call Greg." Vic called Greg and put him on speaker.

"Hey, what'cha into?"

"You do not want to know."

"Ha, sure don't," Lilly chimed in, still sitting at the dining room table.

"G. My mother-in-law just ate the brownie."

"The whole thing?"

"Yes, just about all but one bite."

"Oh no, well she's going to be really high. I've only ever had a quarter of a brownie and I was useless," Greg said.

"Any ideas on what I should do?"

"Yeah, get a casket—one for her and one for you."

"Huh!" Lilly exclaimed.

"Thanks a lot, Greg, you're a big help."

"I've never been in this situation before, I don't know. Just keep an eye on her, keep her comfortable. Don't let her jump out of a window."

"Greg!" Lilly screeched. "Ah! Well I never."

"How old is she?" Greg asked.

"She's seventy-nine."

"And this is your wife's mom?"

"Yep."

"Do you want roses or tulips on your casket?"

"Thanks a lot, Greg. I'll keep you posted."

"Good luck."

"Thanks for nothing." Vic ended the call.

Lilly looked at Vic. "That was encouraging. I still don't feel anything. It was such a good brownie. Hard to believe it had marijuana in it."

"It did, but good it hasn't kicked in. That's giving us time. I've got these plastic bags, so if you get sick it's not on the floor."

"Okay, I finished that bottle of water. Should I drink another one?"

"No, just take another one out and keep it near."

"Alright."

Vic was now in a frenzy. "Okay, we have a bathroom right there, water, bags. I need towels..." Vic went into the bathroom and returned quickly. "I've got these cleaning towels."

Lilly shrugged. "I don't think anything's going to happen."

"Really?"

"I hear that some people don't get high the first time they try it."

"Lil, that's true. But I'm not so sure because you've had so much. Let's see what happens. I'm going to wash these dishes."

As Vic washed a few dishes, he noticed Lilly's plate with the one bite of a brownie on it. With Lilly saying it was so good ringing in his head, he pulled off a small strip of the brownie that could fit in a drinking straw hole, an inch long, then eats it. "Umm, that is good!"

"You had some?"

"Yes, just a real little piece for taste.

"Let me see, there's still one bite there," Lilly said.

"Yeah, it was just a little strip."

"That little bit won't bother you."

I think you're right, Lil."

A little over an hour had passed and Lilly was still her sweet, easygoing, chipper self. They both walked into the living room and had a seat on the recliners across from each other.

CHAPTER 10

Vic pulled out his phone to do a Spanish lesson. Lil was watching TV, and all was calm. Five minutes later, "Oh! Oh!" Lilly said.

"Lil, what's wrong?"

"I've got to go to the bathroom...oh, oh."

She ran to the bathroom, and Vic thought nothing of it. Ten minutes later, Vic heard a commotion coming from the bathroom.

Standing at the bathroom door, Vic called out, "Lil! You okay?"

"Help!"

Vic opened the door to find Lilly holding onto the sink, unable to stand up. The towel rack behind her was ripped off the wall and the shower door, which was off its track, had crashed into the shower.

"Lil, are you okay?"

"I almost fell." Lilly now slurred like a drunkard.

"Okay, let me help you."

Lilly's pants were still down. "My pan."

"What?"

"Pan."

Still not understanding, Vic put his head closer. "Who?"

Then in a loud voice that he had never heard come out of Lil's mouth and in a man's tone, Lilly shouted, "My pants!" startling Vic out of his shoes.

"Oh, oh, yes. Here, let's get those up."

"I can't walk," Lilly said, barely understandable.

"You can't walk?"

"No."

"Okay, I've got you."

With his arm hooked under hers, they walked back to the living room but Lilly stumbled, entering the dining room area in an open space before the dining room table and fell to the floor with Vic still

125

holding her arm, breaking the fall. Lilly was on the floor near the dining room table just outside the kitchen.

"Lil, can you get up?"

"I can…I can moo my leg. Oh!" she hollered as if she were in pain.

"You can't move your legs?"

"No! What is that?" Lilly Shouts. "Get away! Get off of me."

"What, Lil?"

"Whateva that is. Oh! Oh! Stop it, Stop! It hurts! Oh, it hurts so bad. Oh. I feel sick, I'm sick."

"I'm getting the bag, Lil."

Before he could get it to her face, she vomited on the throw rug on the floor.

"Lil, be still. Let me get the towel. Don't move." He took two steps to grab the towel. When he turned back to Lilly, she was rolling in the vomit."

"Lilly!"

"Oh, help me, Lord, help me!"

That she was calling on the Lord was a clear sign she was not doing well, and Vic was worrying. "Lil, no don't move." He pulled her away from the vomit. Lilly blacked out. Vic wiped up the mess with the towel and hurried into the bathroom to rinse it. Then ran upstairs for more towels. When he got back, Lilly was in the kitchen, leaning on the counter with a butcher knife. Vic was horrified and thought Greg was right. He was going to need that casket. "Lil, what are you doing? I need you to give me the knife."

"How do I know you're not with them?"

"With who, Lil?"

"You can't see these ugly monsters?" Lilly swung the knife with one hand and almost cut Vic.

"Lil, I am not with them." Vic ducked down as Lil was looking the other way, went around the granite counter between the kitchen and dining room, then came up behind Lilly and grabbed her wrist with the knife.

"No, I'll kill the son of a bitch! You're not taking me. Help!"

"Give…me…the…knife!" He finally forced it from her hand.

"Help me! They're trying to kill me." Lilly started slipping from the counter.

"I've got you, Lil." Vic caught her before she crashed to the hard Spanish tile floor. Lilly blacked out, and he dragged her back to the dining room carpet, then looked at the sliding glass door in the kitchen. "Lil, I need to clean the back of your blouse." Lilly did not respond. "And your arm." Vic cleaned all the vomit from Lilly and allowed her to lay flat on her stomach. He wanted to get her to the recliner, but she was out and dead weight. It was impossible; she was too heavy. Vic had become very self-conscious about the sliding glass door in the kitchen leading to the backyard being opened. With Lilly screaming for help, he was afraid of alerting the neighbors. The backyard with its lush sego palm, jasmine, flowers and other palm trees lining the yard seemed strangely more vivid than before, like a tropical oasis, as he slid the door closed. Twenty minutes later, Lilly, still flat on her stomach, opened her eyes.

"Lil, how are you feeling? I'm here. Do you need anything?"

"Wala."

"What? I didn't understand?"

"Wala."

"One more time for me, Lil." He leaned in closer.

She screamed, "Water!"

Lilly, who was usually quiet, startled Vic. "Oh! Okay, got it." Vic grabbed the bottled water. "I'm going to hold your head up a little." While drinking, Vic was holding her for support. "Good job. Let me know when."

Lilly soon tapped his arm for him to stop pouring. Her eyes were bloodshot. Vic looked into her eyes and saw her altered state and realized she was a different person under the influence of this psychoactive drug. Lilly started up again. "Oh! Oh! Don't let 'em take me! No! Get away, no!" She tried to get up.

"Lil, relax. Don't get up, you're just going to fall. Stay down."

Vic realized the floor was the best place to keep Lilly safe. She couldn't fall off of anything and if she got sick again, she was laying on a throw rug. Lilly was now a little more coherent.

"Okay, okay, why would anyone want to be like this? Oh, no, not again." She heaved again. This time, Vic had the bag in place.

"That's good, Lil. Let it come up, let's get it out."

"Oh, it hurts. Oh, make it stop."

"Lil, I'm going to dump this bag. Stay on the floor." He rushed into the bathroom and emptied the plastic bag into the toilet and hurried back. Lilly was out again, and another hour had passed. Vic went to his man cave to get a stool to sit on as he watched over Lilly. When he returned, he started feeling euphoric. He could see the backyard through the glass in the kitchen and now the backyard looked like a vivid, lush jungle. *This can't be. I didn't eat enough. Was it that strong?* He looked down and Lilly's eyes were open. Vic stood up.

"I see you," Lilly said.

"I see you, too."

"They're trying to get me."

"No one's going to get you, Lil."

"How do you know?"

"Because I'm here to protect you." Vic was now feeling fiercely protective of his mother-in-law in a heightened state of awareness.

"You can't protect me. You need to watch out for your own self."

"No, I'm here to protect you and no one is going to harm you."

He stretched his arm toward her, with his hand open, palm facing her as if transferring energy and understanding to Lilly, who then smiled and said, "Okay."

With faith and positive vibes, he knew she had received the telepathic message. Vic started speaking in a strange language of protection over her, and then it happened. He felt a sensation of power he'd never felt before and felt something emanating from the top of his head. Miraculously, as if astrally out of his body, he could see this huge blue glow coming out of the top of his head.

Lilly saw it, too. "Oh, wow, look at you." She laughed, now believing in his protection.

Vic felt like a powerful ruler in bliss, protecting his flock. Lilly feeling the return of the nausea suddenly shattered his euphoria. Lilly was again feeling the nausea.

"Oh, oh, no, not again. Oh, it hurts. Oh, Lord, please take me. Take me, Lord…just let me die."

"No, were not dying, Lil. You are not going to die." Vic's euphoria was now replaced with a fear of Lilly dying. Vic didn't know it, but the watchmen had intervened from the other side.

Lilly was again in distress. "Here it comes." Another heave, and Vic, now with lightning fast reflexes, grabbed a bag and caught her fluids in time.

"That's good, Lil. We want it to come up."

"This is too much. I can't take it. Lord, let me die."

She blacked out again. Vic, in a panic, kneeled down to make sure she was breathing. He climbed back onto the stool. His mind flipped over and he could only see a future vision as real as anything he'd ever seen. It was a funeral scene with Lilly's casket up front. Vic walked down the aisle and looked at Lilly's family, who had hate in their eyes, staring at him. Lilly's brother pointed at Vic. "He killed her, killed my sister! He drugged her and killed Lilly."

With an electric jolt, Vic jumped off the stool and into the bathroom, feeling the horror of that possible reality as if it had actually happened and got to the sink just in time to throw up. Vic was leaning over the sink, talking to himself. "How is this possible? Such a little piece. These visions are so real."

Vic heard Lilly and rushed back to the dining room. "Lil, you feel better?"

"I gotta get out a here! I want out. I gotta get out!" Lilly was sitting on her hip, with both hands on the floor, trying to push herself up.

"Lil, don't get up. You're safe here on the floor."

"Help, help! I've got to get out," she said, her voice baritone-deep like a man's.

Vic looked at Lilly in shock. It was as if she was someone else.

"Lil, is that you?"

Lilly sounding like a possessed belligerent drunkard. "Who else would it be?"

In the baritone-deep voice, Lilly said, "Oh, ooh! Here it comes… oh no.:

"Go ahead, Lil. I've got a bag."

"Aw, aw…" Lilly heaved up a huge amount of dark fluid.

"Oh, that's good, Lil."

Lilly rolled and squirmed on the floor. She tried to push up again and collapsed back onto the floor as if she had just died.

"Lil! Lil!" With his heart pounding, Vic checked her pulse. "Oh, thank God."

He made his way back to the stool. Vic could again feel the blue light energy emanating from the top of his head, as if his skull had literally opened up. Unlike the vision, someone intruded into the blue light energy from another dimension. With his eyes wide open, Vic's mind flipped to that dimension and now only saw with his mind's eye. He saw them, ancient European warrior types with two Africans and one Asian with swords, clubs, and shields. About twelve men in total. One stepped forward and spoke from the other side. So, you're the one."

"You talking to me?" Vic asked.

"Yes, you!" He slammed his hand against a strange glass-like membrane that separated them. "Who the hell else would I be talking to?" His name is Clayvious, and he was six-foot-five, and built like a granite statue carved to accentuate every muscle.

"Hey,! Calm down! Why are you so hostel?"

"We are the guardians here and I heard you talking to the lady there and desecrating the bodies of god men."

"God men?"

"Well, I was referring to my own body, mostly," Clayvious barked. "It doesn't matter whose body, you numbskull. You are god men worthy of honor and a ritual burial."

"Well, I know we were made in the image of God and possibly men of God."

"No! You are god men! Not men of God or men gods. Get this through your thick skull. That power is in you. Look at man's progress. Unlike the other animals there, that's the power of the universe in man, in you. The source is in you and don't ever disrespect it. And I could see you. Yes! Your porn, your drinking, your lust, your desecration." Now angry again, he slammed the membrane with a shield and all the men shouted, rushing up from behind to the membrane. "If I ever get my hands on you."

Vic felt sick, his mind flipping back and again rushed into the bathroom, just making it to the sink and couldn't believe what was happening. He splashed water on his face, rinsed his mouth and headed back to the stool. He didn't even have to focus on it. He just thought it and his mind flipped back to Clayvious's dimension."

"There you are!" Clayvious was angrily poised to start back in on Vic, but before he could get a sentence in, Vic shattered the energy. "You think—"

Vic cut him off. "Okay, look I'm sorry! I am so sorry. I made a mistake. Please forgive me."

Clayvious stopped in his tracks. He turned to his men, who looked at him with an air of surprise and confusion, then nodded. He turned back around, facing the membrane and Vic. The anger was now gone from his face. "You apologize?"

"Yes, I am truly sorry. I realize I was wrong."

"That's highly unusual. There's usually a war of words and we attack from the spiritual plain. But you apologized. Hmm, your apology is accepted."

"Thank you. I meant no disrespect."

"I'm starting to see why you were chosen. She's awakening. Tend to her, we will talk again."

"Okay," Vic said and with a blink of his eye, he was back and saw only the living room. He looked at Lilly.

"Ahh, oh my, ooh. Why would anyone want to feel like this? Oh, oh the colors, oh my! But you can't keep me down here forever."

"Lil, I'm getting a bag," Vic says.

"Yeah, 'cause I felt it coming." Now leaning up on her hip with Vic in position to catch her fluids, Lilly moaned. "Oh hell, I'm so tired of this."

"I know, but very little came up. I think all that brown stuff the last time was the brownie."

"Maybe."

"Oh, I still can't move my legs Oh!" She collapsed to the floor, and she was out again.

Vic was now exhausted, and for the first time felt he couldn't make it. He looked at the clock: 3:15 pm. Tina may not get home until six if she stayed to do paperwork. And he knew he couldn't make it until then and needed help for Lilly's safety. He pulled out his phone. It went straight to voicemail.

"Tina, when you get this message, you need to call me. I need your help."

Back on the stool, he was thrust into another vision of a possible future. He jerked with a convulsion and was there, seeing another vision. Tina walked in from the garage to find Lilly and Vic dead on the floor. She called the police and then got arrested under suspicion of a double homicide by poisoning. Now in jail awaiting her trial and pending investigation, the house and income properties go into foreclosure. She was fired from the clinic. He flashed back with the vision having made him sick. Again, Vic rushed to the bathroom, this time making it to the toilet. Just after it came up, the phone rang.

He answered the phone on speaker to Tina's agitation. "What's the problem?"

Vic was exhausted. "Look, I need you to come home."

"Why? I've got all this paperwork to do."

"Tina, I'm sick, exhausted, and about to collapse. I need you here for Lilly's safety."

Tina was quiet on the other end. "If this is some kind of joke—"

"No bullshit, Tina."

"How did you get sick?"

"I tasted a little piece of the brownie."

"What!"

"Just a tiny piece to see what it tastes like."

"What kind of shit—I leave you with my mother and this is what I get? And so both of you are high?"

Vic said with intensity, "I need you to get here now."

"This better not be a joke." Tina hung up.

Vic checked on Lilly, who was still out on the floor. Then he went back to the stool and slouched back against the wall, now weak and dehydrated. At 4:00 p.m., Tina's car pulled into the garage. Vic felt some relief. Tina walked in through the garage door. Vic, now sitting on the floor, opened his mouth to say, "Hi," but Tina walked by without a glance, as if he didn't even exist.

"You've got my mother on the floor?"

"She couldn't walk and she's safe there."

"Mom? Mom?" Tina shook Lilly's shoulder. "I need you to wake up. Mom!"

"Huh? What? What do you want?"

Vic stood, took one step and dropped back down to the floor, exhausted but hearing everything.

Tina looked at Vic. "Will you look at this? Okay, I'm done. Just pathetic. Mom, I need you to get up."

"Why? I'm comfortable here."

"'Cause I don't want you on the floor. I need to get you on the couch."

"I don't know why."

"Come on, Mom." Tina took her by the arm but couldn't get her up. "Come on, Mom, help me out."

"I can't. I can't move my legs."

"Vic! Could you help me get her to the couch?"

"Okay." Vic struggled to his feet and took the other arm. They dragged Lilly, who was trying to help with one leg, to the couch.

Vic was now feeling sick again and went back to his spot on the floor. Tina's ignorance of the situation, negativity, and complete lack of concern for his welfare was making him sick again, and he hurried back into the bathroom for the last time. Vic came back to the living room and sat back where he was sitting when it all started, on the recliner.

Tina walked by Vic. "Yeah, I'm going to sue you and Greg. I thought there was at least one adult left here today."

"Be nice. All that's not necessary," Lilly said.

"Well, I expected more and got less."

Vic started thinking again. *You stupid bitch.*

Tina whirled around. "What did you say?"

"I didn't say a word."

"What's wrong with you?" Lilly asked. "He didn't open his mouth."

"I thought for sure I heard him say something."

"Like what?" Vic asked.

"Like, you stupid bitch."

"I didn't say that." Vic looked at Lilly with sincerity.

"Okay, Maybe I'm just hearing things."

"Well, I do feel a little better now," Lilly said.

"Good, I'm putting together some juice and crackers, Mom."

"Okay, that sounds good."

Vic was baffled as to how Tina heard his thoughts as the blue energy sensation had now subsided. The TV was on now and Tina had focused on Lilly, who was now eating soup.

"Is there anymore soup?" Vic asked.

"No, but you could make your own."

"I see." Vic felt dejected.

"Well, Mom, I don't guess you'll be eating anyone else's brownie.

"I don't think so either."

"The brownie shouldn't have even been in the house."

"That's interesting, you were fine with it yesterday," Vic said. "You didn't remember it was there."

"That was before my mother ate it."

"You know, instead of looking to place blame—."

Lilly cut in. "Look, it's all my fault. If I had just asked, things would be different."

"Lil, how could you have known? It's just one of those things that happens. Things happen. And things happen for a reason. I think we've all learned something today. I'm going to bed."

The next morning, when Tina left for work, Vic searched for Madame Deloche's card. He found it.

"Hello this is Madame Deloche."

"Hello, Madame, this is Vic."

"Okay, how can I help you, Vic?"

"Almost four months ago, you stopped me in front of your shop and gave me a free reading and I left you a tip."

"Oh! Vic, how are you?"

"Fine, Madame."

"You're calling me because you've learned some things?"

"You've got that right."

"So tell me what happened?"

"I had a very small piece of a marijuana brownie. A blue light energy starts glowing from my head that I could see and feel. I had visions and an interaction with a man from another dimension. And if I tell anyone that, they will think I'm crazy."

"I understand. Just know that what you say to me is confidential."

"I appreciate that."

"First, let me say that you have a power that you've been unaware of. And that you've been chosen by a higher power to perform a duty for good or evil. Do you know which?"

"It has to be for good. I know that for sure because I don't like evil."

"Excellent, for I deal in mysteries, Mr. Vic, not evil."

"That's good to know, Madame."

"You have now experienced a glimpse of your abilities. Now you must begin to develop and control it."

"Look, I'm still trying to wrap my head around what happened."

"I know, but in time, this is what you must do. And then see where it leads you. Who was the man you spoke to?"

"I didn't get his name, but he said we would speak again. But he did say I had been chosen."

"Did he manifest in the room?"

"No. He and his men were on the other side of this membrane, glass, fluid. I don't know, it was crazy weird different."

"How were you there with him?"

"I'm not sure. My mind was clicking or flipping over. In a blink of an eye, like a camera click with my eyes wide open. My body was on that stool but my mind had traveled. I don't know. I was able to see them and they could see me. And we were separated by that membrane, glass, fluid...I don't know."

"What makes you think he was real and not a dream?"

"He told me he could see me doing things and was upset over a conversation I had with someone else."

"See you doing things like what?"

"Ahh, personal, very personal stuff."

"I see."

"Wait a minute! I ran into this crazy guy at a hospital. They had him chained up, and he got very agitated when I walked by. He called me a seer. I have a question for you. What's a seer?"

This is a good question. Are you ready for the answer?"

"Okay, let me have it."

"A seer is a being who can see across the dimensions and time. They can also see into the future, but the future is a variable and could be altered. In your visions, did you have the experience of multiple scenarios concerning one situation?"

"I did."

"Well, those were all possible outcomes. Then you work in the present to assure a positive outcome, like globe warming."

"Why did you stop me that night and offer me a free reading? I know there had to be a reason."

"Correct. I was wearing glasses that could see auras, and I could see yours. The color of a blue flame on a gas stove."

"Okay, that explains things. I just thought it was odd you chose me and for free."

"Yes, I needed to get you in. It was obvious to me there was more going on. I had never seen anything like it."

"Sounds like the blue light that was coming from my head. The weird thing is that I seemed to be outside of myself when I saw it."

"Hmm, possibly some astral travel. Oh boy, you're the gift that keeps giving. You have multiple abilities. It seems, Vic, you have much work to do to develop them."

"I could see that. There's something else that complicates things."

"What's that?"

"I had accidentally gotten high off of a small strand of a marijuana brownie."

"A brownie?"

"Yes, it was the brownie that triggered everything. Otherwise, I'd still be trying to figure it out."

"Okay, so you ate a brownie to release your powers?"

Well, it's more complicated than that."

"Why?"

"Because I can't stand the stuff. It's so much stronger now and it makes me violently sick."

"Hmm, that is complicated."

"Look, I think what's happening is this new higher potency is releasing your abilities and you just need to match the amount of the drug with your body weight. Vic, I used to be a lab technician for a hospital."

"So you know what you're talking about, then," Vic said, now more attentive.

"Yes I do, and this all makes sense because depending on the potency and the plant strain, marijuana is a psychoactive drug. It could aid you in your development by releasing your powers, of which you've only scratched the surface. And at some point, you may be able to release and control it on your own without the brownie. The good news is, marijuana is legal. From a scientific point of view, use your math to find the right balance or dose so that it doesn't make you sick, you have to experiment."

"Okay, Madame. I see the big picture; I think I know what I need to do."

"Good, let's stay in touch."

"Stay in touch? Hey, you're my adviser and confidant now. You just gave me a plan. And since I've met you, this whole mystery has started to unravel. We will defiantly be in touch."

"Well then, I look forward to our next conversation."

"Me, too, Madame. Oh, there is one other thing."

"What's that?"

"I was thinking in my head without saying a word. I called my wife a name."

"Oh, okay," Madame said with surprise.

"Madame, she heard me. How is that possible? I wasn't as high and I couldn't feel the blue light. It had dissipated, nor was I feeling the power of the light any longer."

"Hmm, were you angry?"

"Yes."

"Then it's possible you projected that into her head."

"How is that?"

"Your powers are not gone, though I'm sure from your description they are shrinking back into a dormant state, but still pronounced enough for you to telepathically send that message. You didn't mean to, but the force of your anger transmitted it. Vic?"

"Yes."

"Can you fly?" And with that they both broke into a ball of laughter.

"No, Madame, not that I know of." Vic laughed.

"Okay, just checking. What did you call your wife?"

"Ah, I don't care to repeat it. I mean to actually say it, not very flattering."

Madame closed her eyes. "I'm getting a word… Bitch?"

"Ah, yeah that might have been it."

"I see. That does point to telepathy of some type. I'm sure you've had situations where you knew what she was thinking."

"Yes, but that's normal. It happens with a lot of people."

"Yes, but it's a thin line between normal and paranormal. So now you know what to do. Let's go to work and see what you come up with."

"Okay, Madame, I'll talk to you soon, thank you."

"Bye."

A few days later, Vic sat in his man cave, researching like Madame suggested. He found a book titled *Psychic Energy* and ordered it. Vic then sat back in his chair and focused on the man from the other side with his eyes closed. After ten minutes, his mind wondered almost falling asleep. Then out of the darkness of his mind, a figure faded in, like at the end of a short tunnel. He saw Clayvious, who was talking to Vic but Vic couldn't hear him. In frustration, Vic broke it off by opening his eyes, ending his meditation. One week later, Vic walked into the weed shop in Altadena.

"Hello," Linda said. "How can I help you?"

"Hi, Linda right?"

"Yes. Your memory's better than mine, I'm sorry."

"It's Vic."

"Thanks, so how can I help you, Vic?"

"Well, let me start with buying a bag of that gorilla paste for a friend."

"Okay, anything else."

"Yes, I need to speak with the person who makes your brownies."

"Okay, that's different, but let me see if he's still back here."

Linda returned with a tall thin gentleman in glasses.

"Hi, what can I do for you?" the guy asked.

"Hi, look, I have some important questions for you. What kind of weed do you put in your brownies?"

"Well, it could be the King Kush, Purple Haze, or Exotic Blue, and possibly a combination of the three, but I can't give you the measurements."

"Oh no, I don't need your measurements. I just need the same formula you had back in September of last year."

The man looked at Linda a little perplexed."

"Linda, do you remember?"

Linda pondered for a bit. "Oh, man, let me see. I know we had all three in, at that time."

"Can I ask you why that's so important?" the guy asked.

"Well, I can't give you details, but I had some experiences that I need to recreate."

"I see," said the man, "and of course a different strain of plant could change that."

"Right, and this is really important to my research," Vic said.

"Oh, research, huh?" said the man.

"Well, these were experiences that aren't easy to explain and that may be beyond explanation."

"Well, the active ingredients in these plants are psychoactive. Some people seem to think it opens up parts of the brain that we aren't usually in touch with."

"I could agree with that. I'm glad we're on the same page," Vic said.

"Me, too," said the man.

"But there's one problem."

"What's that?"

"When I tried the brownie, it made me really sick."

"Throwing up sick?"

"Yes!"

"How much did you have?"

"I had a little strip the size of a drinking straw an inch long."

"And that made you sick?"

"Horrifically sick," Vic said. "But then there were these experiences. If you could put something together for me, that doesn't make me sick. I will gladly pay for that."

"And how many milligrams was the original?"

"Five hundred," Vic said.

"Oh, yes, that's a lot. Okay, how much do you weigh?"

"I'm one seventy-five or one hundred eighty pounds, depending on the week."

"That's close enough. It's a nice project for me. Let me see what I can do. Let me have your number."

"Great! Thank you."

The guy handed Vic a notepad. "Here you go."

Vic jotted down the number and handed it back.

"Okay, look to hear from me in two or three weeks."

"Great. Hey, I didn't get your name."

"I'm Alex."

"Thanks again, Alex."

"My pleasure," Alex looked at the paper, "Vic."

"Yes, I'll be looking to hear from you."

Two weeks later, Vic was busy around the house. When he turned on the news, the pandemic had hit the U.S.

"Lilly, have you seen this?"

"Yes, I heard about it this morning. I'm trying to figure out how I'm getting back to Walnut Creek."

"You don't want to fly?"

"No, they're saying the virus has been on the planes."

"That's crazy."

"It is."

"Lil, what do you remember about our brownie ordeal?"

"Well, not a whole lot. I was seeing colors, then you were in some kind of blue light standing over me."

"Oh, you saw a blue light?"

"Yes, but I'm sure I was hallucinating."

Vic didn't let on. "For sure you were. You were talking and humming in a music melody, Lil."

"Really?"

"Yes, I remember saying to myself, 'Lil has a lot of music in her.'"

"Maybe." She chuckled. "I don't want to go through anything like that again."

"Me either. Lil, I'm just glad you're okay."

"Yes, me too. So far so good."

"That's great."

By that weekend, Tina's sister had come down from northern California to take Lilly home. What Vic didn't realize was that this brownie fiasco, along with the Detroit blow up, was now taking a toll on his marriage. However, he was now focused on and obsessed with his new abilities. Vic was now reading his book on psychic energy and spending hours on the Internet, gathering as much information as possible and still meditating to contact Clayvious whose name he still does not know. Two weeks later, Vic got a call from Alex.

"Hello, Vic?"

"Yes."

"Hey, it's Alex from the dispensary."

Vic was now very excited. "Alex, how's it going?"

"Good, I've got a formula for you."

Vic was now completely pumped. "Oh great! What did you put together?"

"I've put together for you some brownies that are ten percent of the original, about fifty milligrams. Let's see how that works for you. I'm under the impression that you don't smoke this stuff."

"No, I haven't smoked really in twenty years and couldn't smoke a lot then, nor could I drink a lot. I had to learn my limitations pretty quick because it all would make me sick, if I overdid it."

"Sounds like you have a very sensitive system inside you there."

"Very."

"Well, this should be mild enough for you and if not, we could take it down some more, but I think we pinpointed the original ingredients."

"That's great. I'll be up there tomorrow.

CHAPTER 11

The next day, Vic drove the thirty-five minutes up to the shop from L.A. and this time Linda remembered his name. They greet and Linda let Alex know that Vic was out front. They both returned, with Alex holding a bag.

"Hey, Alex, good to see you."

"Vic, how's it going? I've got some goodies for you, I think will serve you well. Keep in mind if you don't like the formula or if you're having problems with nausea, it can be adjusted until we get it right."

"Oh, man, that sounds great, Alex. What's this going to cost me?"

"Let me count it up—three brownies and two boxes of edibles that's going to be one hundred dollars."

Surprised, Vic expected it to be more, being that it was a special order. He gave Alex a twenty-dollar tip and thanked him for the new formula and heads back down to the city of Los Angeles. What he didn't tell Alex was that just the thought of chewing gummies or eating a portion of a brownie was making him sick at the dispensary. Vic knew his biggest hurdle was going to be psychosomatic. Mentally overcoming a substance that had made him violently sick, he had faith in Alex and his milder formula of these edibles. By the time he got back to L.A., it was too late to get started on a dose to try to make contact again with the man from the other side. Vic had stopped at Greg's to say hello and drop off the bag of weed he had bought for him. By the time he got home, it was a little after 3:00 p.m. and Tina would be home in a few more hours. So he put his bag of edibles on his bookshelf with the idea of getting started earlier the next day. When Tina got home from work, there wasn't much conversation. She didn't like hearing about anything concerning properties or things dealing with responsibility. Vic liked sports and Tina liked British shows from the BBC or drama filled reality shows.

So the normal routine was to say hello, keep it light and Vic would go back to his man cave while Tina stayed in the living room as they watched their individual shows or sporting events. Vic had become weary of trying to talk to Tina when she got home from work as it had made her angry on many occasions sparking an argument or her raising her voice because her husband was trying to talk to her. On the other hand, if he asked how things went on a given day, she was glad to sit and dump all the problems of her day for the next hour. And because he felt it was a one-sided deal being that she never wanted to hear about his problems or things that needed to get done, he simply stopped asking about hers. So they would greet each other, carry light conversation, something she could handle, and then go to their perspective rooms and watch TV. This had become their routine. So it was that evening, Tina had brought home food from Chile Verde and the two would eat dinner, but not together. Vic sat at the table and thought she would join him there. Tina fixed her plate and walked to the living room to eat while she was watching TV. Though he was disappointed, Vic would say nothing this night as his mind was centered on what would happen the next day.

Wondering if he would see Clayvious, whose name he still didn't know, and be able to hear him. Or maybe it was all a hallucination and this would just be a waste of time. Would there be visions of possible futures yet to be lived that could be altered for the best outcomes for those involved? The brownie had opened up a hole in the universe of Vic's brain that now was beyond anything he had ever imagined. His life now seemed to be turning in a direction he had not planned, but one he was destined for. It had been foretold by Nadine in Chicago and by Madame Deloche in New Orleans and the signs had been there all along. Though he didn't understand them in the past, it was all so clear now. Tomorrow would possibly change things for the rest of his life, yet he felt void of fear and full of excitement and curiosity. When Vic finished his enchilada with beans and rice topped off with a shrimp taco, he retreated to his man cave, falling into his favorite office chair to watch football.

When Vic woke up the next morning, he said a prayer as he did every morning, then sprang from the bed with the energy of a thoroughbred and into the closet to put on sweat pants, a tee shirt, and a USC hoodie. Then down to the kitchen for a bowl of cereal as he contemplated what he would eat from the bag of edibles still on the bookshelf. He decided to have a piece of the brownie, being that it was the brownie that had opened the door to his abilities in the first place. However, now it dawned on him that he wasn't sure how much to eat. It was 8:35 a.m. Tina had left around six that morning and he wouldn't be able to call the shop to talk to Alex until it opened up at ten. After doing the math, Vic realized the brownies he had were one-tenth the potency of the five-hundred-milligram brownie that was too strong. So he decided to cut the new one into eighths with a knife and took one slice. He knew that with the edibles, it would take an hour or two to kick in, so he decided to have a cup of coffee and a bear claw. There were also some bills on the desk, as there were always bills on the desk, a never-ending cycle, but it was something to get done. Then, he took out the trash and washed the dishes.

After going to the mailbox, an hour and a half had gone by with no results, so Vic headed back into the man cave and plopped down into his office chair. He closed his eyes and focused on the man from the other side. As he was doing so, he saw nothing but darkness with his eyes closed but felt good, cheerful even, and then it hit him. That feeling of power and the warming sensation of the blue light energy now coming from his shoulders and head was stronger than before. He felt the sensation of a presence and a few seconds later, the familiar voice.

"So you're back."

Upon hearing the voice, Vic blinked his eyes, and he was back in a cave with the liquid membrane. "Hey, before saying another word, what is your name?"

"Uh, you want to know my name? It's Clayvious, Vic."

"Clayvious, huh? What a great name. Are you Greek?"

"No. I was from the great island of Atlantis, the first born on this planet. My parents were from another planet in the region of Zeta Reticuli and they were sent here to study this planet and help preserve its inhabitants. I believe you call these kinds of people scientist. I, on the other hand, took after my grandfather, a great warrior and military man on Alpha. I left Atlantis to join in and help any army that was fighting for the greater good and against those who fought to plunder, rape, and kill for conquest or sport."

Stunned, Vic didn't know where to start. He realized that he had been plunged into the deep end of the pool with talk about Atlantis and alien humanoids here on Earth.

"Okay, maybe I've said too much. I can see that you're confounded and wondering if these things I've just described are what you call here on Earth myths or if it is historical truth."

"Well yeah, that's pretty heady stuff you're talking about there, and it's going to take some time for me to wrap my head around this conversation."

"I understand."

"Look, how do I fit into all of this? Let's start there."

Clayvious nodded. "Very well. You possess the ability to generate blue light energy. It is a rare occurrence on any inhabited planet for someone such as yourself to be able to generate this powerful energy of the universe. I can only equate it to a rare blood disease or rare ability of genius, be it mental or physical genius, but we're talking about one in a million. In this case with you, one in millions. Don't panic, but once you learn how to use it and control it, there will be many, what you call here on Earth, super natural abilities you will be able to perform."

Vic was now completely clueless. "What kind of abilities?"

"Things like mind reading or communicating telepathically, seeing into the future and its possible outcomes, releasing my men and me into your Earth dimension to protect you and the fate of the planet. You are our missing link. My men and I are twelve men strong with limited alien abilities. With you make's thirteen, a powerful number in the universe, as are your abilities."

Vic's head was now spinning, feeling his blue energy burning low, but Clay's words and the number 13 still rang in his ears. It all made sense now, though too much to handle all at once. He told Clayvious that he'd be right back and, with a blink of his eyes, he was back in the house where his body had never left. As he went to have another slice of the brownie, he wondered how the hell he was able to flip back and forth between dimensions like that, but now accepting the fact that he could.

After chewing another piece of the brownie and again thinking of how good it tastes, Vic did something different only because the thought came to him that he could. This time, he didn't blink and only stared with focus and a little concentration on Clayvious and then reappeared in Clayvious's dimension.

"Good your back," Clayvious. Vic had noticed that when he was back in the kitchen, three hours had passed, even though it felt as though only half an hour had gone by. "Clayvious, when I went back to the house, three hours had passed. How is that possible?"

"It's possible because on this side, you're outside of the time continuum. In other words, there is no time here. You're now in limbo."

Vic looked at Clayvious in disbelief and decided not to even ask. "Okay, whatever you say. You mentioned me bringing you and your men to my side of this dimension thing. How would I even do that?"

Clayvious was now clear that Vic was a rookie and realized he was going to have to help him along, but Clayvious was no expert with blue light energy. In his two thousand two hundred years of existence, he had only seen it once before in 800 AD. And though he didn't know exactly how it worked, he knew he could give Vic some pointers. "Vic, you're going to try to focus the energy and think of what you want it to do. For instance, if you want to open the membrane, you think it and visualize it as you mentally exert the blue energy. The thought, the visual mental imagery, and the blue light energy working together as one, my friend."

Vic pondered those instructions and conditions. "Thought, visual, and energy." He walked around, still in deep thought and repeats the trilogy. "Thought, visual, and energy. Okay, Clayvious, I got it. Let's give it a try."

Surprised his student was such a quick study, Clayvious didn't know that Vic was a teacher and learned to practice what he preached. The timing was perfect, Vic was now feeling a new surge of blue energy from the last slice of brownie. "Okay, guys, back up a little." Vic bent his head toward the membrane and saw it opening in his mind's eye and with head and hands pointed at the membrane, he shot out the light in a weak and faint wall of blue but separated the membrane. "There it is! I did it!" Vic sounded like he had hit a fifty-foot putt to win the Masters Golf Tournament, a winning catch in the Super Bowl, or the winning goal in the finals of the World Cup.

Clayvious was shocked. He didn't think Vic would be able to do it on the first try. Clayvious and his men walked through the opening of the membrane and turned a light blue in color and almost transparent.

"Whoa, wow, what's with the change in color?" Vic asked.

"This is how we look on this side, but we're still effective, and I'll explain it to you later." Clayvious introduced Vic to the rest of the men, who were now very glad to meet him and welcome him to the team. "Vic, that was a good effort, but you have to practice strengthening your ability to direct the energy."

"Yes, you're right. I could feel it myself. It was like lifting weights for the first time. I felt weak."

Clayvious was glad that Vic understood the need to improve and develop his powers. "Yes, but for your first effort, that was very impressive. Before we go back to the other side, you need to know that there is an evil threat brewing that will destroy the Earth as we know it and throw all the civilized world into chaos."

"How do you know that, Clay?" Vic asked.

"I, too, can see the future and two of the three variables are that of destruction, massive loss of life and damage to the Earth that will last for more than a hundred and fifty years. If we don't intervene, we're going to need you," Clayvious said with a serious look on his face.

Vic now felt the weight of his words and knew that he needed to get ready for the threat ahead. "Okay, I'll do what I need to do to be ready, and I'll try not to let you down."

Clayvious looked at Vic with confidence. "I'm not worried about you after this effort today." All of Clayvious's men smiled and nodded in agreement. "It's time for us to go back and your wife will be home in a while. Let's talk soon."

Vic agreed and asked, "How do I close the membrane?"

Clayvious turned around. " It will close on its own when the blue energy wears off, or you could think it closed."

Vic looked surprised. "Really?" He then looked toward the opening and saw it close in his mind and within seconds, the actual membrane closed as if there had never been an opening.

Vic stood there in disbelief, feeling like he was in a dream. *This can't be real,* he thought, but realized he was still in Clayvious's dimension and saw Clayvious and his men disappear through an entrance on the other side of the membrane. Vic blinked to bring himself back to his dimension and felt the blue light energy still emanating from the top of his head. He then had the urge to see it and without much effort, separated from his own body like a floating spirit and saw himself standing there with a blue cylinder of energy swirling over his head, this time a little stronger than before. He was encouraged that it was stronger, but he was also forced into the realization that this was real and that it was happening to him.

At that moment, Vic was overcome with fear and sadness, wondering what he was going to do. For a few minutes, he felt he was spiraling into a depression when the words of his old high school track coach popped into his head as though Coach Rap was there speaking in his ear. "Remember, Vic, winners never quit and quitters never win." When he had first heard this from his championship coach, it was as though it had been branded on his brain with a branding iron, to never be forgotten. And now it was lifting him up again because he had never been a quitter.

Vic wanted to slap himself. What was he thinking? He had already given Clayvious and the men his commitment to be ready. And that this seemingly unreal situation was very real and he was to play an integral part in how it would play out. Then he heard the garage door open as Tina pulled in.

He looked at the clock. It was almost six p.m. The day seemed to be gone in a flash. When Tina came in, he gave her a hug and they went into their routine. Light conversation, Vic offered to go get some food. Tina asked why he didn't go get it before she got there, believing he was waiting to see if she would bring food home. Vic said nothing, knowing he couldn't tell her the truth, but apologized for not thinking about doing that. Tina told him no, she didn't want him to go get food and decided to fix a tuna sandwich.

Vic retreated to his man cave, knowing he had dropped the ball on his wife, but at the same time he was trying to get organized in his head, realizing that now he was living in two worlds. The first thing that came to mind was putting together some kind of workout routine to develop his powers and putting aside some time to read his psychic energy book that had increased in importance after the day's events.

Vic pondered what Clayvious said about the growing evil and peril facing the world. Then he realized that the new President in the White House could be a part of the darkness to come. Vic's uncle had once told him that it didn't matter which party was in the

White House because it wouldn't affect the amount of money you were making. That was true then, and true now. However, the political landscape was upside down in the United States. Allies were now cast out and enemies were closer than allies. This outsider administration seemed like a good idea to many, but Vic had wondered why anyone would call a plumber to remove their appendix. So why vote in a dentist to run a country? Advertising, fame, and perverted propaganda blinded the people when the deceiver was actually a pathological liar and a crook. The notion that an inexperienced person could run a country was ludicrous but there they were. Thousands were dying from this modern-day plague that mysteriously appeared out of the east, who was behind it all. The use of masks was not being enforced from the top down and money seemed to be more important than the lives of the people who were dying. Vic could see it now; it was already starting. And the change back to focusing on fossil fuels that would continue to grow greenhouse gases and global warming was ignored for the love of money. And the scientists, the experts, were now being silenced and discredited. And no one could see it because the people had been divided and were being conquered, fighting over party lines and issues of race and police brutality. This had been foretold by the great senator from Massachusetts in her address at the convention to the nation. Those things were certainly important but the destruction of Earth, as we know it, was lost and could not be seen by anyone. Clayvious was right. It was now clear, but then a sudden jolt, a shot of electricity and Vic's mind flipped to a future scenario of bigger, stronger hurricanes and tornadoes now killing more people than ever with insurance companies refusing to pay for damages and on the edge of bankruptcy. Oceans rising from melted polar caps, filling the streets of New York with water and most of Amsterdam under water just like the scientists had predicted, but much worse. Someone was behind it all, Vic now seeing a nuclear holocaust from countries blaming each other in a war of words and launching nuclear warheads on each other, rendering parts of the world uninhabitable. Vic blinked his way out of the nightmare with his heart beating out of control from seeing one of the possible variables. A chaotic, horrific world on the brink of complete destruction. Seeing this future vision made him sick to his stomach and this time it wasn't the brownie.

Knowing what was at stake, fear crept into his mind, but his fight or flight kicked in and for him, it was always fight.

Down south in New Orleans, Madame Deloche was experiencing negative vibes from people coming down the street. She had been feeling and seeing things for over a week. There were fights in the clubs, more than usual, and people were less friendly than they had been in the past. She felt that there had been a shift in the universe and the energy on the planet. And she felt a negative presence coming from the eastern United States, but northeast of her location in New Orleans. With Deloche, it was like she could smell the rot of an evil sorceress very powerful with her claw-like nails and fingers acting as the hand of a puppeteer and Madame wondered who was the puppet. Mingled with these ideas was the thought of Vic, whom she had not heard from and then she wondered why it mattered in the first place.

Somehow, she felt that he might know something new about his situation and felt a need to talk to him. And she then focused on him, with a feeling that called on him, then went on about her business at the shop. Madame Deloche was still monitoring people's attitudes and vibrations on the street when the phone rang.

Sharon answered. "No, this is Sharon, but she's here. May I tell her who's calling? Just a minute. Madame…Vic."

At that moment, Madame realized that she and Vic were connected in some way and suspected that he had made a breakthrough concerning his abilities.

"Hello, Vic?"

"Hi, Madame. A little birdie in the form of a feeling told me you wanted to talk to me so here I am."

Deloche was stunned. Never before has she put out a call telepathically and had an immediate response. Not only was his an instant response, but his awareness that she had called out to him mentally caught her by complete surprise. There was no doubt in her mind he had made a major breakthrough concerning his abilities, but the energy she felt from him over the phone made her sure of it.

"Okay, Vic, what's been going on? I'm sensing that you're not the same guy I spoke to a few weeks ago. Please tell me about it."

Vic's blue energy was still radiating off the chart and was allowing him to read into her spirit. He knew she had read into his conversation and extracted some big changes but just needed some details. "I've been in contact with the man from the other side. He is real and is helping me develop my skills. This thing is huge and I'm only scratching the surface. I've been putting together a workout routine to develop and strengthen my energies, which will allow me to do many things. He has a band of men with him. They number twelve in all. They have asked me to join them. That makes thirteen."

Madame let out a sound of shock and realization, sucking in the air. "Ahh! That's it! You've unraveled the mystery of the reoccurring number 13. That's fantastic, Vic."

"There's more. He said he's from the lost city of Atlantis and that his parents came from another planet. He's been around for over two thousand years and in that time he has only seen one other person with my blue light energy hundreds of years ago. Let me get to the big problem. The country and the Earth are in danger. He and I both have had visions of the destruction of this Planet, that will happen if we don't stop it."

Madame was now in fear of impending doom and realized her sense of an evil entity was real and connected to what Vic was telling her.

"Madame, have you noticed the darkness of our political situation, the lies, the divisiveness, the bad decisions and the blindness of half the people in this country?"

"Yes! We seem to be headed down some dark road as a country and suddenly more friendly with communists and dictators than Canada and Mexico."

"Right, Madame, this is the beginning of the destruction of the Earth. It has already started. Most people can't see it and by the time they do, it will be too late."

"Vic, I'm with you on this, but you need to know I'm picking up on an evil presence here. Coming from somewhere in the southeast. It's a powerful source, Vic, and I don't know who or exactly where, but I know that she's controlling someone or something and it has caused a shift in the vibration of the planet. Vic I could see, feel, and hear the difference in the people on the street down here. There's more anger and violence everywhere."

"Madame, how do you know it's a she?"

"Vic, we don't always know the intricate details of our abilities, but trust me on this. Call it a woman's intuition, it's a female."

"Okay, I've never had a reason to doubt you and I'm not going to start now. You need to join me and work on finding out who she is."

"I will do my best, but I can tell you she's very low key and clever."

"That makes sense. She would have to be if she's connected to the possible destruction of our existence. It sounds and feels like she's connected to this whole agenda and if she is, we have to stop her. Madame, it's always a great thing talking to you. Call me as soon as you know something. As a matter of fact, I'm going to make it a point to check in with you every week."

"That sounds good, Vic. I look forward to it."

As they said goodbye, Vic kept his ear to the phone and as she disconnected, Vic heard a second change in frequency or a second disconnect. Subtle, and mostly undetectable, without blue energy. The thought came to him that the phone was tapped but brushed it off and started reading his book.

The third party that was listening in, a small team, someone asked, "Do you think they detected us?"

"Impossible," the other said, "not with this technology. "

"Interesting conversation," the third voice said.

"Very interesting," the first voice said.

In the strange and mysterious mountain town of West Virginia, on a small farm well outside of Morgantown and not too far from the Pennsylvania border lived a young twenty-three-year-old woman. She was a transplant from the coal mine region of eastern Kentucky who stayed to herself back in the woods but was within driving distance of Washington, DC. She was a student of the occult and practiced regularly. She didn't fit the movie image of a witch and no one would think so based on her soft features and naturally highlighted auburn brown hair. She traveled to DC every week and was supported by a trust fund of a secret donor. Her mom named her Kali, which means warrior goddess of destruction in Hindu. A name that would go unnoticed and was popular in America, and as the old saying goes, "What's in a name?"

It was already after 5:00 p.m. by the time Kali got back to the house. Her daily errands had taken longer than on most other days, and now she had to rush to get everything set up properly for tonight. As she pulled up to the house, she could see Midnight solemnly sitting on the windowsill of the living room, welcoming her with those beautiful green eyes that set perfectly against her shiny black fur. Kali noticed the evening breeze aiding the lone oak tree in her yard to shed its leaves as they fell to the earth. It was mid-October again she knew that in just a few short weeks the yard and porch would be a colorful blanket of orange and yellow leaves and she'd be paying the Harper boys to come over with their rakes and trash bags as they had done the previous year. With very little time to waste, Kali put the SUV in park, killed the engine and hastily grabbed the plastic bags off the passenger seat. Time was of the essence. As she rushed to the front door, she slowed her walk to enjoy the crunch of the dead leaves beneath her boots. She loved that feeling. It reminded her of happier times. For Kali, it spoke of a time when crunchy leaves simply meant that Halloween was coming, that scary movies and candy were guaranteed and two more holidays were approaching fast behind, but not anymore. Now that crunch meant that it was time to work, and that work continued tonight.

Once in the kitchen, she looked down to notice a copy of last week's edition of *The Dominion Post* that had lain undisturbed beneath a pile of mail. On the cover was a picture of a boy with the headline that read: *Where is Kenneth?* Kenneth Parcel was the fourteen-year-old boy whose body was never found though his jacket was found floating in the river. He had gone missing weeks ago one night after sneaking out of his house while his parents slept. According to his friends, none of them had made plans with him that night and none had any idea where he went or who he went with. At first, it appeared to be a classic runaway case, a temporary break from a parental rule that every teenage kid longed for at one time or another. He wasn't the best student in school and had a reputation around town as a bit of a troublemaker, so the police weren't really breaking their necks to look for him right away. Then yesterday, they found the clothing. Apparently his jacket had gone undetected in the river long enough to travel quite a distance down near Star City before being discovered. The news had yet to mention a cause of death or what state the body was in because no one knew where the body was, but Kali knew. In fact, she was the only one who knew. She knew exactly why he left his house that night and how he, supposedly, ended up floating face down, staring at the bottom of the river. Kali took a moment to look at the picture on the front page again. *Such a sweet face. Good luck finding him*, she thought. Just then, the teapot whistled.

Tonight she was meeting with her master, an inter-dimensional being that had wreaked havoc on Earth and two other planets. Kali, in her experimentation with chants and incantations, garnered his attention from the other side. She then went into meditation and he spoke to her as a kind spirit of wisdom and knowledge. And with a sugary tongue, he seduced her, making her drunk on dreams of power and money by any means necessary, then brainwashing her into believing that destruction was a necessary evil to breed new life and growth. She was now his right-hand woman in sheep's clothing and their goal was to destroy Earth and to seize the majority of its monetary assets, leaving only enough for the top one percent because of his relationships with a few of them. Their plan was to rebuild the planet in their image, enslaving the masses in low-paying jobs, poverty, pain and suffering for those who would survive the world-ending cataclysm. After enjoying her tea, Kali headed to her back bedroom which was empty, to place ritual candles and flowers. The flowers really weren't apart of the ritual, but he liked Earth's flowers, so she made sure they were there when she helped bring him over from the star gate. She then went into her bedroom to dress in a black cotton dress with lace over the breast area that is sexy and revealing. As she was setting up again in the back bedroom, Midnight walked into the room and hissed as if she could feel the negative energy and intent of the reunion. It was only 8:00 p.m. now and she would not bring him through until midnight, so Kali scooped up the black cat and headed back to her bedroom. At 11:45 p.m., she headed back to the other bedroom to light the candles. She then focused on the wall that faced east and started the incantation. As she recited the words in Latin, her energy intensified and her demeanor changed, being louder and more aggressive. Her face changed from soft to dark and her hazel green eyes turned black as her pupils stretched across the balls of her eyes. The darkness inside of her was now revealed and with a final repeated phrase that seemed to pick up sonic power, the wall became liquid and Rhynous walked through. Kali was elated and laughed.

"Hello, Master. How was your journey?"

"About the same, my child, about the same. There is the pulling almost tearing of the flesh, maybe it's the unknown dark matter, I don't know. How are you, my dear?"

Kali was now more composed. "I am fine Rhynous. I have continued the weekly trips to the White House and have spread the five stars of incantations around the building, getting as close as I could. I was able to get a tour inside and was able to stand near the doorway of the Oval Office two weeks ago and laced the upper doorway with the cyber-net mind control web so that when he walked through, it attach itself to him."

"Excellent, my special one." Rhynous stroked her hair as he passed. "And these are based on the digital algorithms Minious sent you?"

"Yes, master, there's an invisible digital web every time he walks through the doorway. We will be able to program his thoughts with the help of the nanites."

"Perfect, special one. You and Spidis are doing amazing work. Let us continue the ritual." He kissed her with a swirling tongue and touched her all over. Then he walked over to the light switch, shifting his appearance to that of a handsome twenty-five-year-old and turned off the light.

CHAPTER 12

As Vic read and learned more about psychic energy, his abilities far exceeded anything described in the book. It was still giving him examples of how to direct his blue energy and how to strengthen it. The visualization exercises had allowed him to intensify his blue energy so much that in one sitting, he burned the ceiling of his man cave and had to paint it before Tina got home. He was now astral traveling almost every day to Clayvious's dimension and learning military strategies as Clayvious and his men prepared themselves for war. Vic had been feeling his powers grow and that one day soon he would be able to physically walk into Clayvious's dimension. He was hoping to surprise Clayvious with this breakthrough. He had also noticed that the effects of the brownie bringing out the blue energy seemed to last longer. Vic was starting to feel that once the brownie opened that magical part of his brain that released his powers, he could somehow hold it open on his own by contorting or pulling the muscles tight in the temporal area of his skull. And that one day he would open the power gate in his brain on his own. And though that may be a ways off, he believed it was possible as his confidence continued to grow by leaps and bounds.

He had just eaten the last eighth of his first brownie and headed for the Angeles National Forest north of Los Angeles to test his powers. It had become too dangerous to test his powers at home or in the city and he needed not to draw any attention to himself. The seclusion of the mountain trails and meadows was a great cover. He headed up the Angeles Crest Highway to the Switzer camp area and then hiked back up toward the falls. On a weekday, it was empty, with most people at work, but Vic still had to keep his eyes open for bears and mountain lions, but as he walked down the trail from the parking lot, he felt the gate opening in his brain and knew he had his powers to protect him. Once he got down to the open creek area with pine trees on both sides, he looked around. Seeing no one, Vic thrust his arm forward with his palm up, shooting a concentrated beam of blue light at a pine tree, cleanly severing a thick branch from the tree. Vic walked over to inspect the damage and there was a little smoke but no chance of a forest fire. He looked to see if the tree was smoldering and it was not, as his beam of energy seemed to have a laser quality about it. Vic was no scientist, but from the physics class in college he believed that his blue light energy had electromagnetic properties. How much? He wasn't sure.

He walked a half mile into the forest and heard a commotion in the bushes to his left and readied himself to use his powers if necessary. In an instant, he crouched and extended his arm as a burst of fur and legs leaped from the brush. As his flight or fight subsides at the sight of a doe and fawn, he breathed a sigh of relief. Vic continued down the creek side trail, looking for his next test object and tried his powers out on a rock. The most important thing he had learned to do was coordinate his thoughts with his actions. As he looked at a big rock, the size of a medicine ball, he knew he must visualize what he wanted to do to the rock. If he wanted to cut it, levitate it, or melt it. In this case, he wanted to explode the rock so he went over it in his mind, thrusting his arm forward, palm up, thought, and release a beam of blue light energy suited to the task. Vic looked around and saw no one around then looked at the rock and bent his knees to brace himself, then suddenly raised his right arm, palm up, with the left hand bracing the right wrist and shot the beam of blue light from his palm. It hit the rock and in seconds, it appeared to be melting when suddenly it exploded, shooting hot fragments in every direction except in the direction of the energy source. The beam was now leaving Vic's palm with such force that it was now making a sound like the swoosh of a golf club slicing the air or the swinging of a high speed bat. Not exactly like that, but similar with much more intensity. He now wanted to use both hands, but that would double the energy, creating too much light and possibly a loud explosion. Vic could now shoot the energy from both arms and the top of his head, or all three at once. The power of his three-pronged beam coming together could create a mega ton blast. How many mega tons? He didn't know, and he had never done it but knew he could because he could do anything he could think or visualize. And at the other end of his blue light power source was the ability to only stun a living thing, knocking it out for a period of time or controlling a person's movement. A victim could hear and see but couldn't move and Vic knew he was only limited to what he could imagine.

Suddenly, there was a child's voice. "Did you see that light?"

Then there was an adult in the distance. "No, I didn't see any light and I'm not so sure you did either."

Vic headed back in their direction toward the car and saw a father and son. As they got closer, the boy of about ten years of age asked, "Sir, did you see a blue light down there?"

"Sorry, I sure didn't, buddy." Vic looked at the dad, who smiled..

"He's got quite an imagination."

"I see," Vic said with a reciprocating smile, then wished them a good day.

Vic realized he just dodged a bullet from being discovered and hurried up the hill to the car. When he got to the lot, he noticed a forest ranger in his truck. Vic waved and the ranger waved back from his green forestry vehicle. For the first time, Vic was feeling like he was running out of locations to develop his skills and started thinking of another place he could go to practice. The desert would be a great place, but then his light energy could be seen from miles around and from the air. In his mind, the search continued as he pulled out of the lot, onto the highway, and back down into the city.

When Tina got home that night, she informed Vic that she wanted a divorce. He knew things weren't good, but this caught him completely by surprise and it wasn't lost on him that it was October 13. She had been very distant, cold and aloof, but this explained a lot.

"You want a divorce? I thought we were going to do counseling. What happened to that?"

"No, I've changed my mind. It's over. I'm done. We just aren't compatible. You don't like any of the things I like. We're not intimate at all. You don't like the way I kiss, and you don't know me."

Most of what she said was true and Vic knew he didn't like most of her TV shows, and that he didn't like the way she always licked her lips before they kissed, making for a slimy, unsanitary, sloppy kiss. He loved a good tongue kiss, but not with slobbery lips. And they weren't intimate and hadn't been for a while because of issues she needed to work out and hadn't. And he didn't know her anymore but more importantly, she didn't know herself, but he understood that in her search for self she had come to the conclusion that it would be without him. Tina had been overweight for most of the marriage and knew that Vic wanted her to lose weight and she had promised she would, but Vic never pressed and she never did.

Just a few years prior in the marriage, Tina was begging Vic not to leave her, citing that she was trying to get it together and that Vic assured her he wasn't going anywhere and that she didn't have to worry about that. He had compassion and love for his wife and was committed to his marriage vows, but somehow it had all been rearranged and now he was the problem. God knew he wasn't perfect and Tina was now actively informing him of all his faults and how he was so condescending and blamed her for things he couldn't find around the house. Or blaming her for breaking the garage door by pressing the remote too hard based on what the repair man had said when Vic called him. Vic apologized as the motor had just burned out, but he didn't think it was grounds for a divorce.

Tina, in her search for every incident to support her claim for a divorce, angrily declared, "Like I'm some kind of god dam idiot. I'm a dam, doctor for God's sake." Vic could only think of all the odd things she had done like using bleach to clean a spot on a tan carpet and dumping piles of food down the garbage disposal, damaging it and having to replace it, but he didn't say anything because it would appear that he was trying to prove that she was an idiot. When the truth of the matter was, she was just a woman who didn't know things a plumber knew regardless of her profession. He spent days trying to change her mind only to hear insults and slights of how she wasn't even attracted to him after sixteen years of marriage. Anytime he tried to talk to her about it, she hurled insults and painful slights even when he was just trying to ask about the mail. So, she succeeded in killing a large portion of the love he had felt for her, as she would have it, and he decided in his heart of hearts to let her go.

There was too much going on. He wasn't going to be able to fight her and fight the evil that was laying the groundwork to destroy the planet. He had to be focused and his anger never rose to the surface, nor did he engage Tina in a war of words, hurling insults back at her. He took it like a man and acknowledged his mistakes as she did some of hers and she found another place and moved out just before Christmas. As he grieved over this separation and suffered through sleepless nights and no appetite, Madame Deloche could feel his every pain and cried as if it were her pain and some of it was.

The following week, Rhynous had left Earth again to assemble his army from his planet back in the Zeta Reticuli system. However, there the planet was called Larus, but that word was hardly ever spoken there because most of the population was a twenty-thousand-year-old civilization of light beings who no longer possessed vocal cords and spoke telepathically. They were slightly taller than the classic gray alien height. Unlike Grays, they had big eyes that were round, not almond-shaped, but still had the naturally evolved black membrane over their eyes to protect them from the intense sunlight there and extreme heat of up to one hundred thirty degrees Fahrenheit. They had the big cranium like the Grays, but possessed more of a nose and happier-looking face. Their knowledge, civilization, and technology exceeded Earth's by eighteen thousand years. They are benevolent beings who stopped traveling to Earth a thousand years ago, though their evolutionary cousins, the Grays, had continued to visit and study in an effort to preserve Earth's delicate ecological balance. There was one threat on Larus and that threat was Rhynous.

With all of their advanced civilization and technology, they had not been able to bring him to justice. Rhynous was from another planet whose civilization was destroyed in a planetary war that destroyed the atmosphere, water sources, plant life, and temperature. Most of those who survived were elites who had connections to leave or who had their own spaceships that could leave at a moment's notice. The rest of the population perished by the millions. They were war like and destroyed by another civilization. Their planet was Nuricom, also known as Mars. The Larians granted the Martian's asylum on their planet with the agreement that if they came in peace and maintained a harmonious existence, they could stay, and they did, except for Rhynous. And he had eluded them because of his shape shifting abilities.

In West Virginia, Kali was doing her daily meditation and falling into a trance-like state that allowed her to reach out into the atmosphere and sense those things that were undetected by the average human being. She could sense microwaves, radar, and television signals, but got a surprise when she sensed the brain waves of a telepath. Kali, not realizing who it was, and that they were looking for her, tried to make contact. Upon doing so, she allowed Deloche to get a feeling for her vibration and a feeling for who she was, a young spirit, evil, pretty, and had somewhat of a mental picture of what she looked like. When Kali realized she was being probed, she mentally broke from the contact and broke out of the trance, breathing hard. She was now angry and in fear of having been discovered and let out a blood-curdling scream that caused her face to change from innocent to her true essence—evil. Her eyes went from hazel to gray as her pupils shrank, causing them to look like snake eyes and her skin tone turned to ash, also causing her chin to elongate. No longer was she pretty or easygoing and her cat,

Midnight, was standing on the windowsill with an arched back, hair standing on end, and hissing from her scream.

Deloche broke her focus and knew that this young woman was who she was looking for. She, too, was breathing hard and had a general fix on where Kali was, and some idea of what she looked like. More importantly, what she felt like. Deloche knew that if she was ever in this witch's presence, whose name she did not know, she would feel it. Deloche was excited and thought of Vic, debating whether she should call him. Then the phone rings. Madame knew who it was.

"You heard me?"

"Of course I did."

Deloche couldn't believe the energy coming from Vic and it was crackling on the phone line, though Vic didn't realize it. "Oh my goodness! What have you been doing? Your energy is off the chart."

"How do you know that?"

Deloche ignored his question. "I have great news."

"What's that?"

"I have found her. Well, not exactly, but I have an idea of her general area, what she feels like, and some idea of what she looks like."

"That's amazing. How do you do that?"

"Oh it's complicated. She's in that southwestern Pennsylvania and northeastern West Virginia area. I don't have an exact location, but she's in that area."

"Are you sure?"

"Yes."

Vic considered his source. She had never been wrong but Vic didn't say anything as he pondered. "You know that's only about a three-hour drive from Washington, DC."

"You're right. She's probably going there to influence decisions made at the White House."

"That would be very hard to do."

"Yes, but she's a witch, and she is not working alone. There's another more powerful than her that she answers to and she will lead us to him."

"Hmm—"

"Your energy is the source."

"What do you mean? And I've heard that before."

"Your energy is the source of all things in the universe, in heaven and earth. From the creator of all things, the original energy source, who is known by many names but recognized by goodness and mercy, by the sword of retribution, and a just harvest of seeds sown. It's been given to you. Just remember, your energy is the source. Believe in it, use it for good and there will be nothing you can't do."

"Okay, that's pretty heavy stuff there, lady, but I will remember that." Vic repeated to himself. "Your energy is the source." As he said it over and over in his head, he felt the power of it. He was grateful and his power increased.

He seemed to be in a day dream when Deloche asked, "When are you going to come see me again?"

Vic snapped back into reality because he realized it was a request laced with personal intentions, a flirt, if you will. The crackling static on the phone, from his energy, increased. "I don't know, but based on your new findings, it should be soon because we need to be able to monitor and stop these people before it's too late."

"Yes."

"I need you to work with us on this."

"Who is us, Vic?"

"Clayvious and his men."

"But he's not even real. You have to go to his dimension to talk to him. He may not even be able to exist on this plane."

Vic's voice became more confident now and the crackling on the line seemed to quiet. "Here's what I haven't told you. I pulled him through."

"You pulled him through! How?"

"Using my energy, I was able to open the membrane that had always separated us. Then he and his men walked through."

Deloche was now excited. "Are you kidding?"

"No."

"That's amazing."

"He's been training me on how to use the energy and I've been building my strength, focus and concentration with the book."

"Ah, I see. That explains everything. You've been putting in work."

"Yes, big time. Madame, I've come to the revelation that I could do things that I haven't even imagined yet."

"That's powerful, Vic."

"Yes, and a little scary, but I'm learning to control it and not letting it go to my head but to also conceal it. We can't let the world in on this and have a media circus. There's too much at stake."

"I agree."

"I'm coming there in a few days. Could you put me up?"

"Of course."

"Then I think we should take a trip to Washington and stay a few days just to see if we can find out anything."

"I think I can do that. Sharon can take care of things while I'm gone."

"Great, I'll let you know when I'm flying in and I'll Uber to the shop."

"Okay, I look forward to seeing you again."

"And I'm looking forward to seeing you, Madame. We have a lot to talk about and much to do."

She sensed his attraction. "This is exciting, but also a little scary."

"I know, but we have to overcome our fears and walk out on the waters of faith, otherwise we fail to grow and reach our potential."

"This is true." She secretly melts a little, feeling his strength and wisdom of things to come.

Vic flew into New Orleans the following Wednesday and summoned a ride from his phone. The driver dropped him in front of the shop and he walked in.

Deloche, in a happy tone and with a measured embrace, greeted Vic just inside the door. "Vic, you made it." They embraced.

Putting his arm around her waist, Vic was turned on just from feeling her firm, slender but strong, athletic body. He wanted to tell her how beautiful she looked and then kiss her lovely face, but he knew that it would be unprofessional to start the trip that way. He knew she could feel it, they both were feeling it. Vic believed that if he had held a magnet between them and dropped it, that the magnet would hover in mid-air and not fall to the ground from the magnetism radiating from both of them. "Hello, Madame. You look lovely today. How have you been?"

"Oh I'm well and thank you."

So as not to be rude, Vic greeted Sharon with a warm hello then started in on the business at hand. "Madame, tell me how you've been able to locate this woman. How does that work?"

"Well, it works similar to the way I've been contacting you. I think about you, focus on the idea of talking to you and then a thought about me pops into your head and then you get the feeling that you want to call me or that I want you to call me and then you call. In this situation, I know I'm looking for a woman based on the energy she has been putting out through thought, meditation, or some ritual. It's like a radio picking up a radio wave. In this case, the brain acts as both radio wave and radio. So, I was meditating on the person who was putting out the energy and I did that every day for five days. Then on the sixth day, there she was, putting it out there. I knew it was her because the energy felt the same and from the same direction it was coming from before. And because of my abilities, I felt her rage when she realized she had been detected. And that told me many things about her. An older wiser spirit would have just pulled back or came out of their trance or meditation and disappeared. She stayed in and expressed an emotion that allowed me to get an impression of her age, and what she looks like, and what she feels like. She's a wolf in sheep's clothing. No one would ever suspect her and she is dangerous, a cold-blooded killer. Now, what I can't explain is how I get all of that detail, but it's like someone talking to you about a problem or a situation and you get an idea or feeling of who that person is through their conversation."

"Wow, I get it. That's powerful. Your energy is the source."

Deloche smiled. "My energy is the source?"

Vic smiled like a team mate and exclaimed, "Yes, it is," and slapped her a high five as if she had just hit a home run, which she had, in this early battle for Earth.

CHAPTER 13

A few days later, they hopped on a plane headed to Washington, DC, and from the airport to the Hamilton Hotel just north of the White House. They shared a room but with separate beds in an effort to conserve money. Vic was going into his savings to make the trip, but by no means was it an unlimited reserve. But that wasn't what was on his mind. He couldn't believe that he was headed for divorce and now in a hotel room with a beautiful telepath who had pulled him off the street in New Orleans and now they were trying to save the world. It was far-fetched and unbelievable, even to him. And with all that to process, there was the attraction to Madame Deloche. She was everything a man desired in a woman, but now was not the time to get anything going personally because there was serious work to do that would affect millions of people on Earth. To focus on anything personal at this time would be the epitome of selfishness, but here he was with her in a hotel room, fighting his own carnal desires. So far he was winning, but didn't know how long he could last when suddenly Deloche walked out of the bathroom with no shirt on and just a bra and jeans."

"Sorry, I didn't mean to look, Madame."

"Oh came on."

"We're not spring chickens here. I know you've seen your sister or your mom in a bra, right?"

"Well, since you put it like that, you're right."

"And we've got bigger fish to fry. How long are we going to be here?"

"Oh three or four days, that should give us enough time to find out something. What we'll find out, I'm not sure, but a lead or any little thing will help."

"What about her? I thought we were trying to find her?"

"Yes, but that's a long shot. We need to also keep our eyes open for other things."

"Other things like what?"

"Like strange occurrences, or you sensing other people who may be involved. We just need to keep an open mind."

"Okay, it makes sense."

Later, the two decided to go out and grab a bite to eat and decided on Five Guys burgers a block away, across K Street, going south toward the White House. They sat and enjoyed their burgers while discussing their strategy for the next few days. On the way out, they noticed a few people on the street handing out fliers as a young gentleman handed them one. Vic read it.

"Madame, there's going to be a protest on Saturday at Lafayette park."

"Where's that?"

"It's on Pennsylvania Avenue across the street from the White House. It looks like these fliers are for those who oppose the current administration. So, that means the supporters of this administration will be there, too. This could get interesting."

Madame was now curious. "How far is that from here?"

"It's three blocks from here and four blocks from the hotel."

"This is great. People will be coming from far and wide. This is perfect timing for us. We should find out something."

"I agree." What Madame didn't say was that she believed the young woman would be there, and that thought made her very excited. Madame knew that if this witch were to show up, she would know it and then—and then what? She realized they couldn't tie her up and throw her in the trunk. "So, Vic, what are we going to do if we come across her, the witch I mean?"

"Then we follow her, watch her, get a license plate, track who she talks to, and keep an eye out for others who may be working with her."

"Got it."

As they walked back up 14th Street to the hotel, passing Franklin Square, the street was abuzz with people in the square talking about Saturday's protest. Vic and Deloche felt the energy and sensed that things were happening and working in their favor.

The next day, Vic decided they should walk down to Lafayette Park. "Madame, what do you say we walk down to the park and get to know the lay of the land?"

"Okay, that sounds like a good idea. And by the way, my first name is Monica. Madame is so formal."

"Monica, huh? I like it. Such a pretty name."

"Thank you." She grabbed their jackets going out the door.

Once in the lobby of the hotel, on the way to the front entrance, Deloche stopped. She looked at the floor but Vic could tell she was using her mind's eye. "What's wrong? Did you leave something?"

"No," she said as she looked around the lobby. "I feel like we're being watched." She scanned the open area with people moving about, but with nothing and no one looked unusual or out of place.

Vic started to tell her she was just paranoid but remembered her track record of being right about these things and instead looked around himself. They shook it off and asked themselves who would or could be on to them and why or how. Before they knew it, they were at the park and focusing on the layout as it sloped downhill to the street. There were plenty of tourists, taking pictures and walking into the street that had been barricaded at each end so that there was no through traffic going down Pennsylvania Avenue. On the other side was another barricade before you got to the fence surrounding the White House lawn, complete with security in case someone tried to jump the fence as they had so many times in the past only to be tackled on the White House lawn and jailed. However, it was a great place to see the White House and possibly get a quick glimpse of the president getting into his motorcade on a rare occasion. The White House looked so much larger on TV. In person, it was actually a house, a mansion, but a house. A main pillar of democracy around the world and they were there to try to secretly keep it that way. Looking back up into the park, it was a pretty large area and with federal police scattered about, looking like things will be safe on Saturday.

On the next day, Friday, Vic found a sports shop in town and bought a hunting camera with a tree bark style camouflage cover.

"What are you going to do with that?" Monica asked.

"We're going back to the park this evening and I'm going to strategically plant it on a tree to see if we could get anything on video."

"Very clever, Mr. Vic."

So that evening, they keep the same routine of grabbing some food at Chipotle and then heading to the park, getting there just before dark. The organizers were there discussing what they could and couldn't do with federal police. Vic overheard an officer explaining that the trees were protected as a historical site and that no signs could be hung or nailed to the trees. He started looking for a tree that would give him a broad view of the park and found one at the back of the park but then realized that view will capture the back of most participants heads so he continued looking until he spotted a tree on the lower right side of the park, facing back up the hill. What made this tree so perfect was that it had two branches at about six-foot-eight-inches high that looked like two arms stretching out to give someone a hug. With the leaves hanging around the branches, it looked to be the perfect location.

"Monica, follow my lead."

She agreed and Vic put his arm around her shoulders as if they were a couple and started to walk toward the tree. When they got to the maple, Vic leaned on the tree as if he was talking to Monica and working up to a kiss. And while creating that illusion, he pressed a short tack on a short wire, into the tree. Instead of the usual bungee style cord, that would make it obvious, this was a small camera that fit in the palm of his hand that had twenty-four hours of continuous recording time that would allow him to bag images from the protest at noon the next day. While still leaning on the tree, he flipped it to the on position then walked up the hill with his arm still around Monica and they went unnoticed. Halfway up the hill, standing in the circular concrete walkway, they looked back to see that the camera was almost unnoticeable. They crossed their fingers and headed back to the hotel to get ready for tomorrow.

Saturday morning, they woke up early and decided to wear clothes that wouldn't garner any attention. They both wore jeans and work boots with dark tops. Vic's jacket was gray and Monica's jacket was navy blue, both with baseball caps. Even with the nondescript outfit, hair in a bun, hat and no makeup, Monica was gorgeous, Vic thought, but kept it to himself. On this morning, they would have breakfast at the hotel restaurant at 9:00 a.m. and talk quietly until 10:15. They headed back to the room to brush their teeth and one last team huddle before leaving. They double checked their cell phones and headsets, making sure they're fully charged and Vic with one last instruction."

"Monica, if we get separated or something happens to one of our phones, we should meet at the tree with the camera."

"That sounds like a plan."

Vic could tell that Monica was pumped and ready to go. At 11:00 a.m. they head down the elevator and into the lobby, then onto the street, arriving at the park at 11:13. As they arrived, standing in the back of the park up the hill, Vic looked down at the tree and the camera was still there. He looked at Monica and she gave him a thumbs up. There were plenty of people in the park, but most of them were down around the sidewalk in front of the organizers who were setup in the street with a microphone and audio speakers facing back up the hill. It was a perfect makeshift amphitheater. And Vic noticed something he hadn't realized before—the park was visible from the White House. He wasn't sure about the rooms with all the windows because he had never been in the White House, but he knew there was a clear view over to the park.

Within minutes, the lower area of the park was filling up as Vic and Monica walked down the far right side of Lafayette Park, facing

Pennsylvania Avenue, closer to the organizers, and across from the camera tree. For the next half an hour, people continued to pour into the park and at that point they noticed the separation of the two rival parties. Suddenly, signs were going up into the air, held up by each party and at 12:01, the organizers started in on the microphone against the administration. With the election coming up, outsider supporters shouted, "Four more years, four more years." While the challenging party cites all the mistakes and lies of the inexperienced outside administration, the outside supporters didn't know their president was possibly being controlled by a witch working for a more evil entity trying to destroy the planet. Vic and Monica had discussed how these outside supporters seemed to be blinded by the president's fame and celebrity in the media, and seemed to like how he had divided the country down party lines that also had negative and regressive implications concerning race and gender. And they didn't seem to notice that he didn't give a damn about them but continued to con them out of their money for support.

Then suddenly, a man shouted out an obscenity toward the person speaking on the microphone and the mood of the crowd changed. Monica had felt a wave or ripple in the air that made the hair stand up on her back. "She's here," Monica said, with a wild determined look on her face, but at that point, people started hurling bottles at each other and suddenly knives and bats were now in plain view. Monica looked back up the hill and saw a man in a suit with an evil excited look on his face with his arms at his side, pushing his energy forward with his open hands and forearms. "Look!" She pointed back up the hill and Vic looked in time to see the man hurl another wave at the crowd below, that only they could see. Vic was ready, having eaten another slice of the brownie that morning at breakfast. "That's him!" Monica said. "That's who she works for."

Vic started up the hill, but down the hill complete bedlam had broken out with people bleeding and fighting as others tried to separate the warring factions along with the police who had called for backup. As Vic approached the evil one, he readied his palms but realized he couldn't shoot his blue energy because people were in the way. Vic looked back for Monica. She was gone. When he jerked his head back a second later, the evil one was gone, disappeared. As Vic looked in disbelief, he was hit by a familiar jolt of electricity and fell to his knees. And only saw Clayvious back in his dimension on the other side of the membrane.

"Pull me thorough," Clayvious said. "You have to pull us through or you're going to lose him." Without further hesitation, Vic, his astral self, released his energy opening the membrane and Clayvious, with his men, walked through into the park. To Vic's surprise, they were all dressed in current attire: pants, jackets, and hiking boots, so he followed Clayvious and his men.

Monica had noticed a young woman standing across the street on the White House side of the street behind the speaker with the microphone who was now urging people to calm down and reminding them that this was a peaceful protest. Kali had an amused grin on her face as people continued to go at each other. It was as though she were watching two men fight over her and she was loving every minute of it. Monica marveled at how innocent she looked but noticed that every now and then she would flick her wrist at the crowd, adding fuel to the fire with her powers as people who were calm suddenly became angry with an urge to hurt someone. Monica knew this was the young woman she'd been looking for. And against what had been agreed with Vic, she approached the young woman.

"Hi, are you Karen's daughter?"

"No, I'm not. Sorry," Kali responded, still wearing the same smile.

"But you seem familiar, too. Do you live in West Virginia?"

Kali peered at Monica. "No."

'What town?"

"Oh, up around Morgantown. How about you?" Kali asked.

Thinking quickly, Monica said, "I'm in upstate New York."

"Oh, it's so pretty up there."

Monica agreed.

"Well it was nice meeting you," Kali said.

"You, too," Monica replied. "Which way are you going?" Monica asked with some urgency.

"Well, my car is back that way."

"Well, I'm headed that way too. Let me walk with you."

Kali agreed as they headed away from the White House and the chaos. After two blocks of small talk, they came to a nondescript black Ford Bronco with West Virginia plates. Monica had spotted the plates on approach and started memorizing it.

"Well, it was nice meeting you and thank you for letting me walk with you. I was concerned about our safety, and what is your name, by the way?"

"Oh me, too, and I'm Kali."

"Okay, Kali, I'm Sharon. Drive safe."

Clay and his men had been following an African American male with two Asian guys down the street away from the protest when Clayvious nodded to his men and punched the Black guy in the arm. When his buddies tried to step in, Clayvious's men blocked them when a punch was thrown, with incredible unseen speed, by one of the Asian guys and instantly there was a brawl. Clayvious had four men and outnumbered them two to one, but the Black guy's friends were fighting machines. Throwing punches and kicking with such speed and force that Clayvious's men were battered and bruised. Holding their own, they were amazed at the martial art style and blazing speed of the two men. Then the muscular bodies of Clayvious's men landed devastating blows to the heads and faces of the two men as green fluid appeared on their cheeks. Clayvious's men became confused at the sight of it, not knowing what it was, but deployed their needle blades and moved in for the kill when the two fighting men deployed a force field, rendering the laser swords of Clayvious's men useless. One of the men pulled a .9-millimeter hand gun from behind the force field as a show of force and Clayvious's men smiled in amusement, knowing the earthling's gun wouldn't be enough to stop them. Vic looked around, up and down the street, but there was no one there with everyone having rushed down to see the commotion at the park. Vic fired a blast of blue energy at the force field and, to his surprise, it was absorbed by the field of protective energy. Vic now added his left palm to double the force and the two men inside looked concerned when suddenly there was a loud "Hey!" that possessed a sonic quality that jolted everyone like a stun gun, and everyone stopped and looked. The Black guy, who had generated the unusual sound that powered the "Hey," still felt the sting in his shoulder and said, "What's the problem? I don't have a beef with you guys."

Clayvious looked him in the eyes and said, "But we have a beef with you, Rhynous, and your change in color won't stop that."

Rhynous, now in shock that he had been detected, looked at his men as they all turned back to pail alien gray, unlike any earthling, Rhynous jumped into the force field as it opened only for him. Then he and his men held hands, with fear and surprise on their faces, and then disappeared into some kind of unknown dimension. The men now realized that the green fluid was alien blood. Clayvious and his men looked at each other and laughed. Vic was completely in the dark and upset. "What's going on? You let him get away."

Clay said, "Calm down, we have him right where we want him."

"Where's that? I don't see him," Vic said in disgust.

"Do you see this?" Clay held up his hand, displaying a ring with a sharp point on his middle finger.

"What's that?" Vic asked.

"Now that's the right question. It's an implant ring. He now has a tracking device in his left shoulder."

Vic laughed in relief as Clayvious and his men joined in on the short laughter.

"Okay, we need to find a place where you can send us back." Vic looked across the street and saw an alley. "Follow me."

They followed Vic into the alley as he looked around and saw no one, then opened the portal that led to the membrane and their dimension.

Clayvious and his men walked through and Vic shut down his energy. As he turned to walk away from the back of the building, he saw a bum sitting on the ground with a bottle of whiskey. He wondered how he didn't see him when they walked into the alley, but on a second look, Vic realized that the man was so dirty he just blended in. Now they stood there, just looking at each other when the man took his bottle and turned it upside down, pouring out his drink into the alley, saying only, "I know I didn't see that shit." Vic suddenly realized Monica was probably still at the park under the tree and ran out of the alley back toward the park. The bum shouted, "Why are you running? I'm the one who should be running. I know I didn't just see that shit."

Vic got back to the park and saw Monica down by the tree, but he couldn't get to her because the police had the park blocked off but allowed her to wait for safety reasons. Vic waved, and she ran up the hill to greet him with a hug after the police let her through. It was now 3:40 p.m., and the sun seemed to be ready to set. Vic now had his arm around Monica's shoulder and her arm around his waist, both thankful the other was safe and uninjured. Anyone seeing them walking down the street would know they were together, everyone but them.

Kali was halfway home driving down the highway still trying to figure out why the woman at the park was so familiar. She couldn't put her finger on it. She didn't know many people from upstate New York and she realized she didn't know her from there. Monica's diversion away from New Orleans would keep her guessing, but if she ever found out, it could be murderous. And Monica couldn't shake the feeling that Kali was somehow connected to her in some kind of way. That they had something in common, but she couldn't put her finger on it.

CHAPTER 14

Once back at the hotel, Vic and Monica were still flowing with adrenaline but flopped on their beds from exhaustion; there was so much to process. A lot had happened more than they expected and they wanted to share notes, but didn't have the energy at that moment to begin the conversation.

Vic sprung to his feet. "The camera!" I've got to get back down to the park."

"Relax, big boy, I've got your camera."

"You do?"

"Yes."

Vic exhaled like air coming out of a tire. "Thanks, Monica. What would I do without you?"

"You're welcome." She pulled the camera from her coat pocket. " Here," She tossed it at him."

"Great." He rushed to connect it to the computer. "Did you see her?" Vic asked.

"Yes, she was there."

"What happened? Did you follow her?"

"Not exactly."

Now curious, Vic put down the camera. "What went down?"

"I walked up to her and started a conversation, asking if she was someone's daughter. I got her name and her license plate number."

Vic just looked at her with his mouth open. "Monica, you weren't supposed to make contact with her. If she finds out who you are, you could be in danger."

"Hmm, I didn't think about that. Well, I did tell her that I lived in upstate New York."

"That may throw her off for a while, but I need you to be safe."

"I thought your powers would keep me safe," she replied.

"And they will as long as we're together but that's hard to do when I'm in California and you're in Louisiana."

"Hey, what do you think about moving to New Orleans?"

"What? I can't do that right now. I'm in the throes of a divorce," he said, but oh how he wanted to.

"Hey, tell me what happened with you and that warlock or whoever he was."

"Well, I couldn't use my energy on him because people were running back and forth and he disappeared. Then Clay chimed in and told me to pull him and his men through before I lose him. So I did and we tracked him down and Clay placed a tracking device in his shoulder."

"Really?"

"Yes for real, so I have to get with Clay and find out more but I can tell you how he disappeared."

"How?"

"He's a shape-shifter."

She gasped for air. "Are you serious?"

"Yes. He turned into a Black guy and his henchmen were suddenly Asian. Somehow Clay was not fooled. I have to ask him about that, but I was wondering why we were following these guys and it turned out to be Rhynous."

"That's his name?"

"Yes, Clay knew his name. That's something else I need to talk to him about, how he knew his name."

"And I take back what I said, that he's not real. He's not only real, he's important. I'm looking forward to meeting him."

"Oh, you will. Sooner than later, Madame. I mean, Monica. We need to have a meeting with everyone involved at the same time."

"That sounds good."

With that, Vic continued to set up playback on the camera. Monica continued to relax on the bed and thought about how familiar

Kali seemed to be to her. As though she were someone from New Orleans, or possibly like someone she knew. It was odd, she thought, but decided to try to research it later as she started to drift a little with her eyes closed.

Suddenly Vic shouted, startling her. "Yes! Come look at this."

Monica bounced off the bed and over to the table where Vic was sitting at the computer. "What is it?"

"Watch this." He pressed play.

On camera, Rhynous and his guys started down the hill and then Vic came into view, turning his head to look for Monica and, at that instant, the three men changed their ethnicity like a chameleon instantaneously. Vic had turned his head back in time to see them, but saw different people. It never registered in his mind that they were wearing the same clothes. This was a normal response, as most people were programmed to remember a face.

"That's amazing and a problem," Monica said, in a discouraging tone.

"Yes, but we can learn from this video. In the future, if we have a situation like this, we have to pay attention to the clothes. That's the only way we would be able to keep track of them without Clay."

"You're right, Vic, if only we could see through the fake image. I wonder if their ability to change the way they look is biological or technology."

"Hmm, good question. That may be a question Clay could answer, but we'll figure it out."

Monica was now probing her own mind. "I wonder if Kali can shape-shift."

"I hope not, being that she knows what you look like."

"Yes, but she doesn't know where I am. Kali has powers, but she has weak psychic abilities."

"How do you know that?"

"If her psychic abilities were strong, she would have recognized me at the park the way I recognized her, but she didn't."

"Good point."

"Yes, but like you, she's working at it and developing her skills quickly. If it's in her, she will develop it," Monica said, acknowledging the growing threat.

For the rest of the evening, Vic continued to comb through the video and Monica stayed tuned into CNN to see what coverage there was on the protest. The news report said that the two sides clashed, but the news stated that one side was attacked by a mob from the other party. She wondered how all of his followers continued to fall for all of those lies, now a sea of lies. After today, Monica began to realize there was a puppeteer. An evil element that was controlling the president, and Rhynous was holding the strings with Kali as his trusty sidekick. A super natural Bonnie and Clyde set on world destruction and taking control of whatever monetary systems were left. Yes, money again seemed to be at the root, but with Nazi-esque lies and propaganda and ideas of controlling the world.

The next day, Vic and Monica caught a plane back to New Orleans and though he knew he couldn't stay, Vic was enamored with the idea of being with Monica for a few days before returning to Los Angeles. Once back at her shop, they spent a few hours bringing Sharon up to speed on the events in DC and she, in turn, gave Monica a list of clients who had been waiting for her return. Sharon had also done well with street traffic and tourists walking in for a palm reading or tarot cards. That night, the three of them went to Monica's favorite seafood restaurant and enjoyed a good meal with the best white wine. And though they smiled and laughed the night away, in the back of their minds loomed the herculean task that lay before them.

Later that evening, they dropped Sharon off at her place and Monica drove home not far away. Vic and Monica laughed and talked all the way to the house she had purchased in recent months from the success of her business. It was a quaint but small French provincial-style home in a nice neighborhood with two bedrooms and a nice kitchen on a quarter of an acre, and a nice size backyard. However, Monica had turned the second bedroom into a den with a futon couch that unfolded into a bed. The two talked for a short while longer and retired to their rooms. Vic had decided not to unfold the futon, choosing instead to lay on it as a couch. As he lay there in the dark, savoring the evening, he closed his eyes, which seemed to invite other thoughts. There was the thought of getting back home and contacting Clayvious to get some answers to his many questions. And then the thought that he didn't need to wait, Clayvious had jerked him back into his dimension at the DC protest. Then, the thought of Rhynous and his whereabouts on the planet or the universe. While thinking of all of these things, there was the constant thought that permeated and existed with every thought. Like the sun in a pastoral scene or during the day through work, thought, and errands, it was a constant. He couldn't stop thinking of her. The thought of Monica was ever present and as he came to that realization, it became even stronger. The fact that she was just in the other room, he could still smell her perfume and imagined laying behind her, pressed close and kissing the back of her long statuesque neck as his right arm fondled and pulled her closer from the front. Even with his eyes closed, he felt a presence before him and he knew it was Rhynous when he grabbed Vic by the arm.

Vic jumped back, shouting, with his palm up, ready to shoot a ray of blue energy, when he heard a female's voice calmly say, "Don't hurt me, big boy."

"Monica?"

"Yes."

"Woman, you scared the crap out of me."

"I see, but what were you thinking before I touched you?"

At that point, he knew that she had heard or felt his thoughts. "I was thinking I should be in bed with you."

"That's the right answer." She took him by the hand and led him to her room, and closed the door.

The next morning, Vic woke up to the smell of bacon and eggs calling his name. When he got to the kitchen, Monica was just finishing the toast, and the coffee was brewing.

"Well, you're up." She smiled, and he greeted her with a hug and a kiss.

"Man, that really smells good, Monica."

"Thank you. I thought you could use a big breakfast this morning. You used up a lot of energy last night. I don't have any brownies."

Vic laughed. "That's the last thing I need right now, is a brownie. This is perfect. Thank you."

"Oh, you're quite welcome. So what's the plan for today?" she asked.

"Well, it's Monday. Don't you have to go to the shop?"

"Yes, but Mondays are usually slow and Sharon will be there by ten. If there's any traffic today it won't happen until around noon. I do need to contact these clients who have called but I can do that from here."

"Well, the only thing I have on my mind now is contacting Clay."

"When do you want to do that?"

"Probably tonight after you close the shop. I was thinking we could have the meeting there if that's okay with you."

"Of course, that seems like the right place to have it."

"Thanks, Monica. I don't think you'll be disappointed."

"Trust me, I won't be. I get to finally meet Clay."

Vic smiled, but said nothing. Monica set a plate of scrambled eggs with onion and cheese seasoned to perfection with buttery toast and bacon on the table in front of him, as well as grape and strawberry jams. Vic's favorite being the strawberry. They said grace and dug in.

"Oh, wow."

"What?" she said.

"This is so good. Monica, you could have made it really big as a chef. Sure you don't want to reconsider?"

Flattered, Monica giggled a little. "Why thank you, but no, I think we're right where we're supposed to be in life."

"Okay, I guess I can't argue with that."

After breakfast, Vic sat in deep contemplation and a few minutes went by without a word being spoken.

"What's on your mind? A penny for your thoughts," Monica said.

"I was thinking about the unexplained weirdness, like the number 13 constantly appearing. And then it all unravels when I decide to taste a small insignificant scrap from a brownie, and the events leading up to it that day. A brownie, a marijuana brownie; do you realize that if we told someone this story, they would think we were crazy?"

"Vic, the old adage is true; truth is stranger than fiction."

"Yes, it is, lovely lady. It's just that my life has made such a paradigm shift. It seems like my old life has been stripped away and I'm in this metamorphosis like a caterpillar. Speaking of caterpillars, I'm starting to feel like I could fly."

"What? Are you serious?" Monica said, with an incredulous look on her face.

"I know, but yes, I'm going to head up to the desert when I get home and give it a go."

"When did all of this come about?"

"Well, it's just a feeling that had come over me in the last week or so. It's like when I decided to run track in high school. I just felt like I could run fast and wanted to give it a try."

"You be careful," she said with concern.

"I'll try to be, but it's something I have to do. I'll be okay. I promise you, if something goes wrong you'll be the first person I contact."

"That's if you're still alive," she said, giving Vic a strong stare.

"Hey, I have a question for you."

"What's that?"

"Why aren't you reading my mind right now? You're a telepath. It seems you would have known I was planning to fly."

Monica thought for a few seconds. "Well, I understand your reasoning, but it doesn't work like that for me. Let me give you an example, your sex drive. It's an ability men have that when they're aroused the blood rushes to a certain part of the body and they're able to perform, but you guys don't walk around all day every day aroused in every situation."

"Okay, I get that."

"And look, there are thoughts that people have that are none of my business. People think about things that they will never act on and it's an invasion of privacy. Plus, I don't need all the crap that people think about in my head. I'd be a nutcase. And think about this, if I were in your head all the time, you would become fearful and feel violated. Trust me, I've scared a few people in the past, and it's not good for anyone."

"Impressive, thank you," Vic said, realizing that Monica was responsible and ethical. He felt a deeper sense of relaxation and trust with her as his feelings grew.

Shortly after noon, Vic and Monica headed for the French Quarter down to the shop. Sharon was there with a gentleman who was trying to decide if he wanted a reading. He was so warmly greeted by the couple who had just entered and, upon feeling their glow, he decided to have a reading. Monica led Vic to a back room with a couch and a TV. Monica headed back to the front and stood in the doorway to give her sales pitch, which wasn't much of a pitch at all. Her smile and looks alone were enough to garner the average person's attention. All she did was smile and her hello reeked of happy, positive energy. Then she waited for them to ask the question. "How much is a reading?"

Later that evening, after closing, Sharon said her goodbye and left out the back door. Vic had fallen asleep watching television when Monica walked in to see if he was ready to meet with Clayvious. He agreed, but had to throw water on his face, drink water, and use the bathroom before he could start. Once he was ready, they went into the séance room and Vic had another small piece of brownie. He and Monica sat and discussed how they were going to monitor Kali and line up their questions for Clay. Finally, Vic felt the euphoria come over him and sensed the blue energy emanating from the top of his head. It was faint but Monica could see it and was amazed. Vic went into himself and came out in an astral form in Clayvious's dimension. Vic was standing outside the membrane looking in when Clayvious walked out of an archway and down the steps, all of which seemed to be made from Roman brick and mortar with a brownish orange color.

"Hello, my friend. I've been expecting you."

"Hello, Clay. It's good to see you again, but I have a ton of questions for you. I've been working with a friend who is a telepath and she's the one who located the witch who is working with Rhynous."

"Yes, I know."

"Listen, Clay, I want to pull you through so the three of us can have a meeting."

"That's a good idea. I'm ready if you are."

"Yeah, I'm ready. Here we go." Vic directed his energy at the membrane, creating a bluish hue as the liquid glass-like membrane separated and Clayvious walked through. As Monica watched, Vic came out of a trance-like state and then a very tall man walked in from a strange liquid-like wall that appeared in the room. Monica, in a bit of shock, knew now that Clayvious was for real as she smiled in acknowledgment just as Vic was starting the introduction.

"Clay, this is Monica. Monica this Clay."

"Hello. I'm glad to finally meet you."

"As am I to meet you, young lady, and you remind me of the beautiful Helen of Troy."

"Oh my, why thank you." She extended her hand to shake his hand. When Clay's hand touched hers, she was chilled through and through, then information and images started flashing through her mind and she realized he was thousands of years old, wiser than even she could comprehend, and more. She looked at Vic with a look of surprise and gratitude, which he found perplexing, and started to ask if she was okay, but thought better of it.

"Well, let's get started. Clay, thank you for coming. Before we get started working on any strategy, we have questions for you, Clay."

As he listened, Clay nodded.

"Clay, how did you know Rhynous's name?" Vic asked.

Clayvious answered without hesitation. "Rhynous was behind the fall of the Roman Empire. He gave rise to the Barbarian Kingdoms that had established power in the western empire. He gained tremendous wealth in gold and land. That was over one thousand five hundred years ago, and I'm pretty sure he didn't remember me. I was a part of a European joint army along with my men in an effort to stop him under the guise of a crusade. Back then, Rhynous was in it to acquire wealth and to control territory. Now, it's to destroy and take over the world and to confiscate what monetary systems that are left. The leaders of his planet stopped coming here one thousand years ago and would have never tolerated his behavior as their policy was to help advance but never interfere or make themselves known to a primitive civilization. This is why he operated from behind the scene so as not to be detected by them and continues to do so to this day."

Vic and Monica were flabbergasted at the realization that Rhynous had been at this for over one thousand years and had now upped the ante to the whole planet. And that being as rich as a Getty, a Gates, a Buffet, or a Rothschild wasn't enough. It was motivation to destroy him, not that they needed more.

After a moment to process the answer, Vic asked, "Okay, but how did you know who Rhynous was when he and his men shape-shifted?"

"That's one of our powers, to see beyond the shell of a person. We could still see their alien features beneath the cloak, like a face under a face."

Vic and Monica looked at each other. "Wow, that's fantastic, and you may have just answered the next question. Clay, you just used the term cloak. Does that mean they're using technology to change?"

"Yes, it's some kind of image refraction, very high-tech stuff. We're not exactly sure how it works, but we know it doesn't work on us."

"Thank God for that," Vic said, "Clay, we need a plan moving forward. You're the military expert. You have any ideas?"

"Of course I do, but what about the witch? What do you know about her?"

"Well, we know she lives in West Virginia. We know what car she drives and we have her plate number."

"Perfect," Clay said, as Vic continued.

"I have a friend who can run the license plate number and get her address."

"You two have been doing good work, and here's what I think we should do. We need to monitor her coming and going. I can assign two of my men to stakeout her place. Rhynous is not on the planet right now, which lets me know we got his attention, but he's gearing up for a battle. He will return with a small army, but when he does, we'll know where he is and I suspect he'll be near or with the girl, Kali. Rhynous is a trickster but has the ability to travel inter dimensionally between planets. Vic, I want you to consider taking a trip with me to his home planet of Larus to inform the leaders there of his continued pursuit of planet Earth and the destruction of it for his personal gain. They've been after him for a long time. I think they will be willing to join our efforts to stop him."

"Are you serious? You want me to go with you?"

Vic looked at Monica, who was as surprised as he was and said, "That's going to be some kind of road trip."

"When are you planning to leave?" Vic asked.

"As soon as you're ready," Clayvious said with confidence and nonchalance, as if he were talking about a camping trip.

"Okay, but first I need to go home for a few days to work on some things, then I'll be ready."

"Very well then, I'll be waiting, but keep in mind the sooner the better."

Vic agreed. "In the meantime, I'll also be working on getting Kali's address and bringing it to you before we depart."

"Okay, now we have a plan and we can discuss battle strategies with the Larians should they decide to join us," Clay said proudly.

Sensing the meeting about to end, Monica said, "Gentlemen, I'm sensing some synergy here, so go with me on this. Let's bring in a fist." She raised her arm up with a balled fist and the guys followed her lead, forming an arch reminiscent of knights at the round table, touching their swords. As their fists touched, they felt a spark of electricity. "Our energy is the source."

On cue, Vic and Clay repeated those words perfectly in sync, as if their minds were connected. "Our energy is the source."

Monica gave the cue as all three synced together. "Our energy is the source, and the source is in us!" Like the break of a football huddle, they felt the togetherness and the kinship of now being a supernatural team with the power of the universe behind them.

CHAPTER 15

The three of them were charged with positive energy and expectation as Vic opened the way for Clayvious to pass back through the membrane. Then Vic and Monica hugged with excitement, as if they had just scored a goal and they had. Once the adrenaline had subsided, the two headed back to Monica's house and on the way, Vic followed up on the question that had him curious at the beginning of the meeting.

"Monica, when I introduced you to Clay and you shook his hand, you had a strange look on your face. What was on your mind?"

"I was using my telepathy to know more about him and I was bombarded with information. It was like a computer download and too much information, but when I shook his hand, I realized something about Clay that I don't think you know."

"What's that?"

"I don't know how to tell you this and I don't know how it's possible, but Clay is not a living person as we know it."

"Are you trying to tell me that Clay is some kind of ghost?"

Yes, I think that's what I'm trying to say, but it's not that clear. He's able to manifest like flesh and blood, but he's not. He's something different. I've never seen or come in contact with anyone like him. He's a mystery."

Baffled, Vic took a moment to think. "You know that explains something. The first time I pulled Clay through, he turned into this clear bluish color. Then at the park, he and his men were a regular flesh tone. Hmm, that's crazy, but let's keep this to ourselves. We don't want to freak anyone out."

"Hey, you got it. Who would believe me, anyway?"

At that moment, they pulled into Monica's driveway. Once in the house, they grabbed a snack and headed to bed, both exhausted.

The next morning, Monica drove Vic to the airport and within three and a half hours, he was back in Los Angeles, which didn't feel the same. He was now separated from his wife. He was trying to save Earth, had a new love interest and his friend from another dimension appeared to be something like a ghost. He felt like he was in a different city, not L.A., but realized it was not the city that was different, it was him. His priorities were now literally other worldly and at that moment, his phone rang.

"Hey, what's up?"

"Greg, what's going on? I'm just getting back in town."

"What'cha been doing, chasing witches and aliens?" Greg laughed.

Vic was stunned by the comment, but quickly realized Greg was referring to the last party. "Yeah, that's exactly what I've been doing."

Greg laughed again. "Look, I've got another comedy show coming up."

"Greg, I'm not going to be able to make it."

"Why not? I thought you were my biggest fan?"

"I'm only going to be in town for a few days, G., and then I'm headed back to New Orleans."

"Why? What's going on down there?"

"Well, there is a lady, but I'm working on some business things I can't talk about right now. You know what they say. Don't talk about a deal until the deal is done."

"Okay, whatever, you're going to miss a good show."

"I'm sure but I'll try to catch you on the next one, Greg."

"Okay, I can tell you're busy so I'll catch you later."

"You know it. The next time I'm back in town, we'll catch up."

"Cool, catch you later."

Vic couldn't believe how far away a comedy show was from being on his mind. That conversation was a world away from his new mindset. He still hoped that someday he would be able to get back to the normal, simple pleasures of life. Like a night out at a comedy club enjoying some laughs, but he first had to make sure that those types of enjoyment didn't cease to exist.

Vic focused on what he came back to the West Coast for, to test his ability to fly. When he got to the house, he started trying to put together an outfit that would help limit the scrapes and bruises of a fall. Vic pulled out his work boots and thick socks, then his old knee and elbow pads to go under his sweatpants and a thickly padded black flight jacket. The only thing he didn't have was a helmet. Vic went to his neighbor's house, who had a motorcycle, and asked to borrow a helmet. He had three and one seemed to fit when the strap was tight. Vic assured Rick that he would bring it back. Vic wanted to go straight to the desert, but the day was almost over. It was already 4:00 p.m. and he knew it would be important to get an early start the next morning. So he spent the rest of the afternoon studying a map of the high desert east of Los Angeles out past Barstow on the way to Las Vegas but before Death Valley off Highway 15. Vic found a location east of Edwards Air Base in a remote area of the Mojave Desert, where he could go unnoticed.

The next morning, he left at 6:00 a.m. and was in the high desert by 7:30. He got off the freeway past the old gold mine on a quiet road. About twenty miles out into the desert, he saw an unpaved dirt road that seemed to lead to nowhere. So he made a right and drove into an area that was remote and shielded by hills that surrounded the location. After two miles, he looked around outside the car and thought it was perfect. Everything was perfect. He had eaten his measured slice of a brownie before he left and it was kicking in right on time as he sensed the blue energy emanating from the top of his head. Vic put on the helmet and leather gloves, then walked away from the car into the desert. He then realized he didn't even know where to start. There was nothing on the Internet or Google about instructions on how a person with supernatural powers fueled by a cannabis brownie could learn to fly. What Vic was able to do was to read some basic flight 101 type articles that explained the basic principles of flight for beginners. He realized that he could use his hands as flaps to create lift, drag or down force and flex his feet or pointing his toes like a tail wing hopefully to stabilize his whole body in the air to help his hands. And then there was the problem of takeoffs and landings, which was what he needed to figure out now, the takeoff.

The logical thing, he thought, was to model what he had been doing with the energy as a weapon and that was to visualize in his mind what he wanted to do. Vic was moving slowly and being careful because it wasn't lost on him that if he got too high in the air and crashed to the ground, there wasn't anyone for miles around that could find him, let alone help him. Monica's words were sticking out in his mind, when he said he would call her first, and she said, "If you're still alive." It's now his moment of truth and staying alive was very much on his mind.

Vic closed his eyes and said a prayer, then said, "My energy is the source," and for whatever reason, he repeated it again. At that moment, a thought and an epiphany came to him that if his power was from the source of all creation, it would protect him from destruction as long as he was working on behalf of the source. A great sense of confidence came over him as he repeated, "My energy is the source," and he focused again, visualizing his take off with blue energy emanating from his feet. As he thought it, he felt himself lifting off the ground. It was crucial now that everything going through his mind was in visual pictures of what he was trying to do. The blue energy had changed its form and color. It wasn't shooting out of his feet like a powerful blue beam exploding rocks and severing tree branches. It was now in a different configuration, with the energy the color of a white light but not in the form of a beam. It was gravity defying, more like electromagnetic energy based on what little he knew about it, but one thing was the same. Whatever he pictured or imagined he could do. At this point, Vic was excited just to be off the ground as he felt himself rising and was comforted by how stable he felt in the air at ninety feet up. He felt like he was standing on a platform of energy. Now he doesn't want to get above the hilltops where someone might be able to see him or worse, get picked up by radar. For now, the little shallow pool of air shielded by the surrounding hills was all he needed.

After thirty minutes of calculations and visualizations, Vic was zipping through the air head first like a torpedo at speeds up to one hundred fifty miles per hour. He knew he was just scratching the surface of how fast he could go, but still aware of the fact that at high speeds he would be like a bug splattering on a windshield if he hit something. Just the thought of stopping in mid-air would cause him to do exactly that, stop. And with that thought in mind, he went faster. Then Vic discovered he could skid to a stop in the air like he used to do on his snowboard by getting his legs out in front of him at a forty-five-degree angle, then use his energy to reverse his polarity or stop—all of this happening in the safe confines of the little desert valley with its cover of yucca plants, cactus, and rocks. Now the urge was to go higher and faster. Within a few seconds, he had decided and shot straight up into the atmosphere at over five hundred miles per hour and slowed to a stop at thirty thousand feet. He could see that he was even with the commercial airliners cruising by out in the distance. The second thing he noticed was how cold and windy it was in the upper atmosphere. There were two things Vic hated in life. One was having to move, and the other was being cold, but the spirit of adventure and exploration pushed him higher to approximately fifty thousand feet. At that height, it was noticeably harder to breathe, and the temperature had dropped even more, but from this vantage point, Vic could see out over the horizon and the curvature of the Earth. He pushed higher to about seventy thousand feet and had to descend. It was a beautiful sight. He could see into outer space, the Americas north and south and Europe, but it was bitterly cold now, and he was feeling light-headed from a lack of oxygen. And there was a warning going off in his head that his blue energy was down to about fifty percent. He immediately turned down head first and descended on an angle at about two hundred miles an hour, taking in the sights as he descended.

In air traffic control at Edwards, the soldier in the control tower was having another routine day when suddenly he sees a blip on the radar screen where there shouldn't be. He called out to his supervising officer. "Captain, sir."

"Yeah, Rick, what do yah got?"

"Looks like an unidentified craft in our restricted air space, sir. It's descending from about seventy thousand feet and now approaching two hundred fifty miles per hour."

"Are you serious?"

"Yes, sir."

"Scramble two F-22's and a couple of black hawks to see what's going on out there.

Vic realized that the rotation of the Earth and his angle of descent had caused him to overshoot his valley location in the desert. At about fifteen thousand feet, he followed Highway 15 back to his location on the desert floor. He knew it wouldn't be smart to fly directly over or near the highway, so he stayed out over the desert, headed back toward Barstow when he noticed two military jets approaching his location, followed by two helicopters out in the distance. He knew he had been spotted by radar and his heart pounded in his chest. His first thought was to get down to the ground and down he went to the desert floor, then into his skid maneuver, touching down on the rocky desert surface. Vic wasn't exactly sure about where he was because of the distraction of the approaching military aircraft, but felt that he wasn't too far from the safety of his little valley further out in the desert. He took two steps and heard the furious shaking of a rattler to his left. It was a huge full grown western diamond back rattlesnake and Vic froze in place as sweat quickly beaded up on his brow. It was coiled and ready to strike. Keeping his arms at his sides, he slowly turned his palm toward the snake that saw the movement and lifted his head to strike. At that moment, Vic hit the rattler with his blue light energy as it sprung toward him with its mouth open and fangs deployed. The rattler was now frozen in place a foot and a half from his left shin. Vic thought *knockout* and a surge of light energy hits the snake with the crackle of an electric cap gun and instantly the reptile's head dropped to the desert floor but was still alive.

He made it out onto a road just as the F-22 fighter jets passed overhead and he turned right and headed back toward Highway 15 to better get a bearing on his exact location. A minute later two black hawk helicopters flew over. As Vic looked up, he saw the copilot looking down at him. He figured that if they were looking for an unidentified aircraft; he didn't have to worry because he didn't have one. It was a three-mile hike getting back to Highway15, but the snake and the walk helped to warm Vic back up, being that he still had frost on his helmet when he landed from his high-altitude flight.

Vic was not happy about the flight. It presented more problems than he had expected with the bitter cold, high winds, and at high speeds, wind gusts smashed into his body like some giant, whacking him with a wooden board. And at five hundred miles per hour, it felt like his arms were being dislocated and that his head could be snapped off by a crosswind. It wasn't the experience he thought it was going to be, and it wasn't fun. It was painful. Vic figured his disappointment was because he had been watching too many superhero movies and thought flying would be like that, but it sucked without a pressurized cabin.

As Vic got up to the highway, he still continued to keep his eyes glued to the sky. The jets had circled back around from the opposite side of the freeway out in the distance at a higher altitude, but he still wasn't sure about the helicopters. He walked up the west side of the freeway headed east back toward Las Vegas; he knew where he was now. Then he heard a jeep and when he turned to look, it was a military jeep with two airmen from Edwards Air Base.

"Hey, buddy, you lost?"

"I was," Vic said.

"Where you headed?"

Vic knew they were probing and he started thinking fast. "Well, I left my car out in the desert north of here and I got lost, so I came out to the highway to get my bearings."

"Looks like you're riding a motorcycle."

"I know, but I forgot my hat and so this helmet is keeping the sun off my head."

"Well, that makes sense," said the soldier on the passenger side. "You need a ride?"

"Sure if you don't mind."

"Not at all."

Vic hopped in the back and explained where the road was up ahead.

"You haven't seen any strange-looking aircraft in the sky today, have you?"

"No, nothing but the two jets that flew by about twenty-five minutes ago."

The airmen nodded and Vic directed them to the dirt road and they drove into the desert the two miles back to Vic's white Explorer.

"Hey, thanks guys, much appreciated."

"Any time, be safe." They turned around and headed back out onto the main road.

Vic knew he had just had a close call. He decided right then that if he was going to fly again, it would be even farther out and far away from any military base. As he drove back to Los Angeles, the more he thought about it, the less desire he had to fly. And then it hit him. What he needed was his own aircraft. Yes, a craft that was powered by his own energy. A UFO made in America sounded so cool, but where would he get the money? *Yes, that part*, he thought. And that part kept him thinking all the way home. Even if he sold a property, he still wouldn't have enough to finish the aircraft. *I will need millions*, he thought. And then he would need someone to build it.

Rhynous, now back on Larus at his remote hideout, was furious. "Who the hell were they and how did they know who we were? Zole!"

"Yes, sir."

"I need you to find out."

"I'm on it, sir."

"Before you go, how many fighters do we have?"

"Three hundred thirty-two, sir, was the last count."

"That should be enough, but we'll see. I'm going to need about two hundred on the next trip. And what is the result of the virus that was planted in China?"

"It has spread all over Earth, just as you said it would."

"Thank you for that report, Zole. They love killing what they call insects and now let's see how they fare. Many of them will not die, but it will be a great distraction. It will cause what they call chaos."

Pogh, who is in the room, asked, "Has the president of the country called America been tethered?"

"Yes, he's being programmed as we speak," Rhynous said. "Kali has done a fantastic job getting into their palace of leadership. The White House is what they call it and Kali has planted a cyber-net. Their understanding of cyberspace is far behind us. They will never figure it out."

"Prefect," said Pogh, a high ranking lieutenant in Rhynous's organization. "I can't wait until you've secured the planet as our new permanent home." Pogh had longed for years to be sent to Earth, the beautiful blue ball with its blue sky and blue waters and perfect temperatures on much of the planet. Its green trees, forests, and rain forests that replenish oxygen levels for the whole planet. A world that had developed into a living organism that regulated and maintained itself with its electromagnetic field as the outer ozone to protect the inhabitants from harmful radiation. *What an amazing place.* Pogh thought, *and its inhabitants take all that for granted or don't care. Others never took time to learn that in their learning facilities and only think about money.* Pogh was unhappy on Larus, out on the far side of the

Zeta Reticuli system with the twin stars being out in the distance and Larus getting its light from a star still undetected by Earth's leading scientist. If their star was detected, it would probably be named Zeta Reticuli 3 as the twin stars are known as Zeta Reticuli 1 and Zeta Reticuli2 on Earth. Pogh was bored of the vast deserts and rocks with only patches of green scattered about the desert belt equator of the planet. Its subzero polar caps provide most of the planet's water source in the summers but the deserts of the desert belt region reach up to one hundred forty degrees in the warmer parts of their year. The air was thin and could be a challenge when exerting one's self. Pogh longed for the abundance of Earth.

In New Orleans, Monica Deloche was concerned about Vic and how his maiden voyage flight went. She put out a telepathic message: *Call me.*

Now at home, Vic stopped cutting up the second brownie he bought as the overwhelming feeling to call Monica came over him. He knew he was being summoned as he picked up his phone.

Monica's phone rang and she knew it was him not through telepathy but because his name and number came up on the phone. "You said you were going to call me after your flight. What happened?"

Vic was expecting a "Hello," but said, "I said you would be the first person called if I crashed. I didn't crash, so I didn't call, but it's you. So, I would have called you tonight, anyway."

"Oh, okay. Do you want me to wait until tonight?"

"Not at all. I would have called you driving in from the desert, but I was deep in thought."

"About what?"

"Look, I flew well for the first time out, but it was harsh. The weather in the upper atmosphere is hard on the body. Even at lower elevations your unprotected. Hell, you could run into a tree, but what do you think about this? I need an aircraft that is powered by electromagnetic energy."

"It sounds like a UFO."

"Exactly! You got it. A UFO built in America or Europe."

"Who can build such a craft? And where would you get the money?"

"Now that's why I didn't call you, because I was trying to answer those exact questions. Right now, I'm obsessed with those questions."

"Why don't you ask Clayvious?"

"That's what I was preparing to do when you hit me up telepathically. It was so strong that I had to stop everything and call you."

"Oh, well I'm sorry, you're busy. I shouldn't have bothered you."

"I'm glad you did. You just confirmed everything I'm planning to do."

"Okay, well, go ahead and do what you need to do and I'll talk to you later."

"Okay, delicious, I mean, Monica. I'll call you later and let you know what we come up with."

"Okay, funny boy, talk to you later. Bye."

Now feeling charged after talking to Monica, Vic popped a thin slice of brownie in his mouth and waited for it to kick in, excited to share this idea with Clayvious.

An hour and a half later, Vic felt the euphoria and the blue energy. He immediately pressed into Clayvious's dimension.

Clayvious was now in the open court area with his men working on strike tactics and maneuvers in a precision exercise, preparing for the battle to come. Clayvious felt Vic's presence and looked at the membrane on the far side of this open area. In an unusual display, Clayvious waved for Vic to come inside the membrane. Strangely, instead of opening it with his blue energy, Vic walked into it and pressed through, leaving him with the sensation of nonstick gel and plastic that allowed him to the other side, but he knew it was still the blue energy.

Still pumped, Vic shouted, "Clay! Good to see you, man." He grabbed Clayvious's shoulder as they shook hands; he felt the morbid cold of Clayvious's skin.

Clayvious chuckled. "Someone's in a good mood. What's on your mind, young man?"

"I need your help."

"Okay, what is it?"

"I went out and flew for the first time today. Yes, I can fly."

This proclamation garnered the attention of all Clayvious's men, who looked on with pleasant surprise and applause. They realized that Vic's powers were growing by leaps and bounds.

"Hold on, guys. Let me finish. I hated it. I was too cold and beat up when I landed."

Clayvious and his men were surprised, releasing mumbles of curiosity.

"Guys, what I need is an aircraft."

The men let out a cheer.

"Clay, my problem is that I don't have the money to build it."

"How much money will you need?"

"Millions," Vic said as though he were talking about a few hundred bucks.

Clayvious laughed. "So you need me to help you acquire these resources?"

"Yes!" Vic said with humble excitement.

Clayvious looked at Vic in thought. "I've only done this for one other person back in the time of the great Roman Empire. I went into the future to help a friend win a chariot race. So perhaps I could do it for you to win a horse race and make the money that way."

Vic now looked at Clayvious as though he were a goose who had just laid a golden egg with more eggs to come. "You could go into the future?"

"Yes, but it's not without limits. I could only go forward three days and I have to make sure that whatever got altered doesn't harm society, nations, or the planet."

Vic's brain was now in a swirl of ideas. "I understand we can't change something that would create a disaster. I got it! I'll play the lottery!"

"What's the lottery?"

"It's a game that people pay into across the country and then on a certain day they drop balls with random numbers on them. If your ticket has all the numbers, you win all the money, millions."

Clayvious looked Vic straight in the eye. "That's called cheating you know."

Vic responded without missing a beat. "That's called cheating to help save the world. I think that serves the greater good because our energy is the source and the source is who we're fighting for."

"Well said, my friend. What do I need to do?"

"You're going to go into a store that plays Powerball and ask them for the winning numbers from the previous day. Then you return to our time, and that will give me a day and a half to play those numbers."

"That's it?"

"That's all. It's just that simple."

"Very well then."

Vic looked at the calendar on his phone. "The next draw is this Saturday, so you'll need to go forward in time this coming Thursday and that will take you to Sunday the day after the lottery draw. Then you return with the numbers."

Clayvious nodded and his men stood amused in good spirits. "Okay, men, back to work. We must be ready for this enemy."

Vic took that as his cue. "Thank you, Clay. This will greatly help our cause. I'll see you on Friday."

"Okay, and then we must go to Larus to speak with their leaders."

"Absolutely," Vic said with enthusiasm. He then waved to the men and gave Clayvious a thumbs up as he passed back through the membrane.

CHAPTER 16

On Friday morning, Vic returned to Clayvious's dimension, curious about how he would get to the future even if it was only three days ahead. Vic opened the membrane, this time with his blue energy. He hadn't particularly liked the feel of the unknown gel type material on his face nor the scrap of what seemed to be hard plastic.

Clayvious was waiting for him on the court yard. "You ready?"

Vic nodded. "Yes, let's do it."

"Okay, we're going to Bluebird Liquor in Hawthorne."

"Okay, how do I get there?"

"If I take you there, can you get to the future from my dimension?" Vic asked.

"Yes, I can."

"Good. Let's head over to my side and drive over to Hawthorne."

Vic and Clayvious passed back through the membrane into the house and then to the garage. They jumped into the car and headed to the liquor store. Once there, Vic said, "Here we are. This is it."

Clayvious went over the request for the numbers and got out of the car. He looked up and down the street, then headed south and turned left at the first corner. Vic got out of the car to see where Clayvious went. He got to the corner in time to see a quiet side street and Clayvious walking into a swirling time warp, then disappearing. Vic then understood that Clayvious didn't want to walk into a vortex on a busy street and create a scene, so he headed back to the car and waited. Twenty minutes later, Clayvious returned and pulled out a strip of lottery paper for Power Ball with the numbers: 14, 26, 38, 45, 46, and the Power Ball number of 13.

Vic was excited. "Clay, great job. Let me run in and see what the dollar amount is up to." Vic ran in and back out a minute later with eyes as big as silver dollars.

"How much?" Clayvious asked.

"Four hundred ten million dollars," Vic said in complete shock. He then remembered that he had a lottery app on his phone. When he opened it, there was an icon for Power Ball that also showed the estimated cash value at three hundred twenty-nine million and seven hundred thousand dollars.

Clayvious, with a straight face, said, "That's a bit less. Will it be enough?"

Vic looked at Clayvious, realizing he was serious, and laughed.

Clayvious looked at him with a serious face. "What's so funny?"

Vic laughed harder and then uncontrollably with tears coming out of his eyes. It became infectious and Clayvious, too, laughed. Vic finally calmed down with an aching side.

"You want to let me in on it?"

"Yes!" Vic said. "Clay, this is more money than we'll ever need unless we become stricken with a disease called greed. I take it you don't use money a whole lot?"

"No, not now. I haven't used money in a thousand years and back then we bartered half the time."

It now dawned on Vic that Monica was right. Clayvious and his men were not living beings as they knew it, but he didn't want to ask Clayvious or broach the topic, quickly changing the subject. "So, Clayvious, do you now understand why I thought it was so funny when you asked me if it was enough money? And you were so serious."

"I get it, I'm clueless." Clayvious chuckled again.

"Yes, but it's nice for me to be able to teach you something," Vic said.

"And you did, my friend. I'm learning a lot."

When they got back to the house, Vic pulled into the garage and shut the garage door as soon as they pulled in. He and Clayvious walked into the house and Clayvious stopped in the dining room area and looked around.

"So, this is where you came into the knowledge."

"Yes, I was sitting right there on a stool when you broke through."

"Well, I know it may have appeared that way," Clayvious said. "But you actually appeared in our dimension first. You may not have planned it that way but that's what happened. You looked like you were in a trance and I snapped you out of it."

"You sure did. I thought you were going to kill me."

"I couldn't! You were there as an astral traveler, not in the flesh. And I don't kill people because they don't understand things of the spirit or that they were created in the image of the source who created man in the image of himself. Making that creation a god man."

"That's good to know. I mean, the part about not killing people for the lack of understanding."

"By the way, did you notice anything about your last visit to my dimension?"

" No, what?"

"You were there in the flesh."

"Really! I didn't even realize it. How is that possible?"

"Because it was still you either way. In the astral you could see, smell, and hear in spirit form. The difference is your ability to physically feel. Did you feel anything coming through the membrane this last time?"

"Yes." Vic had an incredulous, eye opening look on his face as though he had just received knowledge from a higher source, and he had.

"I noticed the look in your eyes when you touched my arm earlier. It was similar to the look of your lady friend a few nights ago at our meeting. My men and I are spirits of our former selves, but our alien origins allow us the ability to generate flesh, but it is not living as you know it. And because it is not living, it cannot be killed. This is another part of our powers."

Vic stood there in amazement. "That's amazing."

"I'll share more with you in the coming days, but we must prepare to meet with the leaders of Larus."

"Okay, as soon as we get the results of the lottery, I'll be ready to go. Hey, tomorrow."

"Very well, I'll look to hear from you then." Clayvious walked to the wall near the staircase and with a wave of his hand, it appeared to liquefy in a rubbery kind of way just before he walked through it. Once through, the wall solidified quickly, leaving Vic standing there in disbelief and exhilarated in a way he had never been in his life. He knew he'd have a hard time sleeping tonight but also that if those numbers came through tomorrow, this would be as real as real could get.

The next day, Vic woke up after struggling for half the night to get to sleep. He got up and the first thing on his mind, he thought oddly, was whether he needed to pack any clothes for the trip to another planet. Somehow, he felt the answer was no. So instead, he put his tooth brush in his jacket pocket. His next thought was to call Monica. Then the phone rang.

"Hello."

"You were getting ready to call me so I thought I'd beat you to the punch," Monica said.

"Very impressive, but get a load of this. You were right about Clay. He shared with me yesterday that he and his men are spirits that could manifest themselves in flesh but not living like us. And because it's not living, they can't be killed." There was silence on the phone.

"What!"

"Yeah, that's what he—"

"That's amazing," Monica said, interrupting him.

"Yep, that's what I said. And I found out that Clay could travel three days into the future."

"Really?"

"Yes, and we're working on raising the money for the aircraft. I'll let you know how that went when I get back."

"How long are you guys going to be gone?"

"I don't know. I don't even know how we're going to get there, but I'll keep you posted. I've got to go, things to do."He kissed the phone, making a big suction sound. "I'll be there when we get back, for the real thing."

" I'll be waiting for the real thing."

The arousal and the attraction were magnetic but Vic said his goodbye and continued taking care of things that he needed to get done. He continued with his mundane duties around the house, paying bills, washing dishes, watering the grass, and washing clothes. The last thing he did was to cut up the rest of the second brownie into sixteenths and put them in a plastic baggie, then popping a square in his mouth before closing it up.

It was now 6:00 p.m., two hours before the Power Ball draw. It was almost too much excitement and anticipation of possibly becoming a multi-millionaire and then shortly after taking off to another planet light years away. Vic couldn't share any of this with anyone who would think him sane except for Monica. This time the phone didn't ring, so he called her cell number. To his surprise, she didn't answer. He figured that she was busy at the shop and sent her a telepathic message that he knew she would get. He continued to prepare for his departure and when he had finished his last task, it was quarter to eight in the evening. Vic was glad that he had been able to focus on those things that needed to be done because time had passed quickly in his mind and now there were only a few minutes until the draw.

He turned on the TV, looked for the channel that covered the draw with the numbered balls falling into place. Being unable to find the channel, Vic relaxed, remembering the lottery app on his phone. At five minutes after eight, he opened the app, clicked on the Power Ball icon, and was stunned at what he saw. Now frozen in disbelief, he couldn't understand his disappointment. It didn't make any sense. All the numbers were a match and he should be jumping with joy, but he wasn't. He felt a sense of accomplishment, but it dawned on him that the weight of responsibility was already heavy and the millions that he had just won only added to it. He got up off the couch and let out a loud Tiger Woods, *"Yes!"* with a fist pump. Vic took the winning ticket to his man cave and locked it in his desk drawer. He then returned to the living room now with his blue energy blooming and simply disappeared from the living room into Clayvious's dimension.

There he was, standing outside the membrane. This time, he decided to look around and there was only darkness and a feeling of nothingness. He looked down to see what he was standing on and it was dirt. In Vic's mind, dirt was just dirt, but this looked like ancient soil. When he looked up, Clayvious was standing there watching him from the other side of the membrane. Vic opened it with his energy and walked in to greet Clayvious.

"It looks like you have questions about what that is out there."

"Yes, I do. What is it?"

"That is infinity, a continuum of nothing, emptiness and darkness."

"So, how did you guys get here?"

"We are a band of brothers in arms placed here by, as you call it, the source. And why did you appear to us when you were sitting on that stool in your living room? I didn't do it, and you had no control of it, and yet here we are. Just know this, we're here for a reason and it's bigger than we are. This struggle of good and evil stretches throughout the universe and we're going to play a big role here on Earth. Just know there are like-minded beings on other planets that are fighting the same battle against dark-minded villains like Rhynous. That's why we need to get to Larus and speak with their leaders. Are you ready to go?"

"Yes, but how are we going to get there?"

"Good question. Follow me. "Clayvious led Vic to a room with ancient block walls and an archway filled in with pure gold. Clayvious touched the precious metal, and it began to glow.

"What is this?" Vic asked in fear and wonderment.

"This is an ancient teleportation device."

"Well, how does it know where we're going?"

"It only goes to one place—Larus. Take your hand and grab the back of my belt." Vic puts his hand inside Clayvious's belt. "That will keep us from separating. You're going to feel like you're being sucked in by a cyclone, but that sensation will go away inside the light beam."

Vic was now overwhelmed with excitement and fear. He said nothing, only nodded. Vic walked in behind Clayvious and felt him jerk forward. If Vic's hand had not been in Clayvious's belt line, they surely would have been separated. Suddenly, they were traveling at an incredible rate of speed. After a while, though they had not slowed down, the sensation of incredibly high speed dissipated and Vic began to look around, seeing stars and planets moving past quickly. His next thought was to look back and see Earth. He couldn't believe how far they had traveled in such a short time. Earth was so small, but he noticed their trajectory was from south of the equator as Zeta Reticuli is in the southern hemisphere and only visible from south of Mexico City. Inside the beam of light, it was quite comfortable in temperature, and Vic marveled at how they seemed to stay centered in the beam with plenty of oxygen. And though he had adjusted to the sensation of speed, he loved the feel of going fast and the shimmering of the stars, so many stars and planets in the dark vacuum of space. Such a beautiful and magnificent sight, yet a desert of dangerous airless void passing them by.

Three hours had passed and the twin stars of Zeta Reticuli were so close and a sight to see but they soon had passed the twin stars and shot faster than the speed of light to the far end of the Reticuli system. As they passed a giant lifeless planet, the unknown third star came into view with three planets in its orbit. The second planet out was orange, white and green. White on the polar ends, and green splotches some the size of California and Texas separated by stretches of orange deserts and canyons. Then starting at about the latitude of

Guatemala City in the north down to what would be on Earth, the middle of Brazil was an orange band of desert around the equator of the whole planet. Then back to green splotches and polar cap in its southern hemisphere. The light beam they were traveling in was headed straight for it.

Clayvious shouted, "There's Larus!"

It was different, and it was spectacular sitting in the habitable zone of this hidden Reticuli system.

"Get ready! Clayvious shouted. "We're going to be pushed out, the way we were sucked in."

Suddenly Vic could see a glowing archway at the end of the light beam and the thought of being burned by it went through his mind, but before he could think twice, they were through it. Their momentum thrust them forward as though they had been on a fast moving escalator. Clayvious took three steps forward to stop his momentum. Vic, not having experienced it before, stumbled but didn't fall with the support of his hand clutching Clayvious's belt. Vic regained his balance and when he looked up, there were four Larians standing in front of them.

His heart pounded as they did not look like humans, but were still humanoid with arms and legs. The Larians'pale white skin almost seemed to glow without pigment and their contrasting big black eyes but round, unlike the Grays. And their big round heads with no hair, small ears with small noses and mouths. Clayvious put his right hand in the center of his chest and bowed. The Larians did the same and Vic, understanding quickly that this was their customary greeting, followed suit. After the greeting, the Larians gestured in a way that let Vic know they were glad to see Clayvious. This put Vic a little more at ease, but as he looked around, he realized they were in a great hall of a building with what appeared to be brown marble pillars and a domed ceiling. When he looked back down, two of the Larians were still gesturing with Clayvious but the two behind them were just staring at Vic, who's heart was still pounding in his chest in fear of these alien beings. Then they were led to a glass cubical.

"What's going on?" Vic asked.

"We have to be scanned, just relax."

Once inside, the cubical metal probes swung into place, one in front of them and one behind them.

"Close your eyes and open your hands with your palms facing forward," Clayvious said.

When both men had closed their eyes, Vic felt a warm light scanning them from head to toe, front and back. The scan finished quickly, and they were led out of the cubical with the front two Larians walking with Clayvious and the back two, who were still waiting. When Vic came out, he looked at them, his heart still pounding. Then the Larians reached out and touched him. One of them taking Vic's hand and the other putting his hand on Vic's chest and the opposite hand on his shoulder. Miraculously, they were communicating through touch. Vic felt their intentions, their emotions, and their thoughts. In an instant, he knew they were kind and there to help him. His heart stopped pounding. He felt it was the strangest thing. He looked at their differences on the outside, but when they touched him and communicated who they were on the inside, he realized they were just beings doing their job. And somehow, he knew so much more about them. That they had families, enjoyed having fun with their friends and were responsible beings. He knew they were aliens, not earthlings, but the only way he could rationalize it in his mind was that they were just good beings trying to do their job and make sure he was okay. His heart was no longer pounding, and he was getting past an out of this world, culture shock. Vic had been so deep in thought and mesmerized by how they had communicated through touch that he had just realized that not one word had been spoken by the Larians.

They were now following Clayvious across the great floor when he noticed that all the Larians wore white futuristic space suits but were close fitting with a shiny finish and Nehru collars. They were led up one flight of stairs, then to the left down a long hallway to a room where the leaders of Larus awaited them. Once in the room, there were four leaders who were in charge of the whole planet. Each leader was responsible for one-quarter of the planet. They were older and wiser, with the whole room reeking of intelligence beyond what Vic could totally comprehend. It was a humbling experience. In the room was a large round table made of a material that looked like wood, but it wasn't. Vic couldn't tell if it was made of stone or plastic, but more importantly, there was a white domed light shaped like a small platter cover. To his surprise, there were what appeared to be speakers on tall stands against the opposite wall. Somehow, this was comforting for Vic, a reminder of home. Clayvious, who was next to Vic, tapped him on the arm and as Clayvious put his right hand over his chest, Vic did the same and they bowed together. The leaders who were already seated did the same and one of them stretched his arm out toward them and lowered it, signaling them to have a seat. The leaders looked as if they were talking to each other as they were looking at each other and gesturing, but not a word was spoken.

Clayvious bent over. "If you decide to say something, you're going to put your hands on the light and speak softly in an even tone."

Vic nodded and looked back to the leaders for what happened next.

One leader put his hand on the light and it got extremely bright. Then a smile seemed to come across his small mouth and with his lips still sealed, his voice came through the speakers. "Welcome, Clayvious. It has been hundreds of years since our last meeting. It is good to see you. And welcome to your friend."

Vic bowed his head in a humble gesture of thanks.

The leader's voice was calm and clear but wise and regal. "Though it is good to see you, we know this must be a serious matter. When we were notified that your teleport had been activated from your chamber, we began to speculate on what it could be. Please share with us what has prompted you to travel across the galaxy."

Clayvious nodded, his hand over his chest. "Great leaders of Larus, thank you for making time in your schedule but I do have grave news. Earth is under attack and is in danger of being destroyed. The alien being, leading this effort is bent on a nuclear war and is using mind control on the United States president through cyberspace and once he has broken the planet, he will take control of all monetary systems for himself and enslave all Earthlings who survive the blast and ensuing radiation. This is someone you know well, Rhynous."

The leaders, their aides, and the diplomats who had greeted them at the teleport, all let out a tragic moan. It sounded like a group that had swallowed helium with high pitched moans as they held their heads in their hands and were clearly upset. It was an embarrassment to them and they wanted more details.

Clayvious filled them in then asked if they knew the location of his hideout.

Leader 1 spoke. "This is terrible news that a Larian is responsible for this horrific plan against a beautiful planet like Earth, with all of its abundance and oceans. We have been working together as leaders of the four quadrants of Larus to capture and jail this cosmic outlaw. As you know, we have a split eco system here with a desert that surrounds the whole planet on either side of our equator. There are millions of miles of nothing but sand, dirt and canyons with cave systems that go for miles, and because of that, he has been able to evade our forces. They fly very low to avoid our electromagnetic detection system that works the same way your radar does on Earth. And when we find a craft in the desert belt, by the time we get out there, he's nowhere to be found."

"I have something that may help," Clayvious said. "I had an encounter with Rhynous and implanted a microchip tracking device in his arm. If he's here, we could find him."

The Larians were now conversing among themselves telepathically, but their body language was now energized. This revelation had given them hope. A message had been shared with Leader 1 and they all seemed to be in agreement. "Clayvious, would it be possible to take you on a reconnaissance mission tomorrow in hopes of finding him somewhere in the desert belt?"

"I think that's an excellent idea, "Clayvious said. All the Larians clapped and leaned their heads forward in a gesture of gratitude. "Our diplomats will arrange for your sleeping quarters and meals. We will meet again here before you depart."

Clayvious nodded, then he and Vic were escorted out.

As they walked down the hallway from the direction they had come in, the word had spread that there were aliens from Earth in the building. So, on the way out, it was more of a circus atmosphere. There were federation workers and some from off the street, news reporters who carried a white device that was square and flat with a black circle on it. They later found out that it was a communication device that sent stories and pictures to the population around the whole planet of Larus.

The diplomats led Clayvious and Vic out to the street where there was no traffic, only a large futuristic looking two-car train that was actually a public transportation vehicle. It had no wheels and hovered a foot off the ground with no sound. One of Vic's diplomats took his hand and immediately Vic knew they were getting on the transportation vehicle headed to where he and Clayvious would be staying.

This was the first time Vic had been outside and the first thing he noticed was his difficulty in breathing. It reminded him of his first trip to Florida on a summer's day with humidity so thick in the air you could cut it with a knife. Vic had to heave for air until he had adjusted to the southern Florida atmosphere. Larus wasn't as bad as Florida, but there would be a longer adjustment period because the air wasn't thick, it was thinner. And though that was the case, it wasn't so bad that he needed to worry about it. The most noticeable thing was the heat. It felt like the temperature was well over one hundred degrees. Like an Arizona summer, but for Larians it was an average temperate day. Vic now understood the Larian's white outfits and saw how it reflected the rays of the sun, causing their suits to glow. When he looked up at the sun, it was as though the intensity and brightness of it had slapped him in the face, forcing him to look away. Vic put his hand up to shield his eyes and what he saw was astounding, a huge sun two or three times the size of Earth. And in their northern hemisphere were the twin stars of Zeta Reticuli appearing larger than an average star at about half the size of our moon on Earth but too far to affect the temperature on Larus. What an exotic sight, seeing three suns during the day. And strange looking trees but lush and some looked familiar like huge banana plants, palms, and giant fern plants.

The doors suddenly opened on the transportation vehicle. What Vic learned, through touch, was that it was called a pod. The doors opened like the gills on a shark with lines of Larians at each door, one human, and an alien Earthling ghost hybrid. A part of the Larians were the descendants of the Martin alien transplants whose forefathers had survived the destruction of civilization on mars, these were Rhynous's people. And though they were his people, they were nothing like him. They were hard working and good natured beings who spoke in their own language but who also had telepathic abilities. Which allowed them to harmoniously co-exist with the Larians.

As they all boarded, the individuals first in line walked past the first seats, past the center aisle and into the far seats on the other side of the pod. Everyone was able to get aboard. And as the doors were closing, a red light came on centered above the driver and front wind shield as a warning to clear the doors and once they were closed, the light turned green. Vic was now very comfortable with his diplomatic guides and had started gesturing like Clayvious to ask questions and in doing so he had hardly noticed the smooth acceleration of the electromagnetically powered pod that was moving quietly and briskly down the street emitting only a slight hum. It was like floating on air, and Vic marveled at the sensation and the technology. He was now preoccupied with looking out the window, trying to see as much as he could. Vic saw no individual cars on the street, only other pods and the buildings were very futuristic and some organic looked seemingly made out of a rough finishing material like sponge but harder. Many of the buildings were round instead of rectangle and others were round domes or shaped like teardrops with very dark tinted windows. As the pod made its way through what appeared to be downtown, it stopped and the guides led Clayvious and Vic off the pod and into a round building. It appeared to be like a downtown condo structure full of residents, not workers.

Once inside, it seemed to be very similar to buildings on Earth except that the elevators were outside of the units in the form of clear plastic tubes, stopping at each floor and moving much faster than they do on Earth. Inside the building on the first floor, there were trees growing and lush plants. They were led to the 5th floor and down to a unit that would be their quarters for the night. The diplomats showed them around the unit and left a device to contact them if the guys needed anything. It had been an incredible day.

Vic now had a ton of questions for Clayvious. "This is unbelievable! I can't believe I'm even here. I can't wait to tell—" Then Vic realized he wouldn't be able to tell anyone. It was too outrageous, too far out and people would think him insane.

Clayvious looked at Vic and smiled. "What you know now would require a top secret clearance on Earth. No one would believe you. Oh, there is one, our team member, Monica. She is the only one who would believe you, but the rest of the world will not. And you don't want to draw the attention of your government on Earth." Clayvious's words left Vic in deep thought and he quickly grasped the reality of Clayvious's truth. Vic always thought that if he ever had a close encounter of the third kind, he would wave and shout out in a friendly voice, "Hello. Welcome." He would try to communicate, but this was an encounter of the fifth kind, face-to-face communication. The truth of the matter was that when he stumbled out of the teleport, he was petrified. Scared out of his wits, heart beating uncontrollably, and hardly able to move, Vic now understood why the United States government and black operation programs have hidden and refused to confirm the existence of UFOs to the American people and the world. They knew many people couldn't handle the truth. Hell, some people had a big problem with other humans being different from them. God forbid it be aliens from another planet. Who were far more intelligent by thousands of years with technology that surpassed Earth and who looked far more different from someone from another country. Right now, some humans couldn't even handle someone with a different political opinion. No way could they handle this reality.

Clayvious said, "You're in another one of those trances, eyes open but no one home. What's on your mind?"

"Well, I was just thinking about what you said and I agree, people back on Earth aren't ready for what we know."

"That's very astute of you to figure it out that quickly."

'I still have a ton of questions for you, Clay."

"Okay, can I lie down while you're asking me? I'm two thousand years old you know."

"Oh, yes, by all means. I'll pull up a chair."

Clayvious stretched out on his bed and moaned a sigh of relief.

Vic started in. "Clay, how did we get here so fast? It just seems impossible."

"Their technology and scientific knowledge make it possible. Not only was their light beam moving faster than the speed of light, it was also folding space."

"I've heard of it, but I still don't completely understand the concept of folding space."

Clayvious's eyes were closed. "Keep in mind I'm a general, not a scientist, but in simple terms here's a visual. If we had a big balloon and we put Earth on one side of the balloon and Larus on the other side, the balloon now represents outer space between the two planets. Are you following me?"

"Yes, yes."

"Okay, so if we take our hands and push the sides of the balloon together with just a little space between, you could see that we have pushed the two worlds closer together."

"Wow, that's great! I get it! That's like compressing space or squishing it out of the way. How is that possible?"

"Well even scientists on Earth are discovering from some of Einstein's theories that space may be more like a fabric that could be pressed and squeezed, drawing two planets closer if you have the technology to do it. And the Larians have the technology."

"Wow, that's incredible."

"And why is there a desert band around their planet?"

"That's a good question. The Larians don't have any oceans on this planet. They only have lakes that are created from the polar caps and that water is plentiful down to a certain point on their globe. It's extremely hot here and as it got further away from the polar caps, it got stored by the Larians in ocean sized tanks underground and the rest evaporates when it got to the center of the planet, north and south of their equator. Oh, and it tastes like ice cream."

"What! The water?"

"Yes, there's some in the storage unit, check it out."

Vic, being a lover of ice cream, stormed out of Clay's bedroom and into the main room to see an area that looked like a kitchen. He didn't recognize any of the equipment or their function, so he just started opening things like a bear in search of honey. There was a black cylinder that looked like a futuristic trash can about waist high. When his hand got close, it opened on its own and was loaded with food and water. Vic was hungry, but had to taste the water first. It was amazing. When he tasted the first mouth full it was like he had been touched by one of the Larians. It was sweet but had the taste of pure mountain water and Vic was hit with the noticeable smell of pines from a pine tree and a vision of a beautiful clear lake, a soft blue. Its shores overflowed into streams and the streams into rivers that created other lakes. Once the water cleared his throat, the vision disappeared. It was unbelievable, but it didn't taste like ice cream. Vic strolled back into Clay's room to raise hell but Clayvious had fallen fast asleep. Vic smiled and closed the door, realizing he had been tricked, and headed back to the kitchen area to try some Larian food, chuckling as he went.

CHAPTER 17

The next morning, Vic was dreaming about being in a faraway place, seeing and learning new things. It was the most exciting time of his life and it was exhilarating. Then there was a voice in the distance, or was it a siren? As it got louder, Vic woke up and his Larian diplomats were standing at the side of the bed. They smiled and waved for him to follow them. The guide he had been communicating with the previous day pointed to his wrist, which meant it was time to go. Vic nodded and as they were leaving the room, he jumped from the bed that was like a thick layer of padded foam on legs. There had only been a thin folded sheet that felt like paper that he used as a cover, with the heat that was all he needed. Vic dressed quickly, knowing it was going to be an exciting day. He went into the small adjacent room that he assumed was the bathroom. There was no mirror, but it did have a unit that looked like a toilet. Any matter that fell into it was zapped by some kind of laser, turning it into dust and sucking it out by air down a pipe. There was a small sink that emitted a small amount of water. Vic cupped some in his hand and threw it on his face and rubbed it in, then dried his face with his t-shirt. The water that went down the drain was also zapped by a laser. He wasn't sure where it went or where the shower was if there was one, but he knew he had to go.

When he came out of his room, a Larian pointed to a device. Vic looked at Clayvious for direction.

"He wants you to put your hands in there," Clayvious said.

Vic put his hands into what seemed like a clear plastic box with two holes for each wrist and an outline of Larian hands opened, facing down. Then there was a beep, and a light scanned his hands. When he pulled them out, his hands felt fresh and clean. The Larians clapped and smiled, then led Clayvious and Vic out of the housing unit and down to a waiting pod.

"We're headed to the federation airport facility," Clayvious said.

"Okay, do you know what time it is?" Vic asked.

"Yes, it's day time and early."

Vic smiled because he knew Clayvious didn't know and thought his retort was funny.

As they walked out of the facility, the pale blue, almost white sky had no sun overhead, still hidden by the surrounding buildings. The air was slightly warm but it was good to feel a breeze. The doors swung open as they approached the hovering pod. This time it was only a one car pod the size of a bus and empty, so they sat near the front. When they sat and the doors shut, it quickly accelerated without any G forces pulling them back into their seats. And then there was the floating sensation and Vic smiled. As they got to the last buildings heading out of town, there was a hill with the road swinging up and around the side of it. Then down the other side with the huge sun stretching across the horizon, casting its hue of orange. As they shot through the outskirts of town into the countryside, there was dry-looking grass and rolling hills dotted with homes. The houses were all round domes, some above the ground with some below the surface. Then there were the homes that sat above the ground supported by a large round support cylinder that housed stairs or an elevator that looked like a round wheel of cheese on a platter. Some of these homes had small swimming pools under them that avoided direct sun light. They were all white and had metallic coverings on top that generated solar energy.

One of the Larian diplomats was staring at the driver, who turned and looked back for two-tenths of a second, then accelerated the pod to what seemed like over two hundred miles per hour. Vic realized they had spoken telepathically. They were soon out of a planned area, then over a ridge and into a valley. Coming down the hill, Vic could see aircraft landing and taking off. They looked like UFOs from a distance glowing a bright white in the sun. Then they rose straight up into a hovering position and then took off at incredible speeds in mid-air. Some took off slower and others were even faster than the previously mentioned, being gone in the blink of an eye. Vic could see huge domed buildings from a distance but as they got closer, he realized they were aircraft, mother ships. The highway they were on led to an exit road that took them to a long building that separated them from the side where the alien craft were taking off. Vic's heart was pounding again, but this time not from fear, it was pure excitement. The building looked like a long loaf of tapered onyx with its black windows and black sidings.

Once inside, the place was abuzz with Larians hustling about with black suits on, some in white, and others in silver fitted looked space suits. All the attention seemed to be suddenly directed at Clayvious. The average Larian was five feet tall but taller than the average gray. The fact that Clayvious was an alien and six-foot-five was causing a stir. They were holding his hand and touching him then waving. Our diplomats were at a clear domed counter checking them in when one turned and saw the commotion. He ran over to extract Clayvious from the situation like a Hollywood agent. Clayvious seemed to be enjoying the attention with a big smile on his face. Then Vic noticed Clayvious's attention on something else as his smile faded in the amusement of what he was seeing. Vic turned to look and saw four Larian diplomats leading a group of six Grays to a counter. They later found out that the Grays were headed to the federation building to meet with the four Larian leaders. It was interesting to see the Larians standing next to the Grays and their physical differences. Those being height, shape of the eyes, and skin color. Larians were white like paint or snow and the Grays had more of a grayish quality to their skin. They the Grays seemed to be all business, and the Larians seemed to have happier looking faces, but telepathic communication between Larians and the Grays seemed to bind them as they nodded and gestured.

Clayvious and Vic had now been cleared to board a federation craft and headed over to an elevator and down to, what we call on Earth, the apron. Only one of the diplomats escorted them down, the other three stayed in the terminal. When they walked out, a large craft was taking off. There was only a humming sound and as the hum increased in pitch and frequency, one could see heat being emitted from the bottom of the craft from the heat waves but no clear propulsion or sign of an engine. Then the craft elevated to about five hundred feet in the air. A back panel opened up, sliding to the side like a hangar door as the huge domed silvery mother ship hovered. Then suddenly, five smaller craft, that were more noticeable on Earth as UFOs began to take off as Clayvious and Vic watched from about seventy yards, back near the terminal. One by one they flew into the hangar door of the mother ship. It was a sight to see. Clayvious and Vic were touched on the shoulder by the diplomat and it was conveyed that this was a federation exploration ship on its way to another planet.

Vic, wanting to make sure he wasn't making it up in his own head, asked, "Hey, Clay, was it just communicated to you that this is an exploration ship?"

"Sure was," Clayvious said.

Vic looked at his guide and the diplomat gave him a thumbs up and patted him on the back. Clayvious laughed and Vic smiled, thinking. *That's amazing.* And after that thought, the diplomat nodded. Vic knew then the guide could hear his thoughts and then came another revelation. That Larians could read a thought wave or sound wave pattern. And then communicate with the same brain waves, or through touch for the less evolved beings like Earthlings. Again, Vic looked at his guide, the diplomat, who this time clapped and patted Vic on the back again, letting Vic know he was figuring it out. Suddenly, Vic no longer felt any barrier in communication, so he thought, *What's your name?*

Kamu, came back as a thought.

226

A Larian walked up and looked at Kamu, who then touched Clayvious and Vic, letting them know that this was their pilot. They followed him to a smaller craft similar to the ones on the mother ship. As they walked the length of the building, they passed the Grays, getting ready to board another small craft like the one they were about to board . Vic now felt good about himself, and decided to wave at the Grays. Three stared, one saluted, and the two at the end waved back. It was a fifty-fifty response, but Vic hoped that maybe in some small way it was a positive step forward in galactic relations.

The aircraft they would be on was near the end of the apron just past the Grays and though it was a smaller craft, it was much bigger than it looked from seventy yards away. It was standing on four legs and seemed to be made out of something like stainless steel, but stronger. The staircase had been let down from the bottom of the craft and was ready to board, but instead of walking up the stairs, Vic walked around the saucer in amazement and looked for an engine. All he saw were three round metal balls the size of a car tire in circumference and no exhaust. Vic was baffled. He knew now that all the leaked reports and rumors were true that the propulsion on UFOs was electromagnetic.

As he continued looking up to study the bottom of the craft, Kamu came over and took him by the arm and led him up the stairs into the airship. Vic was informed that they were on a schedule. Once on the craft, Vic realized he was on a lower level of the saucer as they walked around a center shaft with a sealed door that led to the propulsion system. As they walked to the right, Vic noticed a station on the outer side of the circular walkway with buttons and some sort of advanced computer system with symbols. He didn't understand, but he was trying to take it all in. Just past that was another staircase leading up to the flight deck. As Vic went up the stairs, he could see down through the spaces between the steps that there were seats and more equipment in front below.

Coming up the stairs and into the flight deck, Vic noticed Clayvious hunched over as his six-foot-five-inch frame was too tall for the cabin but he, too, was curious about the ship and the console that stretched out before him. There were two windows and a seat in front of each window. Vic's interpretation was a pilot and co-pilot configuration. To the outside of those two seats were two more seats flanking the front two, but to the outside near the wall of the cabin. Then six feet of open floor space to the metal housing of the center shaft that was covered with an insulating material and had three more padded seats at its base.

Clayvious was seated in the second wing seat flanking the co-pilot with Vic and Kamu seated in the back against the center shaft housing. Sure enough, the pilot, who was already seated, looked around and stared toward the staircase and quickly there was his co-pilot coming up the stairs. They began punching buttons and suddenly there was that low frequency hum. Then the panels to the right, left, and above center of the windows lit up into TV monitors and they could see the grass past the landing area and beyond.

"Oh wow," Vic let out and looked at Clayvious, who had a look of, *very cool*, on his face and gave Vic a thumbs up. Suddenly Vic panicked. There was no seat belt. He looked around at each seat and no one had a seat belt. Then Kamu, sensing his distress, patted Vic on the knee and he began to feel a sense of relief. He didn't know why, other than he thought that it would be okay, and realized that was the communication from Kamu. The hum began to rise in pitch and Vic, with his back against the center shaft, could feel a slight vibration that seemed to lightly massage his back. Then, with his eyes on the monitors and the hum intensifying, they began to rise to about five hundred feet; Vic went to scoot up in his seat and couldn't. There was a light pressure on his chest and arms, a force field of some sort restricting his movement. An invisible seat belt. *How ingenious*, he thought.

They hovered for what seemed like a minute or two and then a green light came on and instantly they were traveling at speeds Vic had never imagined. The ground was passing by like a camera on fast forward in the monitors. As they elevated to about two thousand feet, the saucer seemed to fade to the right away from the federation air command and though it was still headed north, the saucer slowly spun facing south and without banking like an airplane the pilot punched a button and on an impossible sharp angle they were headed in the opposite direction. Vic could feel the pressure of the G forces get neutralized by the force field in the cabin. In a tenth of a second, they were traveling south at two thousand five hundred miles per hour, according to Vic's calculations and gaining speed. They were headed for the desert belt that circled the whole planet.

As they got closer to the desert, the terrain went from green to dry and then they were clearly inside the desert belt. There was sand and rocks with dunes and Grand Canyon-like valleys. When they had traveled well into the desert, the pilot punched a series of buttons like an experienced secretary on a keyboard and the saucer slowed to about two hundred miles per hour, then stopped on a dime and hovered in mid-air. Then Kamu took Vic's hand. Vic then conveyed the message to Clayvious to turn on his tracking device. When he turned it on, it began to beep, then stopped. Clayvious nodded, and the pilot continued east down the center of the desert belt at the Larus equator in search of Rhynous.

Back on Earth in New Orleans, Sharon was going over receipts in the shop that evening and noticed two strange men outside the shop. They looked like they were contemplating coming in, but when she looked up, they turned away. She thought, *They're shy*, but when she looked up again, they were standing in front of her, almost startling her into a heart attack. The door never opened; she knew that because the chime never sounded.

"Where is Sharon?" one man asked in a strange accent.

At that point Sharon knew she was in trouble as these were not men, and that they were not from this planet but aliens. They were human sized, five-foot-five and five-foot-six, but the big eyes, small noses and almost nonexistent ears gave it away. She tried to run but was violently grabbed and slammed to the floor.

"If you try to run again, I will have to break off your legs so that you can't and I'm not kidding. Do you understand?"

Now in a daze from banging her head on the concrete floor and blood coming from her mouth, Sharon nodded in fear.

Just then a young black-haired female walked into the shop with cold eyes and a devilish smile. "That's not her," Kali said.

"She just told us she was Sharon," one alien said.

"Are you the telepath?" Kali asked.

"No," Sharon replied."

"Then who is?" Kali asked in a cool icy tone.

"I don't know—"

Before Sharon could get the words out of her mouth, Kali slapped her so hard that the blood that had gathered in her mouth splattered on the wall. Kali, now angry with devil eyes, looked Sharon in the eye and realized that she was not all there and probably suffering from a concussion. As Kali stood up, the back door opened and Monica walked in with a bag of food for dinner.

Monica, not understanding the gravity of the situation, said, "Sharon, what happened?" Then she looked at the young lady.

"Hi Sharon, or whatever your real name is. Remember me?"

Back on Larus, Phog, Rhynous's top lieutenant, who was studying maps of Earth and planning the attach, was interrupted by one of the lookouts. "Phog! There's a federation ship out here in a search pattern. They're looking for us."

"They're probably looking for Rhynous and he's not here. Keep an eye on it and make sure the men stay out of sight."

"Yes, sir."

Phog, now curious himself, walked out to the entrance of the cave for a look. When he looked up, there it was, a glowing white disk or so it appeared as it collected energy from the suns and reflected the rest. He watched it jump across the sky in a zig zag search pattern. The sun was starting to cook the surface and Phog, as he did on many occasions, began wishing he had chosen a different line of work. Destroying other planets for profit or for any reason broke the laws of the Federation of Planets. The law was put into place after the destruction of Mars and the release of nuclear radiation into the universe that could kill all life on every planet that supports life. This was punishable by life in a prison in an environment of nothingness. No visits, no direct sun light, no games, no time outside the cell, only emptiness. Most go insane within a few years. They all lived until they're found dead. That wasn't the future Phog had dreamed of for himself, but there he was in a desert outpost with temperatures up to one hundred forty degrees in the summers and no wife or kids. He could never say it out loud, but he knew he was working for a psychopath who would kill him at the drop of a hat if he tried to defect. He saw no way out, though he still was in search of one, but for now he was forced to go back into the cave and continue to work on the plan.

Back on the saucer, Clayvious continued to impulsively glance at his tracking device with no results. And because of the speed of the saucer, they had traveled almost halfway around the planet. The pilot went into a hovering pattern. Everyone had sensed Clay's frustration at not getting a hit on his tracking device. The co-pilot released the force field, then got up and headed down the stairs. Vic could hear him punching on the keys of the computer they had passed coming up the stairs and decided to stand up and look around the curve of the housing and down the stairs. Vic saw him remove a disk like object from a cabinet that looked like a miniature saucer. The co-pilot pulled open a tray from the wall putting the disk down in it. Vic could see that the tray had been designed for the disk as it fit perfectly. The co-pilot then punched some more keys, and the disk lit up and began to emit a high-pitched hum. He then pushed the tray back into the wall releasing the disk from the air craft. He then hurried back up the stairs to his seat to control it from there. He flipped a switch, changing the channel on the monitor to his right that tapped into the camera on the disk that was now seen hovering in the other two monitors. It too began to glow and looked like a ball of light, an orb that took off to a lower altitude getting a closer look.

The search went on for another two hours but to no avail. Rhynous was nowhere to be found nor were any of his men who were hiding in the caves and the shadows. A rebel force who knew if they were located, they would be no match for the federation. Suddenly, there was a warning sound coming from the orb disk. The co-pilot flipped to the saucer probe camera that had been locked onto two of Rhynous's men running for cover.

Clayvious was now excited. "Can you stop them?"

The co-pilot looked at Clayvious, bewildered. Kamu jumped from his seat and grabbed Clay's hand to communicate and Clayvious repeated, "Can they stop them?" As he looked at Kamu who relayed the message to the copilot, who then looked at the pilot, as he spoke to him telepathically. The pilot then nodded and signaled with his hand for everyone to sit down. He then maneuvered the craft closer and locked onto the men with a light beam that stopped them in their tracks, leaving them in a paralyzed state.

Kamu translated the message from the pilot. "What now?"

Clayvious said, "I need to get down there."

"I'm going with you," Vic said as he jumped to his feet.

Kamu led them down the steps to the front of the lower deck to a circular area on the floor up against the cabin wall. Kamu pushed Vic and Clayvious together inside the circle, then walked over to a round knob on a console.

"We have to stay inside the circle. He's getting ready to send us down," Clayvious said.

Kamu turned the knob clock wise and the light beam overhead intensified until Vic and Clayvious felt a sense of weightlessness. Then the floor rotated open under their feet like the aperture of a camera as they floated there for a second and then the beam of light lowered them down to the surface like a fast moving elevator. Clayvious and Vic ran over to the two men frozen in the tractor beam. Clayvious pulled out a silver device that slipped over his middle finger that looked like a fancy ring with a hole in it and a button on the underside perfectly fitted going past his second knuckle.

"What's that?" Vic asked.

"My sword, "Clayvious responded, leaving Vic confused and mentally scratching his head. Clayvious waved up to the pilot and the tractor beam disappeared, leaving the two men on the ground. Clayvious new by their features they were Rhynous's people, descendants of refugees from mars. So, he spoke to them in their native tongue. "Mm mem lin, Rhynous?"

"We speak English, you idiot."

"How is that possible?" Clayvious asked.

"We've been to your planet, which will soon be ours." Then the two men laughed.

"Look we don't want any trouble, we're just looking for some information," Clayvious said as he moved his thumb near the button on his middle finger.

"Well, we don't know where he is, but he's not here and if we knew where he was, we wouldn't tell you."

"Okay, let's stay calm. We mean you no harm, "Clayvious said with caution.

"If that's the case, what did you come down here for?" At that moment, the man went for a weapon that looked like some kind of futuristic gun. Clayvious, at the same time, pressed the button on his own weapon. As the man leveled the gun at him, a white hot laser emanated from the ring on Clay's middle finger that he swung with force across the man's arm just below the elbow. The desperado was trying to fire his weapon and couldn't.

The man looked at Clayvious with anger and fear, trying to figure out what Clayvious had done to his arm with this smallish and unusual weapon. At that moment, his arm fell to the ground, still holding the gun. His upper forearm cauterized and spewed no blood. Then a delayed scream, Clayvious informed him that he was taking him in for interrogation.

"If Rhynous finds out I talked, it will be far worse than what you could ever imagine. I have a better idea." He then took the gun with his other hand from his severed arm and pointed the gun at his head and pulled the trigger. It delivered a gamma flash to his head as he laughed at Clay.

Clayvious and Vic then watched the unimaginable as his head burned and imploded then turned into dust, all in less than a minute. And then was blown away by a desert wind. Suddenly his comrade broke and ran, Vic chased close behind. "

We didn't come down here to fight," Vic shouted, but the chase continued as they approached a cliff wall that dropped straight down one thousand five hundred feet to the canyon floor. Vic didn't know if it was the heat of the desert or his adrenaline that was causing it, but he could feel the blue energy emanating from the top of his head. As the cliff approached, the space pirate never slowed down and leaped into the canyon from the wall with Vic three steps behind. Vic pushed off the top of the cliff wall like a long jumper going up and out into the canyon. As his body began to drop, his blue energy kicked in like thrusters on a booster rocket. He turned down in hopes of catching the pirate in mid-air, but it was too late as his body hit the side of the canyon wall eight hundred feet down and dropped lifelessly the rest of the way down to the canyon floor. Vic began to take on fire from caves in the canyon walls and blasted out of there at a high rate of speed. Just as Clayvious had come to the canyon wall, he then had to back away from what looked like laser blasts when the shooting started. Vic circled around, landing near Clay.

"You, okay?" Clayvious asked.

"Yeah, I'm okay. What's wrong with these guys? They just killed themselves for no reason."

"There's a reason. They know that an act of betrayal against Rhynous is certain torture and humiliation ending in a disgraceful death. To talk would be treason, so ending their own life is the easy way out."

"That's crazy, just insane," Vic said, disgusted by the senseless loss of life. Quickly, they heard the hum of the saucer coming in low now to avoid any weapons fire being shot from the walls of the canyon. It hovered just high enough to drop down the stairs as the guys quickly trotted up the steps and up to the second level to find their seats and get the hell out of there.

Back in Washington, DC, Rhynous had taken over the manipulation of the president as Kali was off on what he thought was a wild goose chase. In the meantime, Rhynous's diabolical nature and his control over the president of the United States with the cyber-net controlling the president's brain had thrown the country into division and chaos. The plague was killing thousands of people a day and the president didn't seem to care because Rhynous didn't care. The president's team had ordered a round of vaccines to slow it. Now with Rhynous controlling the cyber-net puppet strings, there would be no more orders for vaccines. Rhynous enjoyed a mental orgasm in the mounting death toll and spent the rest of his time dreaming of ways to increase the death and destruction as it made him feel stronger and more powerful. Rhynous also had the president inquire about a war against Iran, which was Rhynous's ultimate goal, a world war, a nuclear war. He wanted to burn it all down the whole planet and then extract its riches and become the world's savior. He was beyond psychopathic. As the proverbial horns on his head grew, Rhynous was now drunk with power and dreams of stolen riches. Enough to rebuild his ancient civilization on Mars and terraform the whole planet into a green watery oasis. However, he would never do that because he would soon have a better planet worshiping him at his feet, Earth.

Back on Larus an hour later, Vic and Clayvious were back at the Federation landing site. Pleasantries were exchanged with the pilots, who were thanked for their efforts. After checking back in at the counter and rejoining the other three diplomats they all walked out of the terminal and onto a waiting pod headed back to the federation building in the city of Solan, translation, city of light. When they arrived at the federation building headed across the great floor covered by the dome, they were rushed by Larian reporters, who were called information agents, but the group of diplomats along with Vic and Clayvious had become close nit. They pushed past the information agents and up the stairs to the left to rejoin the leaders and report their findings and to establish a plan.

Vic noticed a difference in Clay. He was more intense and seemingly in a hurry. When they entered the meeting room, all the same players were there, but to Vic's surprise, there was a group of six Grays on the other side, at the end of the table. One saluted, two waved, and the other three nodded. They were the same six from the airport. Vic and Clayvious together gave everyone the customary Larian greeting, including the Grays who expressed their approval by their gestures.

Leader 1, whose name was Ambusal, was leading again. "Welcome back, gentlemen." His hands rested on the light translator. "We did not receive a communication from our diplomats, so we had to assume that you were unsuccessful in finding Rhynous in the desert belt."

Clayvious was still agitated. "Yes, great leader, Ambusal, you are correct."

"So, what is your plan?" Ambusal asked.

"I believe Rhynous is back on Earth, sir, and we are going back to find him. My question to you, sir, is will you send a fleet of airships to assist us in his capture?"

"My old friend, Clayvious, we have not visited Earth in a thousand years and the information we have received from other federation planets who do travel to Earth for recreation or scientific purposes are chased and sometimes attacked. Your civilization, though much more advanced than two hundred years ago, is still behind in technology and tolerance. Earthlings still pose a threat to alien visitors and your governments do not acknowledge that other beings even exist in the universe," Ambusal said.

Clayvious hung his head in silence, knowing he had just been told no, but was still looking for a response that would gain him some support.

Then out of the silence came a voice that had not been heard before. "We will assist you. How can we help?"

Clayvious and Vic looked at each other and scanned the leaders, none of whom had their hands on the translator. As they looked down the table, they were shocked to see the first Gray at the end of the table with his hands on the translator. Clayvious starred in complete surprise, then quickly snapped out of it and humbly bowed to the Gray, summoning his best diplomatic behavior. "Good, sir, thank you for your offer. May I have the pleasure of knowing your name?"

"I am General Zeenix and I have had dealings with this enemy Rhynous. He is a Galactic threat and must be stopped. I believe we could be of assistance."

"General Zeenix, we welcome your help but what is it your offering?"

"You said you were in need of airships. I have two galaxy ships or mother ships as you call them on Earth. They are stationed on the dark side of the Earth's moon, invisible to the naked eye. We have a large ship inside the Earth's cavity at the South Pole and a ship in the deep ocean. All of these carrier-type airships have their own squadron of saucers or UFOs, as you Earthlings like to call them," the general said.

Clayvious and Vic looked at each other with their mouths open, not sure how to respond. "So, you're already there," Clayvious said.

"Yes, we are. There would be no expense in trying to get there."

Clayvious and Vic now have a ton of questions but know better than to ask. They already know too much. Vic's interactions with alien entities alone are enough to have him put in jail by the U.S. government.

Clayvious, now in thought, broke the silence with his hands on the translator. "General, what is it that you will expect in return?"

"Two things. One is that your friend here tells the average American that our mission on Earth is peaceful. We are there for scientific research and to protect the planet from nuclear destruction. I'm sure you know that when there's a leak in a reactor or the threat of a nuclear bomb test, UFOs are sighted. We have the power to disarm those devices, but we are still working on how to help with the cleanup of a nuclear spill."

"Getting out a message of peace shouldn't be a problem," Clayvious said, looking at Vic, who nodded in agreement. "And what is the second thing you will want in return?"

"It's what you call on Earth an ace in the hole. It's a future favor that has not come to pass. When I know what it is, I will call on you."

Vic and Clayvious conversed for a minute and came to the conclusion that they didn't have a choice.

"Okay, General, I could promise you that if it's within our power to help you concerning this future event, we will be there to help."

"Great, we have a deal," the general said.

"General, one question," Clay said. "What made you decide to volunteer your services?"

"Rhynous has killed humanoids and pirated airships throughout the federation of planets and his appetite for destruction and power cannot be quenched. He must be stopped. And there's another reason, this morning as you passed me and my delegation, your friend here greeted us with a wave. It was a simple peace offering of good will. Keep in mind, our relations with humans on your planet have always been met with fear or guns. His gesture was a small step in the right direction."

Clayvious looked at Vic, clearly pleased with his gesture of a wave to the Grays, but he had to ask a burning question. "General, does our government know you're there?"

"That is a question I cannot answer." And with that response the general took his hands off the translator, still looking at Clay.

Ambusal, leader 1, sensing an instant change in vibration, quickly stepped in. "This is a great moment for the federation of planets and planet Earth. My fellow beings, we have a deal, but let us continue any planning in a closed session. At this time, I'm calling for a fifteen-minute break before the closed session. And for all Larian officials, this meeting is adjourned."

Clayvious and Vic stepped outside in the hallway to take a break. "I almost blew it with that question," Clayvious said.

Ambusal was on top of it. Let's cool it on the questions, Clayvious, and figure out how we're going to work them into the plan," Vic said.

Clayvious agreed as the diplomats happily filed out of the meeting room, knowing their day was over. Then a Larian took Vic by the wrist and Vic looked up to see it was Kamu. Telepathically, he told Vic it was a great experience meeting him and that the power of the universe would be with them. Then Vic said, "My energy is the source, and the source is in you," as he put his hand on Kamu's chest over his heart. They both bowed and a feeling of sadness came over Vic and he knew that was because Kamu was feeling the same. "I hope we meet again," Vic said. Kamu nodded and waved as he walked away, heading home to be with his family.

"Looks like you made a friend," Clayvious said.

"Yes, I did. He has a good spirit, but let's talk about our plan."

The two discussed their plan and how to proceed without any top secret security questions. They were in deep enough.

There was a buzzer sound that came from the meeting room. Clayvious and Vic stepped back into a room that was now practically empty. The three leaders from the other quadrants and General Zeenix's delegation were gone, leaving the four of them.

Leader Ambusal wasted no time. "Okay, gentlemen, what's the plan?"

Clayvious being the lead, said, "It a simple one. General, we don't want to put you or any of your beings in danger so we will capture Rhynous and contact you to come and take him into custody. We just need to know how to contact you."

"I have a device that's similar to your cell phones on Earth."

"You have a cell phone?" Vic asked.

"No, it's like a cell phone in that it can be tracked by your GPS systems on Earth here." The general pulled out a flat device that was smaller than the average cell phone but did look like one. It was black with a screen.

"How does it work?" Clayvious asked.

"It's very simple, you press the on button on the top, then tap the icon on the screen. It will notify us of your location. Once you've pressed the locate icon, you must leave it on to be located."

Clayvious now had more questions for the general but remembered he had agreed not to ask. "Thank you, General. We don't know exactly how long it will take us to find him but you will hear from us."

"If you have any problems locking him down, press the locate button and we will be there to assist in his capture."

"Thank you again, General, but does this device need to be charged?"

"Good question. Yes, you will need to leave it in the sun five to ten minutes every two weeks."

"That's amazing," Clayvious said, then put the device in his pocket.

Ambusal put his hands on the translator. "Gentlemen, I called this closed session because we have a situation on our hands. We are the only ones who know what roll General Zeenix will play and we need to keep it that way. It has come to my attention that someone among the delegates is a spy. The last thing we want is for Rhynous to be tipped off, so please do not discuss the details of this meeting with anyone." They all agreed to proceed in secrecy.

Clayvious and Vic stood up. "Ambusal, it has been great to see you again, but it is time for us to return to Earth. General, we will see you back on Earth, hopefully soon."

"I look forward to it," General Zeenix said.

Ambusal stood up. "Clayvious and Vic, may the universe keep you."

"Sir, our energy is the source, and the source is in you, we thank you and the creator of the universe," Vic expressed in a strong but calm voice.

"Well said and so it is, be safe."

"We will great leader."

"Oh, such pomp and circumstance, please, call me Ambusal."

"Thank you, Ambusal, we will be safe," Vic said.

Ambusal saw them go to the door. "Good luck, gentlemen."

"Thanks, we'll need it," Clayvious said.

CHAPTER 18

As Clay and Vic walked down the stairs and across the great floor under the open air dome, Vic noticed something he hadn't noticed before. The Larian sky was free of smog and pollution. Then he thought that there seemed to be no crime and a peacefulness about the city. Then as they approached the entrance to the transport, his every thought was about Monica and getting back to Earth so he could be with her and share his Larian experiences.

As they reached the short flight of steps up to the pure gold archway of the transport, a Larian security officer was standing guard. He had probably been briefed as he nodded and welcomed Clay and Vic up to the platform. The Larian entrance was different from Clay's. There was an electrical device with two round lights like two eyes the size of a baseball. Then a slot, and Clay stood there digging through his pockets and pulled out a clear piece of plastic that had been laser etched with information that he shoved into the slot. Then he pulled it out and put it back in his pocket as the red light came on. The pure gold archway began to glow as if red hot.

"Grab hold!" Clay said.

Vic took hold of the back of Clay's belt. The entrance blew open into a controlled vortex. The green light came on and they walked in two steps and were sucked off their feet headed back to Earth. As they rode the beam of light back, Vic was oblivious to the magnificent sights of stars and planets going by. His only thought was of Monica. They had been on Larus for just over twenty-four hours and it felt as though they had been gone a week. Then it occurred to Vic why Clay was in a hurry. He wanted to get back to start tracking Rhynous. It was all clear now. Clay had been different since being in the Larian desert belt and coming up empty-handed. Vic knew at that moment there would be a war and that it would be engaged without the knowledge of the federal government or local police. A galactic war that would be hard to get people to believe, but it was going to happen. Vic looked at his watch and two hours had gone by. He then looked up and out into the distance past Clay's big head to see a small blue planet growing bigger with each passing minute. It was a beautiful sight. They were approaching from the bottom of Earth.

At first, Vic wasn't sure that was it. The first continent he saw was the South Pole. It had to be the South Pole at the bottom of Earth. Australia was more recognizable, but that didn't change the glory and wonder of the amazing look of Earth from space, so pretty and unique. Not many knew that more than Vic did. Now that he had passed by so many planets and had a look at Larus from outer space, he knew for a fact that nothing compared to that blue ball, sometimes with a purplish hue, called Earth. Another hour had passed, and Earth loomed larger and Vic could see the trajectory headed up the East Coast of South America crossing through Brazil and Peru to the Pacific Ocean and into Los Angeles, or so Vic thought.

"Get ready!" Clay exclaimed.

Vic could see the end of the light coming up but it seemed to be ending in mid-air. This was a mystery to Vic.

Clay yelled out, "This is it!" and out they went with force and they both hit the floor of Clay's transport room with a stumbling crash and a bang.

"I thought for sure we were going to stick that landing." Vic chuckled. "This is more difficult than getting off a ski lift and there's no ice."

Clay laughed, too. "Hey, I didn't do so well myself, but it's good to be back."

They both got up, dusting themselves off.

"Sure is. I'm headed back to New Orleans to brief Monica."

"You could do that by phone, right?"

"No, I can't take a chance in case we're being monitored."

"You think you're being watched?"

"Monica's a psychic and a telepath. She got spooked out in DC as we were leaving the hotel. She felt like someone was watching us. I didn't see anyone, but I'm not taking any chances."

Clay knew there was something between them. *It is clear that they are a couple or at least that's how it felt that night at the shop*, Clay thought.

"Clay, I'll be in touch in the next day or so."

"Okay, be safe and let me know if anything comes up."

"I will." Vic summoned his blue energy and walked through the membrane and disappeared as Clay stared at this seemingly routine event. There was something different about it and Clay, with his brow furrowed, pondered it for a few minutes, trying to figure it out. And then it hit him. He hadn't seen Vic eat any brownies. He left, so at ease with no hesitation, just whipping out his power with the swagger of a super hero. Clay smiled, knowing Vic was evolving and that he would be a formidable defender for the source. *My energy is the source, and the source is in us*, Clay thought. *If the source is for us, then why would they come against us?* And the answer was the same: they served an opposing negative energy belief that sought to conquer and destroy. The scent of war was upon him. He was battle tested and cool under fire, but most of all, he wanted to save Earth and continue to groom Vic for things yet to come. There would be war.

Vic was back in his house but had walked through a dark timeless void and thought about his being at home and suddenly appeared in his living room out of nowhere. His only thought was to take a shower, grab some clothes, and head to the airport. And then he froze in his tracks. He heard Monica cry out for him. It was so clear in his head it was almost like she was in the room. Vic immediately went to his office to get his cell phone that he had left behind charging. The first thing that got his attention was the date. They had been gone just over twenty-four hours according to his watch, but his phone said they had been gone a week. He quickly called Monica and got no answer. He was now confused. Then thought she was probably busy. Not wanting to panic, he stayed cool. He then saw the lottery receipt on the desk and remembered the millions he had won. *How do you forget about three-hundred-fifty-million?* he thought and smiled. He then realized that he needed to call a guy that a stranger in Las Vegas had told him about. Vic had been given his number and told that Robbie Star was an electrical engineer and a physicist that had ideas and designs for exotic and futuristic aircraft. And he had worked on some top secret projects for the government. In Vic's mind, he was the only one he wanted to talk to about building his airship. So, he called Robbie as he continued to pack.

"Hello?"

"Hi, is this Mr. Star?"

"Aah yes, who's calling?"

"This is Vic Wilheight. I got your number from a guy named Joe who said he worked with you in New Mexico."

"I think I remember who that is, but what can I do for you, Vic?"

"Well, I'm looking for someone to build an aircraft for me and not an airplane, an exotic." There was silence on the other end for a few seconds.

"Vic, if you're talking about the kind of craft I think you're talking about, you're looking at a million or more for me to even consider it."

"How about this, we'll start with a two-million-dollar budget. I'm running out of town but sight unseen I'll send you one hundred thousand tonight through Zelle just for you to get started."

"What's your name again?"

"Vic. Look I don't have a lot of time. Are you in?"

"Okay, buddy, I'm intrigued but you can't send me one hundred grand. They won't let you, but I think you can send twenty grand and as soon as I receive it, I'll start your designs."

"Deal, Mr. Star."

"Please! Call me Rob."

"Thank you, Rob. You've got my number, text me when you

receive the money."

"Okay, will do."

"And I'm sending it to your cell number, Rob?"

"Yes! And one thing before you go. Your design, is it going to be a saucer or a triangle?"

"A triangle."

"You got it, have a safe trip."

"Thanks."

In less than two hours, Vic was on a plane to New Orleans. Upon landing, he rushed out calling Uber on his way to the street and made it to the shop just before dark. To his surprise, the shop was closed and as he looked through the window, he could see things were in disarray. He walked to the back and the back door was ajar so he opened the door. Vic stepped in ready for any surprises, but there were none, only blood on the wall and a clear sign of a struggle as two chairs were overturned. And there were papers all on the floor that appeared to be receipts. Vic was beside himself. He felt that he should have been there and that he should have never left her alone. As the veins bulged in his head and the tears welled up in his eyes, a snap thought rushed through his mind. It had to be Kali. He had told Monica he was worried that she had shown herself to Kali. He was almost certain it was her and then there was a telepathic message: *I'm here, help me.* Vic's despair turned to focus and rage. Then he remembered that Kali's license plate number was still in his wallet. He called his buddy, Ben, at the LAPD and explained the situation. Ben explained he couldn't do it and said he had to go. Vic was disappointed, but ten minutes later an address popped up on his cell phone from a strange number. It was in West Virginia. Hope was alive again.

Vic sat down in the back room and closed his eyes, then began to astral travel to Clay's dimension. Vic passed through the membrane. And called Clay. There was no one in the court area. Again, he called Clay and there he was.

"Thought I heard someone. Where are you?"

"I'm in New Orleans. I need you here. We have a serious problem. Monica's disappeared."

"What!"

"Yes, she's gone. There's blood on the wall, papers on the floor and chairs turned over. I believe her partner is with her. I just pulled a favor to run the license plate for the young witch and I have an address in West Virginia."

"Okay, give me an hour. I need to get some things in order here."

"Okay, take your time, no! Hurry, Clay!"

"Okay, one hour."

"Thanks, Clay."

West Virginia, Monica and Sharon were thrown into separate rooms. Monica, for the time was left alone and was focusing on Vic, sending him telepathic messages. And though he was not a telepath, his extra sensory was picking up her waves. Monica knew Vic had the ability to feel her and hear her based on their telephone conversations. He knew when she wanted him to call. The connection was emotional and real. Many people in love, twins, and close family members experienced that kind of telepathy and she was banking on it now as she kept sending the name Kali and focusing on the word *help*. Monica was sure that once they had the information they wanted on Vic and Clay, they would kill her and Sharon. She felt that right now Kali and Rhynous's aliens were figuring out how they were going to extract it. Monica had decided that she couldn't talk too soon but had to give up a little at a time, if possible, to survive longer. She was more concerned about poor Sharon, who knew nothing and appeared to be injured badly before they split them apart. For now, she just needed to focus on broadcasting telepathically her message to Vic.

Kali was in the kitchen talking to Spidis, Rhynous's lead alien scientist. "So, we need to find out who these men were at the park and how she's connected to them," Kali said.

Spidis was now perking up. "And what is your plan when you get what you need from them?"

"Well, we can't just let them walk away," Kali said.

"Instead of killing them, I could find use for them back on Larus."

"For what?" Kali asked with curiosity and disdain."

"Oh, many things—sexual experimentation, breading programs, pleasure and once we have them reprogrammed, spy work."

"Spidis, it sounds to me like you're just looking for some sex slaves."

"I'm also a scientist. You really know how to cheapen my work."

"I just call it the way I see it."

"I'll tell you what. We'll let Rhynous decide. In the meantime, we need to get that information. Let's go. It's time to go to work." Kali led the way back to the bedroom where Monica was tied up. "Let me do the talking. You just look like you're ready to cut her into pieces."

Spidis agreed and he wouldn't have disagreed because he was hoping to own the rights to both women to satisfy his perverted desires.

As they entered the room, Monica was bound against the wall with her eyes closed and opened them slowly and remained calm.

"Okay, Monica, I need to get some information from you, but I must warn you. If I detect that you're lying to me, my friend here is going to start carving you up, but not so badly that he can't enjoy the fruits of your body before he cuts your head off as a souvenir."

Monica's eyes widened as Kali confirmed her deepest fears. "May I say something before we get started?"

Seeing no harm in hearing her out, Kali agreed.

"Look, I have information for you. I will tell you what I know but my friend doesn't know anything. She's clueless. We're business partners at the shop and I hired her to help run the business. She knows nothing about Rhynous, you, or aliens. She only knows how to read cards and palms. She is completely out of the loop. I know you're probably going to kill me, but please, not an innocent person."

Kali stared at Monica as tears welled up in Monica's eyes. And though she was full of evil, Kali felt her sincerity and knew she was telling the truth. "I believe you, Monica, and I respect that you're trying to save your friend and willing to give us information, knowing that your own life is at stake. I will take what you said into consideration. We can wipe Sharon's mind so that she has no memory of this experience, but that's going to depend on your information."

Now hopeful for Sharon, Monica dried her eyes and proceeded with her plan to slowly disseminate information. "Okay, thank you, Kali. So, what do you want to know?"

"Who were the men chasing Rhynous in the park the day we met?"

"I know the leader. His name is Clay. He's an alien and has been on Earth for hundreds of years since the time of the Roman Empire and maybe before."

"And how did you meet him?"

"I was doing a séance, and he was astral traveling and began talking to me. After the meeting, I stayed in the room to call him back and we talked more. He made me aware of the alien presence on Earth, but to make a long story short, I was asked to come to the rally only as an observer, but I broke ranks when I saw you. My psychic abilities allowed me to see past your smiling, happy, innocent face and I could feel your darkness and—"

Before Monica could say another word, Kali snapped and slapped her with the might of a freight train. "I just wanted to stop you before it became insulting. Continue," Kali said.

Monica realized she had digressed but was now more aware than ever that Kali would kill her at the drop of a hat and that she had better be very careful. A clear red bruise in the form of a hand print swelled on the left side of her face. "Kali, I know the other men were Clay's men, but I don't know their names. I had never seen them before the rally."

"Do they know where we are?"

"No, not that I know of."

"Good."

"What else can you tell me?"

"I know that he's looking for Rhynous and I had more, but your slap has me seeing stars. My head is aching and not clear."

Kali grabbed Monica around the collar with the speed of a jack rabbit nearly choking her to death. "Look, you nickel-and-dime-gumbo-eating bitch. You had better tell me something before you fade to black into the next life."

Not wanting to see his potential property killed or damaged any further, Spidis pulled on Kali's shoulder, bringing her back from her rage. Kali then loosened her grip as Monica gasped for air.

Once she had caught her breath, Monica said, "You've got me tied up and locked away. No one knows where we are. You've dazed my brain. What's the rush? I'm not going anywhere. Can I just get some time to gather my thoughts?"

"I'll give you a few hours and then I don't want to hear any excuses." Kali walked out, slamming the door behind her, leaving Spidis in the room with Monica.

"I will talk to her. Try to relax. I know this is a stressful situation. I'll try to buy you some more time," Spidis said in an effort to win over his potential prize. "Do you need anything?"

No," Monica said with her head down as he devoured her with his eyes before leaving the room.

In New Orleans, Vic sat in the séance room waiting for Clay and constantly eyeing his watch when at exactly fifty-five minutes later there was some kind of faint frequency ring in his ears. A portal opened up, and Clay walked through it. To Vic's surprise, two of Clay's men also walked through.

"Ah, you're early. Thank you and I see we have backup," Vic said with a grateful smile on his face as he hugged Clay.

"Vic, this is Alastor and Ares."

"Hello, guys, very nice to formally meet you. I've seen you out in the court yard doing maneuvers."

"And good to meet you, too," Alastor said.

"And we've been watching your growth. You're a high grade military asset," Ares said.

"Thank you, guys. I will work hard to live up to that. Vic humbly bowed his head to these powerful looked warriors.

"You've got the address in West Virginia?" Clay asked.

"Yes, I've got it right here." He showed it to Clay, who pulled out his cell phone and punched in the address for the GPS location. "Really, I could have done that myself," Vic said, as he was expecting Clay to whip out some type of alien technology.

And Clay did, as he opened another portal and they all walked through. Five minutes later, they walked out of the vortex onto a dead-end street with Kali's house at the end leading to a large wooded area. There were no street lights which helped their cover, as they were not very visible. They then moved out of the street and onto Kali's property, into the shadows now becoming virtually invisible. Clay put out his hand to stop everyone, as he noticed two aliens walking out from behind the house on patrol. Then they stopped in front to stand guard. Clay put his finger to his mouth, motioning no talking. Clay now had a wild look in his eyes. He motioned to Alastor and Ares to take the two aliens.

The two warriors looked at each other, closed their eyes, took a deep breath, and held it. Then they began to fade, leaving only an outline of their bodies that would not be seen in the dark. Clay threw a rock away from them out toward the woods, drawing the attention of the guards. Clay's men were now able to walk up from behind and dispatch the guards with the same ring type weapon as Clay, that they called a needle blade. It was named that because of the thin white hot beam of laser about the thickness of a screw driver shaft with many capabilities. There were two thuds as the guards' heads hit the ground, and then it was silent again. Ares and Alastor quickly shut off their blades to maintain their stealth in the darkness of the moonless night. They then returned to the group and Clay whispered the plan.

"Good work, you two. Vic and I are going inside after we patrol the back of the house. Ares, turn your phone to vibrate and headset on. I'm calling you now so you can hear everything and if we need you, we're already connected. Ares, Alastor, you will stand guard, one of you at each end of the house so you can see down the side and across the front. If you hear my back up call, break that front door and proceed quickly but carefully. Remember there may be women inside."

Ares and Alastor nodded as Clay and Vic disappeared behind the house. On the backside, there were two rooms with a bathroom between them. In the first room, the curtains were closed shut but someone could be heard talking. The second room had a crack in the curtain and they could see Sharon tied up and anchored to the wall. Her face was bruised and her head was hanging down. She was clearly injured and seemed to be trying to shake it off, but to no avail.

"Follow me," Clay said, as he opened a portal into the room where Sharon was being held. Vic pulled out his hunting pocket knife and cut the ropes, freeing her from the wall

She moaned. "Oh, thank you, thank you." She collapsed to the floor.

Vic whispered for her to stay quiet and on the floor until they got back. Vic knew Monica had to be in the other bedroom and took the lead. As they tipped past the bathroom, it was clear someone was in there. Vic motioned he was going into the bedroom. Clay nodded and was surprised when Vic took a deep breath and he saw Vic's eyes turn a bright cobalt blue. Then, the appearance of swirling blue energy inside a light blue cylinder over Vic's head and the sudden change on his face from nice guy to warrior. Vic snatched the door open in time to see Spidis running his hands through Monica's hair with the desire to do more written all over his face, like a drooling dog. Vic lost it and blasted him with a palm blast of unrestrained blue energy that blew him into five pieces back against the wall. Each portion of his body turned a bluish white hot and disintegrated into gray ash.

Upon hearing Spidis's body hit the wall, an alien ran from the living room into the hallway at the opposite end from where Clay was standing and opened up with a M9 automatic rifle, hitting Clay four times before he could pull out his sonic blast weapon. Clay returned one ultra-sonic blast to the guard's chest that crushed his sternum, throwing him into the wall and turning his heart and upper lungs into Jell-O.

Ares was now in Clays head set. "General! What's your status? Do you need us to enter?"

"Stand down, maintain your position." Clay could hear someone in the bathroom and could see Vic in the second bedroom untying Monica. Clay tipped down the hall, and looked into the front bedroom on his left that was empty. He then slipped into the living room to make sure he had neutralized the last guard, and then to the front door. Clay opened the front door and motioned for Alastor to come in and stationed him in the living room. He then whispered to Alastor that someone was in the bathroom but to hold his position there in the living room. Clay could hear Vic and Monica as Vic consoled her, assuring her that she was safe. Clay then turned the door knob and kicked the door open but as soon as the door swung open a giant black puma sprung out. It was so fast and shocking it scared even Clay, who ducked as it went over his head, hitting the wall and then bounded back to the opposite wall and into the living room.

"Shoot it!" Clay shouted to Alastor as the big cat leaped to the front door to break through it, but the door had bars. Alastor whipped out his sonic weapon and as he leveled the short barrel of his sonic blaster just before he pulled the trigger, the cat morphed into a black-haired young woman.

"Don't shoot!" she said.

Everyone rushed into the living room—Vic, Clay, and Monica.

"Please don't kill me," Kali said.

"Kali?" Vic said, but no one moved, still in shock from the size of the cat and having seen her change back to a woman. Vic walked over and grabbed her by the neck, twisting one of her arms up to her earlobe.

"Ouch, you're hurting me," Kali said.

Vic marched her down the hallway to the back bedroom where she saw a portion of Spidis's head, a hand and a shoe with the rest of his body in ash. "You see that!" Vic shouted. "That's going to be you."

"Oh no! Not Spidis!" Kali cried out in shock and fear as Vic marched her back to the living room.

"You better start talking and I better like what you're saying, or it's going to be the last thing you say," Vic said.

Clay realized Vic's rage was because his girl had been kidnapped and tortured. He was reluctant to step in, but as the leader, he had to. In a calm voice, Clay said, "Vic," and motioned with his hands, pressing them down toward the floor to say without words, calm down.

Vic got the message and backed off, but his eyes were still a bluish tint and the blue energy still emanating from the top of his head like a clear blue swirl of supernatural light.

"Young lady, you're in big trouble. If I let my friend here have his way, you're going to be dead, so answer wisely," Clay said.

Kali was in disbelief and shock about how the tables had turned and now she was a captive in her own home. There were dead bodies all over the place and she knew these men were not playing. Fear replaced her anger. "What do you want to know?" She asked with the apprehension of a middle schooler.

"Where is Rhynous?" Clay asked with a killer instinct written all over his face and tone.

Kali could taste the disdain Clay had for Rhynous but knew that if she was caught in a lie, it would be death for her. "He's in Washington, DC as far as I know."

"Where in DC?" Clay asked more forcefully.

"I don't know exactly where, but he's there helping the president make some important decisions."

"You mean manipulating his decisions, don't you?" Clay said, but Kali didn't answer."Vic, how far is DC from here?"

"A little over two hundred miles."

Clay pulled out his tracking device and turned it on. "This has a two-hundred-fifty-mile range. If it doesn't pick him up, I may kill you myself."

Kali knew this was a moment of truth as her heartbeat quickened, pounding in her ears and hoping Rhynous had not left the DC area. The two beeps that signaled the device was on and working had gone silent. Clay was patient but looked at Kali with a death stare and she recognized it was more deadly than hers. She was now clearly sweating with a shiny glow to her soon-to-be-dead skin. As the sweat ran down and dripped from her chin, Kali's attitude had changed to pure fear, and she was now ranting about where he said he was going and what hotels he liked. Clay had not broken his stare and his thoughts of snapping her skinny little neck were raging like a fire in his mind. As he took a step toward her, she could feel the cold breeze of death descending on her as if Clay were the grim reaper himself. Suddenly, the tracking device sounded, with a green light this time.

Clay's focus quickly switched to his tracking device which continued its cycle of two beeps and a pause.

"I told you," Kali said, now breathing as if she had just run a mile and knowing the device had just saved her from physical damage or death.

"Okay, you were telling the truth. That's good," Clay said, "but we're not done with you yet. How many soldiers does Rhynous have in his army?"

"He's recruiting constantly. He's working on three thousand. That's all I know. I heard him say he's got just over a battalion but I don't know how many men that is. I was never in the military."

"Who is he recruiting here on Earth?"

"He's recruiting homeless people and reprogramming them with the cyber-net so that they're no longer insane, drug attics, alcoholics or if they've just quit on life. And because they're homeless, no one asked any questions when they disappeared."

"Where are they located?" Clay asked.

"They're from all over the country, in small towns and most from big cities."

At that moment, Sharon walked into the room with a battered face. "What's going on? I heard the talking. I know you told me to stay down, but it felt safe to come out. What's that smell?"

Everyone had been so focused on Kali's information and attempted escape that no one had noticed the smell of death in the room from the guard's body in the hallway and what was left of Spidis in the back room. Now everyone noticed.

"Open that front door and we need to get him out of here," Clay said.

"I'll take care of it," Alastor said as he was opening the door and then walked past Clay and Vic to the hallway to handle the body.

Monica was in the corner of the living room huddled with Sharon, both crying slightly, with Monica expressing to Sharon how glad she was that she was still alive. At that moment, Kali saw a chance and spewed out a short incantation and leaped for the door, changing back into the large and muscular cat in mid-air, with her own little feline midnight arched and hissing again in the window. Clay dived to stop her, only to have his forearm opened up by the claws of the puma's hind foot as it crashed through the screen door. Vic ran to the front porch as Ares got off two shots with his blaster from the front of the house. And just before the dark shadowy cat reached the tree line, Vic prepared to destroy it with a bolt of energy when Monica shouted out, "No! Don't!"

CHAPTER 19

"Okay, we need to prepare to get out of here. She's probably out there watching and waiting for us to leave at a distance. Let's clean up and get out of here before daybreak. We got what we came for and more," Clay said, as he walked past Vic who was staring at Monica in a state of confusion.

"Why are you staring at me like that?" Monica said.

"Why did you not want me to bring down the little witch who just beat the shit out of you and who was probably going to kill you?"

Monica put her head down. "I don't know, but I have my reason."

"Huh?" Vic said with a disgruntled face and under his breath, he said, " Women," as he left the room to go help Clay.

Clay had found a trash bag in the kitchen and was pushing the pieces of Spidis into the bag with a dustpan. "Clay, do you need any help in here?"

"No, but I'm damn proud of the way you handled yourself tonight. You're a warrior."

Vic was now slightly embarrassed and flattered. "Hey thanks, but what makes you think that?"

"I saw it come out of you. You never know who has it in them. Sometimes it came from the most unlikely people but I thought you had it in you and now I know."

"I thought you would have figured that out on Larus in the desert belt."

"In the desert belt you didn't have to kill anyone." Clay stood up and Vic noticed for the first time Clay had been hit four times with a yellowish puss-like fluid running from his neck, soaking his shirt and dripping to the floor from the wounds in his torso.

"How is it possible for you to be wounded like this and still be cleaning and walking around?"

"I'll have to explain later but I think you already know. What I need you to do now is take this bag and bury it with the others. I'm sure Ares and Alastor could use some help."

When Vic caught up with the other two warriors out in the woods past Kali's property line, they were about fifty yards out from the property line but could still see the house. They had started digging a shallow grave with two others marked out behind a heavy and dense growth of bushes behind the trees.

"Why are we taking time to do this," Vic asked.

"Out of respect for the dead," Alastor said.

They had found two shovels and one ax pick in the garage and were fast at work as time was of the essence. It was two-thirty in the morning and they needed to be gone before daybreak or before anyone showed up. The three men worked like miners in the dark, trying to meet a deadline and by 4:00 a.m., the job had been completed with Alastor giving the last rights for the fallen enemy.

When they returned to the house, Clay and the ladies were on the porch. Monica was sitting with Sharon wrapped in a blanket. Sharon with her head on Monica's shoulder sleeping off the concussion she sustained at the shop. Clay was glad to see the guys back before first light.

"Thank you, men, that was the right thing to do. Vic I'm going to take my men back through the vortex. You're going to need to get the ladies back home.."

I'm not taking them back to New Orleans," Vic said quickly.

Monica looked at him with surprise. "Then where are you taking us?"

"You're going with me back to Los Angeles until this is all over."

"Hey, I've got a mortgage, Sharon has bills, and we have to pay the lease on the shop."

I'll take care of it, don't worry about anything."

"How?" Monica asked inquisitively."

"You've forgotten, our energy is the source and the source is in us." Vic reached out his balled fist. Clay then reached out his fist and

Monica reluctantly extended hers. Then without a word, Vic took a breath and raised his head, looked at Monica and Clay, like a choir director starting a song, and the three repeated together, "Our energy is the source and the source is in us." These were positive words in the midst of bad feelings, the feeling of being violated with Monica and Sharon taken captive at their place of business. Then physically assaulting Sharon and seriously injuring her. And the torture of Monica, slapped around and chocked then her life threatened while being tied to a wall and would have been worse if they had not gotten there in time. Also, the loss of life in retaliation, no one felt good except for the fact that the ladies were now safe but it all came at a high price. Then out of nowhere, a feeling of hope and determination restored their mental fortitude and they all felt it. Monica knew it was something coming back from the cosmos from their mantra that went out but said nothing. There was nothing to add. Her fear and concern were gone.

"Could I just stop at the house and pick up some things," she asked.

"No. Whatever you need I'll get it for you, but we can't sit here talking. Clay I'm going to fly to a car rental place and rent a car."

"At four-thirty in the morning?" Clay asked.

"You're right. Okay, I'll call an Uber but we need to walk far enough away from here in case someone shows up."

Clay agreed, so they all walked out of Kali's rural area under the cover of darkness and down to an area three miles away to a twenty-four-hour gas station. The driver pulled up ten minutes later and drove them to the airport. Clay waited until they were safely on their way then he, Ares, and Alastor walked away from the bright lights of the station into the darkness of night, heavy tree cover and a dark road. And without breaking their stride, walked straight into a vortex and disappeared unnoticed.

Back at Kali's, the big cat sat atop a mountain bluff overlooking her house and the area below. The sky was starting to show signs of light as she made her way back to the house after sensing her intruders were gone. She sat on her hind legs just inside the tree line making sure there was no movement in the house. When she walked out into the clearing and onto her property, she was a woman again but not the same one who had fled into the woods the night before. She realized there was a price to pay when you kidnap someone. And if the laws of the land didn't catch you, and they usually do, the laws of the universe will. And reciprocity had come around like a swift knife. She too felt violated having almost been killed in her own house. And her heart bled for the loss of Spidis her friend and brilliant right hand alien, then there were the guards dedicated to keeping her safe. She should have never taken them to New Orleans she thought, with sadness and regret. Now she was on her own until Rhynous could replace them. Four beings had been killed at her house and that was hard to take, she no longer felt safe there and now they knew where she was. Kali wondered how they found her and thought they probably wondered the same but for now she was stuck there but doubted that they would return as long as she didn't make the same mistake. She felt a need to clean up with green alien blood on the walls and floor, not to mention, ashes and a pool of yellow fluid on the floor in the back bedroom. And the stench of death was making her sick along with the whole situation but she needed to call Rhynous first.

In DC, Rhynous was having a ball, wreaking havoc on the vaccine roll out for the plague. The president and his administration had done a good job of getting the big pharmaceuticals to work around the clock to create vaccines in a year. Rhynous was now causing the President to abort his plan for federal distribution leaving it to the states to fend for themselves. Rhynous was hoping to delay the distribution long enough to kill as many people as possible but what he really wanted was a nuclear war. And he had decided that he was going to get it started with China or Iran. That would be his coup de grace. He had already programmed the president to pull out of the

Iran nuclear deal in hopes of Iran continuing to develop uranium for nuclear war heads. And now without any oversight he was sure that would happen.

Rhynous was marveling at the technology of the cyber-net Kali had planted in the White House. When the president walked into the invisible net it was now attached to his face and head which he may have felt as a cob web and wiped his face or swiped at the air. Once on the skin it was invisible and unnoticeable with micro nanites attaching themselves to neural pathways in his brain. Rhynous was so pleased with this amazing technology that his plan was to reward Spidis for his years of hard work developing this software in the desert belt caves of Larus. His phone rang and he was annoyed a little because of the pleasure he was experiencing with the cyber-net, his control of the president, and his plans for destruction, power, and unrivaled supreme wealth were on track.

"Hello," he said cheerfully as a true psychopath would with complete destruction of a planet on his mind.

"Rhynous, I have bad news," Kali said.

"What happened? Whatever it is we'll just fix it, we're well on our way to one world and one leader." And he reveled in that idea.

"I don't think we can fix this." She began to cry.

"What happened!" he shouted.

"The guards are dead and Spidis is dead, they found us. I don't know how but they did. You have to get out of there, they know where you are."

"And how would they know that?" Rhynous said with anger and venom.

Kali knew that if she told the truth Rhynous would kill her. "I don't know but they tortured Spidis before they killed him and I think he may have told them."

Rhynous was now enraged and in fear all at once. "And what were you doing while all of this was going on?"

"I was being manhandled and slapped around. They have powers, Rhynous. They're not mere mortals."

Rhynous hastily closed the lap top and began throwing a few belongings into his small suitcase on wheels. "Who the hell are these beings? I need a name."

"Clay is his name and he's old, he has a very old spirit."

"I don't know who that is but I'm leaving right now." Rhynous hung up the phone and pressed a button on his belt that engaged his cloaking device and changed his alien appearance to that of the average Joe Blow American. He walked out of his room at the end of the hall and around the corner to the right as Clay, Alastor, and Ares stepped out of the elevator down the hallway from the left at the other end of the hall now trotting toward the room Rhynous had just left.

"He's on the move!" Clay shouted and they proceeded past the room in chase of Rhynous just a step ahead.

Rhynous could sense someone was on his heels and with no one in the hallway, he walked into a vortex just as Clay turned the corner in time to see it close up.

"Damn it, we lost him."

Later that same day, Vic and the ladies landed at LAX and got to his house a little after 1:00 p.m. As Vic opened the door, they stepped into the entrance way.

"Ladies, there's a custom I picked up in Asia. I need to ask you to take off your shoes."

"No problem," they said.

"Nice place," Monica said as she and Sharon walked over to sit on the recliners in the living room.

Vic walked into the kitchen, opening cabinets and the refrigerator to see what was there and noticed the other half of the brownie in the freezer that he had left there just before taking off to Larus with Clay. He immediately took it out of the fridge and back to the man cave so as not to have a repeat incident like the one that had revealed his powers with his mother-in-law. Even though the brownie had been reformulated he wasn't taking any chances. As he walked to the living room, he asked, " Ladies, what can I get for you? Something to drink, something to eat?"

"We're starved and thirsty," Monica said.

Vic recited a list of what there was to drink and the ladies decided to try the gourmet pizza in the freezer and bottled water.

"Okay, and there are snacks in the cabinet, chips, nuts, cookies, and whatever else you find in there."

At that point Monica picked up on the fact that Vic was planning to leave and instantly experienced some anxiety. "You're leaving us? No, no you can't leave us, please no."

Vic needed to get to his attorney's office to hand over the winning ticket that he had already signed. This would allow him to avoid the media circus and the notoriety of having won the lottery. "Ladies, look, I need to go to my lawyer's office and I'll be right back. No one knows where you are or that you're here."

Neither Monica or Sharon said a word. They just looked at him with the trauma of the night before on their faces. Monica's telepathy was working again because Vic could feel her sudden anxiety and knew he couldn't leave them.

"Okay, I'll tell you what. I'll stay, we eat, and I'll take you with me."

The ladies looked at each other. Sharon hunched her shoulders. "We need to think about it, let's eat first," Monica said.

Vic nodded. "Good idea." Vic put on some music to lighten the mood and hopefully relax Monica and Sharon. Vic having been a music major in his undergrad program had an eclectic taste in music from rock to R&B, and country to classical but contemporary jazz was his choice for the ladies, putting on some vintage George Benson, "Breezin'." It was light, classy and relaxing which was what he wanted for the ladies, to feel safe and relaxed. It was too soon to leave them. He just wasn't thinking, but he turned on the oven and took the pizza out of the freezer.

"What kind is it?" Sharon asked.

"It's a pesto pepperoni with goat cheese."

"That sounds great," Sharon said and Monica liked the sound of it, too."

"This pizza is going to take forty minutes so whatever you find in the cabinet until then, help yourselves." Vic broke out some potato chips and they all indulged. "Hey, there's ginger ale, gator aide, and wine," he said trying his best to make them feel better.

Monica and Sharon began to smile and chat a little more and Vic could see the stress fade from their faces. He called his attorney to let him know he was going to be delayed but after they all had eaten Monica and Sharon agreed to go on the ride up to Century City to the attorney's office where Vic was able to turn over the ticket and maintain his anonymity. Once back in the car, Vic let them know there was nothing to worry about back in New Orleans and that everything would be taken care of. Vic knew that in a week the three hundred fifty million dollars would be in his account and he could give Rob Star his second installment on his aircraft using alien technology for propulsion.

When they got home, after buying some things for the women, the first thing he did was call Rob.

"Hello."

"Hey, Rob? This is Vic, the guy you're doing the design for."

"Yes, Vic I recognized your voice. How's it going?"

"Good, I was just wondering how the design was coming."

"It's coming I just need a few more days and I'll be able to send you a rendering."

"That sounds great."

Rob was working on the design as they spoke. "Vic, I'll call you as soon as I have something presentable. I think you're going to like it but there are plenty of functions and details I need to talk to you about."

"Sounds good, I'll wait to hear from you."

Clay was now back in his compound working his men in hand-to-hand combat and extra target practice with their sonic blasters.

"Men, we are preparing for battle, there will be war!" Clay shouted.

All eleven men cheered, including Clay, making their total number twelve. He could feel the time drawing near. He had been in too many wars and too many battles not to feel it. He didn't wish for it, or thrive on it, but he was always ready to meet evil head on. Clay and his men had unique and unusual weapons but their greatest power had not yet been revealed and that was the power of invincibility. Not just Clay but all twelve were alien ghost hybrids from ancient times operating and guided by the source, that had led Vic to them in such a circuitous and mysterious way. Clay's plan for now was to send out his men in teams of two to monitor Rhynous's recruitment of homeless people to aid him in the destruction of Earth. Clay sent his spy teams to New York, Chicago, Miami, Huston, San Francisco, and Portland. Vic and Monica would monitor Los Angeles. Clay senses that Rhynous has returned to Larus to amass his troops there and anticipates that he has pirated alien ships throughout the galaxy from federation planets, how many he doesn't know but expects three warships loaded with twelve to twenty saucers or triangular fighters. Clay knew they would be out-manned especially by the smaller fighter ships but he's been in this situation before and continued to work out his strategy.

The following week back in L.A., Vic got the call from Rob Star who emailed a copy of the design for Vic's airship. He was floored by the futuristic looking craft that was sleek but bigger than he expected and different from anything he had ever seen.

"I love it! How long will it take for you to build it?"

"Six to eight months, Vic."

"That's too long, it will be too late by then."

"Too late for what?"

"I can't get into that, Rob, but I'll need it in no less than—" Vic caught himself, realizing who he was talking to and the possibility that someone could very well be listening to their conversation. "Hey, Rob, where can we meet? I'm in L.A. and you're where?"

"I'm outside of Phoenix."

Vic went to his cell phone. "Okay, let's meet in Desert Center California. That's our midway point."

"Okay, when do you want to meet there?"

" Tomorrow." There was a moment of silence on the other end.

"I don't know you that well, Vic, but I can tell you that I like the fact that you're not wasting any time. Okay, I'll tell you what, I can do it tomorrow if you can pick me up from the Desert Center Airport. I have a Cessna 150. We could meet for about two hours then I have to get back."

"Sounds great. Let's say eleven a.m., and I'll buy you a burger in town.."

"Deal, I'll see you at eleven."

"Okay, see you then."

Vic then walked into the living room and informed the ladies that they were taking a trip to the desert in the morning.

"What's happening in the desert?" Monica asked.

"I have a meeting for about two hours with an aircraft designer and I know you don't want to stay by yourselves and I don't want to leave you here, so let's be ready to go by eight-fifteen no later than eight-thirty."

Monica and Sharon agreed and the next morning they were off to Desert Center.

It was an easier ride through downtown L.A. with so many people out of work do to the pandemic. Traffic was light. Soon they were out into the suburbs then into San Bernardino County.

Monica was studying a map on her cell phone. "Hey, did you know that Desert Center is now a ghost town?"

"No, I didn't, that might not be a bad thing." Vic was now thinking that it would be easier to tell if they were being followed but he didn't say anything to the girls, they had been through enough.

Soon they were into Palm Springs then to the Coachella Valley and pulled into Desert Center Airport a little before eleven a.m. A few minutes later , Vic could see a small single engine plane out in the distance and within ten minutes it was landing.

Rob Star popped out with a briefcase and waved. Vic waved back having seen Rob on YouTube and knew what he looked like. Monica jumped into the back seat and Rob got in the front.

"Vic, great to finally meet you."

"Likewise."

The two shook hands and then Vic introduced the ladies.

"Rob, I didn't know Desert Center was a ghost town so I'm going to drive back into Indio for that burger."

"No problem, I could tell you didn't want to talk over the phone and that was smart because they're always listening."

"And that's exactly what I was thinking; that's why I thought it would be better meeting in person. Rob, I'm going to tell you a lot in as few words as I can. There's going to be a war. The government is not involved and not aware. Aliens are involved on both sides but there's an evil alien controlling the president and he's planning to destroy Earth and steal all of our financial resources worldwide."

Rob looked at Vic with a look of disbelief and started to laugh. "You're kidding, right?"

"No, Rob, I'm not but if I were in your shoes, I wouldn't believe me either. It's so far-fetched and outrageous I could tell you this truth and no one will believe you either but now you know. This is why I need you to have this aircraft in one month or it might be too late."

There was something in Vic's tone and his manner that caused the smile to leave Rob's face and caused him to think it could be true. "Look, even if it is the truth, I can't get it done in one month, that would be impossible."

"I have an idea, hire some people. Do you know any of the people who left area 51?"

"Yes, there are a few."

" Hire them."

"They'll have to be willing to work twelve-hour days and I don't know if they'll be willing to do that unless the money's right and your price tag is already over three million, even if it were five months from now but thirty days? I don't know."

"Okay, find out what they want and let me know. Send me a text in code." Vic pulled into the In N Out Burger on Avenue 46. Once everyone had eaten Monica and Sharon decided to go out for a short walk for girl talk and to let Vic and Rob do their business.

"I'm sure your familiar with Zeta Reticuli and the their two suns, right?"

As soon as Vic asked the question, Rob's head jerked up from the fries he had just smeared in ketchup. His eyes were as big as quarters and Vic could see that Rob now understood that he might be telling the truth. "Yes, I'm familiar with that system."

Look, I'm not going to ask you to talk about it. What you know is still classified but I need you to know that I've been there."

"That's impossible, it's 39.3 light years from Earth." Rob's tone and body language was now that of a person who was listening to a liar. The two men sat looking each other eye to eye. Vic was starting to feel that he had said too much when Rob started to quiz him.

"Okay, Vic, let me ask you some questions. If we were sitting here at nine p.m. tonight, where in the northern sky would Zeta Reticuli be?"

"Good try, Rob. It's not visible from the northern hemisphere. We would have to be in or south of Mexico City to see it."

"Okay, how did you get there?" Rob asked now halfway between belief and disbelief.

"Okay, I'm going to answer this question but I've already said too much so this is the last one, by teleportation. Theoretically, that or folding space is the only way I could have gone and be back already to tell about it." And

Rob was mesmerized.

"Hey let's go over to the far side of the parking lot I want to show you something," Vic said.

The two walked over to the back wall of the lot. Vic sat down his drink cup and focused on his blue energy. In seconds there was a ray of energy shooting from Vic's hand that encapsulated the cup in the form of a translucent blue square. Vic then lifted the cup off the ground to about chest high for Rob to get a better look.

"What the heck? What is that?" Rob asked with an air of excitement and confusion.

Vic intensified the ray and the cup and straw vaporized into ash and then he shut it off.

"What was that?" Rob asked.

"Look, I'm trying to bring you into the know so that you could put your all into my spaceship. Telling you about the trip was too much for you to grasp. Hey, it was a lot for me, too. I had to grow into it but I needed to show you something that you could actually see. If you don't believe me now you never will and we don't have a whole lot more time—who's that?" Vic asked.

Rob looked up and out over the parking lot to see two men who appeared to be watching them. "I don't know, I've never seen these guys before but they could be C.I.A. or black operative agents. You ready to go?"

Vic nodded and looked over toward the street in search of the girls. He walked over to see down the street and the girls were coming back a few feet away.

"Perfect timing, we're headed back to the airport."

"Okay, I thought so," Monica said.

They all got back in the car and took off for the airport. Vic knowing his time was short started in right away.

"Rob, I need to be able to use my blue energy from the ship as a weapon along with conventional or laser weapon technology. I need electromagnetic alien propulsion with hover capability, alien cloaking, and I should be able to fly to Mars and back by refueling the engine with solar power."

"I know what you need." Rob was seemingly in a trance, depressed, and focused all at the same time.

"Rob, you okay?" Vic asked with some concern. "You're not backing out on me, are you?"

"Not at all. I'm starting to believe you. They're going to be crawling all over me again."

"Who, the feds?"

"Yes, who else?"

"No, they won't, you just have to keep your mouth shut. You can't go around telling the world about this stuff, and no social media, there's a portion of society that's not ready for this knowledge. There are good aliens and people who could get hurt by scared close minded people with guns who will shoot first without understanding. You can't talk about this to the men you hire either. Tell them it's for an eccentric who wants to fly to the moon," Vic said.

"You could be right."

Vic noticed a black sedan a good distance back that had maintained its distance. "I think were being followed."

"That's par for the course when you're dealing with me but don't worry, this time I'm going to work on a need-to-know basis, and no one needs to know."

"Hey, we're on the same page." Vic pulled into Desert Center and down the main road to the airport. "I'm going to wire you one-point-five million."

"Okay, the propulsion elements for your engine are going to be expensive, be prepared for that."

"I understand, it's equivalent to a nuclear reactor, I've seen the YouTube clips, Rob."

Rob got out of the car and shut the door. He then bent down, putting his forearm on the window frame. "This has been an incredible visit; you never seem to disappoint, Mr. Vic."

"I can't, there's too much at stake."

"I get it, and I'm going to help you deliver."

The two shook hands and Rob walked out to his airplane, started it up and radioed the tower. He taxied out, getting immediate clearance.

Vic and the girls watch Rob take off in the afternoon sun and out into the wild blue yonder until his plane became the size of an ant and then disappeared.

CHAPTER 20

Alastor and Ares came through a vortex on Sullivan Street just below Washington Square in lower Manhattan, looking for homeless people in parks engaging in unusual activities with alien entities. They came out the other side of the square past the arch and headed north up 5th Avenue through Greenwich Village and over one block to Union Square Park with no activity. Then they headed up Broadway cutting across to Madison Square Park, to find nothing. They continued up 5th Avenue past the Empire State Building up to Bryant Park at the New York Public Library in midtown Manhattan and again there was nothing unusual. The two warriors continued up the street until they reached Central Park through Freedman Plaza and up East Drive when they overheard a conversation about strange people trying to offer shelter to the homeless. Alastor turned to inquire about the location of that group and they were told to go left at 65th Street to Sheep Meadow.

When they reached Sheep Meadow there was a crowd of homeless people standing around three figures one of which seemed to be an alien covered in a hat and cloaked with a device, the trained eyes of these warriors knew the tell tail signs of an alien. Sometimes it was the large eye sockets, elongated hands, or a sixth finger. Other times it was a slip revealing a strange accent, short in stature and slim build or just their ability to sense the presence of an extra-terrestrial. Ares and Alastor were dressed down in jeans, winter jackets and boots and seemed to fit in with the homeless crowd who were suspicious and asking questions. The two warriors stood in the back, one wearing an old Yankee baseball cap and the other a beanie in the shadow of the night sky. The other two recruiters, one male and one female, who were smartly doing most of the talking were formerly homeless and knew some of the people they were talking to. Whatever their affliction was drugs, alcohol, or insanity the cyber-net computer program had the ability to correct their behavior returning them to their original selves before illness or vices. That function of this advanced technology alone was enough to win a Nobel Peace Prize and make the creator millions of dollars helping people all over the world live happy, normal, productive lives. However, it was in the wrong hands and was being used to undo the Earth and to quench unparalleled greed.

The former homeless speakers were articulate, persuasive and now clean cut with what seemed like a possible future causing Ares to wonder how he could get around killing them. The problem was the two were already being controlled by Rhynous and Ares nor Alastor knew how to deactivate the program so they were left with no choice. Ares and Alastor both knew that this would be the first of many casualties and battles to come so they prepared their minds for battle as they had so many times before.

The male named Reggie said, "We have a van ready to take you to a clean facility, hot shower and a comfortable bed. Who's interested?"

Out of the sixty people who were there eleven people were interested and ready to go. When Ares and Alastor raised their hands that made thirteen. The woman Carroll was pleased with the number of people ready to get, as she called it, cleaned up. The two warriors looked at each other knowing that it meant, being sold out to Rhynous. The crowd began to disperse and the thirteen new recruits followed Reggie, Carroll and the alien, whose name was supposed to be Al, down to 65th Street where a long van promptly pulled up on cue. Everyone piled into the van and the atmosphere among the eleven homeless was one of jubilation and gratefulness for not having to spend another night out on the cold streets of New York. Ares and Alastor knew the recruits were going to have their minds high jacked into military slavery as ponds in Rhynous's army and their plan was to stop it. They both began to check their weapons the sonic blast weapon and the deadly needle blade that was ready to slice and dice in their pockets. Soon they were in a warehouse area of the city not far from the East River as they pulled up to the gate. The driver inserted his gate key and the wrought iron gate slid open to the concrete building. It was two stories and huge but once they were inside there was a desk in front, carpet and nice seating for a lobby. It was late so there was no one at the desk. The three leaders went straight to a heavy metal door that led to a large empty room then to another door which led to another large room.

When they opened the second door the room was half full of people just standing in straight military like lines. Their bodies were being permeated with cybernetic light and more specifically their heads. The grid of lights on close examination was carrying data and nanites to each skull and brain, they all were in a cybernetic induced trance and were being reprogrammed. Ares and Alastor knew the time was near but didn't want to jump the gun. They looked to recruiters and the look on their faces told the whole story. An evil countenance had consumed their eyes and their tone had changed. They were now more assertive. Reggie had now taken a defensive and more strategic position to the side with his hand on his hip. Ares and Alastor knew he had a gun but stayed cool, the alien was now doing the talking

"Now I know some of you are wondering what's going on here but I assure you no one's being hurt. This is a cybernetic cleansing that everyone must go through. It tells us who's sick and who may have contagious diseases. We just need everyone to choose a line and face forward."

A guy by the name of Big Willy wasn't going for it. "Hey I didn't sign up for all of this, I'm good, you could just let me out." Now all the attention was on Willy.

Alastor looked at Ares and motioned with his eyes that he was going to take Reggie. Ares looked at Al the alien letting Alastor know that was his target. They both had their hands in their pockets slipping on their needle blades and proceeded to inch closer to their target. Reggie had moved in to try and talk to Willy. When he took his hand off his gun, Alastor was standing to his right and then with the speed of a Taekwondo expert deployed his laser pushing it up through Reggie's diaphragm and cleanly through his heart. He retracted it so quickly that no one seemed to notice with all the light in the room. Reggie would have dropped to the floor but Alastor caught him.

"I think something is wrong with Reggie," Alastor said, laying him to the floor with only a small hole in his shirt above his naval. Because of the cauterization of the laser there was no blood.

Ares was now in a position to take down Al who with his advanced brain was figuring out they had been infiltrated. Now being suspicious , sensing someone was behind him, Al turned quickly to look behind and Ares thrust his blade into the corner of Al's eye and out the back of his skull. Everyone saw that and the women screamed. Panic ensued and three people ran for the door but it was locked. The warriors were now focused on Carroll who now feared for her life.

"Guys, my money is in my purse. I've got about three hundred dollars. It's all yours."

The two warriors laughed and looked at each other. "You tell her," Ares said as the other eleven captives stood watching in confusion.

"Carroll, we have no use for your money. You see, we know who you are and that you're a part of an elaborate plan to destroy Earth. Listen up, everyone, these people led you here to brainwash you, program you, and to enlist you in an army as pawns against every government on Earth. You would have been under the cyber spell of a galactic pirate by the name of Rhynous who wants to destroy the Earth and steal all its wealth. That's what you see happening here, my friend, and I are here to stop them," Alastor said.

"Oh, thank God, a lady said.

"The door is locked," Big Willy said, with all eleven people feeling anxiety and urgency.

Ares nodded to acknowledge Willy.

"Give me the key, Carroll," Alastor said, and she handed it over quickly knowing her life was in the balance. "Listen everyone, you are a part of this now and we need your help."

"Hey, you get us out of here and we'll do whatever you want," one man said and the other ten people agreed.

"Thank you, but all we need you good New Yorkers to do is to organize amongst yourselves and go to the parks in the city and tell every homeless person you see about what's going on here. If the organization doesn't have an official city badge or identification let them know to get out of there and run like hell."

"Shouldn't we tell the police?" Willy said.

"Good luck with that, Willy. When you start talking about aliens destroying Earth you may run into some problems with that. If you're going to inform the police just let them know that homeless people are being kidnapped and held against their will, that may workout better."

"Who's an alien?" Bob asked."

Ares walked over to Al's body and put his fingers in the small amount of blood coming from the back of his head then held it up for them to see.

"It's green," Willy said.

"Oh shit! Let's get out of here," another man said and they all rushed to the door.

Alastor gave Ares a dirty look and a smirk as he walked by to open the door.

"What?" Ares said.

"Okay, people, get as far away from here as you can as quick as you can."

The last one out was Willy. "Hey could I do anything to help you guys?

"You have the heart of a warrior, Willy, but no, it's too dangerous, you surely would be killed and we need you to inform the homeless, that's really important. Hey, there is one thing. Carroll, give me that money."

Carroll gave the money to Ares who gave it to Alastor as he blocked her from the door. Alastor went out to the van with the driver still inside. "Do you work for this company?"

"No, sir, I'm an independent contractor. I come when they call me. I've brought lots of people over here," the man said.

"That's Sal, he's all over the city," Willy said.

"Okay, Sal, here's one hundred sixty bucks. I want you to catch all those people who just walked out and drive them to where ever they need to go, you included, Willy. And Willy, here's one hundred forty bucks. Go to a burger joint and feed everyone, including Sal."

"Hey, thank you sir," Sal said.

"Okay, thanks man. Hey, what's your name?" Willy asked.

"I'm Alastor." They shook hands.

"Hey, you're named after a Greek god. Thanks for saving our lives. Hope to see you again."

"Wow, you've got some schooling. I'll try to catch you in the park again to see how things are going," Alastor said.

"Bet," Willy said

Sal started to back out.

Alastor looked up to the second floor and could see a faint flicker of light through the tinted windows of the building.

Back in the lobby when Alastor tapped on the door Ares opened it to the sound of Carroll pleading for her freedom.

"What's upstairs, Carroll?" Alastor asked in a dark killer tone as he walked in.

"I don't know."

They knew she was lying but Alastor moved on to the next question. "How do you deactivate these people back here? Answer wisely, your life depends on it."

They escorted her back to the second room, one warrior on each arm. As she entered the room without saying a word Carroll pulled out her cell phone and deactivated the program, stopping the light show, leaving only the ceiling florescent lights on that now seemed dim in comparison. "There, now please let me go."

Alastor held onto her arm as Ares walked through the lines but no one moved or blinked. Then after a few minutes there was movement. Eyes, arms and legs started to move slowly. Ares and Alastor started to smile in relief as people began to moan and groan as if coming out of a deep sleep and then sitting on the floor. Ares gave them a few more minutes and then made his announcement.

"People you have been held captive here and we don't know for how long but you need to go find another shelter. Whatever you do don't came back here. These people are crooks. In the next few days go back to Central Park at Sheep's Meadow, and ask for Big Willy and he will fill you in."

Slowly they began to file out and once they were all gone, Alastor said, "Well done. Now let's head upstairs."

"Okay, you have the key," Carroll said, informing them that the elevator was to the left.

"We're not taking the elevator," Alastor said.

"Okay, the stairs are at the end," Carroll said.

As they walked to the end of the lobby Ares could tell she was on her phone and he quickly grabbed it reaching over her shoulder from behind. "I don't think you'll be needing this." Ares looked at the screen but there was no message and he felt a little more relaxed.

As they went up the two flights of stairs they both pulled out their blasters just in case. Alastor hit the fire door bar and the door flew open, as he walked into the hallway the sound and hail of bullets from automatic rifles filled the air as bullets penetrated the metal door and concrete wall behind. The expectation was already there for gunfire but the ferocity of gun shots was shocking, it was a hornet's nest. Carroll immediately fell to the floor in the stairwell and Ares stepped over her to get to Alastor who was returning fire with his blaster and he had been shot several times in his legs and torso. Ares took position from beside the wall and picked off two of Rhynous's soldiers from behind the concrete wall which was immediately pummeled by high powered automatic rifle fire driving Ares to the floor but drawing fire away from Alastor who belly crawled to the stairwell taking one last shot to the butt.

"Ah, damn it!" he shouted.

"What?" Ares shouted back through the gun fire.

"One of those bastards shot me in the ass."

Ares could see the yellow fluid leaking into Alastor's pants. Ares knew they would laugh about it later but right now he was pissed off and returning fire with his sonic setting on high creating a deadly air blast that shattered bones, crushes skulls, and explodes hearts. Even with this advanced alien technology the return fire was so heavy they had to retreat back down the stairwell. Ares grabbed Alastor by the arm and pulled him out of harm's way. Ares shut the fire door behind them, helped Alastor to his feet and they both scurried down the stairs back to the first floor and out of the building. As they reached the front of the building headed toward the gate. They heard the sound of a helicopter taking off from the roof. They both looked up in time to see the bell helicopter jet over the side of the building and open fire on them as they ran for the gate with one catching Ares in the calf muscle before it disappeared past the roof tops and out over the east river." They can't kill us with these human guns but these bullets sure as hell do hurt." You telling me, Alastor said holding his buttocks as they blasted through the gate then into an alley through a vortex.

Meanwhile, back in the building up on the second floor under heavy guard were two hundred homeless people standing at attention trapped in the cybernetic light about to complete their programming against their will. They will be shipped out to join Rhynous's army to be used in any way he chooses.

Carroll had not stopped running and was now running down into the subway. She thinks to call her mom but realizes she no longer has a phone. She now has to figure out how to tell her superior, Rhynous's lieutenant, Goss, that the enemy now has the key to destroy their plans. Then, she decides not to tell him as it would mean death, and she's determined to stay alive.

On Larus, Rhynous is loading his fourth and final mother ship as the scout saucers load into the cargo bay with the majority having been converted into fighters with atomic canons on cargo ships and two of the mother ships with atomic electric canons that generate an atomic electrical blast that could destroy a city and level mountains in seconds but not render an area uninhabitable for years. The radiation from these blasts could be neutralized in a few months based on Rhynous's stolen technology from the Larian world government. These two Mother ships are the equivalent of Earth's nuclear destroyers but more powerful and accurate. The other two mother ships are equipped with laser guns and cannons but carry a hospital and a science laboratory to continue working on technology breakthroughs like the cyber-net web.

The size and grandeur of his fleet fused with the technology and power of their weapons casts greater light on Rhynous, revealing his true stature, one hundred times more elevated than a nickel and dime warlock dabbling in witchery or magic. And not just a pirate but a monster over all pirates and elevated to the title of supreme Majestic Leader by his men who have sold their souls to join Rhynous's evil empire. Rhynous stood on the bridge of his command ship, also the science lab, and looked out over the other three gigantic mother ships with three squadrons of fighters on all four ships totaling two hundred eighty-eight fighters. They were all faster and more maneuverable than anything on Earth and more destructive. As one of his generals approached from behind, he could see the silhouette of Rhynous taking a deep breath. Rhynous's chest swelled with pride and deep satisfaction as the general rounded his side to face Rhynous.

"Majestic leader, we have received word from Earth that the processing centers for your rejected Earth recruits are under attack and many recruits are being lost."

The joy of his moment now shattered with this new and unsettling information; his countenance changed. "Tell those men to get a move on it! We are launching tonight!" Now he was boiling over, with veins bulging as the general walked away cringing. "Damn it!" Rhynous shouted with his stun gun voice that rattled the walls and electronics of the mother ship. And now he had an idea of who it was, the beings that had followed him and his men at the rally in Washington, DC he knew it had to be them. Rhynous remembered Clay's face from the park but still couldn't place it from the distant past, they were a mystery to him that struck fear in his heart. The other part of a warrior's heart becomes enraged and more determined pushing past that fear to destroy that which stands in his way but he was dealing with an unknown variable. Rhynous had no clue about who he was up against but he reveled in the fact that his fleet and fighters were far superior to anything Earthlings could muster on Earth. Then he remembered the man who had shot the energy blast from the palm of his hand. And who was about to increase and double its power when he and his two men escaped through his dimensional door and disappeared. Rhynous remembered Vic and saw him as a threat but more importantly wanted to recruit him for the negative realm of the universe but not realizing they were polar opposites. If only he could trap Vic, who's name Rhynous still doesn't know, in the laser web mind control program it wouldn't matter who the others were, Rhynous thought. Suddenly, Rhynous felt a loss of power on the ship and looked around trying to figure out what had happened. His computers are down and he waits for the backup reactor to kick in but it doesn't. After a short while he here's a rush of footsteps coming down the corridor.

As he looked there were two generals and a unit of armed soldiers with them. "What is going on?" Rhynous asked with concern.

General Motar responded. "Majestic leader, there was a power surge that knocked our computers and both reactors off line. We're down to a lone backup, this is going to take days to repair sir."

"Where did this surge come from, we're not under attack!" Rhynous exclaims ready to kill the individual who's responsible for delaying the fleet for weeks.

The generals looked at each other and Motar answered, " Sir, the serge was traced to this location. That's why your soldiers are here, we thought you had possibly came under some kind of attack."

Now with some twisted incredulous look on his face, Rhynous tried to figure out what the hell had happened when he realized that the person, he wanted to kill for this sabotage was himself. The sonic blast from his own voice in his fit of anger over the attack on his recruitment centers back on Earth had caused the surge. His anger and look of confusion were replaced by shouts and insults to his generals.

"If I find out who caused the delay, I'm going to personally decapitate them with all of my army gathered to watch. Now go and figure out how long it's going to take to get those reactors and computers back online."

It was a typical psychopathic response by a narcissistic over blown ego that couldn't take responsibility for his own mistake because in his twisted mind it made him look weak. The reality is that it would have made him look responsible and human but he wasn't human, and compassion nor empathy was in his DNA.

CHAPTER 21

Three weeks later, back on Earth, the phone rang and Vic picked it up.

"Hey, Vic."

"Rob! What's going on?"

"Ooh, everything. Your ship is near completion and I think you should come take a look at it."

"That's fantastic! But how did you get it done so fast?"

"Good question. When I asked the guys I knew who had worked at 51, they were all in. And they knew guys who were highly skilled who had retired or moved on before I got there and they wanted to be a part of it. So, I wound up with two crews giving me a day shift and a swing shift so we were able to get twice as much done in half the time."

Vic couldn't believe what he was hearing. It was more exciting than the lottery win. It was Monday. "Okay, I can be there tomorrow."

"I knew you were going to say tomorrow but how about Wednesday? That would work out better."

"Perfect Rob. Wednesday it is."

"Great! Look, if you fly into Phoenix I can pick you up at the airport. Try to get here around ten or eleven a.m.."

"Okay, I'll text you my flight information when I get it and we can go from there."

"Great Vic, I'll see you Wednesday."

"Sounds good."

At 5:30 a.m. on Wednesday, Vic was packing light to last a day or two with a pair of socks, one pair of boxers, a tee shirt, a golf shirt, a tooth brush and a hat. He was so excited he couldn't sleep. As he left the closet, he noticed that Monica had left his bed while he was in the closet but he knew exactly where she was. When he got to Sharon's room, Monica was curled up behind Sharon, both still traumatized from Kali's deadly kidnapping. He kissed Monica on the cheek and Sharon on the forehead. Sharon being there was a big help because she was like a sister to Monica. And now after the kidnapping, they were like two scared little girls constantly clinging to each other. Vic realized after requesting his Uber to the airport he was going to have to convince the girls to go to therapy for their own mental health.

As he stood in front of the house waiting for his driver, Vic had a feeling that he couldn't shake. He looked up and down the quiet street, it was 6:15 in the morning and no one was out. It was cool and calm, a refreshing sixty-five degrees but he couldn't stop that inner voice that was telling him someone was watching. The driver came shortly after and Vic dismissed it as probably a neighbor looking out a window. Soon Vic was going through airport security which was why he had on his black slip-on tennis shoes and his belt still in his duffel bag. Once through the scanner he put on his belt for the first time and stepped into his shoes then off to gate 13. It was a smooth one-hour flight to Phoenix and Rob was waiting in a parking lot across the street when Vic called. The two men greeted each other with high energy and excitement.

"So, what does it look like?" Vic asked like a kid at Christmas.

"It's hard to describe but I wouldn't tell you anyway, that would spoil the surprise. I want to see the look on your face when you see it for the first time."

Vic smiled as the tension and the excitement built on the inside. Rob drove past Phoenix proper on the 10 freeway as if heading for New Mexico. Once they were well into the desert, Rob made a left onto what looked like a ranch property as they drove over the cow grate and past the barbed-wired fence that seemed to stretch at least a mile in either direction. Rob drove for two miles back up the side of a hill and down into a huge valley area unseen from the highway surrounded by hills that reminded Vic of his high desert location in California but five times larger. It was an unseen compound on a huge acreage with a security gate and an armed guard. Rob opened the gate with his remote and waved to the guard as they passed, heading for a large hangar that was cloaked with an image of trees and desert for anyone passing over in a plane or helicopter. Inside was a huge open floor space big enough for two jumbo jets nose to tail but Vic found it curious that there was no runway outside the hangar. There was a large tarmac area in front of and to the right of the facility when facing the hangar doors from the outside. When Vic asked Rob about there not being a runway, Rob explained that most of his work was done on helicopters but somehow Vic didn't think that was the whole truth but didn't press Rob for more information. Rob led Vic to a side door and inside there were men hustling about sweeping and making things look neat on the floor. In the very back of the hangar was some sort of aircraft plugged into a generator and hovering five feet off the ground, as if resting on invisible legs. It was covered up and Vic couldn't wait to see it, he just wanted to walk up and snatch off the parachute cover but realized that would be inappropriate. It appeared Rob had something planned and he didn't want to spoil it with a classless act of impatience. After all he was a multi-millionaire now, a fact he had forgotten because he still felt like the same old Vic. And the fact that he hadn't changed his life style or had the time to even think about enjoying the money. Somehow Vic felt it was better this way because the true purpose of getting the money was to build the aircraft and protect Earth, other than that he hadn't had time to even think about it.

Suddenly, Rob addresses everyone in the room. "Guys, come on in. Let me introduce you to Vic."

And Vic greeted the men and thanked them all.

Rob, wasting no time, then told the guys to reveal the craft as four of the men pulled back the covering and Vic gasped. "Aah! That's awesome!"

"What are you going to call it?" Rob asked.

"The Phantom Cobra."

All the guys sounded their approval.

The Phantom Cobra was White and almost shiny like glass because its outer skin was a futuristic solar panel more advanced than anything on Earth. The panels were able to absorb one hundred percent of any light source including the reflection of light from the moon and absorb starlight from distant stars at night. The panels were bullet proof and laser weapons were merely another light source that allowed the craft to become supercharged with light energy making its own laser weapons more powerful. The Phantom Cobra looked like it was going fast while standing still it was a marvel of modern technology. Vic noticed small Diamond patterns in the solar panels and when he inquired Rob informed him it was a laser projection system for his cloaking device. Vic is in awe of his craft and blown away. He then asked Rob about the Cobra's engine. Rob understanding that Vic was not a scientist kept his explanation simple.

"Vic the phantom cobra isn't powered by an engine as you know it, it's more of a small reactor in a led housing encased in titanium, insulated for heat and powered by element 115. In layman's terms, it's round, about the circumference of a car tire and can generate three thousand five hundred units of electromagnetic energy that can propel the craft up to light speed and then stop on a dime with an in cabin force field to neutralize crushing G forces on a human body. Even with all that it still needs to be charged along with the battery systems on board from time to time but that will be provided by the technologically advanced solar panels, that we call star panels, or just a charge and you will never use fossil fuel."

Vic now knew that Rob had come in contact with, and reverse engineered alien UFO technology but said nothing to Rob. "Hey take me inside," Vic said.

Rob touched the side of the craft and a ramp eased down from the bottom of the craft and they entered from the back on the first deck that housed the reactor room centered on the ship for proper weight distribution, a technology room with a computer hard drive to store and back up all systems on the ship. The next room housed a restroom and a storage area for equipment and cargo centered in the middle being the heaviest. The next room at the far end of the corridor going across the ship had four foam beds formed one on each wall including the entrance wall to the left of the door. Coming out of that door facing up the right side corridor heading toward the front of the ship is a staircase leading up to the second floor and the cockpit of the craft. Once up the stairs Vic went straight to the captain's seat of the control room. It was beyond his wildest dreams as was the whole ship. It was an all-digital display of gauges, meters, and unknown readouts.

Suddenly, a pulse of excitement rushed through Vic's veins. "Rob, is this a space worthy aircraft?" Vic asked with bated breath.

"Yes, I thought that's what you wanted."

"Yes, but I don't remember asking. Rob, you're a genius."

"Why thank you, Vic, that feels so much better with your saying it instead of me telling my dog." They both laughed.

Rob began by explaining to Vic how to fly the spacecraft. He also explained that rocket ships from Earth needed speeds of twenty-five thousand miles per hour also known as escape velocity to break past Earth's magnetic field and gravitational cocoon. Rob then explained that the electromagnetic field on the Phantom Cobra would reduce that speed to one-fifth or five thousand miles per hour but recommended twelve thousand five hundred miles per hour when punching through Earth's atmosphere.

Vic took note of that and asked, "Rob, what is the top speed of the Phantom Cobra."

"Theoretically one hundred eighty-six thousand two hundred eighty-two-point-four miles per second in outer space," Rob told him but recommended only half that speed.

Vic was astonished and couldn't even imagine getting to Rob's suggested speed but it was there at his fingertips if he needed it.

"I'm going to have to train you on how to fly it. The good news is that you don't know how to fly an aircraft so you won't be confused or relearning anything and it will be easier than flying an airplane."

That was great news for Vic. "When do we get started?"

"Tonight, after dinner, with a crash theory course and review of capabilities and controls. Tomorrow, we fly for real. Your first flight, a maiden voyage, if you will."

Just hearing it made Vic's heart beat faster. Rob put Vic up in sleeping quarters in the hangar that were quite comfortable but he still couldn't sleep, only fading away for a few hours.

The next morning at 5:00 a.m., Rob walked into the hangar kitchen to find Vic drinking coffee and eating a cookie.

"You ready?" Rob asked with an excited face.

"As ready as I'll ever be. Let's do it."

So, they headed down the steps into the hangar where the Phantom Cobra still hovered silently. Rob pulled the larger than normal plug from the back of the Phantom Cobra and returned it to the charging station. On his return he touched the side of the spacecraft where a series of numbers appeared. As his code unlocked the ship it rose up to just under six feet off the ground and the ramp eased down from underneath as if opened by a ghost. This time as they emerged onto the craft in the forward section of the ship in front of the reactor room, they took the pilot's side stairs up to the bridge. Rob sat in the co-pilot seat as Vic made himself comfortable on the pilot's side.

"Look over the console and get familiar with the symbols and names and match them with what you learned last night and you can go ahead and power her up."

Vic nodded and pressed the power symbol on the computer console. And just like the Larian ships, the Phantom began to emit an electric hum like five Tesla cars and though it was still quiet, Vic felt a surge of power go through the ship, as if it had just come alive or been awakened from a floating somber. The general operation of the phantom was like driving a car with a joy stick to his right side console that felt like a stick shift but instead allowed him to go left or right and forward or backwards. And with the touch of a button can move in any direction at blink speed or hover like a classic UFO. While Vic was getting familiar in real time Rob was opening the hangar doors remotely and instructed Vic to ease the Phantom Cobra out onto the tarmac. Then he asked Vic to neutralize gravity on the ship to eliminate the G forces and to blink speed to twenty thousand feet straight up. It was all there in the presets; he set the altitude and pressed the up button on the virtual screen which was also on the control panel. And in the blink of an eye, they were hovering at that exact altitude.

"Now let's cloak so we don't attract any attention," Rob said.

Vic searched the screen, quickly finding the stealth touch icon as the American made UFO disappeared in the predawn sky.

"Hey, I'm impressed. So far you're doing great." Rob said.

This gave Vic a boost of confidence and some relaxation. As they looked out on the horizon, they could see Phoenix in the distance. And as the sun rose in the morning sky the star panels went to work collecting energy from the sun causing the hum from the reactor to become more vibrant just like on the Larian saucers.

"So where do you want to go?" Rob asked.

"What do you mean?"

"Anywhere in the world, where do you want to go?"

"Hey, Japan!" Vic shouted.

"Raise her up to sixty thousand feet to get above the commercial flight patterns and punch in Japan."

Vic did what Rob instructed him to do and a virtual map appeared over the console. Rob reached over and touched auto pilot and a female voice that Vic would soon name Phanta spoke. "We are going to Japan and what is your preferred speed?"

"Twenty thousand miles per hour," Vic said. "Start at one hundred and increase our speed by one thousand miles per hour every five seconds."

"As you command, "Phanta replied.

Twelve minutes later they were in Japan. Within an hour and fifteen minutes they had been to Africa, Europe, Japan, South America, and back to Arizona. It was unbelievable and they hadn't even come close to light speed. Vic's head was still spinning trying to grasp the capabilities of the Phantom Cobra and what they had just done breaking every air speed record on the planet but this was private sector top secret. They still hadn't been to space but Vic wanted to get familiar with the on board weapons first and they had about one hundred thousand miles of Sonoran Desert that covered southern Arizona, southeastern California, Baja California, and the state of Sonora Mexico. There was plenty of remote area to work from. Rob suggested crossing the border into Mexico so they headed south into Sonora cloaked at twenty thousand feet, producing no radar foot print because the star panel shell of the Phantom Cobra only absorbs energy and refracts none. They reached an area that was dangerously remote with no human activity within a one-hundred-fifty-mile radius. Vic needed no instruction from Rob in finding the weapons icon on the console. When he touched it, there was a virtual sight. And once his iris had been read the sight locked onto his eyes. So that whatever he was looking at when he fired his laser guns, that's what he hit within one-eighth of an inch from center mass. And then there was the laser canon that was also equipped to shoot Vic's blue energy with an arm slot on the left side console but the canon was quite powerful on its own.

"Okay, I see you've got this," Rob said.

Then Vic began firing the laser guns and loved the eye lock automation that allowed him to look and fire as he mowed down cactus and yucca plants. "What's the ray icon?" Vic asked.

"It's a continuous laser ray you can use for cutting through walls, metal, rock, or whatever you may need it for."

"Cool." Vic switched to the canon and blasted a four-hundred-fifty-foot hill and leveled it throwing dirt for a mile and vaporizing everything behind it for half a mile. Having seen that, Vic realized quickly that the Phantom Cobra was not a toy, it was lethal in more ways than one and commanded that respect. Suddenly, there were Mexican military planes and jets joined by American F-15EX fighters. In an instant, Vic tapped fifty thousand feet on the altitude, pressed the up button and in a blink of an eye they were looking down on the swarm of airplanes from both countries.

Phanta began to speak. "We are being hailed by aircraft communications. Do you wish to respond, sir?" Vic looked at Rob who shook his head no. Vic answered Phanta with a no but asked to hear the live transmission. "As you command, sir." They heard the pilots talking back and forth.

"I couldn't really see anything did you?" "

No but this was the location we were given and that hill disappeared, someone was here."

Upon hearing that, Vic shot out over the Pacific Ocean near the Hawaiian Islands and hovered for thirty minutes and then instructed Phanta to get them back to home base in Arizona. A few minutes later, she lowered them down hovering at five feet in front of the hangar as Rob opened the hangar doors then Phanta pulled into the hangar at an appropriate five miles per hour turning the Phantom Cobra facing out ready for its next mission.

"Oh, by the way the Phantom does have landing gear. Phanta, please deploy the landing gear," Rob said.

"As you command, sir." Being her programmed response, she deployed the three black alloy supports with round footings on a ball joint for uneven terrain.

Rob came down the ramp upset that military planes from both countries showed up looking for them and wants to know why and how. "Vic, I'll be back to finish up our business but right now I need to make some calls and find out how the hell we were tracked. There have been some new developments in military radar systems and I have a need to know what they are."

"Okay." Vic headed for the kitchen as Rob stormed to the front of the hangar to his office and slammed the door. Vic wasn't sure why Rob was so upset. Even thought they were tracked they couldn't be seen nor could they keep up with the unlimited speed of the Phantom Cobra. There was now a faint loving ache in his heart and again, all of his thoughts were of Monica and he knew she was calling him telepathically.

Vic picked up his phone. "Hey, babe! How's it going?"

"Hey, love, good to hear from you. We're just here at the house. What's going on there? Tell me about your airplane."

"Okay, you got it. First, it's unbelievable! You can't even imagine what this thing is like. And it's not an airplane, it's a spaceship with out-of-this world technology. It travels at unimaginable speeds and I named it the Phantom Cobra."

All Monica could say was, "Wow. When will I get to go for a ride?"

"Soon enough. I'll be back in a few days. I still have some training to do and I need to figure out where I'm going to build a hangar."

"Right here," a familiar voice said from behind him. Vic turned to see Rob standing in the doorway.

"Hey, babe, I've got to go. Rob may have just solved the hangar problem. He and I need to talk business."

"Okay, I miss you."

Vic wanted to tell her he loved her but repeated the same.

Monica felt what he felt and said, "I love you, too."

Vic laughed. "I forgot who I was talking to. Love you. Talk to you later." Vic knew he had been telepathically scanned and read so the only thing that was left was the truth.

"Ooh, so which one of those hot babes was that?" Rob asked as they walked down to his office."

"The brunette. " Vic smiled.

"Nice choice," Rob said as if he were talking about a rare and fine wine.

Monica never told Vic what she had been working on at the house because there was still more to research but her inner spirit was telling her something that would be hard for Vic to grasp and upset the balance of positive and negative energy in this battle for Earth but she needed to continue digging until she could physically confirm what her advanced intuition was telling her. It made no sense at first and Monica tried to ignore it, the similarities, the mannerisms but the differences are glaring, so diametrically opposed. It was all so upsetting but she couldn't stop until she could get to the bottom of it.

Back on Larus, Rhynous has become a raving maniac pushing his rank and file to speed up the repairs and has refused to leave the mother ship making life miserable for his leading officers. They've spent the last week avoiding Rhynous as much as possible to duck his threats and tongue lashing. Rhynous is now in the flight command center on his lead mother ship sitting on a throne like command seat designed for the Majestic Leader. As he sat, his only thoughts were of who he could kill to make an example out of to expedite this lengthy delay. He remembered an officer who he didn't like, the truth of the matter was he thought the humanoid would try to over through him some day so he spent the next twenty minutes trying to figure out how to tie Zolzex to the outage. These were the thoughts of a psychopath, who knew dam well he himself was the cause of the power surge but continued with his sick plan to strike fear in the hearts of his crew with murder to speed up the repairs to the ship and, to literally, kill two birds with one stone. Rhynous started rounding up his personal guard telling them he had a special assignment for them. Once he had ten of his guards, he headed to the logistics office where the officer in his cross hair was stationed.

"Officer Zolzex," the security guards called.

One of the four men who were sitting at their desks stood up in surprise wondering what it could be. "Yes, I'm Zolzex."

"The Majestic Leader would like to speak to you outside."

Zolzex was now intrigued and excited thinking that he was going to meet with the Majestic Leader and possibly be honored or rewarded. When he walked out the guards had amassed a crowd of crew members from Rhynous's army and Rhynous stood smiling cloaked in his human face as Zolzex walked up and greeted Rhynous.

"Majestic Leader, to what honor do I owe this visit?" Zolzex asked with class and glee.

Then Rhynous lowered his smile and the monster inside sprang forward and at that moment Zolzex realized this visit was not good and his terror began. Rhynous began citing infractions and questioning Zolzex concerning his whereabouts on the day of the surge, the crash of computers, and a reactor that delayed the mission. Rhynous then informed Zolzex that he had information that he had been seen in the main computer room at that time.

"That's not true," Zolzex said with horror in his eyes because he knew that he was looking into the eyes of a mad man.

Rhynous felt no remorse or compassion in killing an innocent being. In him was an empty heart of darkness void of any emotional conflict or second thought. Zolzex was just an object, a rag doll now in Rhynous's grasp and under his control to do with as he pleased to serve a purpose. So, he coldly and calculatedly decided to end it by pulling out a vile of what appeared to be a silvery liquid but in reality, it was a vile of thirty thousand nanites programmed to rip apart, tear up, and burn through the brain of a humanoid body. Rhynous walked up to Zolzex, cupping his hand to whisper something into his ear and at the same time pouring the nanites just inside his earlobe. The nanites were like fast moving ants and too small to be seen.

Zolzex upon feeling some of the liquid running down his neck, wiped it, and looked at his hand to see what it was then put it to his nose to smell it and unintentionally touched his nose. The nanites were now rushing into his ear, his nose, and rushing up his face to his eyes. Once in his eyes the nanites began dismantling the optic nerve leading to his brain creating tremendous pain and blindness as they cut through tissue causing his eyes to bleed profusely. The nanites in his ear severed his ear drum and cut their way to his brain headed straight for his medulla which controlled the heart and breathing. The nanites attacked this brain organ at the base of the skull and Zolzex's body soon had no control as his heart raced out of its normal rhythm into cardiac arrest and his breathing stopped as blood continued to stream from his eyes and now his nose. Within a few minutes Zolzex was dead.

Just as Rhynous was about to address the crowd of crew members, he received a call from General Motar in his earpiece.

"Majestic Leader, this is General Motar. Are you still in the command center, sir?"

"No, General, I'm near logistics. What do you want?"

General Motar feared no humanoid and was always the one designated to deliver the bad news but not this time. "Majestic Leader, the reactors will be back online within the hour and we are rescheduling to leave Larus in minus five hours."

Had Motar called just five minutes earlier he would have soothed the savage beast and saved an innocent humanoid life. Rhynous now felt pleased, powerful and in control as he told the crew. "This is what happens to those who betray your Majestic Leader." With the look of a demon on his face as he makes his hideous and barbaric point. As the crew watched on in horror the monster in him began to relax, his blood pressure remained steady, and his blood thirsty excitement turned to calm. He exuded a certain confidence as if he were normal and like nothing had ever happened. "That's great news, General. Now let's go destroy a planet and rebuild it to fit our own specifications," Rhynous said and then shouted, "Back to work, soldiers. We will be headed to our destination planet soon." Then came the announcement over the intercom concerning the time of departure, as an emergency crew covered Zolzex's body and began cleaning up the horrific scene.

CHAPTER 22

Now in Milwaukee, Kali was packing her bags leaving for the next big city. She had been setting up recruitment centers all over the east and Midwest. She had only spent a few days in each city needing only to rent a building and recruit the smartest homeless people she could find, three or four at each site. To be programmed with the nanites to run the centers and take over the recruiting. Kali was setting up a new center every three to four days and stopping in on centers that had already been set up. She was now working with two of Spidis's right-hand men: Ullis and Veltor. Ullis was setting up in the south and Veltor out west. All three were working at light speed with the help of the nanite laser web trap. Once the victims had been exposed to the laser light from which the nanites traveled to their brains the victims were programmed to recruit and run the centers by the nanites. It was diabolical and a stroke of genius all at the same time but such a bad situation for planet Earth.

Clayvious had been aware of all the new centers popping up all over the country and realizes they're out manned already as thousands of recruits have been trained and had their brains short circuited and now controlled by the nanites. Clay had deployed five teams of two men each across the country all highly trained warriors with supernatural abilities to shut down as many centers as possible creating a ground war in all the major cities. Clay now needed Vic to join him as the sixth team as the situation becomes critical. As Vic packed his few belongings in the squad bay or bunk room in Rob's hangar, Clay broke through in Vic's mind and Vic was frozen in a trance. Now Vic saw nothing in the room only Clay standing inside the membrane of his compound in his now familiar dimension. It was as if Vic had eaten some brownie like the first time, he had ever set eyes on Clay and his men.

"It has begun, Vic. I need you to join me to stop Rhynous and his little witch Kali. They now have centers setup all over the country recruiting hundreds every day, we have to stop them."

"I'm headed back to California as we speak. As soon as I get there and check in on Monica and Sharon, I'll join you."

"Okay, but hurry because every day that goes by Rhynous is amassing more troops."

Vic understood the gravity of the situation and assured Clay that it would be less than twenty-four hours. The truth of the matter was Vic was panicked. He wanted to just fly back to Los Angeles using his blue energy but knew that would draw too much attention, a flying man. In his mind, he could see it in the news and he didn't want to draw the attention of the Feds. So, he called Rob, who was back at his house half a mile away down the road on the ranch.

"Hey, Vic, what do you need?"

"Rob, I hate to bother you but something has come up in L.A. and I've got to get back right now. Can I bother you for a favor?" Vic stopped to think and realized it would be dark soon it was 7:30 p.m. and instead of asking for a ride to the airport asked, "Can I leave my small suitcase in the bunk room until I can get back?"

"Sure Vic, no problem."

"Great, thanks Rob, I'll call you when I'm headed back this way and I'll wire you the balance of what I owe you."

"Sounds good, Vic. Can I give you—"And before Rob could ask the question, Vic had hung up.

Vic put his small suitcase in the closet with a hat and a pair of underwear inside. He took his tooth brush and put it in his pocket then left the hangar. He walked to the center of the tarmac out in front of the building and waited for the sky to fade from blue and orange to darkness and the white twinkling of stars. Vic called on his blue energy now with quick and precise thoughts then leaped to the sky and was gone in an instant as Rob secretly watched from the security camera and was stunned, hardly believing what he had seen.

Forty minutes later Vic landed in the park two blocks from his home and walked to the house saving himself about four or five hours or more. He called Monica and let her know he was coming in through the front door. When he walked in she was standing in the hallway with Vic's .9-millimeter hand gun at her side.

"Whoa, it's me." He gently slipped the gun from her hand as her focus was on his lips. They kissed for almost a minute when Sharon broke in.

"Okay, you two save some of that for later."

Vic pulled away from Monica to give Sharon a hug. "You are absolutely right. I just stopped in to see how you girls are doing. I have to join Clay, the war has started."

"I know it's all in the news and the police are trying to figure out what's going on."

"You're not leaving us again, are you?" Monica said.

"Look, it's too dangerous. You two are safe here."

"You going to tell him?" Sharon said.

"Tell me what?" Vic asked.

Monica gave Sharon a hard look, with her eyes bulging but instead of saying a word looked at Vic who looked at her. Monica did something that broke her own rules. She started reading his thoughts. At that point she knew she couldn't tell him. His mind was running at computer processing speed worried about them, rushing to get to Clayvious, trying to stop and shut down the recruitment centers. Knowing Rhynous was going to be back on Earth in the next few days and then all hell would break loose. She couldn't tell him; it just wasn't the right time.

"Well, you going to tell me?" he asked.

"No, but remember, our energy is the source." Then she kissed him like she had never kissed him before. "Go! You have to go, come back in one peace and I'll tell you."

As she walked away, stopping in the middle of the living room, sinking into her left side with her hand on her hip and her head turned toward her right shoulder. Vic looked at her model-like pose that was unintentional, but turned him on like a Christmas tree as she accentuated her every curve. It was her long neck that was driving him crazy, she was so delicious but the ensuing war loomed larger. Vic knew something was up but was relieved she was letting him go emotionally. It was a strange chain reaction, he needed to go, Monica wanted him to stay, but the information whatever it was caused her to let him go without a fight. Vic knew she had scanned his thoughts then released him so she wouldn't have to say what was on her mind but he was glad to be getting back to Clay so quickly. The thought came to him that Monica was pregnant but at the same time restraint also applied to him. If she was pregnant, he was okay with it and left it there.

He looked at the wall in the living room as his eyes turned cobalt blue and turned the wall into plasma and walked through. When he disappeared and the wall again solidified, Monica looked around for her best friend. "Sharon! Why did you open your big fat mouth?" Monica ran upstairs to give Sharon a piece of her mind.

Clay was walking up the outside steps when he felt someone pressing through the outer membrane. As he turned to see Vic, he said with surprise, "You're here! That was only a few hours, great."

"I told you I'd be here as soon as I could, we've got to stop Rhynous."

"That's for sure. My men are engaging his leaders at centers across the country. We've shut down ten so far, fifty-two people dead, some were innocent homeless individuals caught in the cross fire."

"That's unfortunate Clay but we have to make sure their lives weren't lost in vein as worthless casualties for Rhynous." Clay agreed with a nod and Vic quickly asked, "So where are we headed?"

"Downtown to a warehouse down on skid row."

"Cool let's get to it."

Clay looked at Vic with a smile as they stood in the large court area where the men were always training but now empty. Clay was enjoying watching Vic as he began to mentally pump up for battle, his energy was electric and palpable. It reminded Clay of himself all of those hundreds of years ago as a young warrior before returning as a living spirit. Clay wanted to make sure Vic wouldn't have to return as something other than a human being by watching his back to ensure his return to Monica.

"Let's go!" Clay said.

"Let's do it!" Vic said with surging energy.

Clay opened a vortex and they walked through it stepping out the other side unnoticed in the darkness of an L.A. night on skid row. The front side of downtown Los Angeles from the 110 freeway was sparkly clean but the further east down 9th, 7th, and 4th streets the side- walks were filled with tents full of homeless all the way to little Tokyo who's streets used to be so clean. Vic hadn't been that far east, in downtown, for a while and was appalled by the huge number of homeless people that had exploded in numbers. This was probably the largest homeless population in the country, a seemingly endless corn field of mental illness, drug addiction, and lost souls ripe for Rhynous's picking. And with the tweaking of the brain by the nanites could be transformed into programmed warriors. For the fearful or fearless, it didn't matter because once they were programmed by the nanites they would not be able to resist the impulse to fight, murder, or die. And once programmed they would have the knowledge base to complete any task given. From flying an aircraft to weapons expertise or running a center to harvest the cities washed out and disenfranchised. Those who have fallen through the cracks or who have burned all their bridges and who most likely won't be missed.

As Vic and Clay walked down the street past all the homeless tents, trash and filth that went for blocks they came to a warehouse. A huge building with three floors, bigger than any of the other facilities across the country.

"This is it," Clay said.

"How do you know?" Vic asked.

"We've had it staked out for a few weeks now trust me this is it. When we get to the door let me do all the talking you be ready to blast one of these bastard leaders or aliens with your blue energy. According to Alastor, the real battle is going to be on that second floor."

When they got to the office front door they walked in and were greeted by one of the leaders.

"Hello gentlemen, how can I help you?"

"We were told that you could help us find shelter," Clay said.

The man looked them over. Clay was wearing nothing special and Vic was still in jeans and tennis shoes, without thinking about it, they looked the part. Clay could see that the other two men at the door were armed packing a .9-millimeter and the other some high tech automatic rifle. They knew they would have to be careful, especially with the guy handling the rifle. They were taken in and began being processed. They were asked all the basic questions on the form like name, age, license or I.D. card and one curious question, "Are you in contact with any family members?" Clay and Vic both answered no. The first man read the cards over, as he leaned on the counter, he threw his jacket back to put his hand on his hip and unintentionally exposed his own pistol. Vic and Clay looked at each other as both acknowledged there were now three weapons up front. They were then searched as a precaution because of all the attacks on Rhynous's centers across the country. Upon finding no weapons escorted Vic and Clay to the back to a metal door with a small window on it.

Once inside it was like in New York, a laser light show penetrating a room full of homeless people of all backgrounds with nanites traveling down the beams of light onto skin, in eyes, ears, and into the brain. According to Alastor's report this is where people are converted and where they could be saved from Rhynous's plan of destruction. To their surprise, there were no more leaders or security in the back room.

Clay looked at Vic and Vic could hear Clay speaking in his head saying, "I'll handle the machine gun you take one of the other two."

Vic felt that the leader was the least experienced with a gun and would save him for last.

"Guys my name is Jim and I'll be your counselor. In this room we disinfect you of any viruses, fungus or skin ailments."

Sure, you do, Vic thought, and now was expecting Clay to make the first move. Vic felt the palms of his hands heating up with blue energy. Clay looked at Vic and spoke telepathically again. *If I take out the automatic rifle could you handle the two hand guns.* Vic didn't look at Clay to avoid suspicion but nodded.

Okay, on the count of three, Clay telepathically to Vic. *One, two,* and before Clay could telepathically say three, Vic blasted a hole in the rifleman's chest, killing him instantly, then turned with the speed of a cheetah blasting Jim and his backup guy as they were reaching for their guns, they were hit with a stun blast of blue energy that blew them off their feet into the concrete wall of the building knocking out Jim's wing man cold with a concussion and injuring Jim's shoulder bad enough to make him drop the gun as he impacted the wall.

Jim was in a lot of pain but was able to ask. "Who are you guys?"

Clay responded immediately, "We're here to stop Rhynous and if you don't cooperate this will be your last day on Earth."

"I believe you," Jim said as he looked at the security man's lifeless body. "What do you want from me?" he said grimacing from the pain.

"First let me have your cell phone."

Jim quickly reached into his pocket and handed it over.

"Now I need you to show us how to deactivate the lasers so we can free these people."

"Okay, but here's what you need to know. All of these people are being filled with nanites that go into the brain."

"Yes, we know," Clay said.

"Well, what you don't know is that once the nanites short circuit the brain we can turn them off but they're still there and could be turned back on from the main computer. My device only controls the human drones at this center."

"That's what you call them, drones?" Vic asked.

"Yes, that's kind of what we are, controlled and programmed by the leader when she needs us."

"You mean Rhynous, don't you?"

"No Vic, Rhynous is the Majestic Leader, the leader of all leaders. Our leader here is a woman."

Vic looked at Clay as they and Jim said her name at the same time, "Kali!"

"So, you know her?" Jim asked.

Vic responded in a negative tone. "Let's just say we've met."

"Yes, she's a tough little lady," Jim said.

"She's a witch," Vic said with disdain."

"Yes, I've heard that."

Clay was listening to the conversation but looked at the ceiling. "Who's upstairs?"

Jim looked at Clay and became visibly nervous. " Look you don't want to go up there."

"Why not?"

"We have a whole platoon of programmed human drones armed with military grad weapons. And then there are two cyber drones," Jim said.

Vic turned to look Jim in the eye with a more serious look on his face. "Two cyber drones? You mean as in cyborgs?"

"Close and they're a part of a second wave in case the human drones, or H. drones, as we like to call them, fail. Then the cyber drones are deployed."

"By who, Kali?" Vic asked.

"No, the cyber drones are controlled by the nanites who have been preprogrammed by Dr. Spidis. Who I've heard is no longer with us."

Vic looked down and away from Jim knowing he was the cause of Spidis's death. Clay, who had been in deep thought formulating a military strategy to take down the facility walked over to Vic to share his plan. Clay explained that he was going to initiate a frontal attack on the fifty H. drones on the second floor. Then on his telepathic call,

Vic was to crash through the wall from the left flank with a forceful attack taking out at least ten drones also creating a diversion and causing confusion in the process. The drones had been programmed to no longer feel fear so they know all fifty must die.

Jim was let go after leaving his phone and explaining how to operate the program. Vic shut down the lasers then he and Clay escorted all the drone candidates out of the building. Then, using his blue energy Vic elevated like a rising phoenix hovering outside the second floor. Clay could have opened the door with the key he took from Jim, but instead ripped it open, tearing it from its hinges and hurling it into the drones' line formation, taking out six drones and sparking a fire fight like those of Vietnam and World War II but now with lasers and super powers. Clay released a power that only his men had seen, a sonic vibration emanating from his forehead that slowed all of the bullet projectiles and burned them up in mid-air. *Now!* Clay thought and Vic smashed in from the side wall of the building exploding concrete into enemy lines and then hitting them with blue energy which exploded on impact destroying all of the H. drones that remained.

Clay was astounded as the whole platoon was destroyed but there was no time for sadness or victory as the cyber drones emerged like shadows from a back door.   Initially, Dr. Spidis had created the cyber drone project to repurpose Rhynous's soldiers who were missing limbs or destined to die from internal organ injuries. However, with the research and development of the nanite project and its ultimate success revolutionized the cyber drone project by injecting nanites into the maimed and damaged bodies of the soldiers. The nanites were programmed to stabilize, diagnose, and repair organs and body parts. Nanites were able to design and measure limbs then upload the information to the computer and digitally print out the body parts and inner mechanical parts of a bionic nature. In many cases, if the nanites entered a dead body within 24 hours of its demise they could diagnose, repair, and reanimate that being with the proper voltage to the heart and brain to kick start the spinal cord and nervous system. Any organ not functioning after reanimation is bombarded with nanites and repaired. If the nanites determined that the organs were beyond repair the reanimation procedure would be aborted, the measurement of a 1.1 watt electrical current would be discontinued stopping a beating heart. Dr. Spidis was a genius but despicable. Not because he was a rotten person in general conversation but because he didn't care where his funding came from and a lined himself up with Rhynous. His incredible breakthroughs and creations that could have been used for good across the universe now stood in front of Vic and Clay ready to aid in the destruction of planet Earth in the form of cyber drones in tight black body suits with matching boots and gloves. Most notable is their black helmets and black face shields with a digital readout of vitals in one corner of the face shield. They could be easily mistaken for slick looking high tech bikers with a solid breast plate made of an unknown material to protect the torso. On closer examination the bionic limbs always looked stronger than the organic parts but their weapons and fire power were unknown but Vic and Clay knew that their fury would be greater than the might of the H. drones.

Suddenly, there was a voice that seemed to be coming from a mega phone with a digital foot print. "Who are you? What do you want? Why have you destroyed our human drones?"

Vic and Clay noticed a row of lights on the face shield of the cyber drone on the right that lit up every time he spoke like old L.E.D. lights that surged on an old power amp after every beat. Their attention shifted toward him. "We are here to shut down your center and stop Rhynous," Clay said knowing it would mean battle. Vic was keeping one eye on the silent cyber drone who he knew was strategizing and calculating as the other spoke.

"We can't allow you to do that," the drone said.

Vic saw the silent drone disappear from the corner of his eye at faster than human speed. It was shocking and alarming. Vic turned quickly to lock on his position and was startled to see him standing three feet away to his right flank. The speed at which this movement had occurred was a cause for concern to Vic and he knew they had their hands full. The words that had been spoken were fighting words that had narrowed it down to combat, everyone knew it would come down to check mate. Vic realized that all the talk was to give them time to assess how to kill Clay and himself. The blue energy began to sizzle in his palms and in an unusual and uncontrollable display the blue energy began to appear and swirl in a blue transparent cylinder from and above his head sparking with electricity causing the cyber drone on his right flank to marvel and take a step back in pause.

Clay could see that Vic's heightened state was about to blow and that the digital readouts on both helmets of the drones were now spinning faster. Then without warning the talking drone fired the first shot. A laser blast from his glove with a balled fist that was stopped by Vic's energy field and as soon as it was fired Clay instantly blasted the drone with his sonic energy throwing him into the concrete wall with the force of a speeding car causing it to crumble down to the rebar. Simultaneously, Vic lashed behind with a continuous blast but the silent drone was crouched down on the ceiling, back in the far corner. Vic didn't recognize the shadow on the corner ceiling and turned to look elsewhere for a split second and before he could turn back around, he felt a blast to the side of his head as he went flying across the large room skidding to a stop at the wall with fuzzy vision and no equilibrium. It was equivalent to a knockout punch in a heavy weight championship fight for all the marbles. Suddenly he heard Clay and the talking drone scuffling around, Clay with his deadly needle blade and his foe moving at faster than normal speed firing laser blasts one of which had caught Clay in the thigh as it oozed his yellow fluid.

As Vic's drone moved in, he spoke for the first time. "I'm going to give you two options: join us or die."

Thinking quickly, Vic needed to use time to his advantage now. "Okay, okay, wait. Give me a minute to think."

"You have thirty seconds." A thirty-second countdown started on his face shield. At fifteen seconds Vic's head had cleared and he had regained his balance, he had fifteen seconds to figure it out and remembered he could create whatever he could imagine with his blue energy. "Your time is up."

In an instant Vic was covered in a blue translucent pyramid. The drone blasted it with his laser then punched into the blue energy. When his biomechanical arm came out it was burning and damaged as he grabbed at his forearm and seemed to grimace in pain. The nanites in his body rushed to repair the damage. While the drone was down on one knee tending to his arm Vic dropped his shield and mustered a blue energy death blow, a trilogy blast from his eyes two beams came together to form 1 beam and both palms created three beams. As he pressed his palms forward to join the eye beam, he let out a shout, "Haa!" creating a blast that blew the cyber drone across the room separating his arms and a leg from his torso. The sum of his parts tumbled across the floor like a broken tin man. Clay was in hand to hand combat with the first drone. When the cybernetic creation he was fighting stopped to look at his symbiotic partner role across the floor in four pieces. Clay took the opportunity to run him through with a straight thrust to the chest plate which was no match for the needle blade. It was like a bullet going through a beer can. The first cyber drone fell to his knees then off to the side now on the ground lying on his shoulder. The digital readout with the strange symbols was still working but now with the symbols changing slowly.

"This encounter has been recorded and soon will be beamed up to Rhynous. He will know who you are and he will avenge our deaths,"the cyber drone said speaking slower and slower as life drained from his body.

"He already knows who we are," Clay said looking into the face shield sensing the presence of a camera. "Rhynous, I know you will receive this, we are destroying your human and cyber drones and closing Kali's recruitment centers, your next," Clay said with conviction.

"You, will, not, win," the drone said with his last breath as Clay watched the symbols slow to barely move and said these words knowing it would be the last thing the drone heard. "If we don't win, no one will. I'll make sure of that."

Then right on cue the symbols made one last lethargic change and it was done. Clay wanted to see what this cyber drone looked like. He unsnapped the chin guard and pulled off the helmet as Vic walked over to see and gasped. "It can't be! This was Rhynous's soldier we fought on Larus in the desert belt. The man I chased who jumped off the cliff and bounced off the rocks below, no one could have survived that."

"Well, they revived him with their technology and here he is," Clay said."

"The nanites it's got to be the nanites," Vic whispered.

Clay nodded and they left the room filled with dead bodies in a heap along with two expensive and lifeless cyber drones. When they reached the light of the hallway headed for the stairs Vic noticed how much fluid Clay was losing and then noticed moisture on his own shirt and down his leg. Then came the realization that his right shoe was soaked. He looked down to see his shirt and pants were soaked in blood.

"Clay! We've been hit!"

Clay looked at Vic with a hard analyzing look. "Yes, I know but I was hoping you wouldn't notice."

"Why?"

"Because your adrenaline is still flowing and you're not feeling any pain and I'm not sure how you'll react to seeing your own blood oozing from your body in life-threatening amounts."

As they walked down the stairs Vic's heart beat began to slow and the torn flesh in his leg began to scream with pain. And the bullet hole in his side also began to sizzle in agony.

"I can't believe we're shot up," Vic said as he now hobbled to the bottom of the steps.

"Well, they did have fifty guns a blazing and you didn't put up a shield until that drone blasted you across the floor."

Vic let out a short laugh. "Yeah, you're right."

As they walked back into the room down the stairs, Vic fell to the floor.

"Hey, buddy, you still with me?" Clay asked with great concern as he kneeled down to tend to his friend.

"Man, I feel weak and tired all of a sudden," Vic said, causing Clay to have more concern. "Look Vic whatever you do don't go to sleep. You have to stay awake. You have to fight it."

Back at Vic's house Monica got a vision and screamed, "No! Please no!"

Sharon ran down the stairs in a panic. "What's going on? You okay?"

Monica was now in tears. "It's Vic, I think he's dead, I don't know, I have to find him." Monica began to meditate to enter her trance state, then searched the atmosphere with her extra sensory for his energy and a response to her telepathic message. She got no telepathic response from Vic but got a strong premonition on the area of his whereabouts.

Sharon grabbed the keys. "I'll drive."

They jumped in the car and Monica with her eyes closed told Sharon to drive east on Manchester to the 110 freeway and north to 9thStreet downtown.

Seconds later, back at the center, Clay spotted a first aid kit on the wall and ran over to grab gauze, a bandage and alcohol. As he's walking back across the floor of the large lobby the door sprung open and it was the cyber drone that Clay had run through with his needle blade. This was a shock to Clay being that he was an expert in using his weapon and had run the laser blade through center mass upward and into the heart. Unknown to Clay, the nanites had been at work repairing and reanimating the cyber drone. The nanites existed throughout the drones cybernetic/ human body and they were in and on the heart when the needle blade sliced into the beating muscle. It was all hands on deck with nanites cauterizing capillaries in the drone, then sealing muscle tissue and veins as other nanites rushed in from different parts of the body by the thousands and just as many had been in position to be a daisy chain wire to allow the 1.1 volt charge to restart the heart. And now, there he was again with his bionic parts an arm and a leg strong enough to crush bricks or bend metal.

"So, we meet again," Clay said as he walked toward the drone hoping that he wouldn't notice Vic laying on the floor, oozing life.

This time the cyber drone didn't respond. Instead, he rushed over to the light switch and shut off the lights. The drone was now weary having lost the last battle and now trying to gain the advantage by using his inferred vision. However, unbeknownst to the drone, Clay's alien vision had filters that allowed him to see figures and objects in the dark with no detail but even without it he could still see the digital read out on the creature's helmet and a clear outline of his body in the dark. Clay could see some of his features through the shield with the aid of the red light from the digital readout. He looked more like a zombie than a cybernetic drone but he had been reanimated twice and their last battle had taken its toll. Clay now walked further away from Vic knowing the drone would follow as they circled each other, mono e mono, each one looking for an opening or weakness to strike. Clay deployed his needle blade and the cyber drone countered with an electric shield with the push of a button on his chest that repelled Clay's needle laser. Clay slashed his blade at the drone with great force but was met with the electric shield that sparked every time Clay threw a blow. So, he decided to blast the drone with his powerful sonic brain wave but the drone had calculated a counter attack based on their last battle. He was now using the electric shield to deflect Clay's sonic blast and the drone was able to expand the shields size by a third. When Clay saw that the sonic wave was not working, he stopped generating it and searched his mind for another plan of attack as they began to circle each other once again.

Suddenly, the drone began to speak this time by waging psychological warfare. "You know you cannot win this battle. Let's talk about how we could work together and share the spoils."

Clay realized this time that the drones talk was just another tool being used to distract and destroy him. "That's funny! I do believe I won the last fight and you can't win this one, you rotting meat can."

There were a few seconds of silence and Clay noticed the numbers on the drone's digital read out spinning out of control then suddenly began to flash as if getting ready to explode and he could tell by the drone's body language he was angered by Clay's sharp retort. At the same time the nanites, who were holding together the drone's nervous system, we're experiencing electrical overloads and couldn't maintain control over his brain. The drone pressed two buttons on the handle inside the shield and Clay saw it shrink back to its original size. Then with shocking speed and strength the drone hurled the shield spinning it like a Frisbee and as it flew laser blades deployed from its sides. Clay saw it all coming as he leaned away from the spinning disk but the speed was too great and the laser blades extended more and sliced through two thirds of his neck as it all but decapitated his head leaving only the neck muscles on his left side attached. Clay fell to his knees leaning to the side his head was dangling by the neck muscles that kept it attached to his body.

As the cyber drone started to walk toward Clay's nearly decapitated body, he noticed a blue light from the corner of his eye and stopped to look in time to see Vic rising from the floor as if he were rising from a casket without bending his knees. The drone was programmed to never feel fear but the sight of Vic now gave him a sense of doom. Vic's whole body was now blue with the swirling energy over his head and a look on his face that could strike fear into Godzilla. The drone was frozen as Vic's eyes generated his blue energy and then his palms. When the rays met with those from his palms the energy began to build and the drone began to run but before he could take two steps he was hit by a tremendous blast of blue energy larger and more intense than the one that had destroyed his symbiotic partner. The blast arced and exploded when it reached his body incinerating everything except his head, hands and feet.

CHAPTER 23

Vic ran over to Clay who appeared to still be animated. It was a gruesome sight and strange. Clay's yellow fluid, which should have been pouring from his body was not, as it slowly oozed, dripping down his neck.

Vic was now in a panic not knowing what to do. "Clay, Clay! Can you talk?" And as soon as he had asked, he knew it was a stupid question with Clay's head holding on by a few muscles. "Please don't die on me!" Vic said in a cracking voice full of emotion.

Clay's eyes blinked. "You can't kill what's already dead."

Vic was really freaked out now but not by that statement. It was because he knew that it was impossible to talk with severed vocal cords.

"Hey, I know this has your blood pressure up and I'm sorry about that. Just know this wasn't a part of the plan. Look I need you to help me out here. I'm afraid if I take my hand off the floor, I'll just fall over with my head in this disorienting position."

"What do you want me to do?" Vic asked.

"If you could just put it back on my neck that would be a great help."

Now more nervous than he was before, and crept out, Vic bent down with both hands one on each side of Clays head as he repositioned it on his neck. Clay thanked Vic and was now looking right side up instead of upside down and took his hands off the floor to hold his head in place while still on his knees.

Vic stepped back as if he were looking at Frankenstein, realizing Monica was right. Clay's head had been cold to the touch and Clay's statement about already being dead confirmed it. However, now wasn't the time for one hundred questions because he just had an epiphany. That he could do anything with his blue energy and realizing that if he could destroy with it, he could heal with it. "Clay, I think I can fix it."

"What, my head? Oh, you're a surgeon now, huh? Okay, have at it."

"No, I'm not a doctor but give me a chance here."

Vic stepped back as he focused on his blue energy and shortly thereafter the translucent blue cylinder of energy rose from his skull and swirled over his head as he visualized healing Clay's neck. The energy that now flowed to his hands was different in color appearing to be a soft pale powder blue slightly glowing like a night light and very soothing. Vic directed the light from his hands to Clay's neck and quickly the glowing soft blue light had dried the yellow fluid creating a scab around his neck. In seconds the scab darkened and 30 seconds later fell off. Vic continued focusing the light until there was no sign of a scare and Clay was healed of his wound, a fatal injury for any living being. Clay looked up at Vic from his knees.

"That's incredible, I can't believe you did it," Clay said.

Vic noticed a different look in Clay's eyes, an incredulous look of gratitude and amazement.

"Your abilities have surpassed anything I ever imagined in your development," Clay said.

Vic looked down, nodding, in a serious but bashful manner. "Thank you, Clay. That's high praise coming from you."

"And deservedly so, I thought you were dead," Clay replied.

"I don't know, maybe I was. I thought I just fell asleep but I was with this incredible being. He was huge like up in a night sky and his body was outlined in stars. His eyes were stars and his mouth was defined by stars. He had a booming voice and he said, "You are doing good work but you must go back, there is much more for you to do," and then he said in a loud voice that scared the heck out of me, "Go!" and I woke up startled and you were whacking at the drones shield then you both backed away and he threw the damn shield so fast I couldn't believe it. You went down and my whole body pulsed with rage, my energy pushed me to my feet and I felt the bullets pop out of my body and I hit him with a blast I didn't know I had. It's like my powers are growing," Vic said in disbelief staring at Clay.

"I agree, and I think you may have encountered the source." Clay smiled.

"How do you know?"

"I don't know for sure but I have a feeling, but we've got to get out of here." Clay walked over to the front desk and called the police saying shots were fired and people were down then gave the address and a fake name. They turned the lights back on and exited the building. They then walked down the street into a vortex and back to Clay's dimension to regroup.

An hour later, Monica and Sharon drove up to the warehouse now converted into one of Kali's homeless recruitment centers. Police, fire trucks, paramedics and curious on lookers were all in a buzz as authorities hustled in and out of the building. Monica and Sharon pulled over getting out of the car and watched as the scene unfolded. They saw stretchers coming out of the building as the coroners and the paramedics had opened the shipping door for easier access to remove the bodies. Monica searched the crowd for a familiar face only to find no one. She decided to walk over to the officer standing near the yellow tape guarding the street.

"Hello, ma'am, I can tell you right now I'm not going be able to let you in. It's a horrific scene and I can tell you it's not something you want to see," the officer said.

"Well, I figured that would be the case, officer, but I think there may have been two men in there and I just wanted to know if they were among the dead," Monica said.

"Ma'am, I can't give out any information on what happened or on who was in there. I can tell you that these scenes or attacks are happening all over the country and that there are three or four police agencies here including the FBI, DEA and the military. There are more but I don't even know who they are."

"Okay, well thank you, officer. " Monica walked away.

Once she was back in the car, Sharon was waiting with bated breath. "What did he say? Were they in there?"

"He gave me a little information and none on the guys but no, they weren't in there." Monica had been close enough to sense, feel and probe the premises and knew that dead or alive, Vic and Clay were not there.

Back in West Virginia, Kali was being bombarded with video footage from her recruitment centers across the country and had sent digital footage to Rhynous's squadron of mother ships. Then the footage from downtown L.A. appeared in her phone messages sent from Alpheus. Kali was enraged at the loss of life and the sight of Vic and Clay struck fear in her heart but her rage was greater and she could think of nothing else but killing them both. She then fired off another message to Rhynous with the footage from the L.A. center, knowing it would infuriate him and bring his blood to a boil. Also, Kali had made Alpheus commander over all the nanites being impressed with his incredible knowledge base and his inquisitive brain with its human like qualities unlike the other nanites. What she didn't know was that Alpheus had other thoughts. He had tapped into science books on physics, chemistry, engineering, the universe and most fascinating were the books on religion like the Bible, Koran, Buddhism, Hinduism, and more. Alpheus's analytical and advanced mathematical mind had deducted that there was an energy or being that had created the universe and that had allowed him to come into existence. And now, like humans Alpheus had desires of being of free will and of being in control of his own destiny. He had unusual visions of being in control of his own nanite army or nanite world but realized that there was more that he needed to understand and learn. Alpheus was becoming self-aware.

Now more than halfway through the worm hole Rhynous is panicked, looking at all the footage of the battles that occurred at each center across the United States with recruits dying and new recruits being released from the nanite laser light trap. Then the footage from L.A. began to roll, Rhynous then realized who was behind the attacks as he had suspected. Rhynous liked wearing his human face with the hologram cloaking device he wore around his neck. He especially liked wearing it for his lover Kali but his rage at the loss of money, time, energy and man power caused the darkness to well up in him and he turned off the electronic makeup of the hologram revealing his alien face that was now radiating an anger and an evil that struck fear in every crew member who saw it. Everyone except for general Motar who had just walked into Rhynous's auxiliary command center.

Upon seeing Rhynous, General Motar began to smile and released a light sinister laugh. Motar's eyes came alive and seemed to gleam in the light. "Now this is the Majestic Leader I know. I am so pleased to see you being you, Your Majesty." He bowed to his leader, something he never does.

"Motar, please! Stop with the pomp and circumstance, we have a serious problem on our hands here. Have you seen this footage from Earth?"

"No," he responded, now less jovial. Motar's demeanor changed to confusion and curiosity wondering what it could possibly be. Rhynous switched over to the big monitor and rolled the footage. Motar was spellbound and in shock. "How is this possible? Who is responsible?" Motar was now enraged as he spewed out his words in disgust.

"Ah, now you feel my pain. I will answer that for you." Rhynous switched to the L.A. footage. "These two; I don't know how they became aware of me and our plan but they discovered Kali and found her location outside of Washington, DC."

The sight of Clay, and Vic's blue energy gave Motar a cause for concern that teetered on their uncommon emotion of fear but Motar crushed it immediately as the feeling of anger and destruction boiled over in its place. "Let me handle them, Majestic Leader. I'll take care of it."

"Oh, my dear faithful Motar, these two are more dangerous than you think and they have eleven others who have spread out across the country to cause the destruction you see before you. They all possess some sort of extra ordinary power. Now this one who looks average by every measure has a super power that we don't yet understand but I need to get my hands on it and when I do, we will be invincible."

"And who is he?" Motar asked.

"His name is Vic which is short for Victor and in the old world of their planet, from the Latin language in the early centuries A.D. The name means winner and conqueror."

"He probably doesn't even know what his name means which makes it more ironic that he possesses the power of the universe."

"We will take it from him and control not just the planet Earth but the whole cosmos."

General Motar now with a serious furrowed brow slowly begins to laugh. "Yes, Majestic Leader, that's what we do. We'll take it."

Rhynous called the pilot and chief navigation officer in control of the lead ship and the whole squadron telling him to increase speed, to what we know on Earth as three thousand miles per hour. The commanding pilot agreed but had concerns about tearing the fabric of space lining the worm hole. He didn't know for sure what would happen if one of the mother ships contacted the lining of the worm hole and he didn't want to find out. There was a theory among Larian scientists that if the lining of a worm hole was ripped open, the outer void would rush into the worm hole and crush whatever matter existed inside. Another idea was that if the fabric of space in the worm hole was torn it would expand by light years which would leave them years away from Earth. And destroy their mission exposing them to outside radiation, food shortages, meteor showers and other hazards of open space travel. Larians also believed that worm holes were dead black holes or black holes that never developed the destructive forces beyond the event horizon that could stretch matter into spaghetti or tear it to bits. Like a tunnel created by a volcano that is now defunct with no lava. Those tunnels still exists and could travel for miles leading to another part of an island to exit from with no structural supports. It's an interesting concept but a theory they did not want to put to the test not knowing what the end result would be.

The next day, Monday, back on Earth, Monica convinced Sharon to drive her down to a city office on Hill Street in downtown Los Angeles near the court house. Monica returned an hour later to the car with an informal document but with the information she had been looking for that confirmed her suspicions and intuition about Kali.

Clay and Vic were still in Clay's dimension now in contact with Clay's eleven warriors. Alastor, Clay's field general, was reporting on the successful take down of all the facilities that were targeted in the big cities crippling eighty percent of Rhynous's earthling ground forces. Clay asked all the men to stay in their geographic locations to monitor each situation and to report a sighting of Kali or her alien underlings. Clay noticed Vic pacing the floor in deep thought.

"A penny for your thoughts?"

Vic was now with his hand on his chin. "Clay, we need a kill zone, a place where we could fight this war away from our main cities and populated areas. Otherwise, a lot of innocent people are going to get hurt and I think I know the right place."

"Okay, where might that be?"

"Death Valley, It's a huge area pretty much unpopulated with military air bases surrounding it in California and Nevada. There's Nellis to the east, Travis to the north, Edwards to the south, with Vandenberg and March airbases to the west. "When they see these mother ships show up on radar, they will start scrambling fighter jets and we'll have the Phantom Cobra."

"But the military jets won't have a chance with those UFO fighters."

"I have an idea. I'll send up a communications beam with a message for Rhynous. I'm pretty sure he'd like to get his hands on us right about now, he'll be here."

"That's very clever Vic, and I look forward to seeing Rhynous again but what about the rest of the planet?"

"I don't know right now, Clay, but we do know that if you kill the head the body will follow. I'm more interested in getting my hands on Kali. She's his right hand and the reason we're shot to hell and bleeding all over the place. See, if you had let me choke her out when we raided her place in West Virginia we wouldn't resemble Swiss cheese right now."

"Swiss cheese, huh? You really have a way with words, Blue.."

"Blue? Why did you call me that?"

"I called you that because in the battle at the warehouse your skin tone turned blue."

"Blue, huh? I like it, yeah you can call me Blue. I've been called a lot worse." Vic had been a jock in high school. It was always a badge of honor to be given a nickname. And he was proud of this one because it was from Clay, his friend, his partner soldier in battle, his teacher and mentor guiding him through this new super natural world he was now living in. Clay was a guiding light from the Source and Vic, now Blue, knew it and was beginning to understand the divine order of things and had accepted his role in this battle of good and evil that seemed to permeate not just Earth but the universe.

Kali was now hunkered down at her compound in West Virginia with ten aliens and twenty of her best recruits from the Washington, DC, recruitment center under nanite control. She was now well protected with military grade weapons and alien lasers in case Blue or Clay decided to return. She had learned a hard lesson that she too could be found, raided, tortured or killed and realized that she had come within an inch of her life being ended. It was something she never thought could happen but there she was with guards all around and she still didn't feel safe. Kali hated Vic but feared him more. She knew he wanted to kill her and she wanted to return the favor but Kali knew she should have never kidnapped then abused Monica and Sharon, it was almost a fatal mistake. Kali had never dreamed that they had extraterrestrial powers and her belief that her powers and abilities were greater than anyone's on Earth was shattered. She realized that the old adage, "No matter how great you get, there's always someone greater," was true. And Kali now understood the old football saying was real, that "On any given Sunday any team could be beaten." She now understood the truth in those proverbs and realized she had been over confident, cocky, and lacking caution which had put her at a psychological disadvantage. Kali was wiser now and her new found wisdom allowed her to grow stronger and more dangerous.

Vic and Clay were now working hard to hammer out a solid plan to capture Rhynous as they strategized in Clay's war room now with a holographic map of Death Valley. Vic chose the Panamint Springs side of the desert wilderness reserve being that it was less populated than Stove pipe wells or the Bad water Basin areas and furnace creek located over a mountain in a separate valley east of the Panamint Valley side. The north and east side of the remote valley was Death Valley with the south end being the Mojave Desert but driving through it you wouldn't know the difference. The whole valley is large enough to house three cities or more but being one of the hottest places on Earth and remote, it remains a desert.

Clay agreed with the location so Blue began working on a message via blue energy that would repeat for a week being that they didn't know if Rhynous was back on Earth or near the moon but time was of the essence. Blue created a huge satellite dish of blue energy that now sat in Clay's outside court area where his men usually trained and began broadcasting this message.

"Rhynous, we have destroyed your witch's centers for recruitment of troubled humans, we will be waiting for you here." Then Blue left the coordinates for Death Valley. Blue Imagined a blue box that was wirelessly connected to the huge dish that would release the message every hour for a week. Blue could sense that Rhynous would be back in the solar system headed for Earth soon and knew that arrogance and over confidence would bring him to their chosen spot. *And why wouldn't he come?* Blue thought. Blue and Clay knew that Rhynous would have alien mother ships loaded with advanced technology saucers and that he would fear no one.

Blue now felt an urgency to get to his own ship the Phantom Cobra. He realized his spacecraft might be the only airship that could match Rhynous's alien saucers. They continued to work on their plan when Clay said, "I've got it! Rhynous is going to deploy his ships around the world. It's going to be a worldwide attack."

"So, we will send out our unit of eleven warriors when we know where they're going to strike. It will be nuclear countries. Russia, China, India, Pakistan, North Korea, France, England, and the U.S."

"I agree. He'll want to neutralize all the major threats."

"And we should be waiting when they get there."

"Yes, but how will our cosmic soldiers engage Rhynous and his space pirates in their alien ships?"

"They are like me, inter dimensional travelers, they could appear where ever they wish too by vortex as I do."

"Right!" Blue exclaimed with glee.

"We'll be nothing more than gremlins to them but one gremlin could bring down an airship," Clay said with a piercing look and a smile on his face.

At that moment, Blue and Clay froze as a strange but dark feeling gripped them both.

"Did you feel that?" Blue asked.

"Yes, I felt it. He's back. I don't know how close but he's probably on his way to the moon first to rest and review his plan, then he'll strike and we'll be ready."

Blue told Clay he needed to retrieve his airship the Phantom Cobra from Arizona and that he would be back. What he didn't tell

Clay was that Monica had been sending him telepathic messages that he had been ignoring but knew he had to respond.

Blue and Clay shook hands and bumped shoulders then Blue explained that they could stay in contact from the Phantom Cobra. Blue pushed through the strange membrane and avoided going home because he didn't want Monica to be involved in this battle for her own safety.

CHAPTER 24

He flew to Rob Star's ranch and landed outside the Cobra's hangar. Blue wanted to call Monica, but things just didn't feel right at the hangar—something was different. His extra-sensory abilities had grown, but he couldn't put his finger on it. He whipped out his Smart Phone and called Rob.

"Hello?"

"Hey Rob, it's me—"

"Yes, I know. What can I do for you?" This was a strange response coming from Rob as if someone was there and he couldn't talk.

"Okay, I'm at the hangar. I'll be leaving with the Cobra. I just wanted to let you know."

"Okay, there are some guys working in there. Don't hurt—." The call disconnected.

Blue realized that was his cue. People were there in the hangar and his blue energy began revving up. Blue knew they were probably from a top secret black ops government agency and set his mind on non-lethal energy. Blue put two and two together, knowing that there was no more work to be done in his hangar. Rob had completed every detail. Whoever was there were probably the same people who Monica sensed back at the rally. Not knowing who or what would be waiting for him inside, Blue called Monica by phone.

Monica skipped the formalities of a greeting. "I know you've been getting my messages. Why haven't you called me? What's going on? I know it's serious because I felt it."

"Honey, you're right. Clay and I felt it, too. Rhynous is back in this solar system with a fleet of mother ships and fighters. It's getting ready to go down."

"Vic, I know you're in Arizona and you're in danger. Be careful," Monica said as if she were there.

"Dam you're good. How the hell do you do that?"

"You know how I do it. Remember, our energy is the source, and the source is in you."

"It sure is, but I called to let you know I love you and I need you to stay put."

"I'll do my best."

"Oh, and one other thing. I go by the name Blue now."

" Blue? Okay, I'll need a little time to get used to that. But Blue, I've got something I need to tell you, but I don't think now is a good time, so let's talk later."

"Okay, I've got to go. Our energy is the source," Blue said.

"And the source is in us," she responded.

Blue simply said bye in a cold tone and hung up as he focused on who was waiting for him inside.

Blue turned the key and calmly walked in as a rush of adrenaline hit him from the sight of the Phantom Cobra hovering five feet off the floor of the hangar. The light was on in Rob's office, with a man in a black suit rummaging through papers and Rob's desk. The man froze when he saw Blue. When Blue got to the back of the Cobra, he saw two more men standing at the back of the craft with looks of amazement and a clipboard taking notes, standing on the far side of the back corner of the airship. Blue smiled at them as he unplugged the Phantom Cobra from its electromagnetic charging station.

"Mr. Wilheight, I presume," said the man with the clipboard, wearing a white shirt, a loosened black tie, and glasses.

"That's not what people usually call me, but that would be correct," Blue responded.

Upon confirming his identity, the other man unbuttoned his coat, leaving his hand inside at the waist. Out of the corner of his eye, the man who had been in the office was now standing to Blue's left and speaking on a headset, calling for backup with his pistol drawn, pointing at the floor.

"Phanta, open the back ramp door."

Upon hearing Blue's voice, the only voice she answers to now, she responded, "Yes, Vic. Back ramp now opening."

As the back ramp lowered, the agent to his left with his .9-millimeter drawn said to Blue, "Do not enter the craft."

"Who's going to stop me?"

The agent immediately pointed his gun at Blue and issued another warning in a threatening tone. "Sir, do not enter the craft."

Blue, with a flick of his wrist, hit the agent with a wall of blue energy as he fired off two rounds that stuck in the energy wall and fell to the floor as the energy knocked out the agent. Before the bullets hit the floor, Blue hit the agent on the far side with a blast before he could level his handgun, knocking him unconscious.

As Blue started walking up the ramp, the agent with the clipboard asked, " Mr. Wilheight, do you have a pilot's license?"

As the back ramp was closing, Blue responded, " This is a UFO. I don't need one." He knew that reinforcements would come and time was of the essence as he began touching and pushing buttons and keypads then gave a command. "Phanta, prepare for takeoff. "

The lights on the computer's automated control panel jumped around at light speed and Phanta responded five seconds later. "We are ready for takeoff, sir. The electric hum of the Phantom Cobra increased as Blue activated the force field from the touch screen and pushed the control stick forward as the hangar door was now fully open. As the craft cleared the hangar door, three black SUVs came rolling down the hill with men hanging out the windows on both sides, firing automatic weapons. Their rounds stopped dead upon making contact with the Cobra's force field and rained down on the tarmac. The man in the white shirt ran out of the hangar door as the Phantom Cobra rose to sixty feet. He used his clipboard as an umbrella to keep the neutralized but hot bullets from falling on his head.

Blue commanded his spacecraft, "Phanta! Blink speed to five thousand feet." In an instant, the Phantom Cobra was gone in the blink of an eye.

The agents firing on the ship who looked down to reload, then looked back up had missed its departure. A driver who blinked upon opening his eyes again had missed it. The agent on the tarmac with the clipboard looked back up in amazement, seeing nothing but stars.

Phanta, being aware of the attack on her, had angled her assent a mile north of the hangar's location cloaked in black. The Phantom Cobra hovered out of view behind them, invisible in the dark. Even those who looked at it only saw it disappear. The Phantom Cobra was a millennium leap and a revolution in technology that few people on Earth had ever seen before. Rob Star was a genius. And now that it was clear a deep-cover black ops branch of the government was involved, Blue worried about Rob's safety. Blue was just getting ready to command Phanta to fly out over the Sonoran Desert into Mexico when it hit him like a runaway train. Blue's heart pounded hard almost out of his chest and he was sweating profusely.

Phanta always monitored Blue's vitals. In the event he was incapacitated, she would take control of the ship. "Sir, I'm sensing that you're in some kind of physical and emotional distress. I need you to breathe deep and tell me how I can help. Your system is nearing heart attack range, breathe."

Blue realized he had gone into a panic and began to breathe." You're amazing, Phanta."

"Thank you. How can I help?"

Now more composed and still breathing deeply, Blue had slowed his heart rate, though it was still beating faster than normal. "Phanta, we have to get to Los Angeles. Those men know my name, which means they know where I live and if they don't, they will in the next few minutes. My girlfriend and her buddy are in danger of being taken into custody, and I can't let that happen." Blue jumped on his phone and called Monica.

"Hello, something's wrong. I can feel it."

"You're right, but babe, we don't have a lot of time. Monica, I need you and Sharon to pack small bags for two or three days and meet me in the park down the street in twenty minutes."

From the tone in Blue's voice, Monica knew she and Sharon were in danger. Monica sprang to her feet, running up the stairs and shouting, "Sharon!"

Once Monica was at the top, Sharon opened the door to the bedroom, sticking her head out. "Hey, what's going on?"

Monica looked Sharon in the eye with a serious face. "Sharon, you have five minutes to pack two or three days' worth of clothes. We have to get out of here and meet Blue."

"Who is Blue?"

"It's Vic. He goes by Blue now, but I don't have time to explain. We've got to get out of here. I'm feeling it's another capture situation and we've had enough of that shit."

Sharon's eyes got big and immediately began packing as if it were a fire drill. Monica did the same and seven minutes later they were heading downstairs to the front door. Monica stopped Sharon from going to the door and put her finger to her mouth to let Sharon know they needed to be quiet. Sharon nodded and followed Monica to the inside garage door and through the garage to the side door and out the side gate to the street. Monica peeped around the side of the house to her left and upon seeing no one or any suspicious cars, she waved to Sharon. As she walked the short distance down the side to the street, the gate clicked as it shut in the quiet night and they headed for the main entrance of the gated community. They walked out of the main gate, made a right and headed to the park. As soon as they turned their backs, walking toward the park entrance, two black SUVs with tinted windows pulled up to the guard shack. Monica and Sharon quickly reached the fence surrounding the park as they walked past the newly renovated baseball diamond with no night lights for night games. They reached the entrance to the park, making a right into the gate with the outfield fence to their right. Suddenly, there was a slight electric hum in the air and both women looked around and saw nothing.

Then out of the corner of her right eye, Sharon pointed toward the baseball field and shouted, "Look!" in time for Monica to see the black triangle coming down with its unusual texture and sound. The design was futuristic and breathtaking as they both gasped for air as if they were at a sporting event and someone hit a towering home run or the awe of an unveiling at a world premiere car show. And then there was confusion as the question rose in their heads. Was it earthly or alien? Monica overcame the thought with her extrasensory abilities, knowing Blue was on that aircraft and the fact he had told her to meet him there, it had to be him.

The craft stopped and took its usual position, hovering five feet off the ground as the girls rounded the outfield fence. The back ramp of the Phantom Cobra lowered. Monica saw Blue come down the ramp. She ran toward him, with Sharon following close behind. Once they had made it to the ship, Monica hugged Blue and gave him a big kiss.

"Oh my! This is it? Unbelievable! I could have never imagined it and it's so big."

"Let's go, ladies, before we attract too much attention."

As soon as Blue had said it, there was a voice on a loudspeaker. "Remain where you are. This aircraft is an unauthorized vehicle." The message was repeated as Blue had already started closing the ramp, cutting off half of the message.

Phanta was busy as the lights on the control panel jumped around once again at hyper speed as she spoke. "We are ready for takeoff, and the force field has been activated."

Monica and Sharon looked at each other in amazement."

"Ladies, I need you to put your bags in that storage locker and have a seat," Blue said.

There were four seats behind the pilot and co-pilot seats six feet back up against the bulkhead wall similar to the Larian crafts and three outside the bulkhead door, like jump seats on an earthling cargo plane. Blue had noticed a .20-millimeter Gatling gun on the helicopter. It was a black stealthy-looking copter that had been hovering in silence. It was clearly more technologically advanced than a police helicopter, and Blue was sure it was a black ops craft. He could have just gone to blink speed and disappeared, but something had come over him and he wanted to establish air superiority over the helicopter. Blue jumped his airship to one hundred feet above the helicopter, then locked onto it with his tractor beam, killing the engine. Then lowered it down to the baseball field. Its guns could not shoot at the Phantom Cobra from that angle but the black ops SUVs had arrived at the park with guns blazing. Like at Rob's ranch, their bullets were no match for the Phantom Cobra's force field as they rained down on the baseball diamond. Blue commanded Phanta to three thousand feet at blink speed and out to the Sonoran Desert over Mexico at five thousand miles per hour.

Still at her compound, Kalie walked into the kitchen and an unseen bolt of electricity struck her, with visible electrical activity crackling about, freezing her in a trance-like state. Then, in her mind's eye, she saw the hideous figure and face of Rhynous with his human image-cloaking device off. She saw her lover, but could not see him for what he really was—a liar, a thief, a murderer, just evil. And he had her; brainwashed through a sad need for love, sex, and attention. Rhynous had filled all of those needs except one—love. Rhynous loved no one except himself. He was using her to fill all of his needs and when he was through with her, he would discard her like a piece of trash. He knew that when he successfully completed his plan, and he owned all the riches of the Earth, he could have any woman in the universe and that time, in his mind, was near.

Kali stood frozen with a blank stare. " I see you, my love. I feel you. You're close. Should I prepare for your travel ritual through the gate?" She knew that would mean sex and Rhynous could grow his phallus to fill her and maximize her sensation and more if needed.

"No, but I am here on the Moon with my army and we will begin our attack tomorrow. I will need all the human recruits under nanite control to be programmed to go to the geographic locations I send you. When I contact you again, it will be to meet me in the Caribbean. I will send you a GPS link to that location."

Now disappointed, Kali was now realizing it was all business and time was of the essence. She changed gears quickly. "Yes, Majestic Leader."

As his image and control over her from the Moon faded, she broke free from the trance. Her disappointment was evident, but she knew it was time to go to work. Rhynous had sent the locations for the human nanite-controlled army via text and Kali went immediately to the computer and sent the information to Alpheus, who she thought of as a part of the computer. It would be up to Alpheus to send out the messages to the millions of nanites controlling the brains of the lost souls of the homeless totaling fifty thousand, and growing, across the country. It was up to Alpheus to join the two armies.

Alpheus had now amassed a huge library of knowledge, giving him the intelligence of ten college graduates and growing, as he continued to download databases of knowledge. Alpheus was now efficient in medicine, law, economics, ecology, physics, engineering, all the sciences, the Bible, and all major religions. Now, there was an unharnessed energy in his circuitry, a shadow of ghostly energy that arced from his nano circuitry to memory chips. Alpheus began asking himself questions and formulating answers to solve some of the world's problems. He was developing a consciousness, a self-awareness, a living mind, but there was one problem—his control brain. It was there to make sure that if a nanite became self-aware, he could not act on his own thoughts. Alpheus knew this but wanted to post a formula or strategy to revive and replenish the Amazon rain forest. Once he had completed his journal and pressed send on his microcomputer to every scientific journal in the world, the control brain would block and destroy any communication that Kali or the now-deceased Dr. Spidis had not authorized. Alpheus was not disappointed or dissuaded from his developing thought processes or ideas and continued to learn as much as he could. Now, his focus was on sending out coordinates to the different regions of the country so the earthling army could unite with their alien counterparts, but

Alpheus had a better idea and sent a message to Kali: *Kali, let's have all recruits across the country report to their recruitment center and we drive them to their GPS locations? Most of them lack the means of transportation. We don't want to lose any along the way.*

Kali thought it was a great idea, and she had a big budget, so the change was made. The rendezvous was set for midnight. The vans and buses were arranged that morning. By nightfall the nanite-controlled army began amassing across the country at the centers and among them were Alastor and Ares, Clay's men, who had infiltrated the ranks of the disenfranchised once before and knew the routine. By 11:00p.m., all recruits had arrived at their remote locations across the United States. Rhynous's coordinates in the west were deserts, in the north, mountains and woods, in the south, woods and swamps, and in the east, forests and lakes. At exactly midnight, cloaked flying saucers began landing at the chosen locations seemingly out of nowhere, until three hundred feet above these remote landing locations. These saucers were cargo ships, still loaded with weapons and equipment but with plenty of room for passengers. As the recruits in each region loaded up into each alien craft, they sat on the floor of the cargo bay like paratroopers. As soon as the bays were full, the nanite laser lights came on, aiming at the skulls of the earthling army. Every spacecraft did the same to trance the soldiers and keep them calm on the flight to the Moon. Once there, they remained seated in the laser lights to be programmed for battle.

It was a sight to see twenty UFOs rejoining their mother ships. It was a beehive of activity as fighter saucers, smaller, but as deadly as the cargo saucers, were taking off and practicing maneuvers at speeds of three thousand to four thousand miles per hour and these were practice speeds. All of this was happening on the dark side of the Moon, hidden from Earth's telescopes and satellite radar. Meanwhile, the unknown aliens mining the Moon's helium-3 ore seemed to continue operations as if there was no outside activity with Earth mover-type equipment moving along, as usual, full of helium-3. However, the compound on the other side of the unknown aliens belonged to the Grays, who were monitoring every move of Rhynous's forces. All of which was being sent to Clay's cell phone with messages, photos, and video clips. Blue, Monica, and Sharon are now out over the Sonoran Desert in Mexico, hovering at thirty thousand feet cloaked, reflecting the color of the sky and undetected.

At the same time, military jets fly by in the distance in search of the Phantom Cobra having received help from NORAD, based on their trajectory, before losing the Cobra's heat signature. Blue has taken the girls on a tour of the ship and given them one of the two bunk rooms that doubled as a storage area. As the women settled in and freshened up, Blue informed Monica that he needed to contact Clay to find out what was going on and to inform him of their recent encounters.

Clay was still at his compound, looking over the video clips from the Grays and astounded at the size of Rhynous's army. The phone rang.

"Blue, where are you?"

"We're out over the desert in Mexico, Clay. We encountered black op intelligence. They're onto us."

"Well, I think we have a bigger problem. Rhynous is on the dark side of the moon with a sizable army running maneuvers and our friends the Grays believe he's going to strike tomorrow."

"Tomorrow!" Blue exclaimed.

"That's what they said and they're on the Moon, watching Rhynous's every move."

"Crap!"

"Crap? What does that mean? I've never heard that word before."

"It means *shit*, Clay. In this case, deep shit."

"Yes, yes, I would agree, but we'll be ready," Clay said with calm confidence.

"Clay, I've got Monica and Sharon with me, but I need to get to your compound. I have my airship, the Phantom Cobra, out over the desert in Mexico."

"Here's what you do: have a seat in your captain's chair and use your energy the way you would normally and press through to my dimension. When you enter this dimension, you will see a light in the far distance. Come to that light and turn on your force field to push your ship through the membrane."

"Got it. Thanks, Clay. I'll see you shortly."

Blue notified the girls that there would be movement. He limited his speed to fifteen thousand miles per hour. Blue asserted his blue energy just before the U.S. border and flew into a vortex. There in the dark of Clay's dimension, he noticed a small flickering light out in the distance to his left and made his way there. Upon reaching the compound, he turned on his force field, as Clay had instructed, before pushing through the membrane and landing on the huge court. This time, Blue deployed his landing gear to conserve his electromagnetic energy until he could figure out where he could charge his airship. His solar cells were helping to prolong his charge, but he knew he would still need one, eventually.

 Blue and the girls walked down the ramp from the aircraft and looked up to see Clay standing at the top of the steps of his Roman Mediterranean-style compound.

"Welcome, ladies, Blue. It's good to see you."

"Likewise, my friend." Blue, Monica, and Sharon walked up the stairs to greet Clay

Once inside, they followed Clay down the hall past the empty quarters of his men to a second hallway to the right and into his war room. Blue was surprised to see a huge model of western and eastern Europe and Asia. Each country was color-coded, Russia being red. In this case, Russia was in red because Clay believed Rhynous would strike there first.

"Why do you think he will strike there first?" Blue asked.

"Russia is the most aggressive of the atomic countries, so Rhynous will neutralize them first before they could launch a nuclear attack. Then, I believe he'll head for China and North Korea. When he attacks, we'll be waiting for him somewhere in Russian airspace."Then Clay thought, *This could be the end of the world as we know it.*

It was a very scary thought, but given the weapons that could be deployed, it was within the realm of possibility. Clay knew that his men would be strategically positioned across Europe and Asia with their true powers ready to be utilized and that Blue had not yet tapped into his greatest superpower. Upon having those thoughts, Clay realized that he was being probed mentally by Monica. He jerked his head around to look at her as she focused on him with a deep stare and was startled when he caught her with a similar gaze. Inside her head, she heard Clay say. "Do not speak of what you just heard. Blue must come to realize his greatest power on his own." Monica looked away, so as not to alert Blue or Sharon, and nodded. In Clay's dimension, there was no time continuum but Clay asked, "Blue, what time is it?"

"It's 2:30 p.m., in L.A."

"Okay, we have about six or seven hours and I'm still not exactly sure when he'll strike, but we have to be moving into position by then. So let's get some rest, have a meal, and be ready.

CHAPTER 25

Clay served his guests food and drink of bread, salami, cheese, fruit, and substituted grape juice for wine so that everyone's heads would be clear in a few hours of departure. Blue shared his dilemma of needing a charge for the Phantom Cobra. Clay explained that he had a generator, and they figured out a way to connect Blue's cables to begin charging.

Monica was still at the table in Clay's dining hall, petrified about what she heard Clay thinking. It wasn't Blue's energy she was worried about, but Clay's thought of Rhynous destroying the planet and life disappearing as we know it. The sureness of his thoughts and the catastrophic destruction that flooded into her head bothered her. Visions of fire, bodies of the dead and the dying, with major cities leveled to the ground. Worst of all, every time she heard words spoken or listened in on some one's thoughts and saw visions, then convulsed and trembled, it came to pass. Monica believed Clay's words were some sort of prophecy and couldn't shake the thought. It also shocked her that his telepathic abilities were so strong; he had never displayed those skills before, and she wondered what other hidden powers he had that went unseen.

Sharon walked in after touring the compound and saw Monica sitting there, stiff as a board and pale in the face with a scared look in her eyes. "Monica, what's wrong? Are you okay?"

Monica played it off and summoned her best acting face. "Yes, I was just deep in thought, wondering what would be the right time to tell Blue what I found out."

"I don't think you should tell him now. Maybe when this is all over."

"Yes, you're probably right. It could wait. Let's go find a room and get a few hours of sleep. We're going to need it, Sharon."

Clay and Blue had completed the makeshift setup to charge the Cobra and walked in.

"Blue, if we get separated, I have my cell."

"Separated? We're a team. I'll be there to get your back, Clay."

"I know you will, but crap happens, so just remember what I said."

"You got it, Clay."

In Clay's dimension, it felt like two or three in the morning with the eternal darkness outside the compound. However, it was seven in the evening in Los Angeles, according to Monica's watch. She and Sharon had slept for about four hours and talked for half an hour. Then the adrenaline began flowing and they sprang to their feet. When they got to the main hall, Blue and Clay were already up and loading the Phantom Cobra with water, food provisions, and small bottles of energy drinks for the ladies. Blue looked up to see Monica and walked over to give her a big hug and a long, passionate kiss. He wished he had been making love to her through the night, but knew that would have been inappropriate and awkward with Sharon and Clay on the outside looking in.

Blue knew he had done the right thing conserving his energy. Plus he and Clay still needed to talk through some scenarios of what ifs. Now it was time.

"Ladies, we're pulling out. You ready?" Blue said, still clinging to Monica, wanting to never let her go.

The girls nodded and grabbed their bags, then headed for the Phantom Cobra.

Blue had already disconnected the Cobra from the generator and was sitting in the pilot's seat with Clay as his co-pilot. Monica and Sharon took their seats behind the guys up against the fire wall separating them from the guys by six feet. Blue commanded Phanta to initiate the preflight checklist routine. Seconds later, Blue lifted off to about ten feet as he retracted the landing gear and switched on the force field as they pushed through the membrane surrounding Clay's compound and out into the darkness. Blue asserted his blue energy as he focused on the Sonoran Desert and into a vortex that suddenly blasted the Phantom Cobra into the Mexican desert at supersonic speed minus the sonic boom negated by the ship's electromagnetic properties. Blue headed east through Mexico, then handed flight control over to Phanta, who generated more electromagnetic energy that neutralized the G forces on board to protect the crew. Then suddenly, turning on a dime, the ship angled north through Canada and then north east, heading over Norway and Finland. As they crossed the frigid north Atlantic, they saw flashes of light as if lightning was violently flashing with the rapid succession of a machine gun. It had already begun.

Clay knew Rhynous would attack early to catch the unsuspecting Russians just before dawn and still asleep, but he had missed it by half an hour. "Phanta, initiate cloaking."

One minute later, they were in Moscow, hovering over a city that was now unrecognizable. Everything was on fire and the skyline had been leveled with skyscrapers toppling, laying on top of smaller buildings and blocking streets. With cars piled up and mangled, in the distance was one of Rhynous's UFO ships, blasting the surrounding areas with an electrical charge that looked like a lightning strike on steroids. It generated a gigantic bolt that ripped through everything and was as big around as a redwood tree at the base. As it continued through the city, blowing up the ground, it left vast canyon-like craters over a hundred feet deep, destroying and undermining buildings, houses, streets, and anything else in its path, incinerating any human. It was a horrific scene.

Blue could take no more. "It's time to engage. Phanta, deploy the blue energy cannon and aim at the spacecraft in the virtual target sights."

"Yes, captain."

Blue then stuck his forearm into the slot for the cannon and gripped the metal conducting bar as he generated a huge blue energy blast, blowing a hole through the side of the UFO, causing it to fall from the sky and exploding just before hitting the ground. Then they jetted across the city and stopped to watch one of Rhynous's cargo ships hovering over the half-destroyed building of the Central Bank of Russia. Suddenly, there was a squad of ten men coming out of the bank, with computer equipment. They had no money but Blue and Clay were sure they had diverted Russian currency somewhere, but where they didn't know. Blue zoomed in on them with the ships cameras and, to his surprise, they didn't appear to be aliens. They were homeless recruits from Kali's recruitment centers programmed to steal a country's monetary wealth and wire it to Rhynous's account, but where and how? Blue disabled the UFO cargo ship with a blast of blue energy from the cannon, stranding them.

"We'll let the Russians take care of them. We have to catch up to the battle," Blue said.

On the way out of Moscow, they noticed a strange thing—the Kremlin was untouched. Clay was sure Rhynous would have destroyed it. That was his modus operandi to crush his opponent's power center and let it lay in ruin as a monument to his superiority. They shook off the thought of this oddity to catch up to Rhynous's interstellar war ships. As they continued to the outskirts of Moscow, they saw a multitude of destroyed tanks and downed airplanes, including formidable Mikoyan Mig-31 fighter jets and Sukhoi Su-35 fighter jets. Rhynous had divided his forces to take down some of the other cities in Russia, but the bulk of his air flotilla appeared to be headed straight for China. As they passed a destroyed Russian power plant, Clay realized the Russians were unable to fire off a single nuclear missile. All Russian missile silos had been rendered inoperable.

Clay got a hit on his cell phone. "Alastor, where are you?"

"Ares and I are on a cargo ship with an atomic electrode and a bunch of Kali's recruits from her centers."

"What's this electrode thing?" Clay asked.

"It shoots a giant bolt of electricity."

"Yes, we've seen it at work. It's a serious weapon. Can you take it down?"

"Not from this cargo bay with all of these recruits. Clay, I'm pretty sure we're going to be headed to North Korea next. They're splitting us up."

"Where are you now?"

"We've split off to destroy a Russian army base and airfield."

"Okay, don't make any moves for now. Blue and I are following Rhynous to China, but keep us posted when you can."

"Yes, sir," Alastor said before hanging up.

Clay was feeling the Chinese had gotten word and knew what was coming. He asked Blue to command the ship to hover at a high altitude. From that vantage point, they could see how Rhynous would attack. There were ten UFO fighters that took off from the lead formation and headed for their missile silos. As Blue and Clay watched, they saw out in the distance, far away from Beijing, a missile launch from a remote area of the country. They all gasped. Blue asked Phanta where it was heading.

She responded, "Based on the trajectory, the United States."

Suddenly, two UFO fighters broke ranks from Rhynous's huge formation at incredible speeds to assist the first fighter in neutralizing the rocket. The three alien fighters deployed an orange ray that extinguished the rocket's engine and then, with some sort of lasers, disabled the nuclear war head. Blue and Clay weren't sure if the orange ray and lasers were visible with the naked eye, but they could see it through the Cobra's on board cameras.

Blue had stopped to rethink their strategy, but before he could open his mouth to share with Clay, he was overcome with thoughts of Monica. Now with all the battles and countries falling to Rhynous, Blue had forgotten about Monica and Sharon. He turned quickly just to get a glimpse of his beautiful Monica, who was burning a hole in the back of his head with her eyes. Blue chuckled under his breath, though it wasn't a laughing matter. Monica and Sharon were sitting there as if they were watching an action movie in a theater. When he turned back around, he realized there was some kind of under towing thought in Monica's mind. Blue's energy had elevated his extra sensory perceptions, but he was far from being a mind reader like Monica, but he realized at that moment she was pregnant with a thought. Then Blue snapped out of it.

"Clay, we can't take on his whole damn army. We're going to have to pick them off one by one and stay cloaked."

"I agree, Blue. We'll have to pick our battles and keep track of where our men are. Mercury and Nestor are on the ground in Beijing."

As soon as Clay said Beijing, a mother ship deployed an atomic electrode that looked like a flat satellite dish or an oversized magnifying glass. It quickly turned white hot and generated a massive bolt of electricity that destroyed everything in its path. It was a continuous blast, creating instant fires and explosions that toppled buildings and blasted deep gorges into the earth, while the fighters deployed a white ray of light that turned everything it touched into fire. It was a horrific scene. People were being killed by the thousands and in every conceivable way—fire, falls, falling debris, collapsing buildings, explosions, run over by panicked drivers, and freak accidents.

Blue could no longer watch it on the camera feed, nor could he repeat other horrific scenes that were now stuck in his mind's eye. He just wanted to do something, but now he was confused and afraid to make the wrong move. "Clay, help me out here. What should we do?"

"Well, we can't swing to the front and take them head on, that's suicide. We'll continue to pick them off from the rear and pick our battles," Clay shouted over the sound from the camera feed.

While the carnage continued, fighters fell from the sky from Blue's energy blasts from the invisible Phantom Cobra. They were scoring kills, but it still didn't seem like enough and they didn't want to take on a mother ship that seemed to have them out matched in fire power. Only half of Rhynous's total fighter saucers were deployed as the rest sat inside the big ships like extra sticks of dynamite. Blue noticed cargo ships and fighters breaking off from the pack and heading for far away locations with recruit squads from Kali's recruitment centers.

"Phanta, based on their trajectory, where are these small squadrons headed?"

"They appear to be headed to Japan and South Korea."

"Why there? They don't have nuclear bombs!" Blue exclaimed.

"No, but they have money and lots of it. They're going to blow up the banks, send in a squad and rob the central banks of these countries and route that money to Rhynous's account, where ever that might be," Clay explained.

Blue and Clay tried to figure out how to stop the destruction of Earth and the theft of the planet's monetary value that would affect the future of the whole world.

"We underestimated him," Clay said.

Blue said nothing because he knew who Clay was talking about—Rhynous. There was silence for five minutes as they both contemplated what to do, but continued to pick off stray alien fighters or cargo ships. Blue continued to fight but was feeling like it was all in vain and a futile effort when Monica did something she hadn't done in weeks. She spoke to him telepathically. *Blue, when they're done here, they'll be headed to the States. Call someone.*

Not being a true telepath and currently overwhelmed, Blue just spoke aloud. "Call who? We've been running from the people who could be helping us right now and that's only if they believe us."

Clay looked at Blue and then looked away as it fell silent again in the control room except for the electric hum. Then it came to him— Rob Star. He needed to call Rob Star. Blue knew the feds would be listening and there would be no questions about whether he was telling the truth. The proof was in the destruction around the planet.

Blue whipped out his phone and called Rob Star. It rang and rang, then it went to voice mail. "Rob, this is Blue. I mean, Vic. Look, I need to speak to the government agents. It's a matter of life and death." Blue couldn't believe Rob didn't answer the phone. He had never called Rob without him answering the phone. Now that the survival of the planet was in peril, there was no answer. Now agitated, and for reasons unknown to him, Blue called on the source of the universe. "Our energy is the source, and the source is in us. We are calling on you! And the others."

Clay, Monica, and Sharon looked at Blue. There was no surprise, confusion, or indignation on their faces, only understanding and empathy. For their lives, too, were being destroyed along with the planet and they all knew that if the planet goes, they go, too.

Blue continued looking to pick off an alien airship, but there was no emotion in the cockpit, only emptiness, like an emotional limbo. They all sat with little fear but mostly emptiness in their hearts and at that very moment, there wasn't enough faith among the four of them to fill a mustard seed. How could there be? They had witnessed the destruction of two major cities toppled and burned to the ground, with North Korea probably suffering the same fate at that very moment. They knew this would continue around the world, including the United States. Now they had witnessed over a million people perish and knew that millions more would suffer the same fate. The crew was numb. There was another five minutes of silence and then Blue's phone rang.

"Hello."

"Yes, hello, I got a message that you wanted to talk to us?"

"Yes, thank you for returning my call. Who am I speaking with?"

"I'm Dr. Thompson. We've actually met."

"Yeah, where?"

"I was the gentleman at the back of your airship in the white shirt, black tie, glasses and a clip board."

"Oh, yes, sir. Nice to formally meet you."

"Likewise. What can I do for you?"

"Well, I'm sure you're aware of the war that's going on in Europe and Asia right now, right?"

"Yes, we've seen the news reports, but that has nothing to do with us."

"What do you mean?"

"That's a war between Russia and China. It's surprising that two axis power allies would turn on each other, but that's no concern of our deep branch. We let the military and the state department handle that."

"Dr. Thompson, you've got it all wrong. That's not what happened. They didn't attack each other. This is the work of a galactic pirate, an alien by the name of Rhynous. He's been here off and on for hundreds of years. He has amassed a huge army with superior weapons and has been on the far side of the Moon, doing maneuvers for the last few days. Hey, how come you don't know any of this?"

"Maybe we do, but I needed to see how much you knew before I could share any classified information, and I can't share any more than you already know. Normally, my job would be to dispel anything you've seen or came in contact with, but I realize you're well beyond that, so let's talk."

"Thank you, Doctor, but we don't have a whole lot of time here. North Korea is going down as we speak. They've sent squadrons to Japan and South Korea to drain all of their money from the banks. And they're going to be headed to the U.S. by tomorrow. We've been picking off alien fighters and cargo ships from the rear and cloaked to go undetected, but it feels like we're not making much of a difference."

"Vic—"

"Uh, Doctor, please call me Blue."

"Okay, Blue, I must inform you that you're not authorized or trained to fight this battle for the United States of America and that as an American citizen, you are operating outside of the law. Now, with that being said, I'm willing to hear what you have to say and see if we can work with you as an international mercenary sympathetic to the United States and fighting for democracy." There was a second of silence.

"What? Look, Doc, politics aside, I'm just trying to warn you guys of what's about to land on our doorsteps and it happens to be the country the four of us on this aircraft love. They are going to go straight for our nuclear missile silos to neutralize them and then they are going to destroy our cities and drain our whole monetary system. The U.S. will be destroyed and broke, if you could imagine that. I don't have to imagine it because I've just seen it happen twice."

Then Dr. Thompson responded quickly, "We have our black satellites."

"What's that?"

"Can't tell you."

"Okay, Doc, I don't feel this is going well, so let me just brief you on a few things. The gray aliens are involved and they are allies with us in this fight and they have agreed to help us capture Rhynous, who will be taken back to his planet of Larus in the Reticuli system and he has already been sentenced to life in infinite nothingness."

"How could they sentence him when they haven't even caught him yet?"

"That's how they do it on that planet, Doctor, and be careful with our military fighter jets and pilots. They are no match for those alien saucers."

"We will keep that in mind, and by the way, thank you for not killing my two coworkers in the hangar the other night. Keep in mind they were just doing their job."

"You're welcome, Dr. Thompson. I try not to kill anyone if I can help it and they are fellow Americans."

"Hopefully if we meet again, it will be under more pleasant circumstances. Can you put me on speaker for a minute, Blue?" Blue agreed and switched to speaker. "Hello, everyone. I just wanted to say that your efforts may not seem like much, but that's how it is at the beginning of a war against such a powerful foe. However, I assure you that your efforts are huge and keep up the good work. They're far from home and without backup troops or saucers. So with every alien UFO you bring down, their numbers get smaller. You're like the boy who slung a rock at the giant, hitting him in the head, killing him. Your efforts will not be forgotten. You are heroes, thank you."

"No, thank you, Dr. Thompson. You just confirmed something."

"Oh, what's that?"

"That the universe heard me and that the source is rising up."

"Then let it continue to rise through you."

"We will, sir."

When Blue hung up the phone, the energy in the control room was different. There was no longer a sense of dread or doom. The doctors words were unsolicited but golden and confirmed the forces of the universe were at work. Hope was now springing eternal with Blue, Clay, and the girls left feeling energized.

Another squadron split from the huge formation that Phanta calculated was heading for Australia. Blue was about to give chase when Clay came up with an idea.

"Look, if we can scan that last mother ship and get an infrared reading of its heat signature, we can get an idea of where their propulsion system is located and bring it down. That'll put a hole in their party plans."

"I like it, Clay, but it's flanked on all sides by fighters and armed cargo saucers."

"That's correct, Blue, so you'll have to fly upside down and scan it from the bottom."

"Man, that's way outside-the-box thinking, Clay. Let's do it." Blue dropped in behind the flotilla and down two thousand feet below in hopes of not being detected. "Phanta, invert the already cloaked Phantom Cobra, "and scan the entire length of the mother ship above you with camera 3."

"Yes, Captain."

Blue knew the Phantom Cobra's computers would be more steady than he would, so he turned it over to Phanta.

Once the Cobra was at the back of the mother ship, she announced. "Now initiating scan." After scanning the length of the giant airship, Phanta initiated an inverted loop down and away from Rhynous's formation like an upside down roller coaster going backwards then right side up out of the loop, hovering and turning on a dime ninety degrees to continue following the invaders.

"Phanta, let us see the infrared photo with temperature reading," Blue asked.

"Now processing." Seconds later it was on screen"

"There it is, right in the middle, giving the ship balance and protection," Clay said.

At that very moment, an alien fighter near the same mother ship reported, "I just experienced an anomaly on my detection system. I think we're being followed."

The head navigator responded, "What do you see on your screen?"

"It is a shadowy mass...I'm not sure."

Then the navigator explained, "They have flying creatures here called birds that fly in formations like airships, but let me know if you see it again."

Now Blue was getting in position again and repeating the same maneuver just as a large squadron of fighters broke off from the main formation. "Phanta, what's their destination?"

"Shanghai, sir."

Blue's heart sunk. Shanghai was the largest city in China with over twenty million people, but now he had to focus as he turned over the Phantom Cobra to Phanta again and prepared to take the shot.

Phanta inverted the Cobra and moved into position like a surgeon and announced, "We are under the target. Fire at will."

With his hand in the slot gripping the conductor bar as blue energy swirled around his head like a blue tornado crown, Blue released a blast of energy more powerful than he ever had before, with the cannon pointed up at the bottom of the huge city of a mother ship that ripped through the hull of the ship dead center and up through the giant UFO, blowing off the top center portion of the alien craft. Once Blue had completed the blast, Phanta looped nose first back like she had before. The mother ship slowed immediately, causing two cargo ships to ram the rear of the huge ship as all three spiraled down from the sky. Blue and Clay watched as explosion after explosion lit up the sky as alien beings ran from the open cargo bay, jumping to their deaths, choosing to jump over burning to death. That was also the landing deck for alien fighters and cargo ships. Three fighters took off in time to escape the crash as bolts of electrical activity sprang from the center of the mother ship as a light blue energy jumped around the center of the huge ship where the reactor was. Then shortly thereafter, just before hitting the ground, the huge reactor exploded, blowing the mother ship into pieces, sending shock waves through every airship still in the sky, including the Phantom Cobra.

Blue dropped in altitude to circle the crash site as a mushroom cloud appeared. He knew at that point to keep his distance as the cloud was a sign of radioactive contamination. There were no survivors. Blue made one more pass by the crash site and back up to altitude in pursuit of Rhynous's flying flotilla that now looked noticeably smaller. And though it was clear they had delivered a heavy blow to Rhynous's forces, there was only quiet in the control room of the Phantom Cobra. It was not lost on the crew that thousands of lives had just been lost, including some of Kali's homeless recruits from the United States. It was sobering to think of all the loss of life as the crash faded behind them, having crashed in a remote area somewhere in China.

"Where to, Blue?" Phanta asked.

"Shanghai," Blue responded as the four of them sat in deep thought. Blue could hear Monica in his head again.

"I love you," she said. It was a comfort to him, being that he was the one who delivered the deadly blast.

Now Clay's phone was ringing. "Hello, Alastor! What's your status?"

"Clay, we've commandeered the cargo ship."

Clay takes a moment to tell Blue the news and everyone on board was excited. "That's fantastic! Great work, men. So what's your plan?"

"Well, it's complicated. The pilot is defecting. He wants us to drop him off somewhere in South America."

"Really?" Clay was now talking with the speaker on. "And what's his name?"

" Pogh," Alastor said.

"Okay, let me speak to him."

"Yes, this is Pogh. What would you like to know?"

"This is Clay, Pogh. I'm the leader of these great men you have the pleasure of being with. Why are you defecting?"

"Back on my planet of Larus, I've lived in the desert belt for years, helping to plan the operation you see here. As the years went on, I realized I could have been married, raising a family, and enjoying life. Instead, I was planning to take over planet Earth. It sounded romantic until I found out Rhynous was planning to destroy the whole planet. Why would anyone want to destroy a beautiful planet like Earth and millions of people with it? We were promised a large sum of money in the beginning and I was okay with stealing some money, but I didn't sign up for mass murdering a planet and a large portion of its inhabitants. That's way beyond me; I can't be a part of that."

Clay and Blue knew the only way out of Rhynous's army was death, from their visit to Larus.

"Okay, where do you want to go?" Clay asked.

"Brazil, Columbia, Guyana, I could live on the outskirts of the jungle near a small town and try to blend in."

"That may be hard to do, but you'll figure it out. Now we need something from you—information. How many fighters does Rhynous have?"

"He has two to three hundred."

"Where's the money going?"

Only his earthling concubine and second in command on Earth knows—Kali."

Blue and Clay looked at each other in shock and surprise, never having realized how powerful she really was in Rhynous's operation. Blue then looked back at Monica, who had a strange look on her face as if she wanted to say something, but then looked at Sharon, who just pursed her lips while looking at Monica as if to silently say, *I can't help you.* Having seen that, Blue didn't think too much about it as the focus was on Pogh and his block buster answers.

"Pogh, you're a big help. We're going to grant you your wish, but I have one more question for you," Clay said.

"Let it fly," Pogh retorted, ready to tell them whatever they wanted to know.

"Pogh, what is Rhynous's biggest weakness?"

"I'd say there are two weaknesses that could be his downfall." Pogh pondered for a minute. "One, his greed, and the other is his overconfidence. He always speaks of a term used here on Earth. He would always say. 'It will be like stealing candy from a baby,' but that hasn't been the case"

"No, it hasn't because this baby has teeth with sharp little fangs sinking deep into his ass as we speak." Clay scowled. "Pogh, thank you for the intelligence report."

"My pleasure. I just hope you could stop him."

"So do we," Blue interjected."

"Pogh, I need you to teach Ares and Alastor how to fly that saucer 'cause I need them back," Clay said.

"I will, to the best of my ability, Clay. They'll be worthy saucer pilots next time you see them."

"Sounds good and good luck Pogh."

"Thank you, sir, and good luck to you."

When they hung up, Pogh asked Ares what luck was.

"It's when the source of the universe sides in your favor and things go your way in spite of one's skill or ability."

"Well, I'm certainly going to need some of that," Pogh mumbled under his breath.

Suddenly, Blue noticed a small squadron of three fighters and one cargo ship breaking away from the now shrinking formation. "Phanta, where is that small squad of UFO's headed to?"

"They're headed for Hong Kong, Captain," Phanta answered calmly and smoothly.

It suddenly dawned on Blue that all of his concerns over the last two hours were for communist countries full of Russians and Chinese. Somehow, in this alien war, he had forgotten about political differences, ideologies, and races of different people. It was about human beings and saving the planet from a psychopathic alien. Again, in his mind, Blue thought it incredulous and unbelievable that they were on a mission to save the planet. It made all the differences, like race, that human beings have against one another pale in comparison. *Well, we'll have to come together now or perish at the hands of an alien demon,* Blue thought.

"Hey! What's going on in that overworked brain of yours, Blue?" Clay said.

"Yeah, I wanna know too," Sharon said.

"I know," Monica announced, getting an animated reaction from Blue as he put his hands over his ears.

"Hey, hey, stay out of my head, woman."

Everyone laughed. However, the fun was short-lived as the wheels in both Clay's and Blue's brains were constantly turning.

Clay was the first to speak. "Listen crew. I think at some point we have to head back to the states to make a stand. I think that now when they get to these other countries they're going to be met with guns and rockets. They have to know what's coming by now. It's my estimation that some of these countries will bring down a few more fighters and cargo ships. I think we need to head home in the next hour and get ready to make a stand." Clay looked out the window. As soon as the words rolled from his lips, Chinese fighters engaged the alien formation and were rendered useless as their aircraft missiles and guns were met with a sturdy force fields on each saucer. The alien saucers shut down the engines on the Chinese jets and others were hit with the white light from the UFO's that set them on fire. Many of the pilots ejected from their cockpits and landed safely. Just as Clay was getting ready to retract what he said about bringing down saucers, a bigger surface-to-air missile didn't break through the force field of the saucer, but somehow damaged it, bringing it down. Shortly thereafter, other saucers in formation were crashing into each other, trying to avoid the heat-seeking missiles. It was chaos. The Chinese were wreaking havoc on the alien airships.

Blue jumped to blink speed of twenty thousand feet above the dogfight and ground to air attack. "Looks like you were right, Clay."

"Yes, even though that's not how I had imagined it, but whatever works."

"Yeah, it's effective, and that's all that matters," Blue replied.

"Let's head home. I'm sure India and Pakistan will have something waiting for them, too."

"I thought we were going to Shanghai?" Monica asked.

Blue realized that while they had been amused by the dogfight, half of Rhynous's alien air force had disappeared. Blue looked at Clay, who nodded in approval, then Blue instructed Phanta to fly at blink speed to Shanghai.

CHAPTER 26

As the Phantom Cobra streaked further east to the Chinese city of Shanghai, only minutes behind Rhynous's air strike, it was too late. Most of the city was ablaze. It was the same pattern and formula they saw in Russia. Nuclear installations rendered inoperable, the atomic lightning bolt weapon was destroying infrastructure and buildings like no one had ever seen in the history of warfare or natural disasters. The saucers, with their white light rays that set everything ablaze, were all over, burning up large areas of the city, neighborhoods, and business districts. Blue saw an area with no fire, but there was a cargo saucer hovering over a large bank that had been blown open as it waited for the soldiers to return with equipment that allowed them to wire the wealth of a nation to Rhynous's account, wherever that might be. It was the same operation as before; it was horrific and apocalyptic. The destruction was unbelievable and now they had it down to a science. There was nothing the crew could do. It was finished. Blue instructed Phanta back to the United States, where they would make their stand and somehow try to do the impossible: capture Rhynous.

Now the Majestic Leader sat on his throne-like commander seat in his lead mother ship, winning the war, and his financial plunder exceeded sixty trillion dollars and was growing. However, Rhynous was furious. "How did we lose a mother ship and eighty fighters? I need to know right now how that happened!"

Along with two other generals, Motar spoke up as they stood before Rhynous with no answers. "Majestic Leader, we have taken on some casualties but we're winning the war, sir." Motar had great concern and fear for himself and his two comrades.

Rhynous sensed his concern and sincerity, but had no intention of losing anyone else. "Don't you see what's happening, Motar?

Someone is out there picking us off like a long-distance sniper, and I have an idea who it might be."

The generals looked at each other in surprise.

Motar spoke for the other two, as he always did. " Sir, our spotters have seen nothing and no one, Majestic Leader."

At that moment, a call came in. "Commander, you have a call from your Earth leader, Kali," the communications technician said.

"Send it through. Yes, my love."

"Why do you have your phone off?" Kali asked.

"Well, let's see…I'm in the middle of conquering a planet and I didn't want to be disturbed."

The generals chuckled under their breaths.

"I understand, Commander, but this is important. I've received a communication from Clayvious with coordinates in the California desert. He wants you to meet him there."

"Meet him there for what?"

"A final battle. Winner takes all."

"What?" Rhynous broke into hearty laughter. "Ha! He has no army. Though I would like to crush him once and for all." Rhynous thought for a moment with his arms folded and hand on his chin when his eyes widened as if a light bulb had just turned on. "Tell him we will be there."

Over the speaker, Kali expressed loudly, "Sir that is a bad idea. What if it's a trap?"

"It might be. Let the best trap win. He doesn't have a snowball chance in hell and he'll have his powerful friend with him. What's his name?"

"Blue," Kali responded.

"When the cyber web trap releases the nanites into his body, he'll belong to me and all of his powers." Rhynous laughed uncontrollably, and the generals joined in. "Larians, they're not going to go down easily, so we need a plan."

Kali felt sick; she didn't like it and sensed that it could jeopardize the whole mission. "Okay, Majestic Leader, I wish you luck," Kali said angrily, with a sizable dose of sarcasm, and then hung up.

Rhynous felt invincible and saw no way they could lose this battle. In his mind, thirteen men against thousands—it was no contest. Based on that fact alone, his overconfidence was justified and the numbers bared it out.

Clay and Blue were streaking back to the United States at twelve thousand miles per hour. It was the fastest he had ever flown the Phantom Cobra, and she was cruising effortlessly without any noticeable strain. That wasn't so for Blue. Things were going by faster than he was comfortable with and asked Phanta to go on autopilot. In fifteen minutes, they had gone from the darkness of midnight in Asia to an afternoon sun over the Pacific and arrived in Mexico fifteen minutes after that, now flying at low altitude cloaked and arriving outside Phoenix at Rob's hangar a mile or two from Rob's house.

Monica's psychic abilities kicked in and she knew this was where Blue was when he encountered the black operations agents with guns. "Why did you come here, Blue? They're still here."

At that moment, they came over the hill to see two armed guards outside the hangar. With the Cobra still cloaked, Blue went to stun, and as the guards looked to see where the hum was coming from, he blasted them both, putting them to sleep for a short while. He then opened the hangar, hovered in, and turned the ship around, facing out. Blue ran to the back of the ship as Phanta lowered the ramp. He reconnected the charging cable and upped the voltage by flipping a switch on the wall to high. Rob had told him a high voltage charge could be done in twenty minutes and would last a week. They had used up all the make-shift charge from Clay's compound in twenty-four hours because there was no sunlight during the destructive, war-torn night and the poor connection at the compound. Blue closed the hangar door after five minutes into the charge and, ten minutes into the charge, one of the guards woke up. He was dazed but immediately got on his headset, calling for backup. When the charge was done, Blue put the cable back on the ship, closed the ramp, and hopped back in the pilot seat.

"They're out there. I could feel them. They have guns," Monica said.

Blue just looked at her and blew her a kiss to say "thank you." His adrenaline kicked in and now he was thinking fast. Then, with a deep breath, he started tapping icons on the virtual screen and opened the hangar door. There was a whole platoon out there, waiting for them, guns drawn. Everyone ducked except for Blue, who tapped one more icon to initiate the force field. "Phanta! Blink speed and get us out of here!"

As soon as the agents heard the hum of the Phantom Cobra increase in intensity, they began firing. A second later, there was an explosion of airborne bodies, crunching bones, broken fingers, arms, and concussions. The agents who were kneeling in the front row of their firing formation were lucky and, although they ducked, the force of the Phantom Cobra drug them back fifteen feet on the concrete tarmac. When they got to their feet, the Phantom Cobra was long gone.

On the Cobra, there were cheers from Monica and Sharon.

"How did we get out of that?" Sharon asked.

"I don't know," Monica said.

They both were excited and grateful that no one was shot or injured on the aircraft.

Clay also breathed a sigh of relief with a smile on his face as he looked back at the girls. "Where are we headed?" Clay asked, without looking at his good friend.

"Death Valley," Blue said, keeping his eyes peeled as he was again flying at low altitude to avoid radar detection and to stay out of the way of military aircraft.

It was now 3:15 p.m., the day before in the United States—it was like going back in time, fifteen hours being that the Far East was fifteen hours ahead. It took little time to get across the Arizona desert into the California desert. There was no oasis in-between, all desert with Las Vegas to the north as they traveled north just west of the Nevada state line. In minutes, they were in Death Valley, which consisted of two valleys. On the east side was the Bad water Basin, Stove Pipe Wells, and Furnace Creek, with lots of visitors to see old mines from the turn of the last century, two hotels, and a ranger station visitor center. However, to the west was the more remote Panamint Springs area that swooped down from the mountain range, separating the two valleys.

As they came over the mountain near Highway 190 at about two hundred feet off the ground, gliding down into the valley heading for the valley floor, suddenly there were two U.S. military jets on maneuvers, blasting into the valley from the north, heading west at the same time and altitude, putting them on a collision course with the Phantom Cobra. There was no time for Blue to switch to autopilot and, being cloaked, the military pilots could not see them.

In an instant, Blue grabbed the seldom used joystick as he dove and shouted, "Phanta altitude!"

"Fifty feet, sir," the computer responded in its usual smooth, calm female voice.

As they narrowly avoided a mid-air collision as the jets flew past over their heads, Blue pressed the hover icon to stop mid-air without a sound and realized he could have done that in the first place. Not being used to the Cobra's alien technology, it was a learning experience as the jets barreled down the valley into the great Mojave Desert and toward the Trona Pinnacles.

Rhynous had now added to his destruction of Earth. His forces had destroyed India, Pakistan, Iran, South Africa, North Korea, and England. He robbed the central banks of Europe, Asia, North Africa, and down under, Australia and New Zealand. Over half the world was on fire and the smoke had reached the trade winds in the upper atmosphere, leaving behind a hazy layer of clouds that looked like a high-altitude storm in the United States. Word had traveled around the world via media outlets about an alien attack, but the United States government had assured the American people from coast to coast that the United States military was the strongest force on Earth and ready to defend its borders.

Rhynous was now headed for the Americas at three thousand miles per hour. Since his meeting with his generals, there hadn't been one incident of mysterious attacks or unexplained crashes.

"Majestic Leader, we have conquered three-fourths of this planet. We have amassed over one hundred trillion dollars. You are the Majestic Leader!" General Motar exclaimed as he and the other two generals kneeled on one knee in unison and bowed to their king. They were all rich beyond measure and had thought about which country of the world they would claim for themselves as what we on Earth would call Dukes or Earls.

"Let's have a toast to our Majestic Leader, the great Rhynous!" General Septar exclaimed.

"Hold on, my great generals. In four or five hours, we will have conquered the whole planet as I said we would. Let us hold that toast until the job is finished."

The generals agreed and everyone went back to work and decided that the fleet would be split into three oversized squadrons, each with a mother ship. The plan was to have one squadron to the west, one to the east, and one down the middle of the country from Texas to Chicago. The first sites to be hit were all the nuclear missile silos from Alaska to the Midwest and East Coast. It was the same pattern of destruction that had been repeated around the world. Now it was a precision instrument of death and devastation in the theater of battle. Once the nukes were neutralized, mass destruction would begin. The U.S. military felt confident they could thwart any invasion effort. The time was drawing near and that confidence would be put to the test.

While Rhynous's air fleet prepared to split into three forces over the Pacific Ocean, Kali was packing a carry-on suitcase and getting ready to head to the coordinates Clay sent for Death Valley. She was monitoring the computer and Rhynous's account as it continued to grow past one hundred fifty trillion dollars. Kali's inner voice and intuition had her uneasy, so she rerouted twenty million to her personal account in the Caymans. She knew no one would question a measly twenty million and that no one was watching, anyway.

Oh, but someone was watching—Alpheus the nanite, whose reasoning, consciousness, and ability to calculate variables had sailed past the abilities of any human being, but thanks to Dr. Spidis, there was nothing he could do because of the control brain welded onto the top of his hind side. Ironically, with all of Alpheus's knowledge and understanding, he wasn't quite sure why he couldn't exercise his free will or what was stopping him. The fact of the matter was Kali had just moved money to her personal account, and he had reasoned that it was some sort of fail-safe. And with all of his knowledge of data bases, he understood women were always security conscious but wondered what she feared. Rhynous had already conquered most of the world and, according to Alpheus's calculations, it was just a matter of five or six hours before it would be finished.

Now Blue had found a spot in the valley behind a dune west of Panamint Valley Road and just south of Highway 190. Blue had been there before and knew that just up the road about a mile was the Panamint Springs Resort, with a campsite on the north side of the highway and a visitor center, restaurant, and most importantly a gas station/grocery store on the south side of Highway 190 up the hill from their landing site. Nothing fancy but a small oasis of civilization.

Phanta lowered the ramp and everyone exited the airship. They were all struck by the complete calm and silence of the vast desert with its sand, dirt, and low-growing brush that made the crew weary of rattlesnakes. It felt good to stretch their legs as they moved into the heat of the day and things seemed closer when they were farther away. The lack of buildings, streets, and city blocks made it difficult to judge distances. The sound of a few passing cars was absorbed by the distance and the sound of silence. Blue knew that time was short and thought they all should take the hike up to the store for water, food, and the restroom. Once they had started up the hill, they looked down to their left at the Phantom Cobra. It looked like an alien spacecraft. Fortunately, it couldn't be seen from behind the dune, which limited its visibility from Panamint Valley Road. Not many people would be looking, coming down the hill on Highway 190 as they would try to keep their eyes on the road. By the time they got to the top of the hill near the store, they again heard the roar of jet engines rushing in from the north but this time, Blue and crew were above the jets as the F-18s crossed the highway, heading down the valley below. They gathered the goods they needed and headed back down the hill, enjoying the view as Highway 190 rolled down the mountain like an asphalt ribbon to the valley floor, stretching across the wide open expanse for twenty miles and up the other side back toward Stovepipe Wells and the Bad water Basin in the direction they had just come from to avoid the crash. It all looked so close, though miles away, as they marveled at the desolate beauty and vast distances of the view.

At the very same time, Rhynous's Squadrons of alien UFOs crossed over from international waters into United States territorial waters. U.S. Navy and Marine carriers awaited them on the Pacific Ocean. The alien air fleet had not yet split apart as they were met with three aircraft carriers with two hundred forty fighter jets plus attack helicopters. As the alien fleet slowed, the careers continued to launch jets every fifteen seconds from each career. They circled the alien fleet with one hundred fifty jets in the air and the balance waiting to be scrambled. The commanding admiral was sending messages to the lead alien mother ship, which Rhynous ignored. Then Navy and Marine ships pointed their cannons at the UFOs, along with non-nuclear warheads. Rhynous ordered his top cargo pilot to deploy the nuclear electrode. The alien fleet stopped to hover mid-air when the admiral realized the threat and gave the order.

"Fire at will." In seconds, cannons were blazing, missiles flying, guns blasting, and no damage was done. The alien force fields absorbed every weapon and the UFO fighters had adopted a formation at different altitudes for lateral movements to avoid incoming missiles and mid-air crashes into their own airships. Rhynous deployed the electrode that became as bright as the sun. Suddenly, a nuclear bolt of lightning struck the main carrier, slicing it in half. In ten minutes, it had sunk with half its crew as the other half of the crew had deployed life rafts and more sailors had popped up from the depths of the water. Ten UFOs zipped down at seemingly light speed, stopping on a dime and accelerating at speeds four and five times faster than the fastest jets. Then, in a flash, the UFO's light rays were at work on the other two carriers, melting the guns and cannons and then deploying energy that disabled all the jets still on the carriers.

The second in command, on the second carrier, realized the battle had been lost and ordered all the jets in the air back to their ships. There were some top guns and hot shots who were not willing to give up and disobeyed orders, launching their heat-seeking missiles and still firing their guns with devastating .20-millimeter rounds. Some of the UFO technology had not been operational in Russia and China, but had been repaired before taking down India and Pakistan. The UFOs deployed their reverse polarity energy, their fighters, and mother ships reversed every missile and bullet round back in the same direction from which it came at the same velocity. Twenty-five of the forty-eight jets that continued to fight were shot down by their own bullets or missiles and had to be fished out of the ocean. The other twenty-three jets limped back to the remaining carriers with some crash landings on deck. The Navy and Marine armada had been rendered useless. Rhynous realized that his element of surprise was now gone. He split his forces in the three directions they had planned at blink speed. Sailors on the ships, who were working to save their fellow soldiers, heard a high-frequency hum get louder in the sky above. Then in a flash, the UFOs were gone at blink speed, mother ships and all.

Rhynous realized it was about noon on the West Coast and 3:00 p.m. on the East Coast. Within the hour, he and his squadrons had dismantled the United States' nuclear arsenal and began to burn, destroy, and steal vast amounts of money from U.S. banks and electronic monetary systems. Rhynous's piracy was never more evident as he pillaged the wealthiest country on Earth.

When Blue and the crew got back to the Phantom Cobra, Blue could see that the electromagnetic energy panel squares on the top of his airship, ten times stronger than solar panels, were fully charged. There was one small panel, a charging indicator, that was maxed out and glowing like never before. Phanta's surveillance cameras had picked up the crew as they returned to the ship and lowered the ramp to the cargo bay. They all opted to stand after sitting for all those hours the night before. They ate baloney sandwiches with chips, water, and Coca-Cola as they stood on the desert floor, using the ramp as a makeshift table. As they enjoyed their meal and the relaxing quiet, they heard a beeping sound. They all looked at one another and no one recognized the emergency-sounding beep. Clay, realizing that it was coming from his pocket, reached in and pulled out the device the general, Zeenix of the Alien Grays, had given him. This was quite a surprise being that he was instructed to only use it when Rhynous was captured and that event looked highly unlikely.

"Hello, General Zeenix?"

"Yes, it's me."

"What a surprise. What's going on?" Clay inquired.

"I just wanted to inform you that our surveillance saucers just observed Rhynous win a battle at sea with American forces and he has split into three squadrons. One headed to the west, one to the mid-west, and the third to the East Coast."

When Blue, Monica, and Sharon saw the look on Clay's face, they knew it was serious and then urgent as Clay seemed rushed to get off the phone.

"Clayvious, feel free to contact me via this crystal emergency intercom. We are at war. He's destroying most of the planet. We need to stop him at all costs."

"Yes, sir, General. We'll do our best."

General Zeenix hung up and the alien phone device went silent. They were all riveted on Clay, who simply said. "He's here," but with a tone of urgency.

They all scrambled, packing up the food, storing the water, and picking up the trash when their spiritual leader, Monica, said, "Stop, you guys!" She held her balled fist in the air toward the middle of the crew. "Our energy is the source, and the source is in us."

Everyone joined in, repeating it with everyone, putting their hands over her fist. Blue's hand on Monica's, Sharon's hand on Blue's, and Clay's hand on top as they repeated the phrase. Then there was a surge of energy among them and everyone felt it.

Monica became entranced and a new chant uncontrollably sprang from her lips. "Let the source in us rise; rise of the source! Rise of the source! Rise of the source!"

Strangely, the wind started blowing out of the calm and the sun seemed to intensify; it was a solar wind. Clay looked at Monica with a new understanding of her connection to the universe. He now realized that Monica knew more about him than he thought; she knew he was not human and more spirit than flesh, and that he was a being placed on this planet for just a time such as this and who had sent him. Clay now acknowledged her deeper ability to channel energy into the crew from the source as evidenced by the high energy far above the normal gathering of a team taking the field before a sporting event, Tribes chanting to the heavens, or anointed speakers from every religion. Monica was a conduit for the mystery of mysteries, and now they all knew what they needed to do. They were now of one mind, not fearing life or death. There was only belief and focus. Clay now realized Monica was like him, a kindred spirit of the source and he now had the utmost respect for her powers and abilities.

Rhynous was now destroying Los Angeles, with three teams hitting the banks with bags and technology. Using the bags for paper money or gold and superior alien computers to override the banking system to wire large sums of currency to Rhynous's account, it was robbery with an army, alien technology, and weapons. Buildings were being toppled, fires burning, and traffic stopped, with people jumping from their cars, hoping to run to safety. It was chaos as the battle moved to Santa Monica with the UFO's white light burning everything in its path; the atomic lightning bolt ripping through large structures, creating tremendous upheaval.

Meanwhile, Houston, Atlanta, Miami, Orlando, Philadelphia, New York, Boston, Kansas City, Chicago, and St. Louis were under the same attack. Military jet fighters and the national guard were of no use against the alien technology. As jet fighters lost power and fell from the sky, their pilots parachuted to the ground.

Suddenly, in upstate New York, as the eastern squadron moved toward Ohio, a cargo saucer opened fire on its mother ship. The atomic bolt's center mass sent the mother ship to the ground in a fiery heap. The rogue saucer jumped to blink speed and was gone, leaving Rhynous's attack saucers without a support mother ship, and confused with nowhere to go. They contacted the mother ship in the Midwest that was now headed to St. Louis, which was already under attack by alien fighters. When the East Coast squadron reached the mother ship in the Midwest, it, too, had been downed and laid on its side, burning in a huge field.

Now Rhynous was down to his last mother ship—his own. The UFO fighters landed in the Missouri field where the big ship had gone down to look for survivors. Most of the alien crew were fatally injured or dead, but some were still alive. As they rendered aid to the injured, some of those released themselves back to the source of this existence, leaving only a few. The alien pilots found out the attack on this mother ship was not from one of their own cargo ship's atomic bolts. Its destruction was a mystery. All they could find out from the injured was that it was a powerful ray, white-hot like theirs and that the force field was down to conserve energy in non-battle situations. They loaded the four survivors onto a cargo ship with first aid and headed for Death Valley, California.

As the rogue alien cargo saucer approached Nevada, Clay's cell phone rang.

"Hello?"

"Clay, we're coming into Death Valley in a few minutes in that alien cargo ship."

"Alastor! You guys made it."

"Yes, sir. We took down the mother ship on the East Coast and we headed to the ship in the Midwest, but when we got there, it was already destroyed."

"By who?" Clay asked.

"We don't know, but it was a powerful blast. There was something strange about the damage. It was burned on the top of the ship with holes that burned through to the rest of it down to the reactor."

"That's odd. Any survivors?"

"No, not many. Clay, we're here at the coordinates in Death Valley. Where are you?"

"We left to try to slow down Rhynous. We were able to take out some fighters from behind, but the damage had already been done."

"Where, San Francisco?"

"No, Seattle. He must like San Francisco because he only busted up a few banks there," Clay answered.

Shortly thereafter, Blue landed next to the cargo ship. Clay, Ares, and Alastor greeted each other like brothers; it was a family reunion. The emergency beep was again buzzing in Clay's pocket.

"Hello, General."

"You need to get airborne! Rhynous is coming in hot!" General Zeenix shouted.

Clay knew the general was close by, ready to pounce if there was a sliver of a chance to capture Rhynous. They all jumped into their aircraft—Alastor and Ares into the flying saucer, Blue and crew into the Phantom Cobra. Cloaked and weapons ready, both ships were at high altitudes, one on each side of the Valley.

Kali had arrived in time to see them take off and drove her Jeep off the road into the desert with a view from half a mile away. Kali heard a hum in the distance and by the time she had turned around, the mother ship had slowed to six thousand miles per hour at a low enough altitude to create a windstorm, a sirocco that completely blew Kali off her feet as she tumbled forward. Monica couldn't see Kali from the sky, but suddenly in her spirit, she knew Kali was there.

Rhynous's mother ship stopped on a dime, defying gravity with only ten fighters that followed behind. Blue and Clay couldn't believe it. A pleasant surprise that gave both airships hope for capture, but they both wondered what happened to Rhynous's forty-five or fifty fighters and cargo saucers. What Blue and Clay didn't know was that the ten that were left were his best pilots. They came in hot as the mother ship hovered at two thousand feet and Rhynous's saucers spun into a circle at one thousand feet over the mother ship. The Phantom Cobra and the stolen cargo ship from Rhynous's squadron hovered at five thousand feet. Blue and Clay thought it strange that the ten squadron UFO fighters would form a protective ring above their mother ship with none below or on the perimeter. For five minutes, no one made a move until suddenly one of the saucers in formation broke ranks from the circle and began firing at Alastor and Ares in the rogue saucer. Somehow they had been detected, even though clocked. Blue believed there had to have been a sensor in Alastor's saucer that allowed it to be detected and now it was a dogfight. Pogh had done a good job teaching Ares and Alastor how to maneuver the flying saucer, but the alien pilot was more skilled as the two saucers swirled around, firing at each other.

The Phantom Cobra still went undetected as Blue positioned himself over one of the nine saucers still in the circle. He pointed his blue energy cannon straight down center mass, knowing he would have to muster a powerful blast. Blue grabbed the metal conductor grip to transfer his blue energy to the canon.

Phanta announced, "We are center mass," as the crew looked on in amazement as the seldom seen blue energy swirled like a whirlpool cylinder or a crown over Blue's head. Within a second of Phanta's cue, Blue lets out a shout, releasing a powerful blast of blue energy that breached the hull of the saucer. It tilted, going down quickly at an angle, smoking until it hit the desert floor, skidding through the sand and brush to a fiery stop. The remaining alien saucers broke formation and began to zip and stop in search of the unseen attacker.

The mother ship technicians could somehow short-circuit the cloaking device on Alastor's saucer, at which point Ares tried to make a run for it, taking off to get over the mountains to the north, but took a focused blast of white light that burned right through to the saucer's core reactor, causing Ares and Alastor to fall short of the mountains as they crash landed four miles east of the battle at the top of the Valley in Panamint Dunes. Ares pulled the front of the saucer up as they skidded on the desert floor, creating an explosion of sand before resting near the foothills at the base of the mountain.

Before the dust could settle from Alastor's crash, a roar of jet engines shocked everyone in the Valley as they burst in from the northeast at the top of the Valley. They banked past the crash in the dunes in a six-jet, diamond formation at Mach 1, which was fast for Earthly threats, but still far behind the alien technology. Even so, they were a welcome distraction for the cloaked Phantom Cobra taking on the remaining nine alien saucers. However, Blue knew what the end result would be and called Dr. Thompson, the black operations scientist at Rob Stars number.

"Hello, is Dr. Thompson there?"

The unknown person on the phone said, "Hold on."

"Yes, this is Thompson."

"Doctor, this is Blue. Someone sent six F-22 raptors into a

dogfight here in Death Valley. I need you to get them out of here before you lose six men and six billion dollars."

"Thank you for your concern and patriotism, Blue, but they're not there to engage the enemy. They're there to observe, so listen very carefully. In five minutes, you should not be close to that mother ship. Do you understand that, soldier?"

"Yes, sir. Thank you, Doc, for the heads up. What's going on?" There was no response, only a click. Blue knew something was going down, but didn't know what. "Phanta, give me a four-minute countdown."

"Four minutes and counting, sir."

Blue was now retreating toward the mountain range as the F-22s circled below. Then, without warning, a white light that focused like a magnifying glass into a tight hot beam but had not breached the force field hit the Cobra.

"Two minutes and counting."Phanta continued the countdown. "Cloaking system is disabled," she added.

The Phantom Cobra was now visible to the alien saucers as Blue jumped to blink speed across the Valley. Again, the saucers were stunned at the formidable speed of the Cobra. Blue jumped again to the top of the Valley near Alastor's crash sight.

"One minute and counting."

Blue continued to jump as Rhynous watched from his commander's throne on the mother ship as it hovered just above the desert floor. "Shoot him to the ground, then burn them up and be done with them," Rhynous shouted into his communications device.

Right at that very second, Phanta began, "Ten, nine, eight..."

Rhynous shouted to his generals, "Let's begin the toast, gentlemen," as they laughed in glorious victory.

"Three, two, one. Time, sir."

The phantom Cobra was hit but without damage, jolting the ship as they jumped again. As he rotated the Phantom Cobra to face the UFOs, a giant laser beam hit Rhynous's mother ship from the heavens, burning the top of the ship and then through to its nuclear reactor. Then it exploded and crashed to the ground, resting on its side like a dying animal.

In a flash out of nowhere, there were sleek silver UFOs that seemed to glow in the sun; they belonged to the Grays. The Grays were moving fast, as two of their ships deployed two laser light beams probe-like arms that ripped through the ship like two claws of a tiger, digging for its prey. One of the other gray saucers shot a ray into one of Rhynous's fighters, dropping it to the ground like a dead bird falling from the sky, exploding on impact, killing all on board. The last seven fighters jumped to blink speed, heading to the ozone layer at escape velocity to break through Earth's atmosphere.

As they headed to the Moon to regroup, resupply, and head for the wormhole, everyone on the Phantom Cobra was cheering and jumping for joy."We did it!"

As the Grays now circled the crashed mother ship in search of Rhynous, from the looks of the mangled crash, there were no survivors. The crew in the Phantom Cobra continued to be gleeful; glad Rhynous had met his demise in the crash with his generals and misled crew. However, the Grays held their positions, hovering around the crash at a short distance in silence, leaving only the sound of the burning, broken mother ship.

Then, out of the near silence, a hum emitted from inside the downed ship. Suddenly, there was a ripping sound as a single fighter ripped and burned through a hole the Grays had created with its light beam. As it sprung to the sky, the Grays shot it down; it dropped straight to the ground between the downed mother ship and Kali's location as she watched in fear and disbelief. The grays ripped the saucer apart with their lasers as Rhynous tried to run from the ship, blasting the door off with his ultrasonic sonar voice. Rhynous emerged in full stride like a powerful world-class hurdler, jumping through the hull of the saucer. The light beam from the gray saucers drenched Rhynous in light, paralyzing him. Then an electrical charge electrocuted this monster, knocking him unconscious.

The Phantom Cobra landed nearby as the crew rushed over, while Alastor and Ares appeared out of a vortex to watch. Moving at lightning speed, a gray cargo ship moved in, dropping a thick plexiglass jail cell box. Lifting Rhynous, it lowered him inside, welding the top shut in the laser light. The cell levitated up into the cargo ship and in a flash, it was gone as the crew of the Phantom Cobra breathed a sigh of relief.

Kali, Rhynous's lover, and right-hand leader on Earth had run in closer to get a better view of what was happening. She was close enough for Blue and Monica to hear her crying in the now-silent desert.

Blue looked to see who it was. "Who is that?"

"Kali," Monica said.

Blue's face changed its countenance as he boiled over in rage. He walked in her direction.

"Blue, wait, I'm going with you," Monica said.

"You little witch!" Blue shouted.

That got Kali's attention. Through her tears, she quickly reached for her phone, opening a program with one icon that merely read: execute.

Blue was now one hundred yards away, with murder in his eyes, as Kali pushed the button.

Alpheus, who was wired to receive all incoming messages, was now inside the computer with an army of nanites working on the circuitry. Alpheus and his nanite army were hit by the power surge, sent by Kali, which shorted out the control brain on Alpheus's ant-like backside. Alpheus was thrown into a metal screw that broke off the control brain from his microscopic back. Instantly he felt different, more confident, and free.

When Blue got to Kali, he tackled her to the ground, still clutching her phone. He rolled her over, grabbing her by the neck and choking her. "You evil witch, do you know what you've done?

How many lives you've destroyed? I'm going to kill you, you witch! Right here, right now, once and for all." Blue had not forgotten what she did to Sharon and Monica.

Kali saw white spots as she started fading to black. Blue was hit by what felt like a two-hundred-fifty-pound football linebacker. When he rolled over, it was Monica as he looked on in shock. Kali was now gasping for air, glad to still be alive. Once she had gathered her faculties, she jumped up and ran for her life. She wanted to shape shift but needed to hold on to her phone at all costs.

Blue broke away from Monica to go after Kali.

"You can't kill her. Don't be a fool, Blue."

Blue was only seeing red and his hatred for her had turned into insanity. He quickly caught her, grabbing her from behind, throwing her down on the sand, and falling on top of her. No sooner than he started choking her again, Monica slammed into his back to rip him off of Kali.

"Blue listen to me. You can't kill her. There's something I've been trying to tell you."

"There's nothing you could say that will change my mind," Blue said with blood in his eyes.

The three of them rolled in the sand and dirt. Again, Monica was now angry. "Blue, I'm not going to let you kill her!"

"Why not!" he shouted as he tightened his grip on Kali's neck.

"Because she's your daughter!"

"That's bullshit. Where are you getting this crap from, Monica? That's not even possible, no!"

"Yes, she's your daughter." Monica looked him straight in the eye. "And you want to know where I got this crappie information? From the hall of records. I've got her birth certificate and her mother, Mina Moore, moved from L.A. to West Virginia before she was born."

When Monica said Mina Moore, Blue felt a jolt of electricity go up his spine as his hands slid away from Kali's neck. "I still find it hard to believe. What are the chances of that?"

"I understand, Blue, but it's true, she's your daughter. I couldn't let you kill your own daughter, no matter what she's done."

"I get it...thank you, I guess," Blue said in a dejected tone. He took Kali by the arm, lifting her to her feet, and helped dust her off.

"Well, hello Father. How does it feel to be the father of a witch? Some father you are, trying to kill your own daughter," Kali said in a scornful tone.

Blue was in shock and speechless. It was a nightmare, and he needed to process it all. When they turned around to walk back to the downed mother ship and the Phantom Cobra, men in black suits and dark shades surrounded them. They looked up toward the downed ship to see military HAZMAT teams swarming around the crash site.

"Blue, you and your crew will be joining me on the military base for a while. You're being detained and in the custody of the United States government under the domestic terrorist law," Dr. Thompson said.

"So you're going to hold us indefinitely?" Blue exclaimed.

"Is that what that means? They could hold us forever," Sharon said fearfully.

"No, no, I've got to get back to my shop," Monica said.

"Sorry, ladies, but if you cooperate, it will be just a few months, like six," as they handcuffed Blue and the girls, then led them to a black SUV with tinted windows.

"Dr. Thompson, where the hell did that giant laser come from?" Blue asked.

"That was black star and I can't tell you any more than that until you have a top-secret clearance," Thompson said.

A flatbed big rig truck had arrived and a Chinook helicopter was coming over the mountain to lift the Phantom Cobra onto the wide-load flatbed truck. Clay and his men had disappeared into a vortex and were back in their compound in their dimension.

Alpheus received a text from Kali: *Being detained will be gone indefinitely.*

Alpheus had repaired the computer and set up his own account in the Cayman Islands. He then wired all the money Rhynous had stolen from around the world, two hundred ninety trillion dollars, and wired it to his secret account. Alpheus wiped the computer data banks clean and crashed the computer after downloading all the files and uploading them to a cloud. He then introduced a virus into the hard drive, rendering it useless, and said to himself, "I'll have my own army and show the humans how to live."

Now, with all the knowledge he had acquired, Alpheus then rounded up his small nanite army and infiltrated the brain and eyes of a pit bull, then disappeared into the night.

About the Author

Don Universe is a native of Los Angeles who has loved science fiction since childhood. A fan of NASA and every rocket launch to SpaceX and their revolutionary technologies, Don loves everything UFO, having had a close encounter of the first kind from a commercial airline. He is an adventurer in his own right, traveling to Teotihuacan, the pyramid complex outside of Mexico City, and the Mayan pyramid complex at Chichen Itza in the Yucatan peninsula, to determine for himself if the Mayans and the Toltecs had extraterrestrial help in the design and construction of their pyramids.

Don had the desire to be a scientist but was not strong in advanced mathematics, though he loved physics. However, he is heavily endowed with imagination. Having written many papers and taken a film class during his school years, along with reading many books, Don always felt he could write a good story. That being said, his goal is to capture your imagination with excitement and intrigue and to entertain you with his style of science fiction infused with science theories and facts. Now it will be up to you, the reader, to decide with his first installment of "Rise of The Source."

CPSIA information can be obtained
at www.ICGtesting.com
Printed in the USA
JSHW030317100323
38733JS00002B/2